O9-BUD-347

FIVE SUMMERS

Published by the Penguin Group
Penguin Group (USA) Inc., 375 Hudson Street, New York, New York 10014, USA
Penguin Group (Canada), 90 Eglinton Avenue East, Suite 700,
Toronto, Ontario M4P 2Y3, Canada (a division of Pearson Penguin Canada Inc.)
Penguin Books Ltd, 80 Strand, London WC2R 0RL, England
Penguin Ireland, 25 St Stephen's Green, Dublin 2, Ireland (a division of Penguin Books Ltd)
Penguin Group (Australia), 707 Collins Street, Melbourne, Victoria 3008, Australia
(a division of Pearson Australia Group Pty Ltd)
Penguin Books India Pvt Ltd, 11 Community Centre, Panchsheel Park,
New Delhi–110 017, India
Penguin Group (NZ), 67 Apollo Drive, Rosedale, Auckland 0632, New Zealand
(a division of Pearson New Zealand Ltd)
Penguin Books (South Africa), Rosebank Office Park, 181 Jan Smuts Avenue,
Parktown North 2193, South Africa
Penguin China, B7 Jiaming Center, 27 East Third Ring Road North,
Chaoyang District, Beijing 100020, China

Penguin Books Ltd, Registered Offices: 80 Strand, London WC2R 0RL, England

Published simultaneously in Canada

Library of Congress Cataloging-in-Publication Data is available

Printed in the United States of America

1 3 5 7 9 10 8 6 4 2

ISBN: 978-1-59514-672-4

FIVE SUMMERS

UNA LaMARCHE

An Imprint of Penguin Group (USA) Inc.

For UTAH.

(The girls, not the state.)

Prologue from

Emma

in their Fifth Summer

when the girls are Age 14

During the *Last Night of Camp*

THERE ARE SOME THINGS THAT SEEM LIKE THEY'LL just never happen. There are the little things—like the first spring day after a bitterly cold winter, or learning to tie a cherry stem with your tongue—and then there are the bigger things. For example, my parents (who are giant nerds) sometimes wax poetic about Halley's Comet, which was last sighted a decade before I was born, when my mom and my dad, who hadn't even met yet, both had unironic mullets. You'd think they'd be embarrassed about them, but instead my mom just tickles the back of my dad's neck and says it means they were *bashert,* which is Yiddish for *soul mates*. (Sure, mom. Whatever gets you through those old albums.) Anyway, Halley's Comet apparently won't show up again until I'm sixty-five. Sixty-*five*. I still sleep with a Pound Puppy named

Harold whom I got when I was six, so ever being old enough to get the senior discount at museums feels made-up, like the plot of one of those dystopian action movies; you know the ones, when the voice-over guy starts out by saying, in this *really* grave tone, "In a world where . . ."

In a world where nothing is as it seems, and no one is safe.

My last night at camp felt like that, like a twist ending that caught me—that caught all of us—by surprise.

We were fourteen then, and had been going to Camp Nedoba together for five summers—me, Skylar, Maddie, and Jo, "the JEMS," as we regrettably called ourselves. (In our defense, it was the only way the first letters of all our names spelled something resembling a word. SMEJ just didn't have the same ring.) We were inseparable, and those seventy-two acres of rolling hills, fields, and woods in eastern New Hampshire felt like our Neverland. So our last night was a big deal. Especially since, that year, our last night wasn't just the last night of the summer, with tearful promises to keep in touch and reunite after slogging through another nine months in our "real" lives. It was our last night *ever.* We had to make it count.

Every summer at Camp Nedoba started and ended with a bonfire by the lake, which the camp director, Mack Putnam, liked to joke cost him a lot of extra money in insurance, but which was apparently some kind of meaningful ritual for the Abenaki Indian tribe. Mack is only one-eighth Abenaki but everything at the camp is named for them—*nedoba* even means *friend*—and he's on some special tribal council that holds powwows every couple of months. But if you're picturing Sitting Bull or Crazy Horse, you're way off. Mack looks sort of like Mr. Brady from *The Brady Bunch,* if he became a gym teacher and grew a mustache. He's just really into his heritage. Jo says he went to a spiritual adviser after his wife left him and bought the camp the very next day. And Jo's his daughter, so she should know.

Our last bonfire wasn't that much different from our first, except that we knew all the songs by then and shouted them louder than anyone else—the one about the boy and the girl in the little canoe, the one about Johnny Appleseed, the weirdly upbeat one about the sinking of the *Titanic*. The words came like breathing at that point. But then at the end, instead of watching the seniors get hastily made construction paper certificates from the counselors, *our* names got called, along with titles the counselors gave us . . . which they thought were funny, I guess, but which seemed kind of pointless to me. That kind of thing just shows you how other people see you, diluted down to your most easily identifiable traits, which is hardly ever the same as how you see yourself. Only your best friends know the *real* you, the things no one else can see, which take time to unearth and appreciate. Which is why we had our own ceremony, just the four of us.

We'd been doing it since our first summer, when I started it kind of by accident: a Friendship Pact, a sort of code of conduct that we added rules to each year. The initial pact was just a single piece of notebook paper that we folded up like a fan and covered with stickers, but then the next year Skylar showed up with a thick stack of index cards and a leather artist's portfolio lined with silk that she'd painted over with a map of camp. On the last night every summer, we each added a new pledge. I can't speak for the others, but for me it became like a superstition; as long as we did it, we couldn't lose each other. We wouldn't forget.

It wasn't too hard to sneak away to do our ritual. Mack was a great camp leader, but he ran it pretty much by himself, with a handyman and a nurse around during the day to help out. And of course there were the counselors, but with a ratio of about one of them to every eight of us, there were always holes to slip through if you timed it right, especially on the last bonfire nights when everyone was hopped up on soda and s'mores and the restless energy that comes from knowing you only have one more night to burn it off. Later on I would realize that the counselors had other things on their minds, too, and were eager to have us amuse ourselves with our PG-13 rebellions while they attended to their more mature ones.

We crept through the dark woods—so familiar in the day, not quite so much at night, even though by that time we felt like we owned the place and knew how to blindly bypass obstacles like the dead tree at the bottom of the hill, having tripped over it and tumbled hard onto our palms too many times—moving forward until the shore of Lake Ossipee opened up in front of us, still and calm like a just-washed chalkboard. Soon the counselors would be rowing out to the middle of the lake with a boatload of amateur pyrotechnics for a fireworks display, but for a few minutes, anyway, we had the view to ourselves. We kicked off our flip-flops and sat on the beach, knee-to-sun-browned-knee, in a loose circle. Jo untied the bandana she was wearing around her head and spread it on the pebbly sand, and I took off my backpack and laid the portfolio down carefully. It was so full now it bulged; last year it had taken both me and Skylar to tie it shut.

"Ready?" I asked, passing out felt-tip pens.

"I can't believe this is the last time we get to do this," Maddie said, drawing her freckled knees up to her chest, her pale blue eyes brimming with tears beneath her mop of auburn curls. Out of all of us, she had been the most openly distraught over the end of camp. Even back on our first day that year, when she'd crossed the threshold of Cocheco, the coveted oldest girls' cabin, Maddie had dropped her bags dramatically and cried, "It's my last entrance!" We'd been cracking up over that one all summer.

"You can go last, then, to draw it out," Jo said curtly. She never had much patience for displays of emotion, but then again she didn't often get to act like a regular teenager. She was her dad's self-appointed deputy, and she took the job seriously, which was probably why she got crowned Most Responsible at the awards ceremony. Campers called her "Mini Mack" when she wasn't around, which she knew but pretended she didn't. But she was kind of asking for it, always opting to dress just like him, in beige cargo shorts and a green Camp Nedoba T-shirt, her black hair pulled back into a sleek ponytail.

"Johannah," Maddie said pointedly, raising an eyebrow—Jo hated it when we called her by her full name, and Maddie never wasted an opportunity—"Don't pretend you're not gonna miss me." She swatted at a mosquito that was circling her ankles. (You know that one person in a group who always gets bitten? That was Maddie. Maddie and her sweet Southern blood.)

"Of course I'll miss you," Jo said, scribbling on her card. "But it's not forever. In fact . . ." She held up her offering and read it out loud. "Rule #17: Best friends always come back next year to be counselors with Jo." She tossed it into the center of the circle and crossed her arms, her lips pursed in a defiant smirk.

"Come on, that doesn't count," Skylar said. "We can't promise that." No one was guaranteed a spot on staff except Jo, since her dad had custody for the summer and there wasn't anywhere else for her to go. The rest of us had to write essays and submit reference letters just to apply. It wasn't fair, but neither was the fact that Jo could run a seven-minute mile fueled by a diet of Twizzlers and orange Crush.

"Emma," Jo sighed, turning to me. "I thought we weren't allowed to censor each other." That had been Rule #16.

"She's right, though," I said. "It's not up to us. And the pact has to be made up of rules we can follow."

"Okay," she said, chewing on the end of her pen as she thought. "How about, Rule #17: Best friends do everything in their power to come back together in the place they met each year?"

I smiled and nodded, though I think even then I knew it was a stretch. During the school year, we were all scattered down the East Coast. Maddie lived the farthest—almost nine hundred miles away in North Carolina—which had earned her the night's Frequent Flyer award. It was a title she was disappointed about, since, she argued, traveling up from the South—while rare for a New England camp—was kind of a cop-out attribute. ("It's so generic," she'd grumbled. "I'd rather have gotten Biggest Rack! Which she did have, so we all had to admit she had a point.)

"Can I go?" Skylar asked, clutching her card, which was already smudged with thumbprints of charcoal dust. Skylar got Most Artistic camper, which you could tell just by looking at the acrylic paint and conté crayon wedged under her chipped purple fingernails, a multicolored grime that wouldn't come off no matter how hard she scrubbed—and the showers at Nedoba were communal, so I'd seen it and I knew. That's also how I knew she had the world's most perfect body, and if she hadn't been one of my best friends I would probably have felt like hitting her with a cartoon anvil at all times. She cleared her throat and started to read. "Rule #18," she began, and then smiled. "I like eighteen, it's pastel, kind of orangey."

"Is Rule #18 a Creamsicle?" Jo asked, giving Skylar an affectionate nudge. Skylar always claimed she could "see" colors in numbers and letters. My mom, who has a masters in psychology, says that's called synesthesia, but our joke back then was that the technical term was "being a hippie," since Skylar grew up on an artist's commune in Pennsylvania.

"Shut up," Skylar said. "And you already broke it with that comment. Rule #18: Best friends always treat each other with respect." She added her card to the pile slowly and delicately, as if to illustrate her point. Maddie blew her a kiss across the circle.

"She teases because she loves," she said, giving Jo a look.

Skylar was big on respect that summer, because she'd been hooking up with a guy who gave her exactly none of it—something that would, sadly, become a pattern as she got older. Zeke Tanner was gorgeous, talented, and "brooding," which as far as I was concerned was just another word for "mean." She told me more about him than she told Maddie and Jo, I think because Skylar and I were a little closer to each other than we were to them—it's hard not to break off into pairs even in such a tight-knit group. She and Zeke had been making out since the night of the first session dance, but lately he'd been pressuring her to do more, and ignoring her completely in public while she took the time to think about it. I told her that under no circumstances should she let a manipulative drama queen like that past first base, but Sky promised me that he wasn't all bad. He was a poet, she said, which I thought was unlikely given that I'd never heard him use a word with more than two syllables, but I kept my mouth shut. For the most part.

Skylar had always gotten a lot of attention, not just from guys but from everyone. Even as an adolescent, she was beautiful in the way that everyone wants to be but almost no one is: she never wore makeup (she hated it, in fact, which is ironic considering how much time she spent painting plainer canvases) and still always looked like she just climbed out of a Renaissance painting, the kind where everyone is eating pomegranates on blankets in the grass with cherubs flying around. Fresh out of bed after two days without so much as a perfunctory comb (Skylar was a pioneer of dirty-girl chic), people would ask her how she got her blond waves to look that way. I, on the other hand, was known to a lot of the guys at Nedoba—after *five years*—as "Skylar's friend Emma." Adam Loring had been the one to start that nickname. Or "Zen," if I got lucky and they remembered my weird Polish last name.

I guess I should have at least been grateful *that* wasn't my end-of-camp award. I actually got Biggest Bookworm, which seemed like code for Least Hookup Potential, or Most Consistent Wearing of Night Guard. They only gave it to me because I'd been trying to get through *Jane Eyre* for my ninth grade honors English class the next year, and I'd brought the hardcover with me to breakfast a couple of times. I mean, it's not like I was some fourteen-year-old librarian. I spent a lot of time at Camp Nedoba trying to convince people I was cooler than I looked. Being friends with Skylar definitely helped my case.

"Okay," Maddie said with a theatrical sigh. "I'm ready for my close-up. Rule #19: Best friends are a part of your family." She beamed at us as she placed her card on the pile. None of us had ever met Maddie's family because she always got dropped off and picked up by cabs. Her mom was some kind of high-powered consultant and her dad was a heart surgeon, and they both basically lived at work. Maddie didn't talk about them much, and I remember thinking she must have been lonely, and that maybe she was so emotional because she didn't have much to go home to. It turns out I didn't know the half of it.

"That's sweet, Mads, but . . . that's not really a *rule*," Jo said, pulling a rogue marshmallow out of her pocket and popping it into her mouth.

"Now who's censoring?" Maddie went from sentimental to surly in the span of a millisecond. The way her emotions played out on her face, like electric currents ran just under the skin, always convinced me she'd make a great actress if she wanted to be.

"You guys *do* fight like sisters," Skylar pointed out.

"Sustained," I said.

Maddie seemed placated.

"Okay, Em," Jo said gravely. "You started this, you get to finish it."

"No pressure or anything," I laughed. I looked down at my final offering to the Friendship Pact, a neat line of pink block letters. I was cheating; it was really more of a cleverly disguised wish than a rule. Reading it out loud felt a little bit like hurling a penny into a fountain and hoping against hope that it would turn my luck around.

"Rule #20," I said, pausing for maximum poignancy. "Best friends always help each other follow their dreams."

Skylar raised her eyebrows and gave me a sly smile. She knew my rule came with an unspoken subtext.

"I'll be glad to help you," Maddie said with a wink. "Just tell me where he is."

Okay, scratch that. A spoken subtext. Because on my last night at Camp Nedoba, I was trying to make a very specific dream come true.

I was trying to finally gather the courage to tell Adam Loring that I loved him.

But first, we had to seal the pact.

I reached into my backpack and took out the necessary tools: a Thermos full of "bug juice" that Maddie had siphoned off from the coolers in the back of the cafeteria, along with a plastic cup; four stumpy, misshapen candles Skylar and I had made in the arts and crafts cabin; and a pack of matches—an illegal item that Jo had lifted from Mack's office, where he kept confiscated goods like cell phones, Swiss Army knives, and paperbacks with half-naked muscle-men on the cover.

"Quickly," Jo urged. Off in the woods, leaves were rustling. We wouldn't be alone for long.

It was only the second year we had done the candle part, so we weren't particularly coordinated, but we made it through without setting anyone's hair on fire. I lit my candle and held it out into the center of the circle, and the other three used the flame to light their candles while we recited a little vow we composed our second summer: "You are my rose, never my thorn, and through these pledges, friendship is sworn." (Not exactly Yeats, but give us a break—we were eleven.) Then we passed around the bug juice and each drank a gulp. That detail was from a Celtic ritual Maddie had read about online. Or her aunt's Greek Orthodox wedding ceremony—she couldn't remember which.

We blew out our candles and looked around at one another in the darkness.

"Thank goodness this is the last year," Maddie finally said. "The only way to top that would be a virgin sacrifice."

"Not it!" Jo cried, touching a finger to her nose.

"Not it!" Maddie seconded.

Skylar and I touched our hands to our noses at the exact same time, locked eyes, and started to laugh. And then I looked up at the sky and saw a shooting star. I knew it was a sign. It had to be.

But half an hour later, I was less convinced. "He's not coming back," I said to Skylar. By that point a bunch of other senior campers had wandered down to the shore and were sneaking off, two by two, into the surrounding trees. There were smacking noises, giggles, and whispers that ricocheted off the water. Most of the counselors were ushering the younger campers back to their beds, and the few that remained were out on the lake, loudly arguing about how best to set off the fireworks without blowing themselves up.

"He *is*," Skylar said.

Jo rolled her eyes. Jo rolled her eyes every time we talked about Adam. She liked him—everyone did, it was basically impossible not to—but she hated boy talk. As far as I knew, Jo had never had a crush on anyone but Michael Phelps, and even that stopped when the picture of him smoking that bong hit the Internet. She didn't understand my thing for Adam, but I knew she didn't exactly disapprove, either. After all, she was the one who had begged her dad to let her chaperone the campers on the shore while he cleaned up the fire pit, knowing it would buy me some time.

But I wasn't the only one hoping for a last chance. Zeke emerged from the shadows, his white-blond hair falling over one eye like he was a boy-band backup dancer, and whispered something to Skylar that made her giggle.

"Can I meet up with you guys later?" she asked, already on her feet, not waiting for an answer.

"Don't forget: slumber party in the bunk!" Jo called.

Maddie threw her arms around Jo's shoulders. "Don't worry—I'll be there," she said. "Unlike *some people* I have no handsome prince to whisk me off into the woods for a romantic tryst."

"Neither do I," I said. "I might as well be wearing a shirt that says 'I Had a Crush on Adam Loring for Five Summers and All I Got Was This Lousy T-Shirt.'"

"That would certainly break the ice," Maddie said, this time throwing her arms around me. "But he likes you. I know it."

"Then where is he?" I groaned into my hands. He had left the bonfire to retrieve a hoodie for me but hadn't been seen since. If Adam did like me, wouldn't he be just as eager to find me, to take his shot, to squire me off to a moonlit clearing like Zeke had done to Skylar? He'd probably forgotten about the hoodie. Maybe it had just been an excuse to ditch me.

Jo's head popped up like a bloodhound's, her spine suddenly as straight as her jet-black ponytail, which reached almost to the waistband of her shorts. She held a finger to her lips. "I think I just heard a zipper," she said, horrified. Then: "This was a bad idea."

"Oh, relax," Maddie said. "It's probably just some guy, you know, watering the wildflowers." I smiled, but Jo didn't seem to get the joke. She leaped up and marched off toward the tree line brandishing her whistle.

"Go get 'em, Sarge!" Maddie called after her. Under her breath, she said, "We have got to get that girl another hobby."

A few minutes later, Maddie took my backpack full of pact paraphernalia back to Cocheco. Jo was still busy refereeing the backwoods bacchanal, so I was by myself. Sitting alone in public usually makes me cringe, but that night it felt right. It gave me a minute to say good-bye to the place that felt more like home to me than my own room in my own house. I could see lights on the other side of the lake out in the darkness, like fireflies skimming the blue-black water, and heard the pines rattling overhead like wind chimes. I remember thinking that I'd never want to forget the sounds of camp: the creaking of the storm-battered planks of the dock, the flat smack of rain on the tarp roofs of the cabins. I convinced myself I would even be nostalgic for the famous Nedoba wake-up bell, which sounded to the untrained ear like a toddler banging on a cast-iron skillet with a golf club; or Mack playing taps on the dented pocket trumpet he'd bought at a pawn shop in town for twenty dollars. (He was self-taught, so sometimes it was hard to tell if he was playing taps or if someone was branding a steer at the farm next door, but he kept practicing and generally got a little better every year.)

I knew I should just head back to the bunk and hang out with Maddie, focus on my friends. I don't know why I thought I was going to get some fairy-tale ending that night. Nothing left to the last minute ever turns out the way you want it to; that's when the most mistakes get made.

Adam and I had been friends since the end of our first summer, when we'd gotten trapped under an overturned canoe during my first and last Camp Nedoba boating lesson. And we'd been flirting pretty heavily since the beginning of our fourth summer, probably since I'd just gotten my braces off and he wasn't left with anything to tease me mercilessly about. Adam flirted with everyone, so I knew I could be wrong, but I swore there was something there that wasn't just in my head. The way he looked at me sometimes—staring, without even a trace of his ever-present, lopsided grin—made me want to throw up, in a good way. I'd never had the nerve to actually tell him how I felt, but then again the stakes had never been particularly high. I would always see him the next day, or the next summer. But it was depressing to think about leaving camp without knowing if he felt something, too. I was reluctantly slipping back into my flip-flops, summoning my resolve to surrender, when I heard his voice.

"Emma!" The sand was uneven under my feet and adrenaline shot through my system so fast I was afraid for a second I might lose my balance. But I took a deep breath and closed my eyes and when I opened them again I saw him, walking down the path from the fire pit, holding up a red hoodie with a triumphant smile. His best friend, Nate Hartner, shuffled after him about ten feet behind, trying to keep up in shower shoes while carrying an armful of leftover graham crackers and sodas. Nate's belly spilled over the elastic waist of his basketball shorts and his face was pinched in concentration. Poor Nate. He was so nice, everyone treated him like a lapdog.

I managed to get my shoes on and make my legs work and walked out to meet them halfway, in front of a crowd of campers who were playing spin the bottle with an empty Sprite can. Adam presented me with the grungy sweatshirt like he was wrapping me in furs. His reddish-brown hair was a little shaggy after eight weeks, and it curled up on the ends. He smelled like cedar and sunblock.

"Sorry it took so long," he said. "*Someone* had to, ahem, take care of business."

Nate furrowed his brow. "Dude! That is not cool. This is the last time I'm helping you get snacks for your girlfriend."

My breath caught in my throat. I knew I was a girl and that Adam was my friend, but the compound word hung in the air between us, introducing a thrilling new world of possibility. Adam stuck his hands in his pockets and looked down at the sand as Nate stalked off, and I prayed he couldn't see the flush of color flooding my cheeks.

"I, uh—" He cleared his throat. *Oh my God,* I thought. This was it. He was going to ask me to go somewhere and talk and something was actually going to happen. I pressed my lips together to check if they were too dry, knowing it was dark enough that I could always swipe some lip balm on while we walked through the woods. I was so glad I let Skylar talk me into wearing my hair down, so that if I were, hypothetically, to be on my back at some point in the near future, it would spread out on the leaves and I wouldn't have a hard bump of ponytail behind my head. I felt positively giddy. I had played the scene over and over in my mind, and I knew exactly how I wanted it to go.

"I, um, didn't tell him you were my girlfriend," Adam said finally, looking sheepish. "He knows we're just friends. He's being a jerk."

Wait, that wasn't in the script. But it was too late. The spin the bottle crowd noticed us talking close and someone wolf whistled and then everyone started making that obnoxious, slow-building "Oooooooooooooh" sound that always reminds me of a car alarm you can't turn off.

"What's going on over *here*?" chirped Sunny Sherman, the self-appointed camp gossip, who had the unfortunate combination of being incredibly nosy both figuratively and literally. (Adam used to call her Beak in private, and I always told him to stop, but right then I wanted to punch her in it.)

Mark Slotkin, one half of Nedoba's only set of identical twins and Sunny's on-again-off-again boyfriend, sidled up beside her, saying, "Hey, Loring, you finally gonna hit that?"

Someone squeezed my hand. For a second I let myself hope that it was Adam, but it was Skylar, having materialized from somewhere in the nearby trees, the half-rotten leaf caught in her hair looking like fall's must-have accessory.

"Leave them alone," she said evenly. "Shouldn't you be off someplace showing Sunny that pencil in your pants?" Adam laughed, and even though I knew there was no way Skylar could be speaking from experience, I was shocked by her fearlessness. Then again, she'd hooked up with about ten times as many people as I had. Except that the multiplication doesn't really work out, seeing as how my number was actually zero.

"You're a bitch," Mark said bitterly, and Jo stomped over from her post by the woods, waving away gnats.

"There a problem here?" she asked, resting one hand on her hip, the other fondling the whistle.

"No, ma'am," Mark said. "I just found some virginity over by the outhouse and thought someone might have lost it. But Loring's got his, don'tcha buddy?" He snorted and walked away, Sunny bouncing behind.

"Well, that was humiliating," Adam said once Mark was out of earshot.

"I don't think so," Jo said. "I mean, who's *not* a virgin? Anyway, sex isn't allowed on camp property, and getting caught doing it is grounds for expulsion."

Skylar bristled, and for the first time I noticed that her big green eyes were red and bloodshot.

"Are you okay?" I whispered. She bit her lip and shook her head. I tried to make please-come-with-me-without-saying-anything-obvious eyes at Jo, but she was immune to subtle body language.

"What?" she asked blankly after I'd stared at her for a good ten seconds.

"Give us one minute," I said to Adam, pulling Jo with me. "Seriously, I'll be right back. Don't move."

I linked elbows with Skylar as we walked down toward the water, its soft, rhythmic lapping muffling our voices from prying ears.

"What happened?" I asked.

"Something happened?" Jo parroted. "See, I *knew* this was a bad idea."

Skylar looked out at the lake, the moonlight casting a soft glow onto her tear-streaked face.

"He broke it off," she said, her voice wavering.

"I'm sorry," I said. I wasn't, really, but I hated seeing Skylar in pain. For someone so outwardly confident, she has always had thin skin. My personal theory is that she never had an awkward phase—no glasses, no braces, no acne, no body odor, none of the stuff that hardens you through middle school, the emotional equivalent of walking on hot coals with bare feet.

"It's probably because it's the last night of camp," I said. "It's a breakup of convenience. Obviously he's crazy."

"No," she said. "He said he couldn't ever see us working out because . . . he doesn't find me . . . interesting." Fresh tears spilled over onto her cheeks, and she wiped them away shakily with the back of one hand.

"Oh, please," Jo cried. "Was this before or after you wouldn't touch his crotch?"

"Shhhhh!" Skylar hushed.

"He's a loser," I said, taking the leaf out of her hair and smoothing it behind her ear. "A *pretentious* loser."

"Yeah," Skylar sniffed. "I really liked him, though. And I thought"—her voice cracked again—"he really liked me."

We stood there for a minute just comforting her, and I tried not to let my eyes drift over to Adam, to see if he was looking at me.

"Listen," Jo said. "I need to go check in with my dad. Why don't you come with me and I'll walk you back to the bunk? There's a bag of Cheetos with your name on it."

Skylar smiled weakly. "Thanks," she said. "But I think I just need to be by myself for awhile."

"Okay, but if you change your mind, you know where to find me." Jo started to jog off and then turned, tossing her whistle to Skylar. "Don't be afraid to use it!" she called.

"Nothing says love like a panic whistle," I muttered, patting Skylar's back. "But will you really be okay? I don't want to leave you."

"I'll be fine," she said. "And besides, you've got Adam waiting for you."

"It's not like we . . ." I struggled to finish the sentence. "It's not a big deal." I said, hoping she couldn't tell I was lying.

"It is!" Skylar leaned in and hugged me. "It *is* a big deal, Emma. Adam genuinely likes you. And you've been waiting for this. You're lucky." She pulled back and managed a wan smile. "Now go get him."

"Are you sure?"

"*Go,*" she said.

I turned back once before I reached Adam, and saw Skylar in silhouette against the stars, her hair spilling messily down her back in a tousled waterfall. I wouldn't see her again until the next morning.

"I can't believe it's our last night," I said to Adam as we walked down the beach, each step taking us further and further from what was starting to seem like a foregone conclusion: my hope, my wish, my chance, gaining momentum like a snowball of hormones that compelled me to do things like flip my hair over my shoulder and push my lips out ever so slightly when I wasn't talking, sort of like I was sucking an invisible straw. All it had taken, it turned out, was asking him to go for a walk. It had been so easy: I'd asked, he had said yes. Well, actually, to be technical, he had said "Sure," but it had seemed enthusiastic. Why hadn't I done that ages ago? Why hadn't anyone told me?

"Yeah, crazy," Adam said, but he was kind of frowning, looking at the ground. Not at my lips. His mind seemed someplace else. I spit out the invisible straw.

"Mark's an idiot," I said, rubbing the worn cuff sleeve of the hoodie between my thumb and forefinger. "I think it's nice."

"What is?"

"That you're . . . you know. A virgin." I instantly regretted saying it. "I mean, it's nice when *guys* are virgins," I hedged. "Because . . . I don't know, it's just sweet." Now I was really digging myself into a hole. "Or, what I mean is, girls want a guy who thinks they're special and who's . . . waited for them. You know?" He relaxed a little bit, looked at me, and smiled softly.

"Yeah?"

"Yeah. I guess I can't speak for other girls, but I want to feel special."

"You are special, Emma," he said, looking so earnest it was all I could do to keep from kissing him right then and there. My heart pounded in my ears. I could barely see straight.

"So what was all that with Skylar back there?" he asked as we rounded the bend that led out to the big rocks where counselors sometimes led low-tide explorations during the day.

"Oh. Um . . ." It felt like breaking her trust to tell him, but I figured he'd find out soon anyway. Adam and Zeke were sort of friends. "She and Zeke broke up."

Adam shook his head. "She could have any guy she wants," he said. "I never understood why she picked that douche."

"My feelings exactly." I brushed his hand with mine, accidentally on purpose. "But I think all the adoration can go to her head sometimes. *You* know what that's like." Adam wasn't classically handsome, like Superman or Brad Pitt—his nose was a little big, not that I'm one to talk—but he had a nice face, twinkling eyes, and an amazing smile. Plus he was funny, with that almost imperceptible edge of sadness that's like catnip to anyone with a double-X chromosome. Throughout our years of friendship, Adam always had some not-quite-thing going on with some not-quite-right girl. He had a knack for making everyone feel close to him, when no one really was.

That summer, I had been trying to get him to open up to me about his life back home, with middling results. He'd told me that in sixth grade he'd been diagnosed with mild ADHD and that his dad wanted to treat him but his mom didn't, because she read a book called *The Overmedicated Child* that Adam had found—complete with damning annotations—in the pantry underneath her carb-free diet bars. I knew he had some trouble in school and that his prized possession was his grandfather's Red Sox cap, which was signed on the back by Carl Yastrzemski, and which he had never worn outside the house because he was so superstitious about losing it. But that was basically it. For someone so talkative, Adam didn't say much.

"Oh, come on," he protested, grabbing my hand for balance as we navigated the newly wobbly terrain of slick boulders with our arms outstretched. "I'm not that bad."

"You just got voted Biggest Flirt—by the *counselors*," I reminded him, and he laughed.

"Touché."

The rocks looking out at the western coast of Wexley Island—a supervised overnight campground about half a mile off shore that everyone called "Sexy Island" for the rumored counselor hook-ups that frequently went down there—could be jagged and uncomfortable, but they were also isolated, and they had pretty great views, especially on a clear night like that one, when the stars were so big and unbelievably bright they looked almost fake. Adam climbed nimbly onto a big, flat rock that was conveniently about the size of a loveseat. He cocked one eyebrow and reached a hand down for me.

"Can I can convince you to join me on this luxury boulder?" he asked. I grasped his hand, braced my foot, and swung my other leg up. It wasn't graceful, but at least I didn't fall. I slid next to Adam, and our thighs touched. From our perch we could see the counselors' boat out on the lake in the moonlight. They were singing, and someone was shouting something about finding the goddamn lighter. I could feel Adam looking at me, but I was too afraid to look back. My skin felt electrically charged, and every infinitesimal movement he made set off an explosion in my brain that made me want to simultaneously fly and vomit.

"It's pretty up here," I finally squeaked.

"You're pretty up here." I looked over. He was smiling, but he didn't say it like a joke.

"Stop it," I said. *Please don't stop,* I thought.

"I mean it." He looked at me for a long minute. "Emma—" he paused, like he was trying to figure out what to say next. And then he put his hand on my leg.

I remember the next few seconds happening in slow motion. I turned to him, trying not to look as scared as I was. He started to lean—so slowly I wasn't even sure he was really leaning. Maybe I was just having lust-induced vertigo. His lips parted slightly, those warm brown eyes searching my face for permission, like that time I slipped climbing a tree in the north field when we were twelve and he had to take a two-inch splinter out of my shoulder. I knew what I was supposed to do; I was supposed to cock my head, close my eyes, and let go.

But I couldn't.

It was only once I was in the moment that I realized I couldn't go through with it. My thoughts started spiraling anxiously. Yes, kissing Adam would be amazing, I thought, but then what? The next morning our parents would come and pick us up, and we couldn't exactly have a tender good-bye. And then he would go north to Maine and I would go south to Boston and we didn't even know if we would be back the next year as CITs (a.k.a. counselors in training) together. If we kissed, everything would change, five years of friendship reset in a single second. Everything would change even more than it was already going to. I didn't know if it was worth it. At least the dull ache of my unrequited longing was familiar. I knew what it felt like. I knew I could survive it. But that kiss . . . suddenly, I wasn't so sure.

So at the last second, I turned my head. His lips brushed my earlobe, his nose bumped against my cheek.

"Sorry," I mumbled.

"Oh," he said, pulling back, looking surprised. "No, I'm sorry. I didn't . . . I mean, I thought . . . wow. Sorry." The first fireworks shot through the still night sky like lightning, and Adam shifted away from me. Sparks were literally flying through the air and we had a front row seat, and I was wearing his hoodie, which smelled so much like him I wanted to live in it. I couldn't have asked for a better moment, and I'd just ruined it, so I muttered an excuse about having to get back to help Jo wrap up the leftover s'mores, gave him a stiff, awkward hug, and jumped down to the sand, barely sticking the landing, I was shaking so hard. As I ran back, cutting through the woods so no one saw me, willing the hot tears to wait until I was safe in my bed or curled in my friends' arms, I could still hear the fireworks crackling overhead like gunfire, invisible bullets grazing my heart again and again.

That was the last night I saw Adam. It was also the last time for years that Skylar, Jo, Maddie, and I were all in one place—well, the next morning was, but it was so chaotic and went so fast it barely registered. Our real good-bye had been on the beach, when we sealed the pact, but none of us had known it at the time. If we had, maybe we would have stayed longer, lingered with our toes in the cool sand, listening to each other laugh, letting our candles burn down to our ink-stained fingertips.

Only Sky and Jo came back the next summer as CITs. So did Adam and Nate, and the twins. Maddie had some family stuff to deal with, she said, so she didn't come back, and I applied, but—and it's still hard to say this, three years later—I wasn't chosen. Mack wrote me a nice note along with my rejection, explaining that he just hadn't seen enough of my wilderness skills to be able to confidently hire me, but it stung. In retrospect I guess reading in the bunk all day was a bad call. I cried for a week and then threw myself even more into school, even getting a summer internship from my dad's friend, collating papers at his asbestos litigation law firm (which was as thrilling as it sounds). I told the others I was too busy to be a counselor, but Jo probably knew the truth; I never asked and she never mentioned it. We all kept in touch every few weeks that first year, but then we started to let months go by, which turned into whole semesters. We tried to four-way video chat once, but Maddie's Internet connection kept dropping out. She blamed Mercury in retrograde.

Some nights, later on, I'd find myself lying in bed spooning my laptop and scrolling through Facebook photos Skylar had posted from camp. In them, she was always mid-laugh, her arm draped over someone else's shoulder: a tensely smiling Jo wearing what looked like—could it be?—lip gloss; a slimmer, dimpled, surprisingly attractive Nate. There's one particular photo I always came back to, though, one of her and Adam sitting on the counselors' porch. It must have been taken at the end of the summer, because they're both really tan. They're splayed out in Adirondack chairs, grinning and holding Dixie cups of bug juice. Each drink is topped with one of those miniature cocktail umbrellas, and Skylar captioned the photo "Wish you were here. . . ." It was like she had written it for me.

It was weird seeing my old friends get taller and cycle through different haircuts, but that's not why the photos kept reeling me back in. It was a little heartbreaking to see snapshots of a new Camp Nedoba that I wasn't a part of. Something like Halley's Comet shows up once a century and then disappears again, but camp just kept going without me in it. I knew, deep down, that I could always go back, and that we'd always be friends. But life had obviously gotten in the way. So I was beyond excited when I got the reunion invitation, set for three summers after our graduation. It was an opportunity for us all to be together again, in the place where our story started, away from the stresses and distractions of everyday life.

It felt, in so many ways, like a second chance.

Emma

Reunion: Day 1

Present Day • Age 17

EMMA WAS RUNNING LATE. SHE *HATED* RUNNING LATE. Reunion registration started at eleven, but the girls had set their own pre-reunion for ten thirty, and with the traffic she was hitting as she approached Worcester on the Mass Pike, there was no way she would make it. But she was driving her aunt's car—without *express* permission, although, Emma reminded herself, Aunt Leila had written "What's mine is yours" in the two-page memo she had affixed to the fridge, along with instructions on how to water her azaleas and the preferred ratio of wet-to-dry food mix for her obese and ornery cat, Raoul—and so Emma was sticking to the speed limit. She couldn't afford to pay a ticket, anyway, on her ten-dollar-a-day stipend from what had turned out to be the most disappointing summer job ever.

It had sounded so perfect: an editorial internship at *Miss Demeanor,* a teen-focused literary magazine that featured original essays along with articulate, funny, nonpatronizing advice about issues like sex, drugs, and conflicts with parents. After putting in a long, mind-numbingly boring year editing the op-ed page for the *Reed Memorial High School Voice* ("The Spork in the Road," an argument against plastic cafeteria utensils, was a high point), Emma had been ecstatic to start working at a real publication that wrote about real issues that would look amazing on her college applications *and* was based in New York City, where she could get away from what had become a constant, slow-burning battle with her parents over whether she would retake the SATs in the fall. (2100 was 96th percentile, but they felt that was on the low end for the Ivy League.) She'd harbored fantasies about penning Pulitzer Prize–winning investigative reports—or at the very least getting to write posts for the magazine's blog. But after a week spent making lunch runs and refilling the printer ink, Emma had been forced to readjust her expectations.

"*Editorial intern* is just code for *slush pile slave*," a fellow intern named Jeff had told her on her second day, as they waded through box after box of unsolicited submissions, 99.9 percent of which got transferred directly into the paper shredder, unless the grammatical errors were egregious enough to earn them a place on the conference room bulletin board. Jeff had just finished his first year at NYU, and his blue eyes, brown hair, dimples, and thick black-framed glasses made him look like Clark Kent. Jeff was definitely the best part of *Miss Demeanor* so far, Emma thought with a smile, glancing up at herself in the rearview mirror as traffic slowed to a complete stop.

But work was quickly slipping from her mind the further she

got from New York and the closer she got to the exit that would take her off the highway and through the sleepy main street of Onan, New Hampshire, up to the old oak tree adorned with a threadbare blue flag that signaled the discreet right turn onto Nedoba's private gravel road. Emma couldn't believe she was finally going back. It seemed physically impossible, like how she used to feel about air travel as a kid, waking up in Boston and going to sleep in California. No matter how many times her dad explained the mechanics of flight, she just couldn't accept that magic didn't factor in somehow. That morning, as she'd brushed her teeth in her aunt's narrow bathroom, with a window that looked out on Central Park, Emma had tried to picture lying down that night on a thin, musty mattress, looking up at the underside of a bunk bed, hearing Skylar, Jo, and Maddie's voices, and she couldn't do it. But as she inched the green station wagon down the highway, it was getting more real by the minute, and Emma was equal parts thrilled and terrified.

She'd been texting with Skylar more over the weeks leading up to reunion (*Ten days!* Emma would write, receiving a reply hours later in Sky's hasty typing—*Duuuude cant wait <3 uuu!*), but it had been at least six months since they'd exchanged any real correspondence. The last time they'd talked, in January, Skylar had been about to leave for a semester abroad in Florence, and she and Skylar had made excited plans to apply to Brown and RISD, respectively, so they could see each other again during college, all the time. At the end of the call, like always, they swore up and down to make a weekly phone date, but then Sky had never replied to Emma's e-mails asking for her international number, and Emma had gotten swept up in schoolwork, SAT prep, and internship applications, anyway. Skylar had written a mass e-mail to the girls once, from Italy, which focused almost exclusively on a guy named Carlo, a tour guide she had started dating after he'd taken her on a gondola ride along the Arno. Emma didn't know if he was still in the picture. Skylar's Facebook relationship status was listed as "It's complicated."

Maddie had been even harder to pin down than Skylar. Over the years, she had amassed four different e-mail addresses, and Emma was never really clear on which one she actually checked. Often she would see an e-mail from Maddie in her inbox and get excited only to find out it was a spam ad for diet pills or inflatable underpants to make your butt look shapelier. It was just the sort of prank Maddie would have pulled in their camp days, and it made Emma miss her even more.

Jo was the best at keeping in touch, but her updates were never particularly illuminating. She would e-mail that her team had won the regional volleyball championship or that she was getting certified in ropes course training and was lobbying her dad to set one up at camp. But every time Emma would reply to her with an enthusiastic "How are you??" Jo's response was always the same: "Good." She was good. Things were good. Camp was good. Emma had come to hate the word *good*. It was what people said when they couldn't or didn't want to talk about what they actually felt.

She looked over at the backpack sitting on the passenger seat. It was the same one she'd brought to camp every summer since she was ten: pink canvas with a fold-over flap at the top painted with black seeds to look like a watermelon slice. Despite the fact that carrying it was now highly embarrassing, Emma had spent two hours cleaning out her closet during a visit back home just to find it so that she could bring it with her to camp again. It wasn't so much the backpack as what was inside that she needed: the Friendship Pact. Maybe she had just been reading too many sci-fi novels, but it felt like a talisman, something to help make sure reunion brought them back together again—not just for a weekend, but for good.

Emma had spent a lot of time thinking about when things had started to change. Every summer had brought minor shifts, just the natural effects of increased hormones and responsibilities (even though Emma felt like laughing at them now, those twelve- and thirteen-year-old troubles that seemed so monumental, like finishing a summer reading list or passing a swim test). And of course there were their "real world" friends, the ones they saw every day from September through June and who became more important fixtures in their outside lives as they got older. But those things hadn't made the girls drift apart. Not on their own, anyway. Something had shifted the last night of camp, after Skylar hadn't come back to the cabin. Emma had felt it the next day—and it wasn't just Skylar, although she was distant; Jo was unusually touchy-feely, and Maddie could barely get a word out without dissolving into tears. It was almost like there had been a bad storm while they were sleeping, and the next morning they had woken up to find that things just weren't in the right places anymore.

The traffic wasn't getting any better, so at the next rest area, Emma pulled over to use the bathroom and check her voicemail. As she pushed through the door to the QuikMart, sounding an electronic bell, she felt the clerk's eyes on her. He was maybe nineteen or twenty, with a round, boyish face and a sparse red goatee. He nodded and smiled at her as she turned down the aisle of energy bars and snack mixes that led to the ladies' room. "Morning, gorgeous," he said. She still wasn't used to it.

As she washed her hands, Emma looked in the mirror and tried to imagine what her fourteen-year-old self would think of the seventeen-year-old standing there. Without being too cocky, Emma thought she'd cleaned up nicely. Maybe not *gorgeous,* but the awkwardness of adolescence—the nose that felt ever-so-slightly large for her face, the scrawny limbs and nonexistent curves, the crooked smile—had given way to a prettiness that still managed to surprise her. She'd had to work at it a little bit, of course, learning how to blow-dry her hair, which was normally mousy, to a high-gloss sheen, pluck her eyebrows, and take care of her skin (and she still sometimes wore her retainer at night, secretly terrified that her teeth would shift back if she didn't), but part of it had happened naturally. "You've grown into your looks," was how her grandmother put it. It was a backhanded compliment, but Emma would take it. She put on some lip gloss and smacked her lips together the way Maddie had first showed her when they were eleven. Then she flashed herself a big grin. She thought she looked a lot better, but would they? And—she couldn't stop herself from wondering—would he?

It had taken her a while to get over Adam Loring, but Emma had eventually convinced herself that what had happened on the rocks that night had been for the best. She'd never been quite sure about him, anyway, even if he had been her first real crush. He was such a chameleon, sincere one minute and distant the next. She knew she needed to stop obsessing, so the second semester of freshman year she had made a beeline for Danny Hoffman during the Model UN's trip to Washington, DC. Danny was short, dark, and handsome, and extremely well versed in foreign events. They'd ridden on the paddleboats together and made out in the back of the bus on the drive back to Boston. It had lasted a month. Of course, the next year Danny had decided he was actually gay, but still, it felt like progress. Emma even felt good enough to e-mail Adam at the start of sophomore year, extending an electronic olive branch, and they started chatting online from time to time. He was still flirty, but that was just how Adam was. They never talked about the last night of camp. Mostly they commiserated about the Red Sox or traded complaints about school. Sometimes they talked obliquely about dating stuff, but it was harmless. Adam was still juggling girls and Emma still didn't have a serious relationship. In that respect, nothing had changed, but it didn't make her jealous anymore. She had only saved one of his instant messages, which had popped up on her laptop screen when she'd been in the shower after she'd first gotten to New York that summer: *Can't believe I'm going to see you in a month. Canoe?* It was a stupid inside joke, but it had made her laugh.

Emma was so wrapped up in her thoughts that she almost missed the exit, and as she veered sharply off onto the ramp, causing the driver behind her to lean on his horn, she realized that her heart was racing. She pulled up to a stoplight and took a series of deep breaths.

Reunion was going to be awesome, she told herself. Skylar, Maddie, and Jo had been such a huge part of her life for so long, and their history ran so deep, there was no way they wouldn't be able to pick up more or less where they'd left off. And Camp Nedoba had always felt like a haven—a place she could go to just be herself, where she wasn't defined by her grades or her letters of recommendation, and where people cared more if she could climb a tree than if she could score an 800 on her SAT verbal. That was why, even after three years, she felt like her camp friends knew her better than anyone.

Emma texted Skylar and waited for the light to turn green. She didn't know what the weekend had in store, but she couldn't wait to find out.

Skylar

Reunion: Day 1

SKYLAR SQUINTED INTO THE LATE MORNING SUN and examined her handiwork. She'd painted the reunion welcome banner with the help of her campers (she had the eleven-year-olds that session, in Missiquoi Cabin) the previous weekend, and with the exception of a bright purple *E* that had dripped down to the bottom of the paper, obscuring part of her painstakingly rendered panoramic sunset, she decided it looked pretty good.

"Right there!" she called to Jo, who was standing on a rickety ladder in order to hang it over the entrance to the whitewashed gazebo that separated the camp offices from the infirmary and counselors' lounge. Jo tacked up the last corner and vaulted down, stepping back and craning her neck to look.

"Is that supposed to be me?" Jo asked, pointing to the bottom left corner of the banner. Skylar replaced her pink Ray-Bans and smiled. She couldn't resist putting in a nod to the JEMS, and had painted four girls standing hand in hand like paper dolls: a blonde, a redhead, a brunette, and one on the end with a black ponytail who was yelling into a tiny megaphone.

But Jo didn't have her ever-present ponytail anymore. At the beginning of the summer she'd *finally* let Skylar lop it off—which had been on Skylar's to-do list, along with "Meet Lou Reed" and "Have a show at MoMA"—since she was twelve. The pixie cut Jo sported now (not half bad, Skylar thought, especially since she'd used nail scissors) brought Jo's delicate features into stunning relief, even if from the neck down she still wore her usual "You've got a 'friend' in Camp Nedoba!" T-shirt and beige cargo shorts. Jo had gotten so tall and gorgeous, Skylar sometimes got jealous. But it wasn't like they were competing over guys; Jo still used them for soccer practice, and Skylar used them for . . . a different kind of practice. Her hand fluttered up to her neck self-consciously, and she wondered if the hickey from last week was still there, hiding beneath the strands of her messy chignon. She'd had to tell her campers it was a bruise from getting smacked with an oar.

"No, it's just an *impression* of you," Skylar said, taking a sip from her water bottle. "I tried to use small brush strokes to really capture the changing quality of light glinting off your bullhorn."

"Mmmm hmmm," Jo murmured with a smirk. She grabbed the water and took a long gulp. "Come on, Monet, we've got work to do."

Reunion weekend was always a mixed blessing. It took place every year between sessions, after the first four-weekers left and the next set arrived. (The stalwart eight-weekers over the age of twelve had a choice of going home for the changeover days or going on an intense camping trip known as a WOW, or "weekend out in the wilderness.") Skylar was grateful not to have a bunch of 'tweens harassing her every second of the day for a brief period, but dealing with reunion campers could be even more draining. They were older, rowdier, and much more likely to break the rules. Mack had a strict no-alcohol policy (that admittedly his counselors, Skylar included, sometimes violated), but without fail there was always an incident during reunions, like on one memorable occasion when Gus, the camp handyman, had to clear fifty crushed beer cans out of the old well in the north field. But Skylar knew this reunion would be different. Because it was *her* reunion. And they were all coming back.

Mack popped his head out of the screen door of his office.

"Are you two setting up the food?" he called.

"Yes, Dad," Jo replied in the globally recognized sing-song of the Annoyed Teenager.

"Good," he said with a smile. "In my experience, nerves make people hungry."

Skylar's stomach rumbled. She'd been so distracted, she'd forgotten to eat breakfast. She was debating whether or not to forage in the cafeteria for a granola bar when her phone buzzed against her hip.

5 mins away. Try not to be jealous of my wheels. XO

Emma was probably winding her way up Granger Hill Road at that very moment, Skylar thought, which meant she was just over four miles away. But somehow, the distance between them felt much farther.

Skylar had been mentally preparing to see Emma again for approximately two years and eleven months, ever since she'd watched her ride away in the Zenewiczes' pumpkin-colored Prius on the last day of their fifth and final summer. That morning had been one of the worst of Skylar's entire life.

She'd imagined a few different scenarios for their inevitable reunion. The best option would have been visiting Emma in Boston to spend some time together, just the two of them, but she always talked herself out of actually making the plans. Emma's parents were super nice (if a little dorky), and Skylar knew they would welcome her like a second daughter, but what if things didn't go smoothly? Then she'd be stuck, an unaccompanied minor with no driver's license six hours from home. As year after year passed, even though she missed Emma like crazy, Skylar realized that she was purposefully dragging her feet and that the camp reunion was the only thing that was going to bring them face to face again. On one level it was poignant and fitting—long-lost friends coming back together in the place they first met—but on another, it felt weird, and maybe even a little wrong. So much had happened there. So much Emma didn't know.

Skylar had been avoiding thinking about what would happen when she finally saw Emma's face again in three dimensions. Would she cry? Plaster on a fake smile and act like everything was normal? With the uneasiness that had been building steadily since she woke up that morning, Skylar worried that she might actually puke. But to her relief, as soon as the peacock green station wagon turned into the parking lot, her nausea transformed into near-hysterical excitement. She broke into a run, jumping up and down in front of the car until Jo finally had to pull her out of the middle of the lot so Emma wouldn't run her over.

Just like she had the last time she'd seen Emma, Skylar caught a glimpse of her through the windshield glass. Her hair was sleeker, and her smile, which had always been warm and easy, had reached Julia Roberts proportions, but otherwise Skylar was relieved. It was still Emma. Her Emma.

After some wrestling with her seat belt, Emma threw open the door and grinned.

"Hello, strangers," she said. Skylar had forgotten how far down she had to bend to hug Emma, and how her hair always smelled sweet and familiar, like some childhood candy Skylar couldn't quite place.

"Jo, look at your hair!" Emma exclaimed, trying to take everything in.

"Look familiar?" Jo asked with a wink.

"Don't remind me," Emma laughed. "And Sky, you look . . ." Skylar glanced down at her slept-in tunic, cutoffs, and fair-trade canvas shoes. She hoped she didn't look quite as disheveled as she felt. "Amazing," Emma finished. She stared out at the postcard-perfect scenery, which was framed under the wooden welcome arch with its sun-bleached, twig-lettered sign, and which led from the parking lot to the expanse of rolling lawn everyone at Nedoba called the Green. "I can't believe I'm here," Emma finally said. She looked genuinely awestruck.

"I can't believe you're driving this car," Skylar laughed. She traced a finger along the fake wood paneling. "I'm guessing it's not yours?"

"My aunt's," Emma said. "She's in Spain interviewing flamenco guitarists for her ethnomusicology dissertation, so I'm staying at her place on the Upper West Side."

"Fancy!" Jo said.

"Well, not really. It's rent-controlled. She doesn't have A/C. And I have to share a room with my brother . . ."

"And tell everyone on I-93 that you believe 'Jesus was a liberal,'" Skylar added, examining the sticker on the rear bumper with a raised eyebrow. She silently vowed never to feel embarrassed by the camp van again.

"Right," Emma smiled. "But otherwise, yes, my life is impossibly glamorous." She gestured down at her navy blue tank dress and sandals, which actually did look pretty fancy for the setting.

Skylar tried to remember what Emma was doing in New York. It had been so long since they'd really caught up—before she'd gone to Italy and everything had started to unravel. "Well, you look great," she hedged, hugging her again. "*And* you have a job that doesn't involve picking ticks off children. So you win."

"Hey!" Jo elbowed Skylar, laughing. "That is a *very* important job."

Emma burst out laughing. "I just remembered that time when Nate got a tick on his . . . um . . ."

"Balls?" Skylar finished.

"Yes, balls!" Emma cried. Mack looked over quizzically from the gazebo, where he had started hanging streamers. The girls cracked up. "And your dad had to use a magnifying mirror to burn it off!" Now Emma was almost crying, and the trademark red flush on her cheeks gave Skylar a rush of nostalgia. She threw her arms around Emma again.

"Can we go back in time, please, and can you just stay here like we planned and squat in the barn?"

"We can *definitely* go back in time," Emma said. "In fact, look what I brought." She reached across the front seat, almost dislodging a Frida Kahlo bobble-head doll on the dashboard, and pulled out her old watermelon backpack. "It's still got all our notebooks," she added.

"Our six hundred MASH games!" Jo said fondly.

"Yes, where you marry Gus and live in a shack with six children," Emma said. "Any progress on that?"

"Broken dreams," Jo sighed.

"Ah, well. There's still time." Emma shut the car door and looked at them eagerly. "Speaking of which, I know I'm late, but can we go somewhere and catch up before everyone gets here? I'm dying to hear everything that's been going on."

"I would love that," Skylar said, "but we're supposed to set up the gazebo for the impending vultures." In fact, she was grateful for the opportunity to stall the truth-telling portion of the weekend. Now that Emma was actually there, it was real. She would have to tell her. And she had no idea when, or how, to do it.

"You can help, though!" Jo chimed in. "How does arranging butter cookies into concentric circles sound?"

"It sounds fabulous," Emma said. "As long as we can gossip while we work."

When they got back to the gazebo, Skylar saw that Mack had *completely* ignored her instructions to braid and gently drape the streamers along the beams, choosing instead to hang individual pieces from the ceiling like strips of flypaper.

"How do they look?" he asked proudly.

"Like a car wash tunnel," Skylar whispered to Emma. Emma punched her lightly in the arm.

"They look great, Mack," Emma said.

"Emma Zenewicz!" Mack boomed, setting down his Scotch Tape and giving her a warm hug. He stepped back and looked at the girls, beaming. "It's so good to see you girls together again. This is what I wanted; I wanted the children at my camp to become a family." His mustache, now streaked with gray but just as resplendent as always, started to twitch.

"Dad, don't cry," Jo warned sharply, and Mack laughed his big, deep cackle that always sounded to Skylar like firewood crackling.

"Where's Maddie?" he asked when it had died down.

"Stuck at thirty-five thousand feet," Jo said. "Or, at least, I think she's still in the air. She said she'd text when she landed at Portsmouth."

"Okay," Mack said, patting Jo's shoulder as he turned to head back to the office. "I won't cry until she gets here."

Skylar smiled. Jo hated it when Mack got sentimental, but Skylar thought it was sweet. Her dad was never sentimental. He was whatever the opposite of sentimental was. When she'd unpacked her trunk back in June, she'd found a community college brochure slipped in between the pages of her sketchbook, along with a note that read, in his rigid block print, *We all have dreams. This is for when you wake up.*

"Sky, help me with this?" Jo was struggling to stabilize a folding table. Skylar grabbed one end, relieved to have busywork to focus on, as Emma started opening the plastic sleeves of dollar-store shortbread Mack kept stockpiled in the kitchen pantry for all celebratory occasions.

"So . . ." Emma said expectantly, arranging the crumbly squares on a plastic tray, "tell me everything."

Skylar wondered what Emma would most like to hear. That she'd been desperately missed? That was true. That there was a new foosball table in the game room, one with controls that didn't stick? Or did she want more salacious gossip, like the fact that, over the course of three summers, Skylar had managed to hook up in one way or another with half the male counselors? Skylar and Jo looked at each other, unsure of who should start. There was so much ground to cover.

"Well, my dad's gone totally soft, as you just saw," Jo laughed.

"I love it," Emma said. "What else?"

"Gus finally fixed that rotten board on the dock," Skylar said. "No more butt splinters."

"Come on, I want *real* dirt," Emma smiled. "You know: hook-ups, fights, boyfriends, frenemies." Skylar concentrated on unfolding a checkered tablecloth. She had naively hoped they could skip over those topics, like fast-forwarding through commercials on DVR.

"No, no, no, and sometimes her," Jo said, pointing at Skylar with a smirk.

"Hey!" Skylar cried. She knew Jo was kidding, but it still hit close to home. Since she'd started high school, she'd indulged a little bit too much in all those things.

"How's school stuff?" Emma asked Jo. "Are you still thinking of going into sports medicine?"

"Maybe," Jo said quickly. "I'm busy, though. Especially with camp all summer. This year I did lifeguard training and archery certification. Plus volleyball in the spring and track in the fall. So I haven't had a lot of time to think about college."

"Or boys, I take it," Emma said with a wink. Skylar smiled and shook her head. After three summers, she knew better than to ask Jo about guys.

"What, the ones here?" Jo asked incredulously. "Um, no thank you."

"Wait till you see Nate, though," Skylar whispered. "He got *so* cute. And he likes Jo."

"Shut up," Jo laughed.

"He *does*."

"Whatever." Jo pretended to focus on stacking plastic cups, but she was blushing.

"There must be more than that," Emma said, ripping open another sleeve of cookies and looking pleadingly at Skylar. "I spend my days sorting mail under fluorescent lights. I need to live vicariously." She took a bite out of a discount chocolate sandwich cookie made to look like an Oreo. "Are you still dating Carlo?"

"No," Skylar said slowly. "That whole thing turned out to be kind of a bad idea." She wished she had just called Emma and gotten this conversation out of the way over the phone. It was humiliating to have to repeat it in front of Jo.

"Why?" Emma asked.

"Don't ask," Jo sighed. Skylar ignored her.

"Long story short," Skylar said, "I stopped going to some of my classes, and since my dad pulled some strings to get me into the program, he got notified and was *not* too happy about it." She laughed, but it wasn't funny, and Skylar knew it. Emma knew it, too, from the look on her face.

"What did he do?"

"He made me come home."

"Yikes, will you still have enough credits to apply to RISD?" Leave it to Emma to worry about her college applications.

"We'll see," Skylar said quietly. "My dad is advising me."

"That's great!" Emma finished with the cookies and dusted the crumbs off her hands. "Having another artist in the family must be so helpful. You're so lucky!" Skylar nodded mutely. Her dad had been anything but helpful. In fact, after she'd gotten home from Italy, dutifully humble but eager to show him her sketches of the Duomo and Michelangelo's *David,* and all the other sights that had so inspired her, he had bluntly told her to do something else for a living. Jason MacAlister was one of Philadelphia's most respected gallery owners and had a reputation as a tough critic. But his legion of fans probably didn't know that he had been rejecting his only daughter's refrigerator art for years.

"And are you seeing anybody else since your gondolier?" Emma raised her eyebrows suggestively as she ripped open a bag of balloons with her teeth. Skylar shrugged and self-consciously covered her neck with one hand. It was a question she didn't really know how to answer.

"Nah," she said dismissively. "Nothing serious."

It was, at face value at least, the truth.

Once the other graduates started showing up, giving Jo people to aggressively nametag and Emma people to talk to, Skylar excused herself for a minute to run over to the counselor's porch and text Adam. Emma hadn't asked about him yet, but she knew it was only a matter of time. And she needed to know when he was showing up so that she could run damage control.

The male counselors had spent the morning—unbeknownst

to Mack or Jo—making a beer run with Matt and Mark's shared fake ID ("Mike Slutzky," age 22 and a resident of Intercourse, PA). They were planning on smuggling the contraband to the abandoned toolshed near the bonfire site. Nedoba's staff was incredibly responsible during the day, but as soon as the sun went down all bets were off, and when the kids left for the season it was a free-for-all. The late nights out in the woods or on Wexley Island were legend. In fact, Skylar had spent many of her mornings as a counselor trying not to let Jo know what she'd been doing the previous night, or with whom. Jo wasn't stupid; she knew things were happening, and she even came along on some of the tamer outings, when the staff would sneak out to the north field and just sit around on milk crates trading stories about the campers. But someone had to stay on the girls' side to keep an eye on the kids, and most of the time Jo seemed more than happy to be left behind. "I don't want to know," she would sometimes say to Skylar when they crossed paths at dawn, Jo on her way to raise the flag and sweep the mess hall and Skylar bleary-eyed and hung over, tiptoeing on the wet grass with her bra bunched in her hands.

She was standing on the porch with her back to the gazebo, pretending to be on a phone call and waiting for him to text her back, when the rusty green camp van rumbled into the parking lot and the boys got out looking smug. Apparently the fake ID had worked.

"Hey!" Adam called, jogging over to Skylar. At five ten, he had finally caught up to her height, but except for the stubble sprouting across chin, he looked just as boyish as he had at fourteen. His eyes twinkled as he slipped a hand onto the small of her back. "We're all set. We're gonna bury some six-packs in the sand for later."

"Sandy beer," Skylar said drily, pushing his hand away. "My favorite." Adam shrugged. Everything rolled off him. "Did I miss anything?" He scanned the crowd in the gazebo. "I heard Beak got a nose job."

"Who's Beak?"

"Never mind." He looked over her shoulder, and Skylar followed his gaze. Ironically, Emma was talking to *her* ex-flame, Zeke Tanner, who was still hot in spite of a T-shirt that proclaimed, in big neon letters, "Make art not war." But while Zeke looked like he was trying too hard, Emma just looked naturally stylish and confident. Skylar watched Adam watch Emma and her heart sank.

"You didn't tell me Emma was here!" Adam said.

"You didn't ask," she started to say, but he was already gone. It was an annoying habit of his. By the time she caught up, Adam was already lifting Emma into a bear hug.

"Em!" Adam cried. "I can't believe I'm seeing you in the flesh. I got so used to your instant messenger avatar."

Emma laughed. "You know that's Michelle Obama, right?"

"I *thought* you looked different," Adam said with a wink. Skylar had forgotten how easy their chemistry was. She used to wonder if Emma was kidding herself going after Adam, who was such a flirt with everyone, but there was definitely something there—anyone could see it. And it hurt, the way he looked at Emma.

But not as much as it would hurt Emma to know the way he's looked at you, she thought miserably.

"We were just talking about how much we missed you," Adam said.

"Really?" Emma's eyes lit up.

"Absolutely," Adam said. "You should have applied to be a counselor. It is"—here he looked over at Jo and raised his voice—"the most awesome job ever."

"I'm sure it is when you disappear for hours and don't help clean the bunks," Jo said. "Where were you?" She turned to Nate, who'd arrived from the van bearing a glass bottle of Coke, Jo's favorite beverage, which could only be gotten at the general store in Onan. Nate was so handsome now. His curly, dark blond hair framed his thoughtful, deep-set blue eyes, and he'd grown into his nose since they were kids. He'd also shed his acne and the last of his baby fat. Skylar had to admit that even she stopped to watch when he played soccer on the Green without a shirt on. Jo, as usual, didn't seem to notice. She took the Coke without even thanking him.

"We had to drive into town to get some, uh, supplies," Nate stammered.

"You didn't ask for any petty cash," Jo said, genuinely confused. Skylar smiled. Her obliviousness could be incredibly charming.

"Anyway," Adam interrupted, turning back to Emma. "We missed you."

You said that already, Skylar wanted to scream.

"I missed you, too," Emma said.

"He's the same," Jo interjected flatly. "You didn't miss much."

Adam looked hurt. "That stings, Jo," he said. "You of all people should know that I have blossomed into a beautiful flower as your personal lanyard keychain apprentice."

Jo laughed. Adam's charm worked on everyone, eventually. "Okay," she said. "I'll forget about your 'supplies' if you play some hacky sack with me. I can't eat any more cookies or I'll barf."

"As much as I'd love to revisit the mid-nineties, I'm kind of catching up with a long-lost friend here," Adam said at the same time that Nate practically screamed, "I'll do it!" Jo glared playfully at Adam as she and Nate headed off to the Green.

"So," Adam said, looking back and forth from Emma to Skylar. "What now?"

It was the question Skylar had been asking herself for the past three years, ever since the first time she'd hooked up with Adam. How many times had she snuck out in the dark to meet him, creeping past her sleeping campers, a mini flashlight tucked in the front pocket of her jean shorts? How many times had she told herself it would be the last time? She'd been able to postpone the guilt summer after summer, telling herself she wasn't doing anything *really* wrong—it wasn't like he and Emma were a thing. They'd never even kissed! And that first night, they'd both been feeling so insecure. It had almost been an accident. It had definitely been a mistake. What now? She had to tell Emma, obviously. She needed to make things right. For starters, she would need to keep Adam at arm's length—from both of them.

"Don't you have to put away that stuff you got in town?" Skylar reminded him.

"Oh, right," he said. He turned to Emma. "Then I guess we'll have to catch up later." He jogged off, barely even glancing at Skylar. She shouldn't have been surprised, but it still stung. Actually *talking* to Adam had become a rare occurrence lately. It had gotten to the point where they wouldn't even say hello when they met for their "dates," before he put his hands on her, kissing her, pushing her down onto the grass. Skylar shuddered. She didn't know how to tell Emma, she didn't have anyone she could ask for advice (Jo didn't even know; at least, not the extent of it, not how out of hand it had gotten), and the only person who she thought might understand how she was feeling was suddenly treating her like she was invisible.

Skylar tried to smile at Emma as they wandered over to watch Jo and Nate kick their weird little beanbag back and forth. But she felt worse than ever. The thing was, being with Adam didn't feel so much like a mistake, or even an accident, anymore. Seeing him with Emma again had made her realize that, however inconveniently, she finally felt something real.

Emma

The Fifth Summer • *Age 14*
First Night of Camp

"Friendship Rule: Best friends always help each other follow their dreams."

"I CAN'T BELIEVE WE'RE *SENIORS*," EMMA SAID. IT WAS the first night of camp, and they were all getting ready for their last welcome bonfire in their bunk. Everything was "the last" thing now, and it was their new favorite thing to say even though they were only about six hours in.

"I know," Skylar said, examining her wild hair in Maddie's hand mirror and gathering it into a messy bun. "It's the Summer of No Excuses!" Emma could tell Skylar was using capital letters. When her mood was right, she could be as dramatic as Maddie.

"Is that directed at *moi*?" Emma asked with a smile. She reached into her trunk and pulled out a dress she had bought with her birthday money from her grandpa especially for the occasion. It was red and white striped and had a breast pocket embroidered with a navy anchor. It smelled department-store new. It was also impractical, given the mosquitoes and ticks, not to mention the fact that the bonfire required that everyone sit on giant logs with notoriously crotch-poking stumps, but Emma didn't care; to her, it was optimistic. It meant that this summer—her last summer—would be different, full of the sorts of splendors a girl with a solid A-cup chest who finally had straight teeth and who had finally figured out tampons and who looked like she lounged around on sailboats all day wearing breezy nautical-themed dresses deserved to enjoy.

"No, it's for all of us," Skylar announced. "For instance, I am going to stop making excuses not to go to the pottery studio. I'm going to put in at least two hours a week. You are all my witnesses. I know it's messy and frustrating, but it's something I love to do."

"And Zeke Tanner basically lives there," Maddie said.

"Added bonus." Skylar grinned.

"Well I'm going to perform at the talent show, finally," Maddie said. She had signed up every year only to cancel the night before.

"Clog dancing?" Jo asked hopefully.

"*No,*" Maddie said with a laugh. "Singing 'The Rose,' which is my favorite song, and which you will all love . . . or else."

"I—*we*—" Jo said, "are going to win capture the flag." She gave Emma a look. "Which you will all love. Or else."

Emma groaned. She had always been terrified of capture the flag. She hated all tag-based games, actually, as well as any games where running fast and having good hand-eye coordination were considered important. Her parents were academics and her brother was a film geek, so Emma's childhood had not exactly been full of athletic pursuits.

"What about you, Em?" Skylar asked. "What's your summer goal?"

"I don't know," she said. "I guess to get my swim badge." Emma could swim, but not well enough to pass the Nedoba swim test, which meant that she couldn't go on any of the canoe trips out on the lake. Not that she cared. She was happy to stay on dry land.

"Come on," Maddie said. "It has *nothing* to do with Adam?"

"I don't know," Emma said again. "I think we're just good friends."

"We'll see . . ." Skylar said, pulling on a sweatshirt that managed to be both two sizes two big and flattering at the same time. Emma pulled the dress over her head and smoothed it down over her legs.

"You're gonna be cold," Jo said, tugging on Emma's dainty cap sleeves.

"No, I won't," she said. "Someone zip me up."

"Bossy new Emma!" Skylar exclaimed, lifting Emma's ponytail out of the way so she could fasten the dress. "I like it."

"We're seniors now," Maddie said, dabbing her pinky in a pot of tawny lip gloss. "We're supposed to be bossy."

"How do I look?" Emma asked, spinning around. She wanted to check herself in the full-length mirror in the girls' bathroom, but Jo was already standing impatiently by the door.

"Cute!" Skylar and Maddie cooed in unison.

"You're gonna be cold," Jo said again, tossing back a handful of trail mix.

"I don't care," Emma said stubbornly. "I like it, and, you guys . . . it's my *last entrance*!"

Skylar laughed so hard she cried. Jo almost snarfed a peanut.

When they got to the fire pit—after a last first walk along the winding dirt path that led from the girls' side of camp past the barn and through the woods toward the lake, which led to their last first mosquito bites and ankle scratches and flip-flop rocks of summer—the girls clustered on the big log nearest to the fire that had always been reserved for the oldest campers. With Skylar on one side and Maddie on the other, Emma felt warm and safe as the flames licked at the air near her knees, the reedy thrum of the crickets' song cutting through the still night air.

As seniors, it was their job to lead the songs, which was widely considered an unofficial audition for CIT spots.

"Okay!" Skylar yelled, jumping up and shimmying back and forth, her roomy cutoffs bouncing on her hips. "Who here can spell *chicken*?!" The experienced campers cheered, while the newbies looked confused. Skylar clapped her hands above her head and started singing.

"C—that's the way it begins, H—is the next letter in, I—you're in the middle of the word, and C—you've already heard, and K—now you're roundin' the bend, and E—you're nearin' the end . . ."

Emma smiled at Jo and Maddie as they all shouted the last line. "C-H-I-C-K-E-N! That's the way you spell CHICKEN!"

On the last syllable, Emma looked out across the fire and saw Adam smiling back at her. He started to inch his way around the crowd, and her stomach did a little flip as Jo launched into "Found a Peanut." By the time the narrator was deciding to eat the rotten legume anyway, Adam was wedging himself in between Maddie and Nate.

"Is this seat taken?" he asked rhetorically.

"Is that line still working?" Maddie replied with a sweet smile.

"So it's going to be that kind of summer," he laughed.

"I'm just giving you a hard time," Maddie said. "You know we love you, Loring." She paused. "Some of us more than others."

Emma elbowed her in the ribs.

Across the circle, the brand-new nine- and ten-year-old campers looked lonely and frightened. Some of them had tear-streaked faces, and Emma remembered the terror she had felt the first time she realized her parents weren't coming back for four whole weeks.

"Remember when we were that little?" she asked after Jo finished the last verse.

"The seniors seemed so old," Maddie said. "They were huge, weren't they? I don't feel that big."

"That's because you're a midget," Jo said.

"You're *petite*," Emma said, giving Maddie a reassuring pat.

"I was never that little," Skylar said, tucking her long legs up under her chin. It was true—Skylar had always been the tallest girl at Nedoba, except for Macy Ring, whose mom was in the WNBA.

"Well, *parts* of you were little," Adam said, a smile creeping across his face. Skylar reached across Emma and smacked him on the thigh, hard. "Hey!" he cried, clearly delighted with the attention. "That's too close for comfort. I want to have kids someday."

"Yeah, well, hopefully they'll have the decency not to announce to the whole cafeteria that someone is so flat she doesn't need a bra." Skylar's tone was angry, but she was fighting a smile.

Emma tried to pretend she was having fun, but being in the middle of a kindergarten hair-pulling session was not what she'd hoped her dress would inspire. "Stop torturing her," she whispered to Adam.

"Okay, fine." He paused and then flashed a flirty smile. "Can I torture you instead?"

You do that already, she wanted to say, but instead she shook her head. "If you don't have anything better to do, you can roast me a marshmallow."

"Coming right up!" He left to search for a stick.

"Are you sure you're just friends?" Jo shouted over the din.

"Shhhhhhhhhh!" Emma hid her face in her hands. Adam's friends were sitting a few feet away.

"Sorry!" Jo stage whispered.

"I think you should go for it," Maddie said, patting Emma on the knee. "My mom and dad met at camp."

Emma peeked an eye out from between her fingers. "Are you serious?"

"He was a counselor and she was a camper," Maddie said. "It was *very* illicit."

"Ew!" Jo said, looking stricken.

"They were only a year apart in age," Maddie said.

"Still," Jo shuddered. Maddie shrugged. Mack was trying to

start a sing-along round of "Make New Friends."

"We're just looking out for you," Skylar whispered to Emma, the fire reflecting in her eyes. "Adam's cute and funny, but he's so immature. Everything he does and says is just to look cool."

"I know," Emma said defensively. She thought it was weird that Skylar was suddenly acting so protective, when just last summer she'd offered her five dollars to kiss Adam. (Okay, to be fair, Skylar had bet *against* Emma, but it had still seemed encouraging at the time.)

"I just don't want him to play with you," Skylar said, giving Emma a squeeze. "Even if he's just your friend." Then it was their turn to sing.

"Make new friends, but keep the old, one is silver and the other gold . . ." As soon as the round passed, Emma turned back to Skylar.

"I'm fine, I promise," she whispered. "There's no playing going on. I'm out of the game. I forfeit."

"Okay, I'll back off," Skylar said, looking a little skeptical. "But just remember, it's our last summer. It should be about *us*."

A few seconds later, Adam returned with two sticks speared with marshmallows. "M'ladies," he greeted them as he sat back down. "Anybody up for a joust?" He jabbed the sticks in the air, imitating a fencer. "No one?"

Jo rolled her eyes, and then she, Maddie, and Skylar joined in on a boisterous song about Johnny Appleseed. Emma knew the words, but she was distracted.

"You know," she said, leaning over to Adam, who was just mouthing along. "You can just be normal. You don't have to try so hard." He started to grin, and Emma could see the wheels turning in his head, crafting the perfect snappy comeback. But then he stopped. The smile disappeared and he fell silent.

"I know," he said softly. "I'm sorry. I just . . . it feels like every year I want to try something different. Be someone different, I guess." Emma looked down at her dress. A stray thread spiraled down from the hem; she'd probably snagged it on a branch.

"Someone better," she said. Adam looked at her and smiled, a genuine smile this time, with no trace of his former teasing.

"Exactly."

"Well, we're seniors now," she said slowly. "So that means we're automatically better. Right?"

"If only it were that easy." He blew on the roasted marshmallows and handed one stick to Emma, and she took them, grateful for the warmth. (Jo had been right after all—she *was* cold.) "To being better," Adam said, holding up his stick like a champagne flute.

"To the best summer ever," Emma amended, tipping her marshmallows at him.

"I like your dress, by the way," he said.

She smiled and looked into the fire as she waited for her turn to sing again. Maybe she'd lied to Skylar without meaning to. Maybe she wasn't ready to give up just yet.

Jo

Reunion: Day 1

JO STOOD ON THE BASKETBALL COURT LOOKING OUT at the crowd of former campers assembled on the Green. According to her clipboard spreadsheet, there were almost two hundred reunion attendees, the biggest turnout in Camp Nedoba's short history. And since so many of the former campers came from her graduating year, her dad had put Jo in charge of event planning for the entire weekend. She was both thrilled and overwhelmed. It was the best gift her father had given her since he'd set up a Frisbee golf course in their backyard for her twelfth birthday, but it was also a huge responsibility. She couldn't screw this up.

The dry July heat was unrelenting, and playing hacky sack with Nate had just made her sweatier. She mopped her forehead with her shirt sleeve. People were getting restless.

"Testing, testing, one, two, three." Jo tapped her megaphone, eliciting a squeal of feedback. She adjusted the volume and started in earnest. "Welcome, everybody," she said, raising her voice to reach the back row, where Mark and Matt Slotkin were practicing handstands, "to the sixth annual Camp Nedoba reunion weekend!" There was half-hearted clapping, and someone let out a whoop. Jo put her hands on her hips.

"Come on, guys, that was weak," she cried. "*Omki!*" Everyone laughed. *Omki* was the Abenaki word for *Wake up!* and it was a camp tradition that, every morning, the counselors would gather around the beds of hard-to-rouse campers, stomping their feet and chanting it until consciousness was achieved. If you woke up to the sound of "*Omki, omki, omki*!" it became your job to clear and scrape all the plates from your bunk's table at breakfast.

Jo looked over at her dad, who was sitting on the office porch in his favorite Adirondack chair, watching her with pride as he munched on a bag of the homemade spicy pickle chips he force-fed to the campers at every conceivable opportunity. Mack gave Jo an enthusiastic thumbs up.

"Okay," she continued over the chatter, "we have a lot of fun activities planned, but first I've gotta do a roll call to make sure everybody's present and accounted for before we start." A collective groan rose from the crowd. "I know, I know," Jo said gamely. "But look at it this way—if you didn't get to catch up in the gazebo, this is your chance to see what everyone looks like now, and who you want to buddy up with." A few people snickered, and Jo rolled her eyes. She hadn't meant it like that, but it didn't surprise her that some people were incapable of hearing anything besides sexual innuendo. Jo shook it off and clicked her pen into action. There were check marks to be made.

"Mini Mack!" someone fake-coughed. Jo smiled tightly. Everyone always told her how much she was like her dad. It wasn't an insult, but it got old after a while. She knew what the other campers called her behind her back. Apart from Maddie, Emma, and Skylar—and Nate, who always seemed to be there when she needed help carrying sports equipment or doing graham cracker inventory—none of the other campers had ever really tried to get to know her. They seemed scared she was an enemy spy, just a little adult in a teenager's body. When they looked at her, she thought sadly, they probably didn't even see a girl. Jo had her mom's full lips and high cheekbones, but she had Mack's olive skin, black hair, aquiline nose, and wide-set brown eyes. She was, at least on the surface, only her father's daughter.

Jo's home away from camp, at least according to the post office, was in Danbury, Connecticut. Her mother, Wendy, was a beauty sales executive who commuted into New York on the train every day to place mentions of lip glosses and age-reversing concealers in fashion magazines. The fact that her only child was a tomboy was an obvious source of disappointment. "I have a closet full of vintage Chanel," Wendy would joke to clerks when she took Jo back-to-school shopping at the mall, "but, of course, my daughter has never met a pair of cargo shorts she didn't like!"

Before the divorce, Mack and Wendy had been summer renters in Onan. Jo still missed the big house with the blue-painted porch stenciled with seashells all around the railing. If she stood on the dock on a clear day, she could sometimes see its weathervane peeking out from the trees across the water. Onan was the place all her good memories came from, and if it was up to Jo she would stay year-round, joining the sleepy off-season population of 2,796. As it was, she lived for the summers. It was where her *real* home was. Where her real friends were.

She was halfway through the roll call when a taxi pulled into the parking lot, interrupting the proceedings. Jo hadn't heard anything from Maddie, and her heart leapt at the thought of her best friend finally arriving. Maybe Maddie's plane *wasn't* circling the airport. Maybe she was already there. Jo lost her focus as the cab door opened.

Before Maddie, Jo had never really had a best friend. Being an only child, she had gotten used to playing by herself. Her dad loved to tell people the story of the first day he dropped Jo off at preschool and watched her walk confidently to the toy bin while the other kids wailed miserably around her. By the time the other parents had extricated themselves from their children's anxious grasps, Jo had built a Lincoln Log fort, complete with perimeter security. It wasn't that she *couldn't* make friends—she always got along with her classmates and even had the occasional sleepover with other girls from the peewee soccer league or, later, the Hunter High School varsity volleyball squad. But it wasn't until she met Maddie, Skylar, and Emma that Jo started to understand what all the fuss was about. She wasn't just drifting anymore, rounding out tables of odd-numbered people in the cafeteria. She had her own tribe, like on *Survivor* (except without all the starvation and backstabbing).

But it was hard to learn how to be someone's best friend—let alone three people's—and Jo felt ill-equipped. She didn't have a psychologist mother like Emma's or a touchy-feely family like Skylar's or a no-holds-barred emotional temperament like Maddie's. It was hard for Jo to talk about her feelings or care about how she looked or gossip about boys the way her friends did. She always felt like she couldn't quite keep up in friendship, the way other people couldn't keep pace with her on long-distance runs. But she'd never stopped trying—at least, not until the rest of them had.

Jo was used to feeling left behind. After all, she'd said good-bye to them summer after summer, knowing she wasn't leaving camp grounds for two long, lonely weeks until her mother picked her up on Labor Day. So when the calls, e-mails, and letters dwindled after their last year together at Nedoba (it had been hardest to see the letters stop, those thick manila envelopes with the North Carolina return address, made out to "Ms. Josephine Putnam," or "Jolene F. Putnam, Esquire," jokes Jo's mom never got and in fact seemed annoyed by), the withdrawal didn't feel good, but it also didn't feel new. It was just the way things had always been. And at camp, at least, she still had Skylar, even if their relationship had mostly devolved into odd couple bickering without the other two to balance them out.

As she stared at the taxi, though, Jo realized she wasn't willing to settle for the status quo any longer. Once Maddie stepped out, once they were all back together, she had to do everything in her power to keep them from ever falling apart again.

But she'd gotten herself worked up for nothing. Maddie wasn't in the cab. Instead, a slight brunette hopped out and hurried noisily across the gravel, pulling a gigantic suitcase behind her. Jo let out a deep, shaky breath.

"Sorry I'm late!" the girl panted, waving excitedly to some people on the Green. "Did you call me yet?" Jo studied the girl's face and frowned. She'd been able to identify almost everyone by sight, except for some of the older twentysomethings and a few guys who had grown facial hair. This person *looked* awfully familiar, but Jo couldn't place her. "Uh, I don't think so . . ." She looked down at her clipboard, trying to stall. The girl dropped her suitcase dramatically and opened her mouth in shock.

"*Jo Putnam*!" she cried in disbelief. "It's *me. Sunny*." Mark Slotkin did a hilarious double take, and Jo tried not to laugh.

"Sunny!" Jo said, "Of course! Sorry, the . . . sun must have been in my eyes." In reality, she could see fine—she just hadn't been able to see Sunny's old nose, which had been shaved down to a ski-jump shadow of its former self. Sunny skipped over to sit with Aileen Abrams, Kerry Woodsmall, and Jess Ericsson, three other girls who were bunking in Souhegan. Mack had insisted on making the bunk assignments himself so that Jo wouldn't play favorites, and so she was stuck with Sunny Sherman for three long nights. Jo made a mental note to drive into town later for some earplugs.

Once attendance was finished—everyone had made it on time except for Maddie, and Jo just skipped her name, lest she fall down an introspective rabbit hole again—it was time for the fun part: the itinerary. Jo had agonized over the schedule, but she was happy with what she'd come up with. Ever since she was six or seven she had "played" camp director, overseeing her dolls in a series of organizational meetings, but this was the first time she'd ever really tried to do the job.

"It's two p.m.," Jo announced after checking her watch. "For the next two hours or so there will be CITs in the arts and crafts cabins, the library, and the game room if you want to use them. There's also archery on the north field with everyone's favorite instructor, my dad." Mack smiled as the crowd cheered. "Dinner starts at five thirty sharp," Jo continued, "and at seven we will head to the shore for the opening night bonfire!" She waited for the clapping to die down. "Tomorrow, after breakfast, we'll leave for Wexley Island, where we'll hang out all day before heading back to the mainland for dinner."

"Sexy Island, woot woot!" someone yelled, and everyone laughed. Mack stood up from his seat on the porch.

"Wexley Island was named for John Wexley, who was a farmer on this land before the previous owner founded this camp site in 1976," he announced. "I met Farmer Wexley on multiple occasions and I can personally guarantee that there was nothing sexy about him. He had to have a leg amputated from gout." Mack sat back down and went back to his pickles.

"Thank you for that nugget of history, Dad," Jo said. "You should put that on the website. Anyway, Wexley Island is Friday and then Saturday is an all-day, no-holds-barred capture the flag game"—another wave of cheering cut her off—"with a huge secret prize for the winning team! Then we'll do another bonfire, just because we can, and Sunday morning is checkout. Everybody got it?" She put down the megaphone and looked out at the hundreds of squinting faces.

"Now," she cried, starting to hop back and forth like a boxer, pumping herself up, "can I get a NE . . . DO . . . BA?!" Nate cupped his hands around his mouth and started the chant. "NE! DO! BA!" he yelled. Emma immediately joined in. Adam raised a fist in the air, half serious, half mocking. Soon everyone was chanting.

"NE! DO! BA!" they boomed. "NE! DO! BA!" Mack, whose baritone could be heard from the porch, gave his daughter a one-man standing ovation, and even Gus flashed a smile as he lugged his toolbox back to his van across the parking lot.

Jo blew her whistle triumphantly. If she could successfully rally two hundred people, a measly three would be a piece of cake.

Maddie

Reunion: Day 1

MADDIE'S TAXI BARRELED DOWN THE HIGHWAY. THE cabbie, a sixty-ish guy with a gray ponytail and mirrored aviator sunglasses, was blaring the local rock station, and Maddie was grateful to have a wall of sound between her and any human interaction. She was in a terrible mood. First, her flight had been delayed. This wouldn't have been a big deal if it had been delayed before she got on, when she had a T.G.I. Friday's and a newsstand with fifteen different tabloid magazines at her disposal. But no, the plane had boarded just fine, the cabin had been closed, and then they'd circled around the runway a few times before coming to a standstill due to what the pilot called "unfavorable winds." Maddie learned this information while sandwiched in a middle seat between two men who, if she had to guess, she would say were former college linebackers or WWF wrestlers. The plane sat on the tarmac for three hours.

Then, upon finally taking off and landing, Maddie discovered that her checked bag had opted to stay behind at Raleigh-Durham.

The supremely unhelpful baggage attendant had promised that an airline representative could drive the suitcase out to Camp Nedoba as soon as it arrived on the next flight, but Maddie told them to forget it. She had a carry-on with her toothbrush and a bathing suit and an extra pair of underwear. She was sure she could borrow some clothes from Emma, who was pretty close to her size. And besides, who cared what she looked like? Who cared about her, period? *You can take the girl away from her baggage, but you can't take the baggage away from the girl,* she thought bleakly.

"So, sweetheart," the cabbie said, turning down the music. "What brings you all the way out here?" He had a thick Boston accent, turning "sweetheart" into "sweet-*haaat*" and "here" into "hee-*ah*." Maddie paid a lot of attention to accents, since she was always trying to drop hers. The whole Southern belle, mint julep thing just seemed so cliché.

"I'm going to a camp reunion," she said, making the consonants hard and the vowels soft—the opposite of how her mom and stepdad talked.

"A camp reunion?" He laughed. "I never heard of that before. Whaddya do, hang around in sleeping bags passin' around a flask?" Maddie smirked.

"No flask," she said. "I'm only seventeen. And I don't like sleeping outside."

"Most people don't, sweetheart." He looked at her in the rearview mirror and smiled. "I bet you're used to nicer things, though. I been drivin' a long time. You get good at readin' people."

"Oh yeah? What's my reading?" They had ten more miles to go, and even though she didn't really feel like talking, this was too good to pass up. Plus, Maddie decided, she liked the cabbie. He seemed kind of—to borrow her stepdad's highest adjective of praise—boss. And he hadn't called her "Red." At least, not yet.

"You're a prom-queen type," he said. "Parents got money, nice house, friends, guys knockin' down your door, scarin' your old man half to death . . ." Maddie pressed her lips together and tried to keep a poker face. "But you're quirky," the cabbie went on. "You're like—you ever seen that movie *The Breakfast Club*?"

"Mmmm hmmmm," Maddie said. She could even picture the dusty, peeling VHS cover stacked with other eighties classics underneath her mother's 13-inch TV/VCR combo in the living room. Caitlin Ryland had never bought into the hype of new technology. "Why should I replace all my tapes?" she would say when Maddie or her younger half sisters, Mae and Harley, would beg for DVDs—or better yet, wireless Internet. "This works just fine. They just want you to pay twice for the same stuff." Except she didn't say "stuff." Maddie's mother was a champion curser; to drive the point home after a particularly colorful expletive, she would often exclaim that she didn't give a good goddamn who heard it.

"Well, you're like that redhead," the cabbie said. "She was a quirky prom queen." He merged onto the highway. "How'd I do?"

"You nailed it," Maddie said. She didn't have the heart to tell him that she hadn't ended up going to her junior prom because the week before she found out that her boyfriend had cheated on her with her best friend. Or that the only people beating on her door were collection agents looking for her stepdad, Eddie, who had moved down into the unfinished basement because he'd rather sleep on a mildewy futon than be in the same room with her mom, who routinely came home from her shifts at Kroger smelling like Jim Beam and Kool ultra lights.

"See?" He grinned. "Drive long enough you get to know people just by lookin' at 'em." Maddie wondered how her life would be different if she were a dime-store psychic and was able to see into people's souls. She wondered, for instance, if she ever would have taken up with Charlie Sloan in the first place.

Maddie texted Jo as the cab turned into the Camp Nedoba parking lot. She pressed her face up against the window and took in the hand-painted welcome sign (she'd recognize Skylar's spiral O's anywhere), the sprawling Green and rolling hills, the wooden buildings weather-beaten by the New England winters to a dull gray, except in spots Mack had recently patched or replaced, which shone bright and butter-yellow, like when you carved away the bark of a twig. She rolled down the window to take in the smell of the pines and the earthy dirt pathways leading from camp center to the bunks on either side of the woods.

"Quaint place," the cabbie said as she handed him a handful of cash. "Get some sun, buck up. Take a load off."

"I'll try," Maddie said.

"Call me if you need a ride back to the airport," he said, handing her a card. "Ask for me—the name's Dave. Or just tell 'em you want the guy with the gut and the ponytail."

"Dave," Maddie said, suddenly studying his face with interest. She couldn't see his eyes, but his features looked all wrong—Italian, probably. Plus, he was about a decade too old. But she had to ask. "You ever live down South?" She tried to sound casual.

"Can't say that I have, sweetheart. Too hot down there. And I can't watch the Sox." He gave her a wink and drove off. Maddie hung her head and kicked at the gravel with the mottled gray toe of her dirty white Ked. She couldn't picture her real dad driving a cab, anyway. Or listening to Led Zeppelin. He'd been a math major. And according to her mom, he liked Miles Davis. All she knew was that he'd moved to New Hampshire sometime after she was born. She didn't have an address or even a city. She had a needle buried in a haystack that felt about the size of Mount Everest.

Maddie looked around for a familiar face. Now that she was there, now that she could finally take a breath, she realized she had no idea what she was going to do when she saw her friends, especially Jo. She hadn't told them about the breakup. She hadn't told them about a lot of things, for instance that her mom was a mess and her dad was AWOL. Not minor details, even in the grand scheme of things. And while she could fake a northern accent for a half hour car trip, she wasn't sure she could fake a better life anymore, not even for a three-day weekend. Just then, she saw Mack come out of his office with a stack of folding chairs and she was able to breathe. He was exactly who she needed to see.

"Knock, knock," she said, tapping on the porch railing. He

looked up and took off his sunglasses, and Maddie could see the fresh tangles of lines that sprouted from the corners of his eyes when he smiled, like tributaries from a river.

"Oh my gosh," he said, shaking his head. "I barely recognized you. You look so grown up!" Mack had an expression that Maddie imagined must be what a dad looked like when he saw his daughter all dressed up for the school dance. She blushed.

"The prodigal child returns," she said, dropping into an awkward curtsy.

"You're not prodigal," Mack said, leaning down to give her a kiss on the cheek. "You're a prodigy." Maddie shifted her weight uncomfortably. She didn't know if she could fairly be considered a prodigy at anything. Except maybe for lying.

"Did you find Jo and the girls?" Mack asked, scanning the Green. "They've been jumping out of their skin waiting for you to get here."

"No, not yet," Maddie said. "Before I do, I need to give you something." She took a crumpled envelope out of her purse and handed it to him without making eye contact.

"What's this?" He turned it over in his big, calloused hands.

"It's not the whole airfare but it's as much as I have right now," she said quickly. "I'll have the rest by September, and I can mail it. I would have had it all, but my mom—"

"Honey," Mack said, interrupting her. "You know I won't take this." He handed the envelope back to her, and when she crossed her arms stubbornly, he tucked it into her purse.

"But I owe you," she said, her chin starting to quiver. She had never paid for camp, not a single cent. It was the only way her parents agreed to let her go. She burned with shame when she thought of the letter she had written to Mack when she was nine, after she'd found the Camp Nedoba website while secretly Googling her birth dad on the free library computers. *Dear Mr. Putnam,* she had written, *I am very interested in your summer camp but I only have $57 but I hope we can work out a deal.*

"No, you don't," he said firmly. "You belong here, and how you got here doesn't matter. It never has." He patted her shoulder. "Some people will tell you it's the journey that counts, but as far as I'm concerned, in this situation, it's the destination. So, I think you'd better go find your friends. Don't you?"

She nodded, blinking back tears, and started for the door.

"Hey!" Mack called, and she turned around. "Why don't you tell them the truth this summer? It's never too late."

Maddie grimaced.

"I'll think about it," she said.

Emma

Reunion: Day 1

THE GIRLS' BUNKS LOOKED EXACTLY LIKE EMMA remembered them. Made of sturdy, caramel-colored cedar planks outfitted with rolled kelly green tarps to keep rain out of the open windows and doorway, they were spaced in two even rows of four within a sunny rectangle a quarter mile from the Green, accessible by a shaded, woody path dotted with tiny clearings of crab apple trees. On quiet mornings, she remembered, deer would poke their downy heads out of the woods along the path and sometimes even wander among the cabins searching for food. One time, Maddie had gotten a doe to eat a granola bar out of her palm.

The cabins themselves were about fifteen feet long and twelve feet wide, but now they felt even smaller than they had when she was a camper. They'd always reminded Emma of the log cabins described in the Little House books she'd devoured as a kid—only, drying on the clothesline outside were damp towels instead of fresh venison, stripped from a deer that had recently been killed by Pa Ingalls. All the Nedoba cabins were named for a different Abenaki tribe, and for reunion the girls had been assigned to Souhegan, where they'd lived the summer they were thirteen. Emma could swear it still smelled like the strawberry-flavored lip balm she'd religiously applied for eight straight weeks just in case she got the opportunity to kiss Adam. She cringed inwardly at the memory of all that wasted hope as she flopped down on the bottom bed of the bunk she was sharing with Skylar.

"Does this take you back?" Skylar asked, hanging her head over the side so that her hair almost brushed Emma's comforter.

"Yes! We're even in the exact same beds—look." Emma ran her finger over a tiny piece of writing on one of the slats supporting Skylar's mattress: *E + S = BFF*. She'd used a red marker from Skylar's stash. The graffiti had been the culmination of a nonstop week of rain during which the four of them had spent so much time in the bunk they'd gone stir-crazy.

"You were so scared to get caught," Skylar said, examining the initials.

"Well, you made me do it in broad daylight!"

"At night would have been too easy," Skylar laughed.

"I sort of cheated anyway, though." Emma had refused to use the first letters of their last names so it couldn't be traced back to her, as if she was a criminal mastermind in an episode of *CSI: Camp Nedoba*.

"It's okay," Skylar said, settling back onto her bed. "I knew you weren't big on dares."

Emma frowned. She liked to think that wasn't true anymore.

Moving to New York for the summer had felt risky . . . but then again, she had an apartment to stay in for almost no money. Getting the internship of her dreams had been amazing . . . but she'd been there for over six weeks and hadn't published so much as a sentence. She hadn't even tried.

"I dare you right now to put a thong on Jo's bed," Skylar said.

"No way." Emma glanced over at the bunk bed that was set catty-corner to theirs. Jo was taking a shower and had laid out a new, almost identical outfit on her bottom bed, which had been made with military precision. Above it, Maddie's still-unclaimed upper bunk was adorned with a framed photo of the four of them, along with a sprig of Queen Anne's lace that Jo had picked as they'd carried Emma's bags up the path from her aunt's car. The picture had been taken by their counselor Tara at the end of their first summer, and they all had copies. Emma's was on her desk back home—at least, she was pretty sure it was, buried beneath a precarious mountain of textbooks.

"See? I knew it," Skylar scoffed.

"That doesn't prove anything," Emma said. "I've just matured." She kicked the underside of Skylar's bunk and laughed.

"So how come there's no hot hipster New York boyfriend?" Skylar teased.

"I don't know," Emma said. "My internship is nine to six and then at night I have to do SAT prep and work on my college essays."

"Dude, it's *summer*."

"A Brown early decision applicant's work is never done!" Emma declared with mock cheerfulness. "Plus I live with my brother, which kind of cramps my style." Kyle was twenty-two and spent his days either playing video games in his boxer shorts while eating stale Chinese food straight from the carton or "working on his screenplay" (an activity that did not, sadly, require a wardrobe change), which was a sci-fi action saga set in a dystopian universe in which the sun became toxic and people had to live underground in tunnels. (Emma called that "unemployed," but she kept her mouth shut because according to their mother, Kyle was feeling "extremely emotionally vulnerable right now." Maybe that was why they kept sending him checks.)

"Maybe you could find someone at work," Skylar said.

"It's a feminist teen magazine, so the boys are scarce," Emma sighed.

"Well, maybe you'll meet someone on the subway or something."

"Ew, have you ever taken the subway? The most eligible bachelor I've ever seen was an old guy clipping his nails."

"Was he cute?" Skylar joked. Emma kicked her bunk again.

"You know, you don't need to play matchmaker for me anymore," she said. "I'm fine by myself." It was actually kind of annoying how Skylar seemed to be suggesting that she needed a boyfriend.

Skylar got quiet for a minute.

"Did you feel anything when you saw Adam again?" she finally asked.

"Sky," Emma sighed, "if that's what this is about, you don't have to worry. I'm not here with some kind of grand plan to seduce Adam

Loring." Of course, the thought had crossed her mind, and Emma couldn't deny that old feelings had been stirring ever since he had hugged her in the gazebo. But no one needed to know that. Yet.

"Good," Skylar said. "Because . . . there's some stuff . . . I don't know, I feel like we need to talk."

"About Adam?" Emma asked.

"What about Adam?" Jo breezed in from the bathroom complex with her head wrapped in a towel.

"Don't look at me," Emma said. "She brought him up." Jo turned to Skylar with raised eyebrows as she slipped off her shower shoes, keeping the towel around her body firmly in place with one arm.

"Nothing," Skylar said. "Just that he's frustrating as usual."

"Tell me something I don't know." Jo somehow managed to shimmy into her underwear and bra without dropping the towel. She looked at Emma. "Please don't tell me I have to hear about him all weekend. It's bad enough we're going to have the Sunny Sherman show over there." The other four beds in Souhegan were empty, but Emma knew it was only a matter of time before Sunny, Aileen, Jess, and Kerry lugged their enormous suitcases up from the Green.

"Give me some credit," Emma said defensively. "I didn't drive six hours to see Adam." Old friends were great, she thought, except when they refused to see you as anything other than your old self.

"Good," Jo said. "So let's make this a girls' reunion. No boy drama."

"Sounds great," Emma agreed. (It didn't mean she couldn't *talk* to him, she told herself.)

Jo leveled her gaze at Skylar. "That goes for both of you," she said, drying off her hair.

"What about *me*?"

Emma sat up to see Maddie standing in the doorway. She was as tiny as she'd ever been, barely five feet, maybe ninety pounds soaking wet. Her hair was pulled into a tight bun, but one rebellious curl had fought its way out of her headband and bounced merrily alongside her face. She grinned and put her hands on her hips.

"Is that a *shrine*?" she asked, pointing to the framed photo. "That's kind of creepy, you guys. No offense. I know you missed me and all, but show some restraint."

Jo, still pantless, got to her first and wrapped her in a bear hug, almost knocking Maddie down in the process. Skylar climbed down from her bunk and she and Emma wrapped themselves around the other two.

"Hey," Skylar whispered in her ear, "sorry if I was weird. I'm so glad you're here."

"Me too," Emma smiled.

Everything felt instantly better now that they were all in one place. She felt sure that any tension she'd picked up on from Skylar and Jo had just been a side effect of the heat and the chaos of reunion arrivals. Besides, they would need a few hours to adjust to being around each other again 24-7, like friendship jetlag.

She tried not to speculate on what Skylar had wanted to talk to her about before Jo interrupted them. Whatever it was, she figured, if it was important enough it would come out eventually.

Maddie

The Fourth Summer ◆ *Age 13*
Last Week of Camp

"Friendship Rule: Best friends always send you a postcard no matter where they go."

"MAIL CALL!"

Maddie propped herself up on her elbows and peered through the thin gap between the rolled-up tarp and the top of the window, the most scenic view possible from her top bunk mattress. It looked out on the picnic table in the cluster of trees near the bathroom entrance, which meant that on Tuesdays and Fridays it gave her a view of the milk crate full of envelopes and care packages that the girls' side head counselor, Adri, doled out to the assembled masses at the end of rest hour. Every week Maddie held out hope that someone would decide it was much more efficient to deliver mail by individual cabin—or maybe even not at all. They had to live without cell phones; couldn't they learn to live without letters? Think of all the paper cuts it would prevent! But every week, twice a week, Maddie was forced to climb down from her bed and face the speculation she had come to dread.

"I bet you'll get something today," Jo said as they slipped on their shoes and walked the twenty feet to where all the girls were starting to gather on the grass. The littler kids played hand games and pointed excitedly at the biggest packages, wondering loudly who they were for, while the older girls feigned uninterest and braided each other's hair.

"Maybe," Maddie shrugged. She'd gotten really good at pretending she didn't care.

"Where is she now, anyway?" Emma asked. "London?" Maddie racked her brain to remember the last lie she had told about her mom, who had been promoted from real-life grocery clerk to imaginary "executive consultant"—when she'd made it up on the spot at age ten, Maddie had no idea what that job meant, but she'd heard it on the radio and thought it sounded pretty good—and who spent a lot of her time traveling. In the course of four summers, Maddie had sent her mother to more far-flung countries than most diplomats visited in a lifetime. Her fictional father was a surgeon who spent his fictional time running back and forth between fictional operating rooms saving fictional lives amid highly dramatic fictional circumstances, like the doctors on TV. It was a great way to explain why they didn't have time to drop her off or pick her up in person, or reach out to her in any way. For instance, with a care package.

Care packages were like status symbols at camp. Getting a lot of them made you automatically popular since it meant you had outside goods that other people wanted. Money, electronics, and homemade food weren't allowed (Jo said that last one was because of allergies, but Maddie always pictured some evil stepmother coating candy apples with poison), but packaged cookies, gum, and chips were the highest denomination of social currency. Next came magazines and Mad Libs, followed by flavored lip balms and roll-on perfumes. Clothes were good, too, but it all depended on the style. Everyone had wanted to borrow the tie-dyed leggings Skylar's mom had sent from a sample sale, but no one looked twice at the fleece windbreaker Emma's mom had sent after she'd read about a cold front passing through.

Even though they'd never bothered to spend the eighty-two cents it would have cost to send a postcard, sometimes Maddie idly entertained the possibility that her mom and Eddie would put together a care package for her. Realistically, it would probably contain final sale dry goods, like taco shells and cake mix, that her mom got at an even better employee discount, and maybe some old copies of *TV Guide*, with warped rings on the cover from where Eddie put down his beer. It would be embarrassing, but it would be something.

"No," Maddie said as she sat down cross-legged in what she hoped would become the back row. "I think she's in Paris this week."

"I *love* Paris!" Skylar practically swooned.

"I wish my family went someplace cool," Emma said. "We haven't taken a vacation in forever."

"This *is* my vacation," Jo said with a smile.

"Me, too," Maddie said. "It's my Paris." Skylar laughed pretty hard at that. She didn't realize Maddie meant it.

Adri always did the regular letters first, picking them out of the box at random like one of those models that did the PowerBall drawing on the news. Maddie's mom played the lottery so often that

Maddie had grown up watching little ping pong balls with numbers whirl around in big plastic drums and had learned that the anticipation was always the best part. Every single time, until the numbers came up, it was easy to believe that they would finally be the right ones. Watching the news before the PowerBall came on was the happiest and most hopeful the Ryland family ever got.

"Skylar MacAlister!" Adri called out.

"I hope it's from Cole," Skylar said as she abandoned the waterfall braid she was attempting to weave into Emma's hair and leaped up to collect her prize. Cole was Skylar's boyfriend, and he sent her awful love letters every week that Maddie and Jo secretly read when Skylar wasn't around.

To all of their disappointment (Cole's recent acrostic poem had been the highlight of Maddie's month), it was just a postcard for Skylar's father's new art opening.

"'Imagined Light.'" Emma read the type on the back as all they examined the image on the front, of what looked like a smudge of Wite-Out on a black square. "'An exploration of negative space by Jason MacAlister.'"

"That sounds weird," Jo said.

"My dad *is* weird," Skylar sighed.

"He wrote something, too, but I can't read his writing," Emma said, handing the card back to Skylar, who chewed on a strand of hair as she parsed out words from what looked to Maddie like a series of wavy lines.

"'Skylar, too bad you missed this one, some of my best work.

Hope leaf rubbings are keeping you busy. Dad.'" She made a face and tossed it aside.

"That's . . . nice," Maddie said carefully. She was kind of jealous, even though the message was less than warm. At least he had thought about her.

"No, it's passive-aggressive," Skylar said. "He likes to remind me that my art is kid stuff and his is soooooo important." She pulled a strand of Emma's hair a little too hard.

"Ow!" Emma cried.

"Don't braid angry," Jo warned. "Maybe there'll be something from Cole, too."

But there wasn't. Adri moved on to the care packages. There were only three, the largest of which went to a first-year who squealed as she unwrapped what seemed like enough stuffed animals to fill Noah's Ark.

"Jo Putnam!"

"Oh, great," Jo groaned. "It's here." Jo was the only person Maddie had ever seen pissed off to get a care package. Jo's mom sent her a box of makeup every summer, and Jo took it as a personal affront.

"Aren't you at least going to open it?" Skylar asked when Jo sat back down clutching a shoebox wrapped in brown paper.

"Maybe later," Jo said with a yawn.

"And last but definitely not least, Emma Zenewicz," Adri called. She had been the girls' counselor their very first summer and still always found the time to catch up with them. She was also studying to go to med school and had lots of questions about Maddie's imaginary doctor dad, which Maddie was actively avoiding.

"My parents didn't tell me they were sending me anything," Emma said brightly when she got back to the group. She tore open the thick padded envelope and pulled out a stack of magazines.

"Yes!" Skylar cried. "Did they send *Us Weekly*?"

"Or *Sports Illustrated*?" Jo asked.

"Nope, even better," Emma said. "The *U.S. News & World Report* college ranking issue!" She held it up like an ugly Christmas sweater. "Just what I've always wanted."

They picked themselves up and trudged back to the bunk. It was the same twenty-foot distance, but on the return trip Maddie felt like she was dragging twenty extra pounds. Every week she told herself not to get her hopes up, and every week she failed. She wondered if it would be any easier if she just played sick. Would it be like that old saying about the tree falling in the forest? If no one wrote to her, but she wasn't sitting around to find out, would it still hurt?

She kicked off her Keds and climbed the five steep rungs that led to her bed, hoping she had a few minutes to sulk before the dinner bell rang. But she couldn't lie down . . . because her mattress was strewn with postcards and candy bars.

"Surprise!" Jo yelled.

"What's this?" Maddie asked, laughing. She picked up one of the postcards, which said "*Greetings from New Hampshire!*" on it, alongside a photo of a moose. On the back was a message in Emma's neat cursive. She turned over another postcard to see Skylar's loopy scrawl; sure enough, Jo's slanted print filled a third—she'd written so much, the sentences got miniature at the end as they struggled to fit on the card.

"Sorry all the postcards are the same," Emma said. "That's all they sell around here." Maddie started to flip them over. There were at least two dozen of them, all filled with writing.

"You guys . . ." Maddie stared down at them. "What *is* this?"

"It's your care package," Skylar smiled. "You never get them. And we know your parents are busy, so we decided to take matters into our own hands."

Maddie shook her head in grateful disbelief. She didn't know what to say. She only knew that she was going to have to tell her mom to stop buying those stupid PowerBall tickets, because her numbers had finally come up. She felt like she'd won the lottery.

Maddie

Reunion: Day 1

THE CAMP NEDOBA BARN WAS BUILT INTO THE SIDE of a small hill abutting the north field, overlooking the arts and crafts building. It was a long, low rectangular cabin that had always reminded Maddie of Frankfurter, the lost dachshund she'd had for a week when she was six, after she found him in the yard gnawing at the front wheel of her bike. The outside of the barn was relatively nondescript as barns went—tall, wide, red; the usual—but the inside had always felt like a wonderland: the walls of the drafty, cavernous space were covered in a childlike mural of flowering plants, which made playing tag in there feel like darting around an indoor forest. Mack had never put any real furniture in the barn other than a card table and some folding chairs. It was a rainy day playroom, a makeshift auditorium, and, for the girls, a secret hiding place.

"There's a lot more crap up there now," Jo said as they stepped inside, the cacophony of mid-afternoon noise giving way to a dusky quiet. Sunlight streamed in through the open windows, and particles of dust hung suspended in the hot, still air. Jo closed the barn doors behind them.

"I still can't believe no one ever caught us," Emma marveled.

"I can't believe we never fell off," Skylar laughed.

Maddie looked up at the loft. It was just a wooden platform on the east end of the barn, tucked under a splintery door that had always been nailed shut, although that didn't stop droplets of rain from shooting through the ragged edges of the planks when it rained really hard. There was no ladder, for obvious safety reasons, since it was fifteen feet up. But on one lazy afternoon when they were ten, Maddie had discovered that if Skylar gave her a boost, she could shimmy up the knotty wood beam just as easily as she climbed sycamores back home.

"Where's the rope ladder?" Maddie asked. She squeezed her hands reflexively, remembering the calluses she'd gotten from bracing her feet in the crack where the sloping roof met the loft floor and pulling the rope tight enough to hold Emma's weight.

"Last time I was up there, helping Gus stack boxes, I stashed it under a bunch of blankets," Jo said.

"Okay," Maddie said, grinning impishly at Skylar. "I'm ready when you are." Since Jo was almost as tall as Skylar now, they each took one leg and held her as high as their triceps could stand.

"Thank God you didn't get fat," Jo laughed.

"Can it, sister," Maddie panted as she gripped the beam with both hands, hoping the tread on her Keds was strong enough to grip the sanded wood. "You're talking to the girl who's gonna be holding the rope." The first few feet were touch and go, and Maddie briefly considered giving up, but then, all at once, the skill came back, her hands got surer, and she was swinging a leg onto the platform in no time.

Just like Jo said, the loft was crammed with boxes overstuffed with Camp Nedoba T-shirts, tennis rackets, and the big round clip lights Mack used for the annual talent show. But the little corner they used to huddle in was still there, crisscrossed with cobwebs. Maddie smiled. Obviously no one had been there in ages. It still belonged to them.

She unearthed the rope ladder they'd made—hours spent hunched over an old Boy Scout manual in the woods, not to mention the time it had taken to "borrow" the rope from the tool shed and whittle down branches for the rungs—from beneath a musty pile of blankets and tossed it over the side, whispering "Anchors aweigh!" like she always used to, eliciting giggles from Emma. Supporting weight was easier with the clutter; Maddie just had to shove a box against a beam and wedge herself behind it.

Once they were all up, they stood in a circle and stared at each other, panting and smiling.

"Now it's official," Maddie said. "It feels like we're really back." No one knew where they were, except for each other. The rest of the world seemed very far away.

"You know what I feel like?" Skylar said, stooping to avoid whacking her head on the ceiling. "Alice after she ate the EAT ME cake and got humongous." They settled into a circle on the dusty planks.

"You haven't been up here since we left?" Emma asked.

"Why would I? It's a pain in the ass." She smiled. "Plus, this is our place. Who else would I come here with?"

"It's weird, isn't it?" Maddie said. "Except for right here, in this spot, camp's not really ours anymore."

"It's still ours!" Jo cried.

"It *was* ours," Maddie said. "Now it belongs to some other kids. Some little, bizarro versions of us. We're just passing through, like ghosts." She ran her fingers along the graying wood, suddenly realizing why people were always compelled to scrawl their names onto walls in permanent marker, followed by the words *was here*.

"Don't think of it that way," Emma said brightly. "Think of it as them trespassing on our property."

"Totally," Skylar said. "And we can chase them off in our motorized wheelchairs!"

"Swinging our canes!" Jo added. They laughed.

"I really missed you guys," Maddie said. She swallowed, feeling a lump forming in her throat. Until now, she hadn't realized how long it had been since she'd been among friends. At school, everyone had stopped talking to her after word about Charlie got out. But they hadn't stopped talking *about* her. As she'd walked the hallways, the whispers had glanced off her like airborne paper cuts.

"Hey," Jo said, reaching over to grab Maddie's chin. "I declare this a no-cry zone. We should be happy. We're all here."

"I am happy to be here," Maddie said. "I'm just also overwhelmed. I don't know where to even start." She took a deep breath, knowing she had to be careful. If she let too much slip out, she could end up with an emotional avalanche.

"I have an idea," Emma said with a sly smile. "Let's play ten fingers."

That could be dangerous, Maddie thought, but she'd never been able to resist a good round of inappropriate gossip. "I'm in!" she said, with as much enthusiasm as she could muster.

"Which game is that again?" Jo asked.

Skylar sighed. "You know it; we've played it dozens of times. You just suck at it, is all."

"It's never have I ever," Emma explained. "You know, you turn a finger down if you've done whatever it is."

"*Right,*" Jo said. "Okay, I'll just keep mine up then, because I haven't done anything." She held her hands in front of her like a street mime pretending to be trapped in a box. Maddie guffawed.

"Okay, I'll start," Emma said. "I'm just going to put this out there now, because it's the big one. . . ."

"That's what she said," Maddie whispered. She knew it was a cheap joke, but she couldn't help it; humor became a defensive reflex when she was feeling anxious. Jo, being kind, laughed louder than she needed to.

"Never have I ever . . . had sex," Emma announced. She wiggled all ten fingers. "Yes, I'm still a virgin. Don't all gasp at once."

"Ditto," Jo said.

Well, they were bound to find out sooner or later. Maddie turned down the thumb of her right hand; across the circle, she saw Skylar do the same. Neither one of them looked particularly proud.

Jo gasped. "Wait!" she cried. "You had sex with whatshisname? Your lab partner?!"

"Charlie," Maddie corrected. But it was true. Maddie and Charlie had been paired in sophomore chemistry lab thanks to alphabetical proximity, and after three months spent hovering warily over Bunsen burners, they'd become friends. They'd spent lunch hours quizzing each other on oxidation reactions on the track bleachers and speculating as to whether their teacher, who went by the nickname "Doc," fashioned himself after Doc Brown from *Back to the Future* or after Snow White's smartest dwarf. By the end of the semester their chemistry was soaring, even though they'd only pulled C's in the class.

"And you didn't tell me?!"

Maddie was frankly surprised that Jo seemed so interested all of a sudden. When she'd first told Jo about Charlie, after she swooned over his dark blond curls and bright blue eyes in freshman year homeroom, Jo had barely responded, and she'd never asked about him after they'd started dating. Hell, three seconds ago, she hadn't even been able to remember his name.

"When?" Emma asked. "Is that too personal?"

"Nope," Maddie said. "April 22, Holiday Inn Express, Brantley Boulevard, Fayetteville, North Carolina."

"Wow," Skylar laughed. Maddie just shrugged.

"People say you never forget your first time," she said. She knew she never would.

Charlie had wanted to do it from the very start, of course, but Maddie thought fifteen was way too young, and besides, since her own mom had given birth to her at seventeen, Maddie was determined to graduate high school before engaging in any behavior that could possibly land her in the same situation.

They'd come close once, when Maddie had come over the night Charlie's parents went away to Myrtle Beach for their anniversary. He'd pulled out all the stops, lighting candles, buying flowers, playing soft emo music, and even changing his sheets, and Maddie's heart had felt like it was going to burst out of her chest as she took off her clothes. He'd been gentle and nervous and said all the right things, and they'd gone further than they ever had before. But when he asked her if he should get a condom, Maddie knew she wasn't ready. It felt too fast. He'd assured her that it was okay and held her face in his hands and told her he loved her, and she'd left feeling weightless and giddy, so lucky to have a boyfriend who would wait for her. *With* her. But after a few months, Charlie had clearly grown tired of waiting.

"It's not *normal*," he would say petulantly when she pulled away in the backseat of his Toyota, which he eagerly drove into the woods on days that he could convince Maddie to ditch drama club to fool around. "We've been dating for a year. You love me, I love you . . . it's just what happens next, Maddie."

"How special," she would reply. "Intercourse! The next step in the manual." It had reminded her of health ed class, where the nether regions of the human body were bisected on diagrams, with arrows leading to various canals and ducts with ominous-sounding names.

A week before the junior prom, he'd threatened to break up

with her.

"I'm not a total douchebag," he'd said—inarguably a great start to any romantic monologue—"but I can't pretend it doesn't matter." They'd been standing in the parking lot behind the Super Dog & Dairy, where Maddie worked an after-school shift, and Charlie had looked like he might cry. Maddie had been prepared to stand her ground, but as she'd listened to him stammer about commitment and trust, she'd realized that Charlie was the only solid thing she had in her life, at least since camp had ended. Things between her mom and Eddie were bad, and if they got divorced, Maddie realized she'd probably have to move to Alabama to live with her grandma. So she'd done what she thought she had to not to lose him. Hence the Holiday Inn Express. Hence the turned-down thumb.

"Okay, I've got one," Skylar said, grinning. "Never have I ever... gotten a bikini wax!" Maddie was relieved that the spotlight was off her, and delighted when Skylar turned down her right pointer finger.

"What?" Skylar asked innocently. "Just me?"

"*Why*?" Jo asked, wincing.

"My cousin gave me a spa certificate for my birthday, and I just thought... why not?"

"Did it hurt?" Emma asked. "I once got my upper lip waxed, and..." she shuddered. "Never again."

"And those were just the lips on your *face*," Maddie cracked. They laughed so hard the rafters shook.

"Okay, I have one," Jo said, once the giggling subsided.

"Never have I ever killed a man," Maddie said solemnly, making a stabbing motion with her left hand.

"*No*," Jo rolled her eyes. "I was going to say never have I ever skinny-dipped." They all looked around at each other, but no one turned a finger down.

"Well now I know what we're doing after the bonfire!" Emma laughed.

"I almost did once, but the lake water—ick," Skylar said, grimacing.

"You did that *here*?" Jo asked, raising an eyebrow.

"I just said I didn't do it!" Skylar cried.

"Who with?" Emma asked.

Skylar hesitated. "A bunch of people," she finally said. "But like I said, I didn't, so . . ." She looked hopefully at Maddie. "Got one?"

"I feel bad for Miss Johannah Jazz Hands over there, so this one's for her," Maddie said. "Never have I ever worn a whistle as a necklace!"

Jo gamely turned a pointer down and they all cheered. "I don't want your pity," she said with a smile.

They flew through a dozen more—never had they ever smoked a cigarette (Skylar); kissed a girl (Skylar, Emma—but only for a school skit about LGBT rights, did that count?); had a beer (all of them—where had their innocence gone?). But when it came back around to Maddie on the last round, she decided to tell them what had really been going on with her—well, at least some of it.

"Never have I ever been in love," she said, turning her pointer finger down. She looked around the circle. Emma bit her lip and seemed to consider it for a minute before keeping her six remaining fingers extended. Skylar looked down at the floor and shook her head. She was out of fingers, anyway. Jo's hands didn't so much as twitch.

"Charlie?" Jo asked, nodding at Maddie's hands. She nodded and started to talk.

She told them about meeting him, and falling in love with him, and sleeping with him. And then she told them about how she hadn't heard from Charlie the day after the Holiday Inn. Or the day after that. But she'd assumed that he, too, was processing what had just happened, and maybe even setting up some over-the-top romantic date to show her how grateful he was. In fact, when she'd noticed the e-mail from Christina, titled "Charlie," her first thought had been that they were plotting something together. (*Like what,* her present-day self added witheringly, *a Congratulations on Giving It Up surprise party at the IHOP?*) Right off the bat, the e-mail should have been a red flag. In all their years of friendship, Maddie and Christina had always used their phones.

Maddie had read the e-mail so many times, she knew it by heart and recited it to the girls from memory. It wasn't planned, Christina had written. Charlie had been desperate; he thought Maddie was going to break up with him. He'd needed advice. They'd driven around talking and parked by the creek. He'd had a six pack in the trunk. They'd gotten a little tipsy. One thing had led to another . . .

"I did the math," she explained. "It happened ten days *before* the prom. Which means that when Charlie threatened to leave me, it wasn't because he couldn't wait for me. It was because he *hadn't* waited."

"Oh, Maddie," Emma said, her eyes wide and sad.

"No faces!" Maddie insisted. "It's my after-school special and I'll cry if I want to, but the truth is I don't regret all of it." She looked down at her hands. "Not *this* finger anyway. The other one, maybe."

"I'm so sorry," Jo frowned. "I wish you'd told me. I would have been there."

"We all would have," Skylar added quickly.

Maddie nodded. "I thought about it," she said. "But honestly, I didn't want to talk to anyone then. It was kind of a dark time. I just stayed home cuddling with my cat, Mr. Snitches, and composing scathing monologues about trust and betrayal." Skylar looked pained.

"Did you ever get to deliver one?" Emma asked.

Maddie shook her head. "Maybe one day," she said. At the end of her speech, in an ideal world, the whole junior class would slow clap, and then the police would come and arrest both Charlie and Christina for aggravated betrayal and emotional battery. Also, maybe, Charlie's penis would fall off.

"Sky?" Emma said worriedly. "What's wrong?" Maddie snapped out of her revenge fantasy reverie to see that Skylar was wiping away tears.

"It's just sad," Skylar said. "Sex? Check. Bikini wax? Check. Love? Sorry. Wrong girl!" Snot started to run from her perfect nostrils. "Loveless sex is all I have."

Maddie shook her head firmly. "Don't say that," she said. "Don't *ever* say that. You're so much more than that."

"This game is stupid," Emma said. "I shouldn't have started it."

She moved to hug Skylar, but her cell phone started ringing loudly, to Kelly Clarkson's "Since U Been Gone." It was the perfect tension release, and they all laughed—even Skylar, who started blowing her nose into a spare Camp Nedoba T-shirt from one of the storage boxes, much to Jo's chagrin.

"Sorry," Emma groaned, reaching for the back pocket of her shorts. She glanced at the screen and frowned. "It's work."

"Don't pick up," Jo said, waving as if she could shoo away the cell phone like a bee. "Reception sucks out here, anyway. Blame it on being out in the boonies." Maddie breathed a sigh of relief. Camp had always felt like an escape, but with modern technology anyone could reach you anywhere, anytime. It was nice to think that Nedoba really was in its own little bubble that nothing from the outside world could penetrate. It felt safe.

Emma nodded, but her face got more and more tense as she watched the phone ring, even on silent.

"Do you want me to confiscate that?" Jo asked. "I have the authority now."

"No, no," Emma said. "But . . . I should call them back. Just to remind them I'm unreachable."

"How ironic," Maddie said. Like how she still felt she couldn't be herself with the friends who supposedly knew her best.

She watched Jo lower the rope ladder for Emma, looking down at the steep drop they'd cheated so many times. She'd thought that telling the girls about Charlie would feel like a weight had been lifted, but instead she just felt heavier. Charlie had lied to her, and she would never be able to forgive him.

How could she expect her friends to forgive her?

Jo

The Fourth Summer • *Age 13*
Beginning of Second Session

"Friendship Rule: Best friends never talk behind your back."

THE KEY TO APPLYING MASCARA IS TO START AT THE roots and wiggle the brush through to the tips. Jo looked at her eye, comically magnified by the vanity mirror—a big brown orb filled with concentric circles of gold like tree rings radiating out from the inky pool of her iris—and then back down at the instructions. "Wiggle" the bristles full of black gunk within a millimeter of her cornea? That didn't seem right. But she had no one to ask.

The cosmetic care package from her mother had come with a note, typically brief (if Jo came home after soccer practice to find Wendy not there, she would find a Post-It on the hall mirror with the words "Out. Call 4 emgcy" in her mother's loopy scrawl): *Try it pls. XO, Mom.* On top of the "XO," her mother had left a lipstick kiss, as if to drive home the point. The other girls had been thrilled as she opened the tightly-wrapped shoebox to find neat rows of shimmering lip gloss tubes, silky powders, and watercolor palettes of eye shadow packed in lightly scented pink tissue paper, like in a department store.

"Let me make you over!" Maddie had cried. "Please? You don't have to leave the cabin."

"I just want to see what it would *look* like," Skylar had said, with a smirk that made Jo feel like one of those poor orangutans she sometimes saw on YouTube, wearing bow ties and ice skating to the theme from *Rocky* for a million hits. Not that Jo herself didn't wonder what it would look like, but it seemed too late, and too mortifyingly obvious, to try to do it in public. She was afraid she would end up like her friend Anika, who had a unibrow all through junior high until one day it mysteriously disappeared, and she came to school with two eyebrows instead of one. Jo still cringed when she thought of how much flak Anika caught for just five minutes of tweezing, and decided that she most definitely could not step out into Nedoba daylight looking like she belonged at the tail end of a rags-to-riches movie montage. Which is why she was giving herself a makeup lesson in the barn loft.

She was just starting to get the hang of the wiggling when she heard voices approaching at the southern entrance. Jo dropped the mirror and the mascara wand—which rolled along the planks, leaving a damning jet-black trail, before settling at her feet—and crouched behind a stack of boxes. She heard the floor creak as people stepped into the barn. It was the middle of the afternoon elective hour, which meant that whoever it was was playing hooky. Then again, Jo couldn't really judge; so was she. She had told the girls she was going to the infirmary to check out a freckle that looked weird.

"It smells like hay in here," said a nasal female voice. It was

Sunny Sherman. *Of course*, Jo thought. Only the person she would least like to catch her with one eye looking like a raccoon, clutching a compact of something called "cheek butter."

"Duh, it's a barn, of course it smells like hay." This voice was also female, but deeper and less annoying. Probably Jess Ericsson.

"Well, I don't think we should smoke near dry hay," Sunny said. Jo's eyes widened.

"I don't think we should smoke at all," said a third voice. "We're supposed to be throwing bowls in the pottery studio. Someone's gonna notice."

"Kerry," Sunny said, "if you're not going to be chill, you can leave. But trust me, no one is going to know about this. Everyone is busy doing their stupid arts and crafts. No one is in this gross, hay-smelling barn but us. And it's *one* cigarette, so relax."

Jo heard the click of a lighter, and then a lot of coughing.

"Why do you even smoke?" Kerry asked.

"Because . . . it's . . . *cool*." Sunny wheezed. Jo bit her lip to keep from laughing.

"Well, it smells gross."

"Kerry, seriously, shut up."

"She has a point," Jess said, coughing. "Someone could smell it. What if Mack finds out?"

"He'll send us to bed without marshmallows. I don't know—nothing bad," Sunny snapped, pausing to inhale again. "Mack Putnam is a total pushover."

Jo balled her fists, wondering if a citizen's arrest made by yelling from a low height differential would hold up in court.

"He's nice, though," Jess said.

"Of course he's nice, he's a cartoon character," Sunny sighed. She lowered her voice and adopted a doofy affect in an impersonation of Mack. "Come on, kids, let's sing a song about friendship! Who wants to make a picture frame out of popsicle sticks? Who wants to be friends with my annoying daughter? Bidding starts at one great big hug!" Jess and Kerry laughed.

"I'd be more scared if Jo found us," Kerry said.

"Ugh, I know, that girl has issues," Sunny said. "I heard her mom doesn't even want custody. Her own *mom*."

Jo felt her skin prickling as blood rushed to her muscles, readying her for a fight her body didn't yet realize she couldn't have. And even if she could climb down and surprise them, what would she do? Hit them? Call them names? Tell them their moms probably didn't love them all the time, either? Her mom just didn't want *full* custody; it wasn't that she didn't want *any* custody. And the only reason she hadn't fought for full custody was that Jo begged to still be able to spend the summers with her dad, who wasn't a childlike doofus but a lonely, hardworking man trying to make a living supporting his family while providing kids across the country with a place they could call home—maybe even more than their real homes—for a few weeks each year. Jo was willing to bet Sunny's father couldn't say the same.

"That's sad," Kerry said.

"What's sad are her outfits," Jess muttered.

"Snap!" Sunny cried, obviously delighted. "The claws come out."

"I don't think she's a bad person," Jess qualified. "I just think it's weird how she wears the camp T-shirt every day, like she's one of the counselors."

"Well, she *thinks* she's a counselor," Sunny said. "And he lets her think it. It's definitely a conflict of interest if you ask me."

"*Good thing no one asked you, then*," said a fourth voice sharply, and for a second Jo worried she'd blown her cover and spoken her thoughts out loud. But her inner monologue didn't have a Southern accent. It was Maddie.

"We were just leaving," Jess sputtered.

"Good," Maddie said. "And take your nasty cancer sticks with you."

"Calm down, Little Red Whining Hood," Sunny scoffed. "We were going anyway." Jo heard creaking as the girls crossed over to the back door. She could tell just by listening that Sunny was acting like she wasn't in any hurry. After a minute, though, the barn seemed quiet. She wondered if Maddie had left, too. She wanted to look, but if anybody *was* still down there, moving even an inch would give her away. She was agonizing over how long to wait when Maddie made the decision for her.

"Jo?" she whispered from below.

Jo crawled out and peeked over the edge of the loft. "How did you know I was here?" she asked.

"Please, I've known you four years and you've never gone to the infirmary," Maddie said. She studied Jo's face and frowned. "Maybe you should, though. Is that a black eye?"

Jo froze. She *might* have teared up a little bit when Sunny had made fun of her—but she'd forgotten about the mascara.

"No," she said, "It's just dirt."

"What are you doing up there?"

Jo considered telling Maddie the truth, but she'd already started the lie. It seemed easier just to keep it going. "Nothing," she mumbled.

"Fine, don't tell me," Maddie said. "Stay there and lemme get the ladder." With considerable effort, Maddie lugged Gus's stepladder over from the corner. Jo had to scoot her legs over the side of the loft and hang down to reach the top with her toes, but Maddie stood underneath her and guided her legs with one hand while holding the ladder steady with the other. "P.S.," Maddie said as Jo jumped to the ground, "I thought we agreed never to climb up there alone. You could have gotten hurt!"

"I didn't, though." *Not physically, anyway,* she thought.

"That's not the point," Maddie sighed. Together, they carried the ladder back to its spot, making sure to lean it against the wall at the same angle. Jo waved her hands around in the air, trying to clear the lingering, sour smell of Sunny's cigarette smoke.

"Do you think I'm weird?" she asked Maddie.

"Yes," Maddie said. "But in a good way."

"Do you think my *dad's* weird?"

"No," Maddie said firmly. "Your dad is awesome. And besides, family is complicated. Nobody knows what's going on in a family except for the people in it. And anybody who thinks they can judge anybody else is a dumbass."

Jo smiled. Maddie's indignation always made her feel better. "Okay, just one more question," she said, raising an eyebrow. "Do you know . . . how to short-sheet a bed?"

Maddie's face lit up. "Darlin'," she said, "I thought you'd never ask."

Emma

Reunion: Day 1

EMMA STOOD OUTSIDE THE BARN PACING BACK AND forth, searching for a decent signal. Jo was right, cell service was spotty, and every time she was finally able to reach the receptionist at *Miss Demeanor,* there was so much interference it sounded like she was hang gliding in the Serengeti. She dialed her own voicemail in the hopes that maybe her boss had left a message. "You have . . . one . . . new message and . . . three . . . saved messages," the patient robot voice said. "First new message . . ."

"Hey Emma, it's Jeff. I just read a submission from the slush pile that included the most beautiful simile, and I knew you would appreciate it. Ready? 'Her thoughts tumbled around inside her brain like underpants in a dryer.' Okay, that's all. See you Monday."

Emma grinned stupidly at the side of the barn. She knew she should hang up, but since her signal was still clear, she stalled. "First saved message . . ."

"Hey, Emma, it's Adam. You'll never guess where I am . . . I'm standing outside of Fenway Park! Impromptu road trip with my dad to see the Sox play the Yankees. I was kind of hoping you'd pick up and you'd be here too and we could do a slo-mo hug, but . . . I guess that's not happening. So I just wanted to say I'm in your city. Love what you've done with the place, by the way. Okay, so . . . later, I guess. Bye."

She paused. *I really should delete the message,* Emma thought. It was almost a year old, and it felt like the right time and place to let it go. But out of habit she hit nine to resave and remembered the first time she'd heard it, after spending a Saturday writing an intensely boring term paper on the history of the Quabbin Reservoir, the largest inland body of water in the Commonwealth of Massachusetts. She'd been so intent on finishing it (even though it wasn't due for three more days) that she hadn't even plugged in her phone. The ballpark was less than twenty minutes from her house.

"Hey!" Adam's voice in real life startled her out of her voicemail-induced reverie. He was down on the path near the pottery studio but jogged up the hill to meet her.

"Hi!" She turned her phone off and slipped it into her pocket.

"Going to dinner?" he asked, cocking an eyebrow. "Or just getting nostalgic for our square-dancing days?" He started circling her in a comic do-si-do. Emma laughed.

"Dinner," she said, "But . . ." She glanced up at the barn. "I was waiting for the girls."

"Yeah, Nate's supposed to meet me there, too" he said. "But he's shaving. Between you and me, I think he's trying to impress someone."

"Aw," Emma sighed. "Poor Nate."

"You don't think he has a shot?" Adam asked. "I've kind of been egging him on."

"No, he might." Emma smiled. "It's not an easy shot, though."

"That's cool. Easy shots aren't worth it, anyway." He looked at her and cleared his throat. "So, you're waiting for your friends, I'm waiting for mine. But the last time I checked, we were friends . . . and you're here, and I'm here, so . . . shall we?"

Emma hesitated. It would be rude to leave the girls under normal circumstances, but she couldn't tell Adam where they were without blowing their cover, and besides, they were all headed to the same place. Plus, she had been hoping to get some one-on-one time with him, just to see where things stood. She wanted to stick to her promise not to incite unnecessary drama, but she still felt a pull toward Adam that she couldn't ignore.

"How could I argue with that logic?" she said.

Inside the cafeteria, clusters of friends sat scooping up three-bean chili with corn chips from Styrofoam plates and refilling their plastic cups from communal pitchers of bug juice and water. Emma and Adam grabbed scratched plastic trays and stood in the food line. To their left, Sunny, Aileen, Jess, and Kerry were ensconced at a corner table with the Slotkin twins and Bowen Connors, a husky athlete who'd once kicked Jo in the shin so hard during a pickup game of football that she'd walked with a limp for a week.

"I'm so glad I ran into you. I thought I was going to have to sit with Beak and the meatheads," Adam whispered. "Which, by the way, note to self: *great* band name." He grinned, reaching for a square of cornbread and brushing up against her arm. It sent a warm wave of déjà vu washing down her spine.

A few minutes later they sat down. "To reunions," he said, knocking his bug juice back like a shot.

Emma looked across at Adam. He'd grown into his looks, too. She couldn't pinpoint exactly what had changed, but he was definitely more handsome. She wished she could tell what was running through his mind. Her own inner monologue went something along the lines of, *So, about that night three years ago, when I turned away instead of kissing you? That was a mistake. I was dying to hook up with you, but I was nervous about what that meant for our friendship. I lost my nerve and I ran away and I've regretted it ever since, so with that said, how do you feel about trying again, and maybe, I don't know, deflowering me by moonlight someplace?*

Out loud, she said, "So you're a counselor now. What's that like?" He laughed through a mouthful of bread.

"Um, it's basically exactly like being a camper, only I get to be lazier. And I get paid."

"Sounds like a good deal."

"It is," he said. "Only . . . I have the sneaking suspicion that I'm really bad at it."

"What?" She was genuinely surprised. "I bet you're great with little kids."

"I'm good with the kids, I'm just not good with responsibility."

"Example, please."

"Okay . . . for one thing, I have to keep dozens of tiny humans alive in the wilderness for weeks at a time." She laughed. "But seriously, I can't wake up on time, like, ever. A bunch of ten-year-olds have to do that stupid *omki* thing to *me*."

"You and Skylar both," she said.

"Yeah, she and I are not the poster children for respected authority figures."

"Well, waking up late doesn't sound *so* bad . . ."

"What about leaving my wallet in the woods next to an empty six pack?"

"You did *not*."

"Which some of the thirteens found during a hike."

"NO!"

"Yes. But in my defense, it was very dark and I was intoxicated."

"Adam!" She flicked a bean at him. Emma wasn't really surprised, but their sporadic late-night G-chats had made her think he'd grown up at least a little bit in the three years since she'd left. He sighed.

"It's just not my thing, you know that."

"What, accountability?"

"Well . . . yeah."

"That sounds like an excuse to do whatever you want and never have to feel guilty about it."

He looked at her seriously for a second and then broke into a grin.

"Damn, I missed you," he said, like he was only just realizing it, at that moment. She knew it was a cliché, but suddenly Emma felt like the only person in the room. Everything else blurred to a watercolor.

"I missed you, too."

"You don't let me get away with anything."

"Yes, I'm an excellent hall monitor," she quipped. "It's one of my gifts."

"That's not what I meant," he said. He paused, looking down at his plate like he was trying to phrase whatever came next. "Why didn't you ever come visit camp?"

It was a rare vulnerable moment; he seemed genuinely sad. Emma decided to take advantage of whatever brief window she had before he started shielding himself with jokes again and tell him the truth.

"Honestly, I wanted to," she said slowly, taking a deep breath. "But I felt . . . awkward. I got rejected . . ."

"What?" His eyes widened. "I didn't reject you. In case you don't remember, I actually tried to—"

"Not you!" she said, cutting him off. So much for being brave, Emma thought. But she wasn't ready to talk about the last night of camp. Not yet. "I meant Mack. I applied to be a counselor, and I got rejected." Adam looked confused.

"Wait, I thought you said you got some internship at an asbestos company."

Emma laughed. "An asbestos *litigation firm*," she said. "And I did, but only because I didn't get in here."

"You could have told me."

"I was embarrassed. It sucked."

"I've told you embarrassing things," he said, crossing his arms.

"Getting pantsed in second grade and having everyone see your Superman undies isn't the same as experiencing professional rejection."

"They were Batman," he corrected. "Anyway, I'm just saying, you could have told me." He pushed his plate away and shook his head. He looked angry. "If I had known you'd wanted to come back . . ."

"It wouldn't change anything," she said softly.

"Maybe it would." He looked at her helplessly.

Emma was formulating a reply when she saw Skylar making a beeline for the table, with Maddie and Jo following close behind.

"What happened to you?" Skylar asked, looking back and forth from Emma to Adam. "I thought you were waiting for us."

"It's my fault," Adam said. "I abducted her outside the barn."

"I tried texting," Emma lied. Adam raised his eyebrows.

"No biggie," Jo said. "Save us seats while we get food?"

"Sure," Adam said. Or, that's what he *was* saying when a cube of Jell-O hit him in the jaw with a wet smack. Maddie exploded in nervous laughter, and Skylar jumped back, wiping the neon green shrapnel off her shirt. They all looked over to see Nate standing at the dessert table and doubled over.

"Dude!" Adam stood up and wiped the green goo off his lips. He picked up his cornbread and lobbed it across the room, narrowly missing Nate's groin. "You are so . . ." He looked at the girls apologetically. "Sorry, I have to go hurt someone," he said, and sprinted after Nate, who was now pelting Adam with grapes.

"You're cleaning all of that up!" Jo shouted, following him back to the buffet.

"I really am sorry," Emma said to Skylar. "He just showed up, and I didn't know how to explain where you guys were."

Sklyar sat down, grabbing a corn chip off Emma's plate. "It's fine," she said. "I just thought you said you'd outgrown the whole Adam obsession."

"I am not obsessed." Emma felt her cheeks get red. "He's my friend."

"I get it," Maddie said. "Charlie was my Adam. You never really get over your first love."

"Except they were never together," Skylar pointed out.

"And I don't *love* him," Emma whispered.

"Well, I'd be careful if I were you," Skylar warned, popping another chip into her mouth. "He still has a *very* short attention span."

Emma concentrated on drinking her bug juice, not sure what to say to that. Was Skylar just punishing Emma for ditching her for Adam, or was she actually trying to be protective? What had gone on during the past three summers? The uncomfortable thought dawned on Emma that maybe there were no second chances. Maybe too much had changed.

Skylar

Reunion: Day 1

SKYLAR PULLED THE COVERS UP OVER HER HEAD. It had been a long time since she'd been in one of the bunk beds—now she was used to having her own queen-sized counselor's nest—and her five-foot ten-inch frame felt comically large stretched out on the little twin mattress. She pressed her hands up against the low beams of the ceiling, creating a one-person blanket fort, and the sun shone through the sheets in hazy orange squares. They'd just come back from dinner, and Skylar was feeling oddly jealous. How had Adam and Emma ended up at dinner together? Why were they both suddenly acting like she wasn't even there?

Crushes, Skylar knew, were called crushes for a reason. She still got sad when she thought about the awful things Zeke Tanner had said to her on the shore the last night of camp. But aside from him—and now, Adam—Skylar had always been the crushee, not the crusher. Not that she never liked anyone—it was just that they always liked her back more. But as she'd said in her embarrassing display during never have I ever, she had never, to her knowledge, truly been loved. Then again, she'd never loved anyone either. Thunder rolled ominously in the distance.

"Crap! Is it supposed to rain?" Maddie leaped up from the bottom bunk, where she'd been tweezing her eyebrows, and stuck her arm out the open door.

"Nah, it'll blow over," Jo said. "It might be a little cold, though, so bring sweatshirts."

"What you see is what I got." Maddie spun like a runway model and gestured to her tank top and thin cotton capris. "Thank you, Southwest Airlines!"

"Don't worry, I've got you covered," Emma said, tossing Maddie a denim jacket.

"I have a bolero if that's more your style," Sunny Sherman chirped from across the cabin. Skylar, Jo, Emma, and Maddie exchanged eye rolls—no small feat from four separate bunks.

"Seriously, you couldn't pull strings to get us our own place?" Maddie said to Jo through clenched teeth. Skylar snorted into her pillow.

Jo put a finger to her lips. "It was this or twenty-two-year-olds," she whispered.

Emma made a face. "God, I hope I have better things to do when I'm twenty-two than go to a camp reunion."

"Hey!" Jo said. "Watch your mouth."

"Sorry, I just mean—we'll be in college. We'll be able to live on our own, go wherever we want . . ."

"And drink!" Maddie piped up.

"Right, and drink!" Emma said. "So why would we want to hang out someplace where booze is forbidden and everyone else is underage?"

"Hold that thought," Skylar said. She had an excellent idea to get the evening back on track. She swung her legs over the side of her bunk, jumped down, and strolled casually across the room. "Hey, girls," she said conspiratorially as she approached the other set of beds. Sunny and Kerry looked up from the *Us Weekly* they were paging through. Aileen put down her book on colonic therapy, and Jess turned down the volume on the game she was playing on her phone. Skylar lowered her voice to a whisper and leaned in. "So, some of the guys went into town earlier on a beer run. I can't go right now because of Jo"—she made a face and the girls nodded sympathetically—"but you guys should totally head down to the shore early. I don't know about you, but I can't be sober for the sing-along or I might die of shame."

Sunny nodded. "Totally," she said. "Want me to grab something for you? I can keep it in my purse." Sunny carried one of those enormous leather satchels that looked like Mary Poppins's carpet bag but which probably cost more than some people's cars. Skylar wasn't even sure that someone actually *was* down at the shore manning the stash, but, in the words of her tenth grade drama teacher, she committed to the scene.

"Yeah, one of those light beers, the sixty-four-calorie ones." She flashed an impish grin. "Don't have too much fun without me!" She turned and crossed back to her own side, and the others watched gleefully as the Sunny Sherman section of the cabin cleared out.

"Slow clap, Sky," Maddie marveled. "That was beautiful."

"What did you say?" Jo asked excitedly. "Please tell me you sent them to the HoJos down the road."

"I wish," Skylar said. "But they should be occupied for a while. And now that they're gone, we can safely reminisce without the threat of judgment." She dug in her trunk and fished out the Camp Nedoba yearbook. It wasn't technically a yearbook, just a stapled sheaf of photocopied collages Mack put together, but campers traded and signed them at the end of the summer, just like at school.

"Oh man, I forgot about those!" Emma said, taking the yearbook from Skylar and examining the cover, which was a group shot of the entire Camp Nedoba population. Gus took it every year by standing on the roof of the barn.

"There we are!" Maddie cried, pointing to a row of tiny faces near the back.

"Ha!" Jo said, leaning in. "Look how short I was."

"Look at my hair," Emma said. "Why didn't anyone tell me it looked like that?"

"Because we hate you," Skylar joked. She looked at Emma's shiny grown-up mane and flattering fitted clothes, thinking of all the times she'd shown Emma how to flat-iron her hair and coordinate her outfits. Of course she didn't want Emma to look *bad*, but had she unwittingly created a monster?

"Look!" Emma said. "I wrote you something." She squinted at

the tiny print. "Dearest Sky," she read, "I am going to miss you so much! It's our last entrance! Leading songs, making s'mores, breaking hearts. So much to say, so little time. Wish me luck tonight. Summer of No Excuses!! Haha. :) Can't wait to be a CIT with you, M & J next summer. JEMS 'til the end. Love, Emma." She looked up with a smirk. "Well, I was always a wordsmith."

Skylar studied Emma's face for signs of Adam-related pain. Clearly, the message had been written the morning before the end-of-camp bonfire.

"Let me see," Jo said, reaching for the yearbook. She paged through it, stopping short when she got to a photo of Nate and Adam standing on the basketball court with their arms around each other. "Oh wow," Jo said. "Nate *was* big." Adam looked even scrawnier next to his round friend. He was smiling his lopsided smile and winking. So typical, Skylar thought. Adam was even capable of flirting from a grainy photocopy. Too late, Skylar noticed that Adam had scrawled a message in sloppy block print next to his own face.

"Hey S," Jo read. "Been cool getting to know you more this year. Stay beautiful, Adam. P.S. You're not flat anymore and I'm sure you need a bra. LOL Don't hit me."

"What?!" Maddie laughed.

"Oh," Skylar said, "remember that time he told the whole cafeteria—"

"No, I meant the 'stay beautiful' sign-off. Who says that?"

"Adam does," Emma sighed. "To some people, anyway. To me, I think he wrote 'Keep being awesome.'" She frowned and looked down at her hands. There it was, Skylar thought. Proof positive that Emma wasn't over Adam.

"Wait, who wrote this?" Jo asked. "You are an artwork. A Botticelli beauty. A sculptor's muse. Mine." Skylar covered her hands with her face and groaned with shame. Why hadn't she read the yearbook before parading it around?

"That is creepy as hell," Maddie said.

"It was Zeke," Skylar said.

"It sounds like a ransom note," Emma said.

"It was a haiku. That's why it's so short."

"Still," Maddie said. "Yikes."

It made Skylar feel a little better to realize that Zeke had in fact been a pretentious idiot, but something about the words he'd chosen for his poem really rubbed her the wrong way. Did all guys think she was just some object to be looked at, like a piece of art? To be possessed? "Mine?" And Adam had written "Stay beautiful," like it was some kind of command, like if she didn't have her looks she would have nothing. Suddenly Skylar felt like crying.

"This is just depressing me," she said, putting the yearbook back in the trunk. Her attempt to lighten up the afternoon had been a colossal failure. She felt dangerously close to cracking.

"On the bright side, at least you know guys like you," Jo said, lifting her mattress and plucking out a Charleston Chew lodged in the rusty springs.

"Yeah," Skylar sighed. "Whoop-de-effing-do." She took the proffered candy gratefully and bit off a huge chunk, wishing it was one of the cold ones Mack used to keep in the deep freeze for particularly hot days. The brittle snap of frozen nougat against her teeth was something she would always associate with her happiest memories.

"I'm serious," Jo said. "All the guys here treat me like I have a penis."

Skylar looked at Emma and Maddie and they burst into laughter simultaneously.

"It's not funny!" Jo said, even though she was laughing, too. "I'm a seventeen-year-old nun."

"But I thought you hated the boy talk," Maddie said.

"Kind of," Jo said. "But I don't hate the boys. I think about them just like you guys."

"Jo*hannah*! It's like I don't even *know* you anymore!" Maddie cried dramatically. "Don't tell me you watch *The Bachelor*. Or, actually, do tell me, because I need someone to discuss the final rose ceremony with."

"I might be able to help you out with that," Emma said, shyly raising her hand.

Now it was Skylar's turn to be shocked. She never tried to dish about dumb pop culture with Emma because she figured she'd roll her eyes and go back to marking up the pages of *Anna Karenina* or whatever important book she was reading for extra credit. Maybe she was guilty of pigeonholing people, too.

"But how do you fit it in with all of your work?" she asked.

"Where there's a will, there's a way," Emma said. "Also, Hulu."

Maddie and Emma launched into an analysis of that season's

contestants—who was there "for the right reasons," who might be mentally unstable, and whether "pharmaceutical sales" was a legitimate career or just code for television prostitute—as Jo shared more of her candy stash with Skylar, and the combination of the sugar and the laughter acted like a tonic. In fact, Skylar was just starting to feel hopeful about reunion again when she heard the soft knock on the wood and turned to see Adam standing in the doorway.

She froze. Was he looking for a pre-bonfire booty call? Even though she was jonesing for his attention, the last thing she needed right now was for him to say something that would expose her secret to Emma.

Adam flashed his easy smile. "I hope I'm interrupting something," he said.

"Just girl stuff," Maddie said. "You know: flowers, unicorns, tampons." Adam laughed.

"Well, I'll let you get back to your vagina monologues in a second. I was just stopping by to ask if I could borrow someone for a walk," he said.

He braced his hands on the door frame and leaned in, blocking the light so that the setting sun hovered behind his head like a halo. He looked both angelic and predatory, Skylar thought. He was probably a little bit of both. She felt a shiver of longing. How had she let things get so out of hand? Skylar wracked her brain for what she could say to Emma that would make Adam's visit seem innocent.

But when she looked up, she realized she didn't have to say

anything. Adam was looking right past her. His smile was for someone else.

"I'd love to," Emma said, "but we're all going to the bonfire together." Skylar knew she was the only one who could see the corners of Emma's smile turning down ever so slightly.

"It's fine," Skylar heard herself say through the dizzying hum of blood suddenly flooding her head. "You should go."

"Really?" Emma could barely hide her delight.

"We'll meet you there," Maddie said. "Right, Jo?"

Jo caught a Skittle in her mouth and shrugged.

"I'll take good care of her," Adam said as Emma slipped into her canvas flats and joined him in the doorway.

"Bonfire starts at seven sharp!" Jo called after them.

"See?" she said to Skylar and Maddie. "I *knew* he was going to be a problem." She tossed back another handful of Skittles, grumbling, "No drama my ass."

Skylar climbed back up onto her bunk and buried her face in her pillow. She felt like crying again, but she didn't know how she could explain it to the others. She'd spent so much time worrying about hurting Emma that she never considered she might get hurt in the process.

Emma

The Fourth Summer • *Age 13*
End of First Session Dance

"Friendship Rule: Best friends think you're beautiful even when you don't."

"HOLD *STILL*!"

Emma gritted her teeth as Skylar dragged the brush through her wet, tangled hair.

"OW!"

"I know, I know, and I'm sorry," Skylar said, lisping a little from the bobby pins she was holding in her mouth. "But I promise it'll be worth it." She patted Emma's shoulder. "Now, head down."

Emma stared at the tile floor of the girls' bathroom. It was the only building at camp that had a full-length mirror, and in addition to torturing her scalp, Skylar had brought along a bag full of outfits she was going to force Emma to model. "Remind me again why I can't just have a ponytail?" she asked.

"Because you have a ponytail every single day, and this is the only dance all session and you need to look like you're trying."

"Trying to *what*?" Emma lifted her head and Skylar pushed it back down, working on a snarl at the nape of her neck.

"Trying to look good! I mean, no offense, Em, but you act like you're still ten years old. You don't pluck your eyebrows, you don't shave your legs—"

"That hair is *blond*," Emma protested.

"—you don't paint your toenails, you never wear your hair down or wear skirts, and you sometimes still wear your retainer *during the day*."

"My orthodontist says I have to," Emma said helplessly.

"Well, he's not trying to get someone to kiss him." Skylar put her hand on Emma's chin and tilted her face up to the mirror. "I would never have gotten a boyfriend last year if I wore my glasses to school."

Skylar had not stopped talking about her boyfriend, Cole, since she'd arrived at camp. He was fifteen, but in the pictures she'd taped up inside her trunk, he looked even older.

"See?" she said. She had brushed out Emma's hair and pinned the sides back. "This looks like you're trying, but not too hard. It's very girl next door."

Emma examined her reflection. "I guess so," she said. "But if I'm the girl next door, what are you?"

Skylar smiled at herself in the mirror. She wore a loose, white, off-the-shoulder peasant blouse and a long, gauzy yellow skirt. A silver and turquoise necklace hung halfway down her chest, along with her tangled blond waves. She'd borrowed feathered earrings from their counselor, Sasha. "I'm boho," Skylar said proudly.

"You know that those letters rearranged spell *hobo*, right?" Emma teased.

“Hey, don’t be jealous just because you can’t pull it off.” Skylar brushed her bangs out of her face.

“I’ll never be the third Olsen twin,” Emma sighed.

“Not with that attitude,” Skylar said. “Now, let’s pick your outfit.”

Emma watched as Skylar draped out maxi skirts and halter tops over the closed bathroom stall doors. She felt totally fine in her T-shirt and jeans, but she knew Skylar would make her change into something tighter, something that Emma would spend all night self-consciously adjusting.

“I know you’re trying to help,” Emma said. “But . . . isn’t the whole point that he’s supposed to like me the way I am?”

“You’re still going to be the way you are, just better,” Skylar said. “Try these.” She shoved a handful of dresses at Emma and ushered her into a stall.

The barn was set up the same way it had been for every dance of every summer—folding tables pushed up against the far wall with plates of knock-off Oreos and Chips Ahoy!; pitchers of water and weak lemonade floating with tiny, amoebic swirls of concentrate; and white Christmas lights Gus had strung from the rafters, which reflected onto the polished wood floor in constellations of egg-shaped orbs. Mack’s mix tape—which Jo swore was actually a *tape,* as in cassette tape—flowed out of two big box speakers set up against the northern wall, under the loft. The mix was always the same, and there were never any Billboard Hot 100 hits. It started off with the

Beatles, moved on to Motown, and then took a strange Simon & Garfunkel detour (Emma's dad would have been in heaven) before ending with a slow dance to "In the Still of the Night." That song was the reason Skylar made her dress up. Well, Adam Loring was the reason. But the point was to bring him, the song, and Emma together at the same time.

Emma looked down at the maroon batik maxi dress Skylar had insisted made her look like "a gypsy goddess." It bunched around her (still absent) chest and drooped down to the floor, giving her the approximate shape of a deflated toadstool.

"I feel awkward," she whispered, not budging from the door frame.

"You look fine," Maddie said unconvincingly.

"You have to trust me," Skylar insisted, adjusting the straps and tucking in the tag. "I know it's not your normal look, but sometimes getting out of your style comfort zone is the only way to get a guy's attention."

"Did you read that in a magazine or something?" Jo scoffed. She was wearing the same camp T-shirt, track pants, and running shoes she'd had on all day . . . although something was different. Her eyelashes looked darker and thicker than usual. Emma would have asked if she was wearing mascara if she didn't know Jo so well. Jo would have sooner picked up a sick of dynamite than a makeup brush.

"My mom was a model," Skylar said matter-of-factly. She seemed to take it for granted that everyone's mom doled out fashion advice alongside the mashed potatoes at dinner. Emma's mother wore shapeless cardigans and hopelessly uncool black peg pants, and when Emma had asked her to help teach her how to shave her armpits that winter, her mother had looked at her like she'd asked for a cigarette. "Sweetheart," she'd said. "We have hair there for a reason. Do you really want to mess with evolution just to fit in?"

Just then, a group of senior girls pushed past, and Emma clutched at the fabric against her legs. She had to pull it up a little to avoid tripping on the hem.

"Let's get out of the doorway," she hissed.

"Yeah, I love this song!" Maddie danced out to the middle of the floor, where scattered clusters of campers were swaying gracelessly to the dated music. Dancing had not been exactly what Emma had in mind—hiding in the shadowy corner near the cookies was more her speed—but Skylar and Jo had already followed Maddie, shimmying their hips but laughing at the same time to make sure everyone knew they weren't really trying to look cool. Emma was confused. Was she supposed to try or not try? Or try, but make it look like she wasn't? Either way, she knew she was failing. So she tried not to think about her ridiculous outfit or about the bobby pins pinching her scalp as she reluctantly joined her friends. At least Adam wasn't there yet. She silently thanked the universe for its small favor.

By the time Adam, Nate, and the rest of their bunk showed up,

Motown was blasting from the speakers, and Mack was moving around the barn demonstrating dance moves like the twist and the monkey, to Jo's horror. Luckily, Emma saw Adam before he saw her, so she had time to pin her arms to her sides and look uninterested. But Adam hung back, hugging the perimeter with Zeke and the twins. After briefly conferring with his friends, Nate made a beeline for the girls.

"Hey, Jo," he said. Emma noticed dark stains spreading from the underarms of his blue button-down shirt. It was sweltering outside, and inside was worse.

"What's up?" Jo asked, stopping to stretch her quadriceps.

"Um, I was just wondering . . . do you want to dance?" Nate kept his eyes on the floor.

"I *am* dancing," she said.

This seemed to throw him. "Oh, I mean, like . . . later."

"I'll probably be dancing later, too," she said. Nate stuck his hands in his pockets and shuffled away.

"He was asking you to dance," Emma whispered. "One on one."

Jo looked uncomfortable. "Well, what was I supposed to do?"

"I give up!" Maddie cried.

"This is what you're supposed to do," Skylar said. She turned to Zeke, who was standing a few feet away by the snack table with Adam.

"Hey, Tanner!" she called. "Wanna dance?"

His blue eyes got wide. "Yeah!" he said, tossing his Dixie cup of lemonade into the trash.

"*See?*" Skylar said. She directed it to Jo, but Emma knew the display had also been for her. She had to set her Adam plan in motion. She picked up her dress and walked over to where he stood, slouched against a thick support beam. He had taken care to look somewhat disheveled, with his untucked button-down and flip-flops, but Emma noticed that his hair had been reshaped from his usual hat-head into something resembling a pompadour.

"Hey," she said. "Can I join you?"

"Sure thing." He smiled. "You look fancy."

Emma rolled her eyes. "Skylar dressed me," she explained. "I wish I had just worn regular clothes."

"No," Adam said. "I meant you look nice."

"Wanna join us?" she asked. "Poor Nate's out there by himself." They watched Nate, who had joined another group and was attempting to dance with Jo by proximity, scramble to dodge Maddie's flailing arms, which were encircling Jo in an invisible lasso.

"Sorry," he laughed, "But I'm not going out there."

"Come on! It's fun!" Her entire plan hinged on getting Adam onto the dance floor. She could never just ask him to dance like Skylar had done with Zeke—it would be way too weird—but if they *happened* to be dancing near each other and a slow song *happened* to come on . . . well, that was different. Emma realized she had more in common with Nate than she wanted to admit.

Adam shook his head. "It's lame."

"You didn't think it was lame last year. In fact, I remember you winning the limbo contest."

He shrugged.

"There must be *someone* you'd dance with," she pressed. The corners of his mouth twitched up. "Aha! I saw that."

"Shut up."

"You like someone."

"Maybe." He smiled and wiggled his eyebrows teasingly. Emma knew she was treading in dangerous waters. Adam was a flirt, but she didn't really want to know if he genuinely liked someone else. Then again, they were friends. A friend wouldn't care. And Skylar always said the best way to get a guy to like you was to pretend you didn't *care* if he liked you.

"Okay, spill. Who is it?" Emma steeled herself for the sucker punch she knew she was asking for.

"What if I said *you*?"

Her stomach lurched. Her mouth fell open. Adam burst out laughing.

"Relax, I'm kidding. I just wanted to see your face."

Emma forced herself to smile, and it was so hard that for a second she felt like she still had braces, with rubber bands connecting her upper and lower jaw. "Very funny."

"I still feel weird telling you, though," he said, lowering his voice. "It's someone in your bunk."

"Skylar has a boyfriend," she said, reaching for a cookie.

"You know those aren't real Oreos, right?" he asked.

"I don't care; I love them." She reached for another, almost out of spite.

"Anyway, it's not *Skylar*," he said. "Give me some credit for originality, please."

Emma swallowed hard, the barely-chewed chunks of chocolate wafer scratching her throat. "Then who?"

He nodded his head to the right, and Emma looked over to see Aileen Abrams leaning against the wall, talking to some of the senior girls. Aileen had a brown shag haircut, big brown eyes, and a tiny button nose that made her look like Bambi crossed with Justin Bieber. She was pretty, but not *that* pretty. Not prettier than Emma, on a good day, anyway.

"Aileen?" she asked incredulously.

He shrugged again. "Do you think she likes me?"

"Why do you care what I think?"

He looked hurt. "Because I trust you. And you're a girl, so you know girl stuff."

Emma softened. He was genuinely asking for help. But still, her heart ached. She liked him the most when he stopped trying so hard to impress her.

"I'm sure she likes you, Adam," she said quietly. "Everyone does."

"Aw, you're just saying that."

"No, I'm not." She looked at him helplessly. "You're a great guy. She'd be crazy not to like you." *And I'm crazy to like you,* she thought.

He flashed her a crooked grin. "You're the best, Zen. You know that, right?"

She forced her rubber-band smile again, trying to remember

the last time he'd called her that. It was a nickname you gave to your buddy, not to someone you had a secret friend-crush on. Not somebody you would ever slow dance with, anyway.

Emma

Reunion: Day 1

THEY TOOK THE SCENIC ROUTE TO THE FIRE PIT, cutting through the woods that separated the girls' cabins from the open expanse of the north field. The setting sun cast a sherbet-colored light through the trees, and above them, the thrushes called back and forth to each other, their unhurried notes floating down on a breeze that made the hair on the back of Emma's neck stand up. There was no path, so Adam walked in front, holding branches out of the way and alerting her to wobbly rocks and tangles of tree roots that poked out of the dirt like gnarled fists. Emma couldn't help but marvel at his deftness as he navigated without so much as a second of hesitation. He'd obviously cut through the same path many times before . . . which, of course, begged the question, what was he doing on the girls' side of camp? But she tried to put that out of her mind. She had to, if she didn't want to fall; her ankles seemed to buckle almost every time she took a step.

"I've gotten rusty," Emma said, laughing as she narrowly avoided slipping on a patch of pine needles.

"You're just out of practice," he said, climbing over the low stone wall, nearly hidden by thick green moss that separated the woods from the open expanse of the north field. He reached out a hand to pull her up and over, and as their fingers touched Emma felt a rush of déjà vu.

"I'm sorry about dinner," she said as they waded through the knee-high grasses, yellowed by the dry spell that summer, and onto the dirt path that wound around the perimeter of the field and then out through the woods to the shore.

"*I'm* sorry about dinner," he said. "I'm the one who bolted."

"Yeah, but before that, you seemed like you needed to talk and I didn't let you." Adam didn't answer. "So . . . did you need to talk about anything?"

"I don't know," he said. "I guess I just don't really feel connected lately. Does that make sense?"

"Sure," she said. "Although that's a little vague. Where's the disconnect?"

"Other people, I guess," he sighed. "Camp. All of it." He stopped and looked at her. "I feel like I have a lot of empty relationships."

Emma tried not to react. She knew they were on a platonic walk, and she wasn't expecting some swooning declaration of love, but she also wasn't interested in being treated like the token non-sexual female friend he'd decided to confide in.

"I mean, I've spent all this time here and I'm just the guy everyone likes," he said.

"That sounds rough."

"I'm not trying to sound like a dick," Adam laughed. "I mean, they just like hanging out with me. They don't actually care. They just want . . ." He trailed off.

"Your body?" Emma finished sarcastically.

"No!" He looked at her and smiled mischievously. "Okay, sometimes. But no, I was going to say they just want the fun, party-guy me. I feel like no one really *knows* me."

Somewhere, Emma thought with a smirk, the world's tiniest violin played for the poor, misunderstood playboy. "Adam," she said, turning to face him. "We've talked about this before. The way you act can sometimes be totally different from the way you actually are. If you want people to stop treating you like the fun party guy, then don't be that guy."

"You're right," he said. "Of course you're right. How come you're the only one who gets that about me?"

"Maybe because I'm the only girl you never—"

"Never *what*?"

It had come out before she could stop it, and now there was no avoiding the topic she both most and least wanted to talk about.

"Never liked. That way." She looked down at the path. "You know what I mean."

"I *do* know what you mean, and that's not true," Adam said, shoving his hands in his pockets awkwardly. It was very un-Adam—or, maybe, a rare glimpse of real-Adam. Emma blushed in spite of herself.

They crested the hill at the northwestern corner of the field, arriving at the curving log bench Mack had built, which reportedly formed the shape of a *J* when viewed from above. It was the only spot on the Nedoba property with a panoramic view of the whole camp. The sun was almost gone and the winds from the passing storm—which, as Jo had predicted, had missed them by a few dozen miles—were whistling through the trees. She was glad she'd changed out of her dress and into a long-sleeved tee and shorts, even if it meant she looked, in the parlance of vapid women's magazines, more girl next door than girlfriend material. She sat down and rubbed her arms to keep warm.

"I'd give you my hoodie, but I'm pretty sure you stole it from me three years ago," Adam said with a smile, sliding in next to her on the bench.

Emma still wore that hoodie all the time, even though the lingering scent of his Old Spice deodorant had been washed away years ago.

"Did I?" she said. "Oops."

"It's okay. I have a pair of your socks."

"What?!"

"I didn't keep them on purpose," he laughed. "Remember, you lent them to me that day we waded through the creek and my sneakers drowned?"

"I like how you say *drowned*, like they're people."

"Well, yeah, I had to throw them out, so for all intents and purposes it was a fatal accident."

Emma looked away and smiled into her hand. She had forgotten how good it felt to be around him.

"Anyway, I accidentally packed them in my trunk and so I have them. My mom thinks it's weird that I would own a pair of athletic socks with pink stripes around the ankles, but I like to keep her guessing."

They stared out at the treetops in silhouette against the purple sky. Down below on the main path, campers were streaming toward the fire pit, their phone screens flashing like lightning bugs.

"So if you're so over camp, why are you still here?" she asked.

"I have friends here," he said. "I mean, Nate's been my buddy since we were ten. And I do like being a counselor, mostly. Besides, what else would I do?"

"What do you *want* to do?"

"For the summer, I just want to hang out," he said. "But for a career? I don't know. Do you?"

Emma thought for a minute. She had held three internships over the past three summers, and so far, all they had really taught her was what she *didn't* want to do for a living. "No," she said. "I guess not. I mean, college, obviously."

"Why obviously?"

"Because it's what you do after high school, unless you want to work in food service."

"I'll have you know that on weekends, I man the pancake station," Adam said with pretend indignity.

"No offense, Chef."

"None taken." He patted her knee, lingering for a few seconds more than he should have.

Out of the woods came the sound of taps being played on Mack's pocket trumpet. The bonfire would be starting any minute.

"I guess we should get going," Emma said. Adam stretched his arms, and his fingers brushed her hair. She wondered if it was even a little bit on purpose. They started walking again.

"Hey, since you brought it up, I want to clear something up about the last night of camp," Adam said after a minute.

"You really don't have to."

He looked at her earnestly. "I really do."

Emma stared down at her blue and white sneakers on the pine needle covered path. Each step brought a satisfying crunch, like the first bite of cereal before the milk turned everything to mush.

"I'm glad I didn't get to kiss you," he said quietly.

She wasn't sure what to say, so she just nodded as if she understood. It worked in her German language lab, and Emma was all about applying classroom skills in the real world.

"I wouldn't have known how to handle it," he continued. "I wasn't ready to kiss someone I actually liked."

She stopped mid-nod. Her pulse raced. What was Adam getting at? Was he hitting on her?

"And now that I'm ready, there isn't anyone I actually like."

So much for that. The door of opportunity that had just creaked open after years of being locked closed on her fingers—hard. When she finally spoke, she kept her voice low so he wouldn't hear it shaking.

"So what you're saying is, you hook up with people you don't care about, and you're sad about it, but you do it anyway because there isn't anyone you *do* care about."

He glanced at her and smiled softly. "There's you," he said.

Emma didn't know what Adam wanted from her. She didn't know what she wanted from him yet, either. Seeing him again had definitely reignited a spark, but she wasn't sure if it could last the night, let alone the weekend. It was too early to tell. And what would her friends say? But just in case, just to make sure he didn't take her reticence as rejection, she reached out and squeezed his hand. He squeezed back. The winds picked up.

Maddie

Reunion: Day 1

MADDIE HAD CONSIDERED TURNING OFF HER CELL phone for the weekend. For one thing, the reception problems meant that all communication took five times longer than normal, which meant that the roaming charges she was incurring just to download e-mails from Anthropologie about the latest bandeau harem romper were probably going to cost her the entirety of her remaining Super Dog tips, which were bundled in the toe of one of her snow boots deep inside the hall closet at home. Also, her phone didn't go with the only outfit she had, thanks to her baggage debacle. She wasn't going to carry a purse to go canoeing or to sit around singing songs about Native American agriculture, and she sure as hell wasn't going to stick a big, boxy phone in the pocket of her snug, white capri pants. Finally, everyone she wanted to speak to was at camp anyway, and there were way too many people she *didn't* want to speak to who could reach her in the wilderness thanks to Alexander Graham Bell—and whoever invented texting.

But then she'd thought about her sisters and how she always

told them they could call her if things got bad—which was more than likely, given the state of her mom and Eddie's volatile relationship, which tended to vacillate between mutual indifference and screaming fights. So Maddie left her phone on. Which meant that just as she was leaving Souhegan to head over to the bonfire site with Jo, she heard the chime that told her she had a new text message. And since it was a physiological impossibility for her to ignore a new text message, she looked at it.

Chris is really upset you didn't remember her birthday.

It was from "DO NOT ANSWER!!!!," which was what she changed Charlie's name to in her contacts. She stared at the screen in disbelief. Charlie was texting her for the first time since breaking her heart and publicly humiliating her to try to shame her for not sending the best friend who betrayed her a birthday card? Maddie doubted there was a Hallmark greeting that could accurately express what she wanted to say.

"Mads, you ready?" Jo called from the doorway. Skylar was already waiting outside. Since Emma and Adam had gone on their walk, she'd gotten awfully sulky.

"Coming," Maddie said. She shut down her phone, overcome with fresh hurt and rage. The damage was done.

Outside, girls—well, some of them were in their twenties, so women, maybe? Maddie still wasn't sure where the turnover took place—streamed out of the bunks talking and laughing. Some of them smoked cigarettes and stumbled drunkenly, but if Jo noticed or cared, she didn't let on. Maddie wasn't a drinker, and yet she found herself wishing she could be like those girls, just for one night. She wanted nothing more than to care about getting tipsy and talking to cute guys instead of angstily swatting away mosquitoes and picturing Charlie and Christina out on some romantic birthday date discussing what a heartless bitch she was for not sending flowers, and maybe a pack of congratulatory Trojans.

Maddie glanced over at Jo but couldn't catch her eye. Jo always looked straight ahead when she walked, like she was charging into some historical battle. Even Skylar, who had the longest legs of all of them, had to move fast to keep up. That meant Maddie had to run. She'd worn the soles of her Keds down so much they had almost no tread left, and she felt herself slip a little bit on the dry pine needles scattered across the path.

"Charlie texted me," she panted as she fell in step with the others. Jo groaned.

"Let me see it," she demanded. Maddie turned her phone back on and showed her the message. "Wait, who's Chris?" Jo asked, squinting at the screen in the blinding beam of light that was cutting through the trees as the sun dipped below the horizon and out of sight.

"Christina," Maddie said. "My ex-best friend."

"Ugh, he sucks *so much*. Why didn't she just text you?"

"Because I blocked her." Maddie felt a pang of guilt.

"That's not fair," Skylar said. "Why didn't you block him?"

"She's right," Jo said, handing the phone back to Maddie. "You should have blocked both of them. She's no more to blame than he is."

"But she was my *best friend*," Maddie said. "Best non-camp friend, I mean. I've known her even longer than I've known you guys. She knew me way back before I met Charlie." Maddie knew it was faulty logic, but it felt like Christina had betrayed her more.

"Did she know you really well?" Jo asked.

"Since first grade."

"But did she *know* you?"

Maddie frowned. It was a weird question. "Yes, obviously," she said. Had Jo been acting strangely since she got to camp, or was Maddie just cranky?

They trudged for a few minutes in silence as other girls, who presumably had not recently received soul-crushing text messages, laughed around them. When they came out of the woods, instead of continuing on past the barn, Jo motioned them to follow her down the hill to the cafeteria. They were almost to the double doors when Nate barreled through with a tray full of marshmallows.

"Hey!" Jo laughed, dodging his elbow. "Watch where you're going, Stay-Puft." Nate grinned, and Maddie stared at him, awestruck at how the pudgy, awkward boy she remembered could have morphed into the gorgeous Justin Timberlake look-alike in front of her.

"Sorry," he said. "I was given strict orders to have these at the fire pit by seven, on pain of death." A marshmallow toppled from the stack and landed noiselessly in the dirt.

"I'll take it," Jo said, grabbing the tray from him. Maddie watched Nate's face as Jo's hands brushed his. She knew that look.

She'd had it when she first touched Charlie when he'd passed her a pipette of saline solution.

Inside, Skylar and Maddie stood in front of the kitchen pass-through window as Jo rummaged in the back for graham crackers.

"When did Nate Hartner get so hot?" Maddie asked Skylar, climbing onto one of the picnic tables and resting her legs on the bench.

"I know, right?" Skylar laughed, pretending to swoon. "It was sort of gradual, so I didn't really notice it happening. His acne cleared up the first summer we were counselors, and then he started working out. This year has been crazy, though. All the girl campers are like in love with him."

Maddie nodded her head toward the kitchen. "What about her?" she whispered. Skylar looked surprised.

"Miss Oblivion, you mean? I don't know, she never talks about it."

Maddie shook her head. "What a waste," she sighed.

Jo stuck her face in the pass-through. "Are you guys going to help with these or just stand around?" she asked, shoving a dozen boxes of graham crackers across the counter.

They each took an armful and navigated back through the double doors using their hips and elbows. Once they were out on the path, Skylar turned to Maddie.

"Hey, what did you do?" Skylar asked. "When Christina told you?"

"Nothing. I mean, she e-mailed me. So I didn't respond. It was pretty easy," Maddie said.

"What would you have done if she'd told you in person?"

"I never thought about that. But I guess it wouldn't have been as easy to ignore. I would have had to say something to her."

"What would you say?" Skylar seemed weirdly fixated on Christina, but Maddie decided to ignore it. It was nice that someone cared. She tried not to be hurt that Jo wasn't asking any follow-up questions.

"Nothing Jo's delicate ears could handle," Maddie whispered. Jo managed to flip her the bird without dropping her boxes.

"But do you think you'd still talk to her?" Skylar asked.

"I really don't know," Maddie said, realizing that with every word she spoke she became more and more of a hypocrite. "But I think I'd at least respect her for telling me to my face. She was one of my best friends. She owed me that."

"Okay," Jo said with a deep sigh, the way she did when she was about to be brutally honest. "I am so sorry this happened to you. Really. But I need you to promise me that you won't let him win."

"Win . . . what?" Maddie asked.

"Guys try to throw you off your game," Jo said. "That's what they do. I mean, look at Adam and Emma. He *wants* you to hide and stay in bed with Mr. Snitches eating pretzel M&Ms. He *wants* you to get upset when he sends you a stupid text out of nowhere. It's tactical. The only way to protect yourself is to build up your defense."

"Build up my defense? We're not playing soccer." Maddie looked at Skylar for backup, but she seemed distracted again and just offered a sympathetic eye roll.

"Fine," Jo said. "Don't listen to me. But at least turn off your phone if you don't want to hear from him. Or block him already." For someone so clueless about guys, it was actually sound advice.

"You're right. I should," Maddie said.

"You *will*," Jo replied.

"I will," Maddie parroted. She tried to hold her stack of boxes steady with her chin, but she could tell she was losing her grasp. With each step her fingers slipped further, until she was just waiting for the moment she lost control, and the whole thing toppled.

It was a feeling she was getting used to.

Jo

Reunion: Day 1

"HOW YOU HOLDIN' UP?" NATE SAT DOWN NEXT TO Jo on the log she'd been perched on for over two hours, stoking the fire and compulsively eating fun-size Hershey bars. His T-shirt was soaked with sweat—even though it was a cool night, Nate had been busy chopping wood and hauling heavy coolers of soda back and forth from the mess hall—and clung to his torso like a wetsuit.

"I'm okay," she said. "No second- or third-degree burns so far!"

"Can I get you a drink or something?"

She shook her head.

"Are you sure? Water? Coke?" He coughed suggestively. "Beer?" Jo laughed.

"How do they keep selling to you? I'm going to fax a poster with all of your photos to the guys at the liquor store."

"Please don't." He pulled a can out of the waistband of his shorts and cracked it open with a smile. "Some of us need it."

Jo shot him a concerned look.

"Not like *that*," he said. "I meant some of us need it to, you know...

work up the courage to talk to girls we like."

Jo poked at the dying fire and then waved her stick toward a group of drunk twentysomething girls in a nearby clearing. "I don't think you'll have a problem getting them to talk to you," she said.

Her dad had presided over the bonfire like always, singing "John Jacob Jingleheimer Schmidt" and the rest of his Camp Nedoba Greatest Hits (no, really; there was a CD) in his hilariously deep baritone and passing around skewers of marshmallows for roasting. But then a former counselor named Shane had an asthma attack brought on by smoke inhalation and Mack had driven him to the ER, entrusting Jo with wrapping up the festivities. That had been over an hour ago, and in the interim a sizable portion of the older crowd had gotten rowdy and amorous, starting a game of spin the bottle, which had devolved quickly into a game of seven minutes in heaven—except that instead of seven minutes, each player got approximately fifteen seconds, and instead of heaven it was a stump of gnarled wood surrounded by citronella candles and discarded Solo cups. Now, five or six older drunk girls were simply going around to cute guys and saying, "You get to kiss me," and then dragging them into the bushes.

"My dad would freak out if he saw that," Jo said, trying to control the panic rising in her chest. "He thinks we're all so innocent." She looked at Nate's beer for a second, snatched it from his hand, and took a gulp. "Why not, right? I'm a total failure as an authority figure anyway."

"You're awesome," Nate said, retrieving the beer with an amused smile. "Those kids are just drunk."

"That's my point. If anyone got hurt or sick, my dad would get blamed. They'd probably shut down the camp!" She leaned forward and put her head between her knees. "What have I done?"

"Don't worry," Nate said, resting a hand gently on her back. "I'm going to help you."

Over in the circle, things were getting out of hand. "You get to kiss me" had degenerated even further into a sloppy square dance of making out. The main players were three older girls, Meredith, Allie, and Ruth, and a few older guys whose names Jo didn't know—she decided to call them Thing 1, Thing 2, and The Cat in the Hat for the goateed guy wearing a fedora and sunglasses even though it was so dark even Jo, who had documented 20/10 vision, had trouble seeing. A junior varsity version of the game was being played by Sunny and Co., the Slotkin twins, Zeke, and Bowen. Skylar and Maddie were leaning against a tree on the periphery of the circle, sharing a beer, and Adam and Emma sat in the grass a few yards away. Jo wasn't sure what she was more upset about, the drinking game or the fact that it had only been six and a half hours since their emotional reunion and already the JEMS seemed to have dissolved again—and that none of them, not even Maddie, seemed to want to hang out with her.

Jo stomped into the center of the clearing and waved her arms. She thought about using her whistle, but she didn't want to risk calling attention to the fire pit. Even on the slim odds her dad was already back on camp grounds, she couldn't let him see what a mess his idyllic welcome tradition had become under her watch.

"Okay, guys," she said, trying to keep her voice steady and avoid touching any roving limbs. "Time to reclaim your own saliva."

"Buzzkill!" Thing 2 yelled. The girl he had been kissing—Allie, the blonde—cackled with delight.

"She is!" Allie cried. She pretended to press down on a giant *Jeopardy!* buzzer. "Bzzzzzzzzzzzz!"

Jo looked over at Emma and shrugged helplessly.

"I'll take insanely wasted for $200, Alex," Emma called. Adam laughed as Skylar rolled her eyes and took a healthy swig from her Corona Light.

"Hey, that's funny!" Cat in the Hat said, breaking away from Meredith, who'd been giving him a hickey. He stumbled over toward Emma. "You're *funny*."

"You get to kiss him!" Sunny yelled from a prone position on the grass. Emma looked horrified.

"I don't think so, man," Adam said, holding his hand up like a stop sign. But Cat in the Hat just high-fived him and ran off into the bushes to pass out.

"Okay, okay," Nate said, starting to herd the boys out of the clearing. "I mean it—enough. Time to head back, sleep it off."

Thank you, Jo mouthed. Nate just shrugged and grinned. Maybe it was just the moonlight and all the smoke inhalation from the fire, but Jo was finally starting to see why all her campers always swooned when Nate led their activities. He was *cute*. But she didn't have time for thoughts like that. She marched over to Sunny and helped her up off the grass.

"Time for bed, ladies," she said. "We have a big trip tomorrow and wake-up's at seven a.m."

"Why are you such a killjoy?" Sunny moaned. "Can't you, like, join the army or something so you can get up at dawn and do a million push-ups and leave the rest of us alone?"

"Thanks for the advice," Jo said. She wanted to add, *Can't you, like, go join a sorority or something where other vapid women might appreciate your deep thoughts on nail art and Brangelina?* But she held her tongue; she was in charge, and she had to behave like a camp director. To that end, she marched over to the clique of older girls and started snatching the half-finished beers out of their hands.

"Hey!" Meredith cried. "I was drinking that."

"Sorry, camp policy," Jo said. "Anyway, the bonfire's over, and it's time to go back to the bunks."

"Jeez, who died and made you boss?" she asked. Ruth leaned over and whispered something in her ear, and Meredith laughed and nodded. "I can see the resemblance now," she said, looking Jo up and down. "Neither one of you has any tits!" They exploded in laughter.

Jo felt the color rise in her cheeks, but she clenched her teeth as the girls stumbled back onto the path. When she turned around, she saw Maddie and Skylar walking over arm in arm.

"Where have you guys been?" she cried. "I thought we were going to stick together."

"Me too," Skylar said loudly. "But Emma went off with Adam, and as soon as we got here you and Nate had super secret s'mores business to attend to. So Maddie and I founded the Lonely Hearts Corona Club."

"Yup," Maddie said, taking a swig.

"Give me that," Jo scolded, grabbing the beer. "Where did all of this come from, anyway?" Maddie and Skylar smirked at each other and shrugged. Jo sighed. Why did she always have to be the bad cop?

She looked forlornly at the trash strewn around the campsite. It would take at least an hour to clean up, maybe more. She was tired of being a mini-Mack, or a mini-Gus. Just once, for one night, she wanted to be herself and not to have to care about running camp.

"You know what? Screw it. Let's take a break," she said, handing the beer back to Skylar. "This is my reunion, too."

"Atta girl!" Maddie said. They stepped over the marshmallow carnage and sat together on the log they'd always favored, the one they'd sat on senior year that faced the path down to the lake. The sliver of water that was visible through the trees shimmered in the moonlight.

"Emma!" Jo called, cupping her hands around her mouth. "Get your deserting little butt over here." She took the beer from Skylar and took a sip. Just a few minutes, she promised herself, and then she'd start cleaning up. She just needed a few minutes of feeling like a normal teenager.

Emma appeared, looking sheepish and wiping dirt off her knees.

"You've spent more time with Adam than you have with us,"

Jo said. "That was not the plan." Emma shifted uncomfortably.

"Yeah," Maddie chirped. "Party foul. We're gonna have to install a tracking device."

"Don't do that," Emma laughed. But then her smile faded. "I'm sorry," she said. "I want girl time, I really do. I just . . ."

"Want to hook up with Adam?" Skylar asked. The bluntness of the question seemed to strike Emma like a blow to the kidneys. She sat down next to Jo and rested her chin on her hands.

"I don't know," she said softly. "Maybe. At least get some kind of closure."

Jo had to respect Emma's honesty, but she still didn't quite understand it. Yes, guys could be distracting, but camp was supposed to be about lasting friendships, not short-lived hookups. And it's wasn't like Emma and Adam were meant to end up together, no matter what Maddie said about her parents meeting at camp. Jo was pretty sure that had been a lie, anyway.

"Remember when we rigged that fortune teller to try to get Adam to kiss you?" Maddie said suddenly. Emma put her face in her hands and groaned.

"Don't remind me!" she laughed. Jo had completely forgotten about that rainy day that they'd spent painstakingly writing "You will kiss the person who read you this fortune" in tiny print on the inside flaps of the fortune teller Skylar had folded like origami from a sheet of notebook paper. But then Adam hadn't wanted to play, and when Jo unsubtly tried to coerce him into doing it by promising he'd get something no one else at camp had, Emma panicked and destroyed the damning evidence in a puddle.

"I still say he would have done it," Skylar said. "And then we all would have been spared another year of moaning and groaning."

"Hey!" Emma said. "It's not like *you* didn't have anyone we got sick of hearing about."

"If Zeke asked me to, I would go all the way with him!" Maddie trilled in an imitation of fourteen-year-old Skylar.

"Whatever," Skylar huffed—and then broke into a grin. "I still would." Jo threw her head back and laughed. She felt strange and warm and uninhibited. Maybe she was actually . . . relaxed. It was a weird feeling.

"What's so funny?" Adam stepped into the circle, with Nate following close behind him as usual. Jo wondered why Nate seemed so content to be Adam's sidekick; it seemed like it should be the other way around. In movies, the leading man was always the cuter, quieter one, and his best friend was the zany attention whore with the too-big ears.

"People we want to sleep with," Skylar said. She glugged her beer and looked pointedly at Adam before adding, "*Not* you."

Jo could tell her relaxation was going to be short-lived.

"You didn't miss much," Emma said quickly. "Just a little trip down memory lane."

"Well," Adam said, raising his beer. "Why don't we take a trip down present-day lane and go sit on the beach?" Jo bristled—her inner camp counselor worried about letting anyone, especially people who'd been drinking, near the water when visibility was so low—but she looked around at the others and they all nodded eagerly. Maddie, who was getting eaten alive by bugs, looked particularly pathetic.

"Relax," Nate whispered, crouching behind her. "We're just having a few beers. No one's drunk, and no one's going to get hurt." Jo smiled. It was nice to have someone looking out for her for a change.

"Sure, why not?" she said, and everyone cheered. Cleanup could wait another hour. As acting camp director, she made the official decision to give herself the night off.

Emma

The Fourth Summer • *Age 13*
First Full Day of Camp

"Friendship Rule: Best friends never let you get in over your head."

"I HAVE AN ANNOUNCEMENT TO MAKE," EMMA SAID. She stopped cutting her Belgian waffle and put down her fork. "This is the summer I will get kissed." It was the kind of thing she could only say to her camp friends. If she'd tried a line like that at Prouty Middle School, she would have gotten laughed out of the cafeteria. The few people at her junior high who even knew who Emma Zenewicz was probably remembered her as the Model United Nations delegate from Zimbabwe who threw off the curve on the social studies midterm by performing a traditional African drum solo during her impassioned speech in favor of environmental protection. It had been her dad's idea, the same dad who couldn't understand why his daughter stayed home from the seventh grade dance.

"Oooooh!" Maddie clapped. "I approve. Who's your target?"

"Take a wild guess," Skylar said.

"Adam Loring," Emma stage whispered.

Their counselor, Sasha, was sitting at the head of the table, and since it was only the first day of camp Emma wasn't sure yet if she could be trusted with confidential matters of the heart.

"Ew. Why?" Jo asked, snapping a Pop-Tart in half.

"I bet her five dollars she wouldn't," Skylar said. "Time to bite the bullet."

"That's not why," Emma protested. "He just makes me . . . want to kiss him. I don't know. I just like him. I don't even want to, I can't help it." Even just talking about him made her ears start to tingle.

Jo grimaced. "To have Adam's tongue all over my face you'd have to pay me like a thousand dollars," she said.

"She has a point," Maddie said. "You don't know where it's been. You should hold out for more cash."

"He hasn't kissed *that* many people!" Emma felt her face getting red.

"Yes, he has," Skylar laughed.

"Maybe that just means he's good at it. I mean, obviously he's practiced," Emma said. She practiced her Latin verbs every day, and now she could do even the most advanced exercises in her textbook, *Veni! Vidi! Vici!*, which featured the bust of Julius Caesar against a backdrop of lasers.

"Right, because so many thirteen-year-old boys are awesome at kissing," Maddie said. "Hey, Skylar, didn't you kiss him once during spin the bottle?"

Emma cringed. She'd almost let herself forget about that. She was relieved to see that Skylar looked uncomfortable, too.

"It was like one second long," she said, taking a bite of her English muffin. "And I wasn't . . . you know . . . *trying*."

"You don't have to," Maddie said. "Adam tries hard enough for two!"

"I don't think he's that bad," Emma said. They'd started e-mailing over the winter, and she felt like this year they might really become good friends. The last time she'd talked to Adam in person, at the end-of-camp bonfire the previous summer, he'd tried to give her a piece of already-been-chewed gum, but in his e-mails he was so much nicer and more mature. He wrote most of them to avoid doing his math homework and sent her pages and pages of funny observations about his teacher, whom he called Mr. Pants, and the other kids in the class. Adam was actually a really good writer. Emma knew there was definitely more to him than her friends saw.

"Well, he's sort of cute," Skylar said. "But too short."

"He reminds me of someone's little brother," Jo said.

Just at that moment, Adam came out of the bathroom by the kitchen entrance and made a beeline for their table. He had a haircut that made his ears look even bigger than usual, but there was something more grown-up about his face. As he got closer, she could see a faint shadow of mustache above his upper lip. His Adam's apple seemed bigger, too. Emma felt her face getting red.

"Hey, Em!" he said, grinning. "We have to catch up later. Buy you a bug juice?" He turned to the others. "Good morning, table four. You're looking lovely today."

"Move along, Adam," Sasha said.

"Nice 'stache," Maddie whispered. She and Jo erupted into giggles.

"Be kind; puberty's rougher on the boys," Sasha said with a smirk.

"Can we talk about the Romeo act?" Jo asked. "Was he always like this?"

Only when people are watching, Emma thought.

"It's gotten worse," Maddie said, poking her fork at the jiggly yellow pile on her plate. "He's as fake as these 'eggs.'"

Jo made a face. "Blame my dad. Frozen egg substitute is the cheapest."

"And so is Adam!" Maddie cried. "It's the circle of life." She and Jo fist-bumped.

"Why can't he commit to liking one girl?" Skylar wondered. "I mean, seriously, how hard is it to keep liking one thing for more than ten seconds?"

"I will always love Pop-Tarts," Jo said.

"See? Jo mates for life. Like an albatross," Maddie laughed.

Emma looked back at Adam. Sure, he could be annoying. And he was definitely a flirt. But he wasn't a real player or anything. Even if he acted like it.

"You guys are mean," Emma said. "I think underneath all that... he's nice."

"But he's *nice* to *all* the girls," Jo said, turning serious. "It's like he wants to be everyone's boyfriend."

"And no one's," Skylar said.

"Exactly!" Jo took a bite of her Pop-Tart. "Plus, we're too young to have boyfriends." She looked right at Skylar when she said it.

Skylar had started dating a boy at her school that winter.

"Speak for yourself," Skylar said. "Some of us are more mature for our age."

"I don't want a *boyfriend*!" Emma whispered. She was blushing so much she was almost the color of the strawberry jelly on Maddie's bagel. "I just want to kiss him. That's *all*."

Skylar looked over at Adam, narrowing her eyes and tilting her head like she was taking aim at an archery target. "You should do it right now," she said to Emma.

"What?!" Emma felt like she might throw up.

"Do it now. A guy as confident as Adam needs to have his attention grabbed, and laying one on him in public when he's not expecting it will be way better than trying to make the right moment happen."

Emma shook her head. She needed time—preferably weeks and weeks of painfully drawn-out time—to plan the perfect move.

"Come on, if you do it now you won't have to worry about it all summer. It'll be like ripping off a Band-Aid."

"I don't rip off Band-Aids," Emma said. "I take a bath until they get soft and gooey and I can take them off without it hurting."

Skylar set down her spoon, looking worried. "That's the problem, Em. You can't be afraid to get hurt."

"You can take Adam in the bath, though," Maddie drawled.

"*Maddie*," Sasha said in a warning tone. Jo elbowed her.

"Guys, shut up. I am *not* doing it now, okay? End of story." Emma pushed her waffle away and pressed her lips together, an added barrier just in case Skylar tried to physically force her to make out with Adam.

"I'm just saying you need to be proactive," Skylar said. "Don't be afraid to like him; otherwise it'll never happen."

"I'm not afraid to like him. I like him. You all know I like him." In fact, she was starting to get self-conscious that she talked about liking him too much.

"*He* doesn't, though."

"She has a point," Maddie chimed in.

"What, am I supposed to send him a note?" Emma thought of the little squares of notebook paper that always got passed around in fifth and sixth grades:

Do you like me? ☐*Yes* ☐*No* ☐*Maybe*

She would sooner blind herself with a plastic spork than hand a note like that to Adam.

"There are ways to show someone you like him without *saying* it, Emma," Skylar sighed. She pushed away from the table and walked over to the cereal station. On her way back, she purposefully brushed up against Adam's arm. He looked up at her and she shot him a demure smile. Skylar sat back down and raised her eyebrows. "See?"

"Great, now he thinks *you* like him."

"Oh, he does not. He thinks everyone likes him anyway. But if *you* don't show him *you* like him, someone else will. And then they'll get him and you won't."

Emma knew there was some truth to this. But it infuriated her that Skylar was being so pushy.

"If the only way to get him is to be a big ho, then I don't want him." She balled up her napkin and flicked it at Skylar.

"You don't have to be a ho, just don't be a grandma about it, either," Skylar replied, launching a forkful of egg at Emma's chest.

"Hey, that's ageist," Maddie laughed. "My grandma has a boyfriend!" She threw a globule of egg white at Skylar's arm and they all cracked up.

"Girls!" Sasha yelled. "Were you this much trouble last year or am I just lucky?"

"You're not lucky," Sunny Sherman muttered from the other end of the table, and her friends giggled. Emma started wiping up the egg.

"Nice manners," Adam said a few minutes later as he passed them on the way to clear his tray.

"That's just a preview of what you're gonna get at capture the flag this year," Jo said.

"Yeah," Skylar said. "Watch out for us."

Emma marveled at her confidence. She'd gotten an A in biology that year, but even though she could quote the steps of mammalian mating rituals from memory, she realized that Skylar had actual field research under her belt. And if she wanted to get Adam's attention, she would need to take her cues from someone with more experience. She decided to seize the moment before she could talk herself out of it.

"Watch out for me, especially," she said.

Adam looked at her quizzically, a smile playing on his lips. "Okay, okay," he said, backing away with his hands up. "Don't hurt me."

Emma turned back to her friends and covered her face with her hands. "I'm dying of shame," she whispered through her fingers.

"No, that was so good!" Skylar said. "He was totally caught off guard."

"Really?"

"Yes. He is going to be putty in your hands."

Emma smiled nervously. She felt excited, but she also knew that for the first time in her life she had started a project she wasn't sure she could follow through with. After all, Skylar wouldn't be able to coach her before every conversation with Adam. And she wasn't the only one vying for his attention. Emma would have to show him how she felt . . . before someone else beat her to it.

Emma

Reunion: Day 1

"SHHHHH!" EMMA WHISPERED AS SHE PUT A FINGER to her lips. The distance from the fire pit to the dock wasn't far—maybe a quarter mile, mostly on fine, sandy dirt that gave way silently beneath their feet—and the only animals around were squirrels, scrawny from a summer of dodging stampeding Nedoba campers, out foraging for leftover graham cracker crumbs, but now that it was just the six of them, Emma felt a rising sense of danger that sent nervous laughter bubbling up into her throat. It didn't help that the moon was hiding behind clouds, plunging the woods, the lake, and what seemed like the whole world into total darkness. Emma raised herself up on tiptoe and extended her arms for balance, walking as if she was stepping delicately around a motion-sensor laser maze that protected a priceless artifact like the *Mona Lisa* or King Tut's mummy. In related news, she was tipsy. She'd only had half a beer back at the campsite, but it had been enough.

"I've only ever had alcohol at my cousin's wedding," she whispered to Adam, who was walking a few steps in front of her, balancing a six-pack on one shoulder. "They had dinner rolls in the shape of *swans*. I mean, how do you even make those?" She reached out for him blindly and stumbled over a branch.

"I don't know. Quit trying to touch my butt," he laughed, grabbing her hand.

All of a sudden, it seemed, they came spilling out of the woods, and in the weak moonlight Emma saw the long, skinny finger of the dock lying still on the surface of the water. Upside-down row boats lay on the shore, their wide, white undersides turned up to the sky like the bellies of beached whales. To the east, the lake stretched out for miles, broken only by the dark lump of Wexley Island. Emma was used to seeing it in the daylight, but now it looked ominous. As they got close, she could hear the soft, rhythmic groan of the wood, the gray pylons, wound with thick rope, swaying almost imperceptibly as tiny waves broke against them with a soothing, frothy slap.

"It's creepy here at night, huh?" Maddie said, coming up behind them with Jo and Skylar flanking her on either side. She pursed her lips and blew across the open mouth of her beer bottle, eliciting a deep note that sounded like a fog horn.

Emma looked around nervously.

"Don't worry," Jo said. "No one can hear us."

"Aren't you worried we'll get caught?"

"Emma," Skylar said, patting her head like a puppy. "We do this all the time."

"Well, *I* don't."

"Relax!" Adam said, massaging her shoulders. "Trespassing

can be fun if you have the right guide." He led Emma over to the rowboats and set the six-pack down in the sand. "For instance," he said, flipping one over and gesturing like he was showing off a game show prize, "did you know that this makes an excellent open-air conference room?" He held out his arm and she used it for balance, stepping into the creaky old boat like it was a stagecoach. He gestured for the other girls to get in, and once they were all seated he bowed. "My name is Adam and I'll be your waiter this evening," he said. Emma tried hard not to roll her eyes; this was laying it on thick, even for him. Across from her, Maddie and Skylar hung their heads and were laughing behind their hands.

"Hey, where did Nate go?" Jo asked. In response, a glow-in-the-dark circle flew through the air, and Maddie immediately ducked.

"Is that a UFO?" she cried, covering her head.

"No, it's a Frisbee," Jo grinned, waving as Nate jogged over from the shed down the shore that was generously referred to as the boathouse. She laughed and pointed at Maddie. "I forgot how much you hate sci-fi!"

"I don't know why everybody thinks E.T. is cute," Maddie shuddered. "He looks like an anorexic turd caterpillar!" The girls shrieked with laughter. Adam offered Emma a beer and Emma took it. *Why not*? she reasoned. It was the Summer of No Excuses, part two. Jo didn't even raise an eyebrow. She actually almost looked like she was having fun, which balanced out Skylar's sudden testiness nicely. Emma had been trying to catch her eye to make sure she was okay, but it felt like Sky was avoiding looking at her.

Adam and Nate started a game of what they dubbed Ultimate Night Frisbee while the girls stargazed, and Emma felt a warm wash of nostalgia and intoxication turning her knotted muscles into Play-Doh. Over the years it had become easy for Emma to file her camp memories away in short clips, stringing them together sometimes in a movie-preview montage that made her feel instantly wistful—Laughs! Loves! Adventure! Best friends!—and at that moment she felt like she was living in the trailer of her imagination. The only thing that would have made it more cinematic was a soundtrack.

"How come I never danced with anyone?" she wondered aloud. She could still see the barn in her mind's eye, the rafters strung with white Christmas lights.

"Oh, come on, nobody danced for real," Jo said, passing the beer to Skylar, who finished it in three long slugs and reached over the side of the boat for another. "We just danced together, trying to avoid getting *asked* to dance."

"And watching your dad do the frug," Maddie laughed, shimmying her shoulders.

"I always wanted to," Emma said. "I just didn't want to seem like I wanted to. But I would always look for him, you know. . . ." She blushed. "It's pathetic."

"No, it's sweet," Maddie said. "You should go tell him that."

"I couldn't," Emma said, although she didn't feel the stab of cold fear that used to accompany any suggestion that she open up to Adam. "And anyway, what about sticking together? I meant it when I said I didn't come here for him."

"I know," Jo said. "I was just giving you a hard time. And I know it's important to you." She took a sip of beer and shook her head, as if she couldn't believe what she was saying.

"Sky?" Emma asked. Skylar finally looked up at her with a blank, glassy stare.

"Are you asking my permission?" Skylar sighed.

"Kind of, yeah."

"Why do you care what I think?"

"What do you mean?" Emma asked. "I just want to make sure it's okay with you if I go hang out with Adam for awhile. I know we haven't gotten a lot of time together yet." She reached out for Skylar's knee, but Skylar bristled.

"I can't tell you what to do, okay? Stop asking me to make decisions for you." Emma could tell that she was a little bit drunk, so she tried not to take it personally.

"I'm not asking you to tell me what to do," she said carefully. "I was just being polite." Jo and Maddie looked down into their laps.

"Please, you don't make any decisions for yourself," Skylar groaned. "You don't do anything, period. You'll *never* hook up with him, because you're too scared." Emma felt tears spring to her eyes and turned away just in time to see the glowing Frisbee shoot past her face, missing her by inches.

"Heads up!" Nate yelled as it landed a few yards out in the lake with a splash. Adam ran after it, pulling his T-shirt off as he waded into the black water. Emma wished she could run in after him, just float away until there were miles and miles between her and Skylar.

Then, all of a sudden, she realized she could.

Emma reached out and snatched Skylar's beer from her hands, chugging it and then throwing the rest in the sand.

"Thanks for the vote of confidence," she said, standing up and pulling off her shirt. The blood rushed to her head, but even through her dizzy haze she saw Skylar's eyes widen. Emboldened, she kicked off her shorts.

"Emma," Jo said, standing up. "She didn't mean it. Put your clothes back on."

"No!" Emma said stubbornly. "Never have I ever skinny dipped, remember?" Maddie burst out laughing.

"Don't encourage her," Jo snapped, but Emma didn't hear anything after that, because then she was gone. She ran down the beach, her feet causing tiny avalanches in the peaks of wet pebbles left by the high tide. She reached the water's edge just as Adam turned around, clutching the Frisbee, and he stared at her. She wasn't sure if it was appreciative or uncomfortable, but she dove in anyway.

"Nice night for a swim, huh?" he asked with a smile when she had paddled out to where he stood in the waist-deep water.

"Yup," she said.

"Are you drunk?" he asked. "Because as a trained lifeguard I have to discourage you from swimming under the influence."

"I had one beer," she said, splashing him.

"Even so, I'd feel better with you on more solid ground." He stuck the Frisbee in his teeth and took her hand, dragging her through the cold, murky water until she felt a sandbar rise under her toes. Emma clung to his arm, which prickled with heat under the droplets of water that clung to his skin. Nate and Jo stood watching them from shore, and Adam tossed the Frisbee back, a neon shooting star against the clear night sky. It made Emma think of fireworks.

"Be careful!" Jo yelled. Skylar was still sitting in the rowboat with her back to the water, and she didn't turn around. She was probably just jealous, Emma realized. Against all odds, Skylar didn't seem to have a boyfriend at the moment, and Emma knew all too well how lonely it could get when your best friend is more in demand than you are. But there was no reason to lash out at Emma, even if she was drunk. They would have to have a talk.

"You're stuck with me now," Adam said, crouching down next to her. "I know you can't swim."

"I can *swim*," Emma said.

"You never passed the swim test," he reminded her.

"Whatever, it's basically impossible to pick a dime off the bottom of the deep end of the pool."

"Yeah, if you can't swim," he laughed. He sat down and looked at her. "Remember when we capsized in the canoe?"

"Of course," she said. "It was the first time we met." Emma paused and smiled at him. "I should have known you were trouble. I've never been in a canoe since."

"Whatever," he said, puffing up his chest. "I saved you."

"You did not!" she laughed. "We both cried."

"Ah, yes," Adam said with a smile. "Well, then, I almost saved you. Through my tears."

Back on the shore, Jo and Nate started up the Frisbee toss again, and Emma watched it streak back and forth.

"I always wanted to dance with you," she said.

"What?"

"At the dances, in the barn. I always wanted to slow dance with you. I used to stand near you hoping that when a slow song came on, you would ask me."

He smiled and put his arm around her. "I always thought you stood near me because I was near the snacks."

"That too," she said, nestling into his chest. "I figured I'd kill two birds." She listened to his heart beating under his slick, wet skin. It was speeding up.

"Adam?" she said, turning her face up to his.

"Emma . . .?" He squeezed her and kissed her forehead.

"*Skylar*!" Maddie's voice rang out across the water, and Emma looked out to see Skylar wading into the lake in her bra and underwear.

"Skylar, come back!" Maddie stood on the shore, frantically rolling up her pants and splashing in after her.

"Wow." Adam pulled away from Emma; he looked suddenly panicked. "Uh, party on the sandbar, I guess."

"You guys just looked like you were having way too much fun!" Skylar cried as she got closer, splashing at Adam with theatrical glee. "The water feels so good!"

"She's drunk," Emma whispered to Adam.

"You think?" he muttered.

Skylar climbed onto the sandbar, her long limbs glistening. At least she wasn't wearing a thong, Emma thought.

"Hi, guys," Maddie said apologetically as she reached the sandbar, her only outfit now soaked through from the shoulders down. "Sorry for crashing. This one got away from me." She grabbed Skylar's arm. "Come on, hon," she coaxed. "You'll catch cold, or something will swim up somewhere you don't want it to be."

"Oh, shush," Skylar said, draping her arms around Adam. "I'm just saying hi to my friends."

"Hi," Emma said.

"You are *very* friendly," Adam laughed, taking her hand off his chest. "But maybe we should go in." Skylar whispered something to Adam, and he laughed nervously.

"We need to get you out of the water," he said. "Maddie, can you help me?"

"No, stay!" Skylar cried. "We can play chicken." She attempted to straddle his shoulders.

Emma rolled her eyes and looked to see Adam's reaction, but he was busy gazing up at Skylar's almost naked body with a look of happy disbelief. All at once, Emma felt like she was thirteen again.

"Well, I think that's my cue," she said. She stood up, suddenly acutely aware of the way her blue underwear, now soaked, hung against her thighs like a wet dishrag. Her bra didn't even match. It was black and had a deodorant mark on one side. This was why people like her didn't skinny dip. Or play chicken. Or try to get a guy's attention while standing next to anyone who looked like Skylar.

She stepped off the sandbar and into the frigid, murky water, which pulled at her limbs as she swam back to shore as fast as she could.

"Emma, wait—" Adam tried to untangle himself from Skylar, unsuccessfully. She heard a splash and a giggle, but willed herself not to look back. Instead, she focused on the Frisbee, now sitting still on the sand as Jo and Nate rushed to get towels. If she kept her eyes on its fading light, everything else slipped painlessly out of focus.

Skylar

Reunion: Day 2

SKYLAR SIPPED HER COFFEE AND DUG INTO HER BAG for her Ray-Bans. The sunlight streaming through the windows in the cafeteria was a little too bright. She normally slept through her hangovers, but Jo's phone alarm had gone off at six a.m., and then she couldn't get back to sleep. She had a pounding headache, not to mention a terrible feeling she had ruined everything with Emma. Coffee was helping a little bit, but Maddie's heaping plate of gelatinous egg substitute was not.

"Could you not eat those right now?" she winced.

"Not a problem," Maddie said, taking a swig of orange juice. "The eggs here still don't come from chickens." She looked pointedly at Jo. "I'm lodging an official complaint."

"Whatever," Jo mumbled. Skylar would have looked surprised, if it didn't hurt so much to raise her eyebrows. It was only the second day of reunion and Jo's seemingly boundless camp spirit was already flagging. Or maybe she was just feeling the effects of the beer she'd ingested the night before. Ugh. Skylar couldn't even think the word *beer* without getting nauseated.

She hadn't meant to get so sloppy, but the Emma and Adam situation had upset her more than she'd thought it would. Of course it made sense that Emma wouldn't be over Adam—a crush like that didn't just go away. In Skylar's experience, crushes were like horror movie villains, and every time you were sure they were dead, they'd spring up again and scare the crap out of you. But she hadn't expected *Adam* to be so receptive to Emma. She certainly hadn't expected him to stick by her side all night, putting his arms around her and swimming around half-naked with her while totally ignoring the fact that the girl he was basically dating was sitting right there.

Skylar knew that Adam wasn't in love with her or anything, but sometimes it felt like he didn't even like her. And while she hated to be the cliché girl in the situation, she'd gotten kind of . . . attached to him. At first, back in the beginning, it was just hooking up, and it didn't even happen all that often, but in the four weeks leading up to reunion, things had felt like they were getting more serious. They saw each other every night. They slept together—actual sleeping, not just as a euphemism for sex (which they also had, more and more frequently). It had started to feel kind of like Adam was her boyfriend, and the weirdest part of all had been that it made her happy. Now, on top of feeling sick, Skylar felt tears forming in the corners of her eyes. Thankfully, she finally found her sunglasses and slipped them on gratefully.

"Sunglasses indoors. How very Kanye West of you," Emma said tersely, picking at her pancakes.

Skylar didn't know what to say to Emma now. She should have just told her right away, or at the very least, when Emma had admitted that she was still going after Adam. That would have been hard, but it would have been the right thing to do. The display at the lake had been more "showing" than "telling," but either way, Emma had clearly started to get the message. Even if she didn't know that they were hooking up behind her back yet, she definitely thought Skylar was moving in on her territory. To tell her now would just make things worse. Especially since, as of around midnight, Skylar and Adam were officially over.

The immediate aftermath of the sandbar debacle was slightly muddy in her memory thanks to the drinking, but Skylar was pretty sure that after Emma got out of the water, Jo and Nate had followed her. Maddie had helped Skylar dry off and get back into her clothes, but then she'd left, too. Adam was being kind of quiet, but he offered to walk her back to the girls' side. They had held hands, she was sure of that, and then at one point he'd tried to kiss her. That must have been the moment the last of her buzz had worn off, because Skylar remembered the rest of the night quite clearly.

"Not now," she'd said, pushing him away.

"Are you mad?" he'd asked.

"I'm not mad, I'm just . . ." She'd been hurt, but she couldn't tell him that. "I'm tired," she finished.

Adam had sighed heavily. "You came on to me like a freight train back there. And now you're tired?"

"Okay, maybe I'm a little mad."

He'd flashed his trademark grin, which usually charmed her but which suddenly felt impersonal, like a one-size-fits-all flirtation device. "I knew it," he'd said, going in for another kiss.

"Uh-uh," she'd said, batting him away again. "You don't get to do that and be all over Emma, too."

"I thought we were casual," Adam said. "I thought we agreed we could hook up with other people."

"Yeah, *people*," she'd said. "Not *Emma*."

"You don't get to choose."

"Actually, when it's my best friend, yeah I do," she'd snapped.

"Well, nothing happened. Nothing was *going* to happen." Adam had yawned then, which had really made her furious. As soon as he'd figured out he wasn't getting laid, he'd turned narcoleptic. So typical.

"Don't lie," she'd said. "I saw you all over her."

"Yeah, well, she saw *you* all over me. Thanks for that. Very subtle."

"I made a mistake," she'd admitted. "But at least I wasn't trying to hook up with Nate right in front of you."

"You can do whatever you want," he'd said. "I wouldn't care." As if that was a good thing.

That was what did it. At that moment, Skylar knew Adam would never talk to her the way he talked to Emma, or look at her the way he looked at Emma. He would never choose her over Emma. And she realized she didn't want him to. If the feelings she had for him didn't go both ways, then she didn't want it. She'd been through too many superficial relationships to settle yet again for a guy who treated her like an on-demand movie he could watch whenever he got the urge. She deserved someone who saw something in her that they didn't see in anyone else. Something below the surface.

"Skylar? Hello, Earth to Skylar. You guys, I think she passed out." Emma's voice swam up through her haze of hangover and heartache. Skylar took off her sunglasses and attempted a smile.

"I'll be okay," she said. "Just tired." This time, it was true.

Emma's face softened. "Maybe you should get some more sleep before we leave for the beach," she suggested.

"Yeah, no puking off the side of the boat," Jo said.

"At least not on the way there," Maddie added with a wink. "Sexy Island has a way of making people fly their freak flags."

Skylar closed her eyes. She had never felt less sexy, or less confident. The reunion was not going the way she had hoped, although she realized that she'd been naive to hope it could go anyplace but disaster. Camp could never be the same as it was—and it was all her fault.

Emma

Reunion: Day 2

IT WAS A PERFECT HIGH-SUMMER DAY—80 DEGREES and breezy, with a gorgeous blue sky dotted with clouds like cotton balls. As they hiked down the path to the dock, retracing their steps from the night before, Emma almost couldn't believe it was the same place. In daylight, the dock seemed to bounce invitingly on the surface of the lake like a picture on a postcard. There was no sign of the emotional melodrama that had played out on shore just twelve hours earlier.

Emma looked over her shoulder at Skylar, who was still sluggish despite an hour-long nap. She still looked great, of course, in her peasant blouse and cutoffs, her unwashed hair in a messy bun, and the trendy sunglasses that Emma knew were hiding tired, bloodshot eyes somehow only made her look more glamorous, like a slightly disheveled celebrity caught by paparazzi: Stars—they get wasted and act weird around their best friends' unrequited crushes! Just like us! She'd barely spoken to Skylar all morning, which felt weird, but what was she supposed to say? Skylar hadn't said a word to her about what had happened out on the sandbar, or her nasty attitude beforehand. Things were definitely, officially tense, and Emma knew that a day trip to the beach, no matter how perfect the weather, wasn't going fix it.

"Hey girl," Maddie said, jogging up beside her. "Stop walking so fast. We can't keep up."

"Oh. Sorry." Emma slowed down, and Jo soon joined them, dragging Skylar with her. Ahead of them, the sun gleamed on the planks of the dock. The rowboats, right side up now, were bobbing alongside. Each could hold four people, so the counselors would be making trips back and forth all afternoon. Jo, naturally, had insisted that they be in the first group in order to claim the best hangout spot. Jo was nothing if not strategic.

"I wish there was some way to get to the island that didn't involve a boat," Skylar moaned, massaging her temples.

"Then it wouldn't be an island," Emma snapped. She instantly felt bad and tried to backpedal. "But I know what you mean."

"It's only a five-minute ride," Jo said. "Don't be such a wimp."

They reached the dock and joined the crowd of campers reluctantly donning their life vests.

"Do these come in any color other than orange?" Sunny Sherman yelled to no one in particular.

Maddie sucked in her cheeks and puckered her lips, fanning her face in a dead-on impersonation. "I'd rather die looking *fabulous* than live dressed like a Cheez-It," she whispered as she slipped her vest over her head.

"At least yours matches your hair," Skylar said.

"If my hair is this color," Maddie said, gesturing to the dirty neon polyester, "do me a favor and shave my head, please."

"If you both don't stop talking about life vests like they're fashion accessories," Jo said, "I'm going to capsize us on purpose. Now, into the boat."

Maddie got on first to sit in the rear—it was unanimously decided that Skylar should not be trusted with an oar—where Jo joined her. Skylar was trying to steady herself against the bobbing dock when Sunny's voice rang out again. "Come on, we can make room!"

Emma looked over at Sunny, Jess, and Aileen, who were sitting in a rowboat a few yards away. Kerry was still standing on shore. Since none of them were counselors, they couldn't take the boat out unchaperoned, and with a chaperone they couldn't all fit.

"No, we can't make room," said Tina, the nineteen-year-old counselor unlucky enough to be Sunny's chauffeur. "Four people max. Safety regulations."

"It's okay," Kerry said. "I'll just go with the next group."

"But she's so skinny!" Sunny cried. "So am I. Together we barely make one fat person. And you couldn't not take a fat camper, right? So what's the big deal?"

Tina—who was herself big-boned—looked like she wanted to throttle someone. "I don't make the rules," she said. "I couldn't take four fat people, either."

"Really," Kerry said, getting embarrassed that people were looking, "it's okay."

"Why don't you take my spot?" Emma volunteered. Jo and Maddie looked up at her like she was crazy.

"I need to put sunblock on," she explained. "Plus, I'm feeling a little nauseous, too. I think I need to sit on dry land for a few minutes. You go, take Kerry, and I'll catch up with you."

Kerry looked hesitant. "Are you sure?" she asked.

"Totally," Emma said.

"Whatever," Jo said impatiently. "Just *someone* get in the boat, please."

Sorry, Emma mouthed to Jo as Kerry clambered in. She realized that she needed some time away from Skylar—even if it was only five minutes.

"I have my cell," Maddie called as they rowed away. "Text me when you get there!"

"Okay!" Emma yelled, waving cheerfully. She didn't bother telling Maddie that she hadn't brought her phone. She needed time to clear her head, and besides, camping was supposed to be under the stars, not under the limitless broadband of 4G wireless Internet.

As she sat on the grass near the dock, watching the boats leave one by one, Emma wondered if anyone would notice if she snuck back to the bunk and spent the afternoon rereading *Little Women* and stress-eating instead of following everyone to Wexley Island. Probably, she decided; Jo almost certainly had some kind of clipboard stashed in her backpack.

Emma looked around for other people she knew, but she couldn't find anyone else from their year. She knew she had a tendency to self-sabotage and psych herself out, but it seemed pretty obvious that the day was going to be a waste. The red bikini she had on under her clothes—which was a kind of racy purchase for her, and which she'd bought specifically for reunion (and, if she was being honest with herself, more specifically for Adam)—now felt silly. After all, if anything was going to happen it would have happened last night, when she'd basically thrown herself at him in her underwear. The only person who would care what she looked like in a bikini now was Jo, who would probably say something like, "Hey, Em, didn't anyone tell you they canceled the Victoria's Secret swimsuit catalog shoot?"

Sneaking back to her aunt's car and hightailing it back to New York was looking increasingly attractive, until Emma saw a familiar Sox cap in the distance. Sure enough, Adam, Nate, the twins, and a few other guys were making their way toward the dock from the boys' side path. She thought they were too far away to see her, but then Adam raised his hand in a tentative wave, and Emma's fight-or-flight response roared into action. If she stayed put, she realized, she would have to talk to him about Skylar and the sandbar and her amateur stripping, and the potential awkwardness of that conversation was too much for her to bear. Out of the corner of her eye, she saw a boat with three people in it that was getting ready to leave, and she practically sprinted over.

"You guys leaving?" she panted.

"Yeah," said the twentysomething brunette holding the oars.

"You need a ride?"

"Desperately," Emma said.

The girl looked strangely familiar, but it wasn't until Emma already had one foot in the boat that she realized it was Meredith, one of the drunk girls from the bonfire.

"Well get in," she said. "We need another body anyway, otherwise we'll get stuck with a weirdo."

"Yeah," chirped Allie, whose *Jeopardy!* buzz had decidedly worn off. "And I'll give you five dollars if you row, because my head is killing me."

Emma sat down next to Ruth, the third spin the bottle enthusiast, and helped steer the boat away from shore, just as Adam stepped onto the dock. "Meet me on the beach?" he called. Emma just waved, as if she hadn't heard him.

It didn't take long for Emma to realize that although she'd jumped ship, she wasn't necessarily in for a relaxing ride.

"That guy with the fedora will not stop texting me," Meredith groaned. "Can you say stalker?"

Allie shuddered. "Do not remind me about the events of last night. I am never letting you talk me into tequila shots again. We're not nineteen anymore."

"I just want to curl up on my towel with my Kindle," Ruth sighed as they reached the open water.

"What are you reading?" Emma asked.

"*Anna Karenina,*" Ruth said. "I read it in high school but some of my coworkers started a book club, and this time I think I might actually get it."

Allie laughed. "I did my thesis on Tolstoy," she said. "It's only been a year since graduation and I can't remember any of it. Do you think I can get a refund on some of my student loans?"

"I *so* know what you mean," Meredith said. "I think I've gotten dumber since college. Probably because I traded my brain in for a BlackBerry. Pity the first-year paralegal!" She shook her phone and studied the screen. "I can't get a signal out here. How am I supposed to get in touch with work?"

"You're not," Allie said, slapping at the phone. "Put that away."

"I can't!" Meredith cried. "Some of us have real jobs."

"You don't even *want* to be a lawyer," Allie shot back.

Emma studied the bags under Meredith's eyes and the acne dotting her jaw line. She wondered if she could ever let herself end up chained to a phone, in a job she hated, getting drunk at a camp reunion just to let off steam. Apart from the acne, she realized morosely, that was already kind of her life.

"Sorry," Ruth said to Emma. "This must be so boring for you. What are you, sixteen?"

"Seventeen," Emma said quietly. She felt a stomach-turning flash of motion sickness, the same as she'd felt watching her parents drive away from the Green her first summer.

"You're a baaaaaaaaaby!" Allie cried, attempting to light a cigarette despite the powerful crosswinds.

"Seventeen is the perfect age," Meredith said, nodding down at her phone. "You're old enough to have fun but not old enough to be held responsible." Emma briefly wondered what Meredith's law firm would think about her "you get to kiss me" prowess.

"I guess," Emma said. "But the guys act like they're still thirteen."

"Oh honey," Meredith said. "If you think they're immature now, just wait 'til they go through four years of beer pong and intro psych seminars." Emma bit her lip and concentrated on rowing.

"So who was that cutie on the dock?" Ruth asked. "Is he the one you desperately needed to get away from?"

"Yeah," Emma said. "It's complicated."

"It always is." Meredith looked up for the first time since they'd left the mainland.

"So, what, did you hook up with him?"

"No," Emma said.

"Why not?" Allie said. "He's adorable. And he likes you."

"How do you know?" Emma asked. Meredith put down her phone and touched Emma's knee.

"He practically dove off the dock after us. Guys don't do that anymore when they get to be our age."

"Yeah," Ruth said. "He's way into you. And you're the right age for him. You should go for it. I would if I was seventeen again."

"Don't wait too long," Meredith cautioned. "I thought I would want to spend all weekend drinking and chasing guys like the old days, but it turns out that now all I really want is a beach chair, a decaf soy latte, and my sudoku." She sighed. "I am officially old!"

Emma wanted to remind her that she'd spent at least part of the previous evening giving some guy a hickey in public, but thought better of it. All she really wanted was to get out of the boat and get back to people her own age, instead of these frightening Ghosts of Christmas Futures, with their Kindles and their student loans and their borderline alcohol abuse.

"We're heeeee-re!" Allie trilled, and Emma looked over her shoulder at the fast-approaching shore. Wexley Island looked like an undeveloped miniature of the main camp property, with a short rectangle of flat beach on its south end that led out into a thick forest covering almost all the rest of it. There was an unfinished cabin on the northwest end, but other than that the only signs that human beings spent any time there were a few scattered picnic tables tethered with chains to the trees at the edge of the woods, so that they wouldn't blow away in case of a bad storm.

There was no dock, so Ruth and Emma just steered the boat gently in on the tide until it stuck in the sand. A few other boats were pulled up on shore, but as she climbed out Emma couldn't see signs of Jo, Maddie, or Skylar; all she could see were a few clusters of abandoned towels and some guys playing football.

"Bye, seventeen!" Allie called as the older girls walked up the beach clutching their tablets and bottles of sunscreen. "Don't forget to wait for that cute boy." Meredith, lost in her texting, just raised a hand in a distracted wave.

Emma looked back out at the water. If she squinted, she thought she could see Adam's Red Sox cap peeking out of a boat on the horizon.

She decided to give him one last chance. For old times' sake.

Skylar

The Third Summer • *Age 12*
Middle of Second Session

"Friendship Rule: Best friends ALWAYS kiss and tell!"

"OKAY," SKYLAR SAID, LEANING IN CONSPIRAtorially. "Say when." They were sitting up in the barn loft during the afternoon free period, all four of them high on sugar from a one-pound bag of Skittles Jo had smuggled up in the pouch of her sweatshirt. As the rain whipped against the roof, they had painstakingly pooled them and divided them by color. Skylar liked the reds, Emma got the yellows, Jo took the purples, Maddie got the greens, and they saved the oranges—the communal least favorite—to play Skit-ball, a game they'd invented that involved flicking the candies off the edge of the loft and trying to hit beams on the other side of the barn. But Skit-ball could only be played once, since retrieving the playing pieces took so much effort, and so they'd moved on to MASH, which was more up Skylar's alley. It was Emma's turn, so Jo and Maddie had started a game of spit with the deck of cards they kept stashed under a box of extension cords. Emma closed her eyes and Skylar started drawing a spiral, around and around and around and around and—

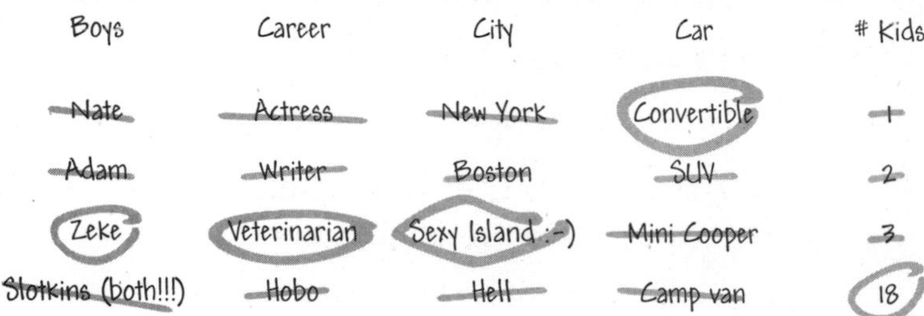

"When!" Emma cried. Skylar counted out the rings.

"Nine," she said, and started x-ing things off. "You're not an actress," she said apologetically.

"What a shocker."

"But you have eighteen children!" Skylar giggled, picturing Emma surrounded by an army of mini-Emmas, as if Emma had asexually reproduced. Skylar knew it was weird to picture your best friend doing it, but with Emma, she couldn't, even if she tried.

"Oooh," Maddie said, not looking up from her rapid-fire card slapping. "You can have your own reality show. That's even better than being an actress."

"Who's the baby-daddy?" Emma asked. She had listed Nate, Zeke, the Slotkin twins (you always had to put at least one bad pick in—those were Skylar's MASH rules), and of course Adam. Skylar knew he was the answer Emma wanted, but the numbers didn't add up.

"Zeke!" she said. "Ugh, I'm jealous." Zeke Tanner was easily one of the hottest guys at camp.

"I guess I'll live," Emma joked.

"Spit!" Jo cried.

Skylar burst out laughing.

"What?" Emma demanded.

"You live . . ." Skylar announced with a dramatic pause, "on Sexy Island!"

"*Wexley* Island," Jo corrected, reshuffling the deck.

"I heard it's clothing optional, like a nudist colony," Maddie said.

"That's not true," Jo said, rolling her eyes. "I've *been* there."

"At night?"

"Well . . . no."

"Then how do you know?" Maddie said. "No one wears clothes, and everything just sort of . . . hangs there." She giggled. "And then if you want to do it, you just make a signal at the person. Like this." She jumped to her feet and swung her hips forward like a dirty hula dancer. Emma cracked up.

"You are so full of it," Jo sighed.

"Fine, but there's one Sexy Island story I *know* is true," Maddie said, "because I heard the counselors talking about it in the bathroom. Apparently one of the girl counselors and one of the boy counselors were secretly dating. And they had a date on Sexy Island and he rowed a *mattress* over there." She paused for emphasis. "On a *canoe*!"

"That's so romantic," Emma sighed.

"Yeah, a moldy swamp mattress. Swoon!" Jo shook her head.

"She probably got ticks in her hoo-ha."

"*Hoo-ha*?" Maddie chortled. "Johannah Putnam, I never."

"It sounds like a dirty Dr. Seuss rhyme," Emma said. "*All the Whos down in Hoo-ha liked Christmas a lot . . .*"

"*But the Grinch who lived just north of Hoo-ha did not!*" Skylar finished. They were beside themselves.

"Well, what do *you* call it?" Jo asked defensively.

"Nothing," Emma said. "I guess I never thought about it."

"My mom calls it *yoni*," Skylar said. "She says it means *origin of life* in Sanskrit." She decided not to mention that her parents also owned a copy of the Kama Sutra, which Skylar had paged through on more than one occasion.

"Your mom is such a hippie," Jo said.

"Well, what does your mom tell you?" Skylar asked defensively.

"Nothing, we don't talk about genitals."

"You'll have to someday."

"I guess," Jo said. "But that's so far off."

Except it wasn't, Skylar thought. She couldn't be the only one who thought about boys that way, could she? She wondered if it was perverted that she'd been aware of sex since she was eight, playing house with Jeremy Walling from across the street. They were pretending to be husband and wife, and lay down together at "nighttime" on a bed made of couch cushions. They'd barely been touching, but Jeremy had gotten . . . excited. She hadn't known what was happening, she'd just known it was awkward by the look on Jeremy's face. It had made Skylar feel kind of powerful to have that effect on him. For the next few months, she'd caught herself staring at the crotches of the boys in her class during gym, wondering if she could do it again.

"Didn't you have to talk to her about it when you got your period?" Maddie asked.

Jo was silent. The others exchanged looks.

"It's not like a race," Jo finally said. "I don't want it, anyway."

"It's a pain in the ass," Skylar sighed. "I got mine when I was nine." Her mother had taken her out for cupcakes and tried to explain human reproduction. But Skylar had been horrified to learn that she had eggs inside her, picturing the big, speckled brown ones her parents brought home from the organic food co-op.

"There should be another sign," Emma said. "Some way to know when we stop being girls and turn into, you know, women." Skylar smiled, resisting the urge to tell Emma she was inadvertently quoting a Britney Spears song.

"Like when you cross into a new state," Maddie agreed. "Like, 'Adulthood Welcomes You!'"

"Or 'Curves Ahead!'" Jo said, pointing at Maddie's chest.

"Hey, these are genetic," Maddie laughed. "It doesn't mean anything, just like MASH can't really predict the future." She stretched her arms and stood up, peering between the cracks in the old hay loft door. "It stopped raining," she said. "I guess we should probably skedaddle before people start wandering around outside."

Jo leaped to her feet and started packing up the cards while Maddie tossed the rope ladder down so that Emma could gather the fallen Skittles.

Skylar looked down at the make-believe future she held in her hands. It was just a series of X's and circles, like a childhood game of tic-tac-toe. It was silly. Of course there was no way to tell when you would become a woman from a piece of paper. Growing up in that way seemed a lot more complicated than having a birthday or a period or a certain cup size or even sex; not just one thing, but a series, like dominos that kept falling down no matter how much you wanted them to stay standing . . . or, maybe, like a big round of MASH with the universe doing the counting for you.

No matter what it was, it was a game Skylar wasn't sure she felt ready to play.

Maddie

Reunion: Day 2

MADDIE LAY ON HER BACK GAZING UP AT THE SKY. The sun beating down on her face felt so good, she wasn't even worried about the fact that she hadn't put on any sunscreen yet, which meant that freckles would soon be spreading across her nose like a constellation of stars. They'd only been on the island for half an hour but had already walked all the way across and back in search of the perfect spot to drop their things—finally, maddeningly, Jo had settled on a patch of beach ten feet from where they'd started. Maddie felt winded, but the breeze was refreshing, and if she closed her eyes and listened to the birds and the soft lapping of the lake against the shore, she could almost take herself back to those days when she and Jo used to spend hours on the dock, without a care in the world except for—

"Attention! ATTENTION, PEOPLE." Jo's voice blared through the megaphone from five feet away. Maddie sat up and shook her head. She'd *told* Jo not to bring that thing.

"I just wanted to let you all know that we have approximately six hours on the island, so please synchronize your watches—"

"Who wears a watch anymore?" Skylar muttered grumpily from her towel, and Maddie shrugged wearily.

"—and meet back at the south shore at five p.m. for return boats!" Jo cleared her throat and placed one hand on her hip. "I *will* be checking names. So anyone with plans to stay on the island overnight can forget it." A couple of people booed.

Maddie caught Jo's eye and motioned frantically for her to put down the megaphone. "I think they get the point, Jo," she said as kindly as she could manage. Jo reluctantly dropped it and started doing stretches, lunging down in the grass like a sprinter on the starting block and then standing up and windmilling her arms.

"What are you doing?" Skylar groused. "I'm getting tired just watching it."

"Warming up," Jo said breathlessly. "For our hike later."

"*Dude.* We've been walking all over the place. Can't we just sloth for one afternoon?"

"You can have a few minutes to rest," Jo said, contorting into a back bend.

"Oh, yay," Skylar said sarcastically and rolled onto her stomach.

Maddie tried to close her eyes again and unwind, but she couldn't relax with Jo's heavy breathing and joint-cracking happening inches from her ear.

"I'm gonna go look for Emma," she said, getting up and putting on the wide-brimmed straw sun hat that she'd thankfully thought to stick in her carry-on. She didn't actually care if she found anyone; she just needed some peace and quiet.

Maddie walked west along the beach, passing Sunny and her group lined up on towels, glistening with tanning oil like string-bikini-clad sardines, and a few older girls in sarongs reading Kindles and doing crossword puzzles. A bunch of guys had already started a game of football and some were wearing their shirts pulled up over their heads, which Maddie thought must be an impulse genetically coded into the Y-chromosome, since the only time she had ever done it was by accident in the dressing room at Forever 21. As she got closer to the woods, she could see Nate and Zeke and a few other guys her age hunched over a towel; upon closer inspection they were maneuvering little toy soldiers in formation, strategizing for capture the flag. Maddie smirked at the boys' frowns of concentration and made a mental note to tell Jo, who would surely be pissed she hadn't thought of it first.

She was looking out at the lake when she saw the cabin out of the corner of her eye. It sat in the distance on the island's westernmost point, its skeletal roof beams peeking out from between the trees. Mack had intended it to be a safe house in case anyone was ever stuck out on Wexley overnight, but he had never gotten around to finishing it, so it was more like an open-air gazebo. Over the years, for obvious reasons, it had earned the nickname Virginity Point.

Maddie had forgotten all about the cabin and had even forgotten about Charlie for five minutes or so, but now the pain bloomed fresh in her chest. She sat down and took a deep breath. She was almost starting to feel better when a football collided with her left shoulder.

"What the hell?!" Maddie looked up to see a stocky guy with white-blond hair and a bright red sunburn jog over to retrieve the ball.

"Sorry," he mumbled.

"Hey!" Nate stood up from his spot in the makeshift war room. "Why don't you guys move it up the beach where you won't hit anyone?" Sunburned Guy looked over at his shirtless compatriots, who nodded.

"Sure, no problem, man," he said. He looked down at Maddie sheepishly. "Sorry again."

A few seconds later, Nate appeared at her side.

"You okay?" he asked. His dark blond hair was windblown from the boat, and with his muscular arms, threadbare tank top, and rolled-up cargo pants he looked to Maddie like a TV castaway, the kind who would grow sexy stubble but always look freshly showered.

"Yeah," she said, massaging her shoulder. "Just a dent—mostly to my dignity."

He sat down next to her and rested his arms on his knees.

"Everyone okay after last night?" he asked.

"Some hurt feelings, I think, and a slight hangover, but everyone's fine," she said. "You should put Adam on one of those leashes people use on toddlers at Disney World."

"Yeah," he laughed. "He's pretty oblivious sometimes."

Maddie examined her fingernails. She and Nate had never really had a conversation. She'd known him for seven years, but only as background color, kind of like the way she knew the table lamp that had always been in her living room.

"How's the flag capturing going?" she asked, nodding back toward his group.

"Oh," he blushed, embarrassed. "Fine. It's stupid."

"No, it's okay. Some people I know take it really seriously, too." Maddie nodded at Jo, who was doing athletic cartwheels down the beach, unwittingly kicking sand into Skylar's face.

"Yeah, she's really something." He smiled and shielded his eyes from the sun.

"I know," Maddie laughed. "She's nuts."

"But in a good way," Nate said.

"Totally. She's just so into camp." Maddie thought for a second. "You know what, I have actually never seen her *not* at camp."

"Maybe she lives here year-round," Nate joked.

"I know, tunneling into the ground like a vole or something."

"Only cuter." He looked at Maddie cautiously. "I mean—"

"It's okay, I won't tell," Maddie said.

Nate seemed relieved. "It doesn't matter anyway," he sighed. "She barely knows I exist."

"That is not true! You guys are joined at the hip."

"I don't know," he said, tracing circles in the sand with one foot. "I just can't seem to get her attention."

"Have you tried a bullhorn?" Maddie suggested. She was only half joking.

Nate laughed. "No. But one time last summer I picked a bunch of wildflowers up in the north field and when I gave them to her she got mad at me for taking time away from my lawn-mowing shift."

Maddie shook her head. That was Jo all right. But even someone as terrified of romantic abandon as Jo would have to be crazy not to notice the attention of a handsome, sweet guy like Nate.

"Did she at least keep them?" Maddie asked.

"They ended up in an empty mayonnaise jar on the pass-through window of the cafeteria," Nate said. "I think some hash browns knocked them over."

Maddie had the sudden urge to hug Nate. She also had the urge to smack Jo upside the head with her clipboard and tell her how crazy she was not to grab Nate before some other girl came to her senses and went after him. *This* was the kind of guy who should be someone's first love. Someone who brought you flowers and refilled your water glass without your having to ask. Someone who watched you across crowded rooms just to make sure you were okay. Someone who loved you quietly from a distance, without pressuring you or wanting you to change.

"Well, I'm her best friend," Maddie said, giving Nate a sympathetic smile. "And I know how tough and stubborn Jo can be. But I hope you won't give up."

"I don't know," he said. "I feel like I'm being so obvious already."

"It's up to you, but I say give it another shot. At least a final Hail Mary. Because I think she needs a guy like you."

Nate brightened. "Really?" he asked.

"Yeah," Maddie said, adding silently in her head, *I think we all do*.

She felt better than she had in months. If for every Charlie in the world there was also a Nate, she thought, eventually probability would be on her side. Maybe, just maybe, there was hope for her after all.

Skylar

Reunion: Day 2

SKYLAR BURIED HER FACE IN HER TOWEL. THE FRESH air wasn't enough to chase off the last remnants of her headache, and she was pretty sure her legs were already burning. To top it all off, her hair still smelled like lake, and she was starting to think everyone was avoiding her. Jo was busy doing some sort of weird capoeira workout on the sand, Maddie had gone down the beach to talk to Nate, Adam was suspiciously AWOL, and Emma had gone out of her way to stay as far from Skylar as humanly possible. Even though she knew yoga breaths would be more productive, Skylar decided to allow herself to wallow briefly in all-consuming self-pity. She curled up in the fetal position and pulled Maddie's towel on top of her.

Skylar had been to therapy, after she got caught breaking into the science lab sophomore year so that she could bleach her hair in the girls' bathroom with hydrogen peroxide (she hadn't realized you could buy it over the counter at CVS), so she knew that parents got blamed for most people's problems. And she had to admit that there was a precedent in her life for a man who treated her like she didn't have anything to offer.

She flashed back to sitting in her dad's studio after her junior art expo, the semester before she'd gone to Florence. The rain had been beating against the floor-to-ceiling windows as she'd sat on a stool and stared at his big, violent canvases streaked with black, red, and white— a series Skylar and her brothers had nicknamed "Snowball in Hell," due to the white blob at the center of each piece that seemed to sit melting in a fiery wasteland. "Where's the point of view?" he'd said as he paced around her work, spread out across the broad, paint-splattered planks of the hardwood floor. It had smelled like turpentine and incense, which served the duty of masking any lingering scent from the joint he liked to smoke while conceptualizing a new piece. "Anyone could have done these, Skylar," he'd finally said, frowning at her, his thick, cracked fingers massaging his chin. "I just don't think you have anything unique to say. But don't beat yourself up." He'd clapped her once on the back and cleared his throat. "We don't choose our talents. You're either an artist, or you're not."

When she saw Maddie making her way back to the towels, Skylar emerged from her cocoon.

"So . . . where is she?" she asked, hoping that she sounded at least semi-casual.

"Who?" Maddie seemed confused.

"*Emma,*" Skylar said. "Didn't you go looking for her?"

"Oh, right. Sorry, I got distracted."

"Didn't you ask Nate?" Skylar pressed. "I saw you talking to him."

"No, actually. I guess I should have." Maddie smiled, as if at an inside joke, and Skylar wondered for a second if there was something brewing between her and Nate.

"It's okay," Skylar said. "I'll ask him myself." She pulled on her shorts and walked quickly down the shore, the beads on the ties of her bikini jangling with each step. As she approached, Nate, Zeke, and Bowen Connors exchanged awkward looks.

"Hey, guys," she said, crossing her arms over her triangle top self-consciously. "Have you seen Emma?"

"Yeah, she was on the beach when we got here around eleven," Nate said.

Skylar could have killed Jo. Their pointless hike around the island meant that she'd missed Emma's arrival.

"Well, do you know where she is now?"

The boys exchanged smirks.

"Um, she's with Adam," Nate said, fiddling with a toy soldier and avoiding eye contact.

Of course, Skylar thought. They were probably off somewhere bitching about her.

"They disappeared a while ago, though," Zeke said.

"Do you know where they went? I really need to find Emma. I couldn't care less about Adam." The last part was both unnecessary and untrue, but she wanted Adam's friends to know she wasn't just a jealous third wheel—no matter how much she was starting to feel like one.

Suddenly, Bowen coughed—except it wasn't a real cough. It was one of those coughs that doesn't try very hard to conceal something that's being shouted.

"Thanks," Skylar said quickly, turning so that the guys wouldn't see her eyes welling up with tears. The words Bowen had coughed were "Virginity Point."

"I need to talk to you," Skylar said to Jo, pulling her aside when she got back to the towels. It was everything she could do not to start freaking out, but she couldn't let Maddie know what was going on—not yet, not after what she'd been through with Charlie. Skylar needed counsel from someone who wasn't going to get emotional or passive-aggressive. They all gave Jo a hard time about being stoic, but in certain situations it was a lifesaver.

Luckily, Maddie was quite happy to lie on her towel and nap while Skylar and Jo took a walk. They cut through the woods to the south, away from the beach and the noise and the cabin where Adam was doing who knows what to Emma. Skylar cringed and put her face in her hands. Mid-afternoon sunlight spilled through the thick tree cover in kaleidoscopic patches.

"Adam took Emma to the cabin," she blurted out. "I think they're hooking up."

Jo frowned. "Isn't that a good thing?" she asked. "Or did I miss something?"

Skylar took a deep breath. Her junior year drawing teacher used to say that once a student shared their work with the class, it didn't belong to them anymore, and she hoped the same principle held true for secrets. Because she didn't want it anymore. She needed to let it go.

"It would be a good thing," Skylar said slowly, "if Adam hadn't tried to kiss *me* last night. And if we hadn't been hooking up all summer."

Jo didn't react, except to look down at her hands. "I thought something might have happened between you guys, but I didn't know it was still going on," she said quietly.

"It's not. I ended it."

"Well, that's convenient." Coming from anyone else, this would have been sarcasm, but coming from Jo it was just a statement of fact. "How long had you two been . . . ?" Jo asked.

"Too long," Skylar said with a sigh. "Three years."

"Shit!" Jo never cursed, so this was a big deal. "I had no idea it was that serious."

"It wasn't," Skylar said. "For him, anyway."

"And for you?"

"I didn't think it was, but I've known him since I was ten. It was always going to be more complicated than just sex."

"Ew," Jo said.

Skylar sighed. "We're not twelve, Jo. Sex isn't gross."

"I'm not ew-ing sex in general, just with Adam Loring."

"Don't knock it 'til you try it."

"Okay, *ew*," Jo said. "And for the record, that one was specific to you guys."

"Are you mad?" Skylar asked.

Jo kicked a pine cone. "Not mad, just . . . why him, you know? Why do that to Emma? To all of us?" Skylar felt a fresh wave of guilt.

"She's going to hate me, isn't she?" Skylar whispered.

"Probably," Jo said. "But I hope she hates *him*, too. I hope you both do. It wasn't just you; it was him." She started to sound genuinely upset. "Adam's been manipulative since he was a kid, but this is going way too far. Leading Emma on, and then hooking up with you, trying to have it both ways. I always knew he had a sleazy side, but I never thought he was a bad guy."

Skylar didn't know what to say to that. Was Adam a bad guy? She'd never thought it either. An unrepentant flirt, definitely. But she'd never thought of him as manipulative. In fact, she always felt like *she* manipulated *him*. It had been Skylar who called the shots, who'd told him when she wanted him and when she didn't, who'd pushed him away when she was done. Throughout their whole relationship, Skylar had felt in control. She had never once stopped to consider the fact that he was getting exactly what he wanted, with no strings attached.

"Maybe he's not that way with Emma," she said. "Maybe he really likes her." The possibility made her both hopeful and depressed.

"I don't know. From the way he was acting last night I'd say he was playing her, too," Jo mused. "Emma wants talk, so he plays up his sensitive side. You want to hook up, so—"

"I want more than that," Skylar said sharply.

"Sorry, that came out wrong." Jo stopped and put her hands on

Skylar's shoulders. "I know you think I judge you, but I don't. And whatever Emma does, I won't judge her either." That gave Skylar a terrible mental image.

"I should go stop them," Skylar said. "I can tell her right now and keep her from doing anything with him."

"No," Jo said. "If you stopped her, she'd just resent you. If she hooks up with him, she hooks up with him. You can't make that decision for her."

"But what if he's just using her?" Skylar protested.

"What if he isn't?"

"I get that you're playing devil's advocate," Skylar said. "But please, just pick a side. None of this what-will-be-will-be crap is helping."

"If you want me to pick a side, you might not like whose side I pick," Jo said.

"I know."

"From the outside, it looks like you tried to hurt her on purpose."

That was too much. Skylar's hands flew to her face, and she started to sob.

"I'm not a bad person," she choked out. "I was just in a bad place." She felt Jo's arms wrap around her, and she held on for dear life.

"I'm not going to cry," Jo warned her after a few minutes of comforting.

Skylar laughed and pulled back, wiping her puffy eyes. "No one asked you to, robot," she sniffed. "But I do need you to lead us back to the beach, because I have no idea where I am."

Jo smiled. "That I can do," she said. She grabbed Skylar's hand.

"Is this the buddy system?"

"It never fails," Jo said.

Skylar interlaced her fingers with Jo's and smiled. Her dad—and Adam—had been right about one thing: you couldn't choose certain things in life. They found you. Like your best friends. She resolved to find Emma and tell her everything, before anything else could pull them apart.

Emma

Reunion: Day 2

"SEE? I TOLD YOU!" ADAM PULLED ASIDE A HEAVY PINE branch and gestured grandly. Beyond it, Emma could see a clearing with an open-air cabin that looked out on a little half moon of beach.

"Wow," she said, impressed. "And here I thought you were leading me into the wilderness to take advantage of me." She grinned and bit her lip. Ever since he'd stepped off the boat, greeting her with a Christmas-morning grin and a grateful hug, she'd been flirting with the kind of intensity and commitment she normally reserved for memorizing SAT flashcards.

"No, I just moonlight as a highly motivated real estate agent," Adam joked. "I really think you'll like this one. There's no roof or bathroom, but I think you'll agree that the natural beauty of the land trumps the need for shelter and plumbing." Emma laughed.

"This *is* nice," she said as they walked around the right side of the cabin, stepping carefully through a thicket of overgrown brush. "But I think I'm looking to settle somewhere . . . less in the middle of nowhere." Her eyes fell on a pair of boxer briefs stuck in a nearby shrub and she shrieked. Adam put an arm around her.

"I'm sorry you had to see that, but that's what happens when you don't have a washer/dryer," he said. "Let's check out the waterfront."

When they got about ten feet from the lake, Adam opened his backpack and pulled out a blanket and a paper bag.

"Wait, were you *planning* this?" she asked.

"Not planning so much as hoping," he said, looking up at her with a wink.

"And what's in the bag?" *Please don't let it be something gross like malt liquor or condoms,* she silently pleaded with the powers that be.

"Just some of those fake Oreos you like. I swiped them from the kitchen."

She grinned. "Aw, you shouldn't have."

He looked at her more seriously.

"I owe you a lot more than knockoff sandwich cookies."

Emma sat down on the blanket and kicked off her flip-flops, digging her toes deep into the gravelly sand. She knew that they would eventually have to talk about what had happened with Skylar at the lake and all the feelings they'd been dancing around since she'd come back, but part of her wished they could just erase everything between when he'd squeezed her hand on the path the night before and when they'd met on the shore that morning. She knew that if she and Adam ended up together, she'd delete that stretch of time from their story. It could be like the five-second rule, right? They'd dropped things for a minute, but they could easily pick them back up. Sitting together in the hazy afternoon light on a private beach seemed like as good a restart button as any.

They passed the cookies back and forth and watched the sun dip beneath the clouds. "Skylar and I . . . have become pretty good friends since you left," Adam finally said, staring out at the lake. "In a way, I feel like she missed you so much she needed me to lean on."

Emma kept her eyes on the horizon.

"And same with me," Adam went on. "I missed you. And she was the closest thing I had to you." He looked at her with a pained expression, the sun hitting his irises at just the right angle to turn them into pools of gold-flecked copper. "But I think maybe for her, that got confused. And when she saw us together, she was sort of . . . jealous, I guess. She's pretty insecure, underneath it all." Emma had often thought the exact same thing, but when Adam said it she sort of wanted to smack him. Did he really think he knew Skylar better than her own best friend?

"Well, nothing happened, at least," she said. "I was afraid she was going to try to kiss you!" She'd meant it to be funny, but Adam just looked more upset. Emma rested her hand lightly on top of his. "Thank you for the apology," she said. It was more than she'd gotten from Skylar.

"I just don't want it to mess things up," he said. "With us."

Emma threaded her fingers through his and turned to face him. It had been silly, she realized, to worry about knowing when her second chance would present itself. It was so obvious it was like an alarm had been tripped in her central nervous system. This was it. She would lean over, part her lips, and—

"Oh, shit," Adam said, pulling his hand away. He rooted around in his pocket for his phone. When he found it he looked at it and raised his eyebrows. "It's five o'clock," he said.

Emma wasn't sure why he suddenly cared what time it was, until it dawned on her. "We missed the boats," she said. She immediately pictured Jo seeing the unchecked names on her list and shaking her fist at the sky.

"Don't worry, Mack keeps a boat stashed down the beach," Adam said. "I know where it is."

"Do you want to go back now?" She tried to hide her disappointment.

"Hell no!" He started unbuttoning his shirt. "Since we're here we might as well have some fun. We've got the island to ourselves. And since our swim was so rudely interrupted last night . . ."

Soon Adam was down to his swim trunks. He wasn't muscular like Nate, but he wasn't scrawny, either. He had a trim swimmer's body, which she could actually see now, since it wasn't pitch black. She noticed that Adam had a patch of chest hair as well as a trail leading from his belly button down below the waistband of his suit. Emma blushed. Pubic hair seemed so personal; she couldn't believe guys got away with flashing it in public.

"You coming in?" Adam ran at the water like he was diving into the ocean, even though the placid green surface of the lake barely registered his presence.

Emma stayed seated as she peeled off her shorts. She pulled her tank top over her head and watched Adam dunk his head below the surface and then emerge, shaking his hair like a dog trying to dry off. She grinned.

"What?" he called, flexing his biceps. "You don't like my bikini body? Get in here!"

She stood, and he took her in, just the way he had the night before. He didn't say anything for a minute, and she was wondering if maybe the red had been a tacky choice, when he put his right hand over his heart and fell backward into the water. Emma laughed. She waded into the lake feeling like the most beautiful girl in the world.

The sun was just starting to dip below the horizon, sending a dazzling reflection shooting across the water. Emma and Adam bobbed farther and farther away from shore, until Emma had to stand on her tip-toes to touch the slick, mossy bottom. Treading water was making them both breathe heavily.

"In case you didn't appreciate my fake heart attack," Adam said, slicking his hair back from his forehead, "you look amazing."

"Thanks, you're not too bad either." Maybe it was the cold water, but she felt exhilarated, like every pore was oozing an electric charge. She was hyper-aware of Adam's body; how close it was; how she could just reach out and—

"Truth or dare?" he asked, splashing her playfully.

"Um . . . truth."

"Did you want to kiss me?"

She bit her lip. Emma had never been stoned, but it couldn't feel more dizzying than this.

"You'll have to be more specific," she said, splashing him back.

"That night . . . with the fireworks."

"Yes."

"I knew it!"

"Okay, your turn," she said. "Truth or dare?"

"Truth."

"Did *you*?"

"Did I what?" He smiled. He was making her work for it.

"Did you want to kiss me?"

"Are you kidding? Wasn't it obvious? I was doing the lean. But I can see how you might not have picked up on that. It was one of my first leans. I'm much better at the lean now."

"Oh yeah?" She couldn't stand it anymore. She had to touch him. She beckoned, and he swam closer.

"Truth or dare," he said. They were less than a foot apart.

"Dare," she whispered.

"I dare you to kiss me right now."

Emma wrapped her arms around his neck and he pulled her in. She tilted her face up, and he moved to kiss her, but she stopped his chin with one hand. She nuzzled his wet cheek and held her lips millimeters from his, so close they were brushing, but only just. He moaned softly, and she shuddered. *Then* she kissed him. His lips were full and warm, and the warmth seemed to radiate out from him and all the way through her—down her throat and through her stomach and out her legs, which wrapped around his back instinctively like a starfish curling around someone's hand. He opened his mouth slightly and she tasted his tongue, salty and sweet. But then she pulled away. The sensory overload was almost too much to take. Adam looked at her with a dazed expression.

"Now you," she said breathlessly. "Truth or dare?"

"Dare." He smiled and reached for her, but she darted back.

"I dare you to kiss me like you mean it." He pulled her in again and put one hand behind her head, pressing his lips hard into hers, his tongue braver this time. She wrapped her legs tighter around his waist and then his hands were moving from her hair to her waist to her breasts. She could feel him through her bathing suit and she arched her back toward him, trying not to fight the tingle that was spreading across her pelvis. As she took his face in her hands, she thought, *So this is why people have sex*. It wasn't a moral choice or a rebellious statement. It was a base, animal instinct. Her body had never wanted anything more. It kind of scared her.

"I dare you to take your top off," Adam said. Emma broke away and swam back a few feet. She grinned at him.

"Only if you take off your bottoms."

"I only have bottoms!" he protested.

"Deal or no deal." She didn't have to ask him again. A minute later he held his swim trunks above his head with a flourish.

"Now, I don't want you to manhandle me," he said. "And by don't, I mean do." Emma suddenly felt out of her depth as she reached up to untie her bikini top. They'd only just kissed, after years of confusing build up, and now things were moving lightning fast, like one of those terrifying carnival freefall rides that lifted you higher and higher until it finally plummeted one hundred feet in two seconds. She wasn't sure she was ready. Still, she dropped her bathing suit top, immersing her bare breasts in the cold water, hoping they were hidden from view.

"You're gorgeous," he said. She leaned in to kiss him again, but more tentatively this time. She didn't want their bodies to touch—she wasn't sure she could handle it. And when Adam reached for her, she knew she couldn't.

"You know, we probably should head back," she said, covering her chest self-consciously with one arm and splashing him. "Jo will just flip out and send a search party anyway." He looked crestfallen.

"I should have known you just wanted to get into my pants."

"I'm sorry!" she laughed. "But think of this as a 'to be continued . . .' on dry land."

"Promise?" he said, fishing for his bathing suit in the darkening water.

"Promise," she said. She made good on it approximately forty-five seconds later, when, top intact and feet firmly planted on the sand, she put her hands on his chest and kissed his neck.

"Mmmmm," he murmured, leaning down to kiss her softly. "Can't we just stay here? Sleep under the stars?"

"Not tonight," she whispered. "But soon." Emma couldn't wait to go on a real date with Adam. She wanted to kiss him on doorsteps, under street lamps, lying down on a proper bed. She wanted to do everything with him. As he brushed her hair out of her face and kissed her again, she couldn't believe she'd tried to convince herself she didn't want him that way for so many years. She wanted—no, needed—to feel this way all the time.

And now I will, she thought, trying to ignore the guilt that tugged at the edges of her consciousness. She'd blatantly ignored Skylar, ditched Maddie and Jo, and had barely thought about any of them all day. For the first time in her life, she'd chosen a guy over her friends—something she promised she'd never do. But they would forgive her—wouldn't they?

Maddie

The Third Summer • *Age 12*
Changeover weekend, second day of WOW

"Friendship Rule: Best friends have to earn your trust."

THE MIDSUMMER HEAT WAS STIFLING AS MADDIE stood at the edge of the creek, trying to figure out how to get across without getting wet up to the waist. There were rocks she could step on, but they were scattered in a zigzag pattern three feet apart, and besides, they looked slippery and sharp. If she'd had time to strip down to her bathing suit she would have gladly just waded in—it was noon and the sun was high, and while trees offered some relief it still felt unbearable, like she was a dinner roll being kept warm in the oven. But she was carrying twenty pounds on her back and they still had ground to cover, so there was no time for a free swim.

They'd been hiking for five hours, since seven a.m., after a breakfast of turkey jerky and canned orange juice. The night before, they'd had to strip branches and build their own shelters using tarps and rope. Maddie's whole body ached, and she was getting blisters not just on her feet but also on her shoulders, in the spots where the metal frame of her pack rubbed against her skin.

"Maybe you should call this trip Weekend of Welts," she joked to Jaime, one of the two counselors leading the expedition. He was exactly the type of person Maddie had always pictured when she thought about camp counselors: clean-cut, outdoorsy, and enthusiastic to the point of being obnoxious. Even though they were in the middle of a seven-mile loop of trail with no one else around, Jamie was wearing a name tag. Maddie was supposed to be wearing hers, too, but she had "lost" it during a snack break.

"How about Weekend of Whining?" he said with a grin, clapping her on the back and tramping through the water so enthusiastically Maddie's face got splashed. "Look alive, Ryland!" Jamie was both an extreme sports nut and a hopeful Marine recruit, and as a result he usually acted like he was starring in a Jeep commercial. He and her stepdad, Eddie, would have gotten along famously.

Thanks for the help, Maddie thought.

It was kind of her own fault she was doing WOW to begin with, of course. She couldn't go home between sessions and she couldn't stay on camp grounds during the reunion that happened over the weekend. It hadn't been something she'd thought about when she'd sent the e-mail to Mack that had led to her enrollment at Camp Nedoba. She'd been nine years old. She hadn't been thinking about anything then, except running away, and for as long as possible. Luckily, Jo had been waiting anxiously ever since their first summer to be old enough to participate in a WOW trip, and she'd begged all the girls to do it with her. So Maddie's misery had company, at least.

"After this weekend," Emma panted, coming up behind Maddie and leaning over with her hands on her knees, "I'm never, ever going to take dry socks for granted ever again."

"I'm never eating gorp again," Skylar said, stretching her right triceps, which was wrapped with a beaded American Indian armband. Her dirty blond hair was woven into twin braids like Pocahontas. "Unless I need to throw up."

"What are you guys waiting for?" Jo asked, breezing past them and hopping from rock to rock like she was carrying a pack full of helium balloons instead of heavy camping gear.

"Nice work," Jamie said, raising his hand for a high five on the other side. Every minuscule accomplishment received a high five from Jamie. Sometimes, for variety, he mixed it up with a fist bump. "Now, come on," he said. "We're holding up the team." The other campers on the trip, two girls and six boys who were all thirteen and fourteen, along with the second counselor, Tallie, had all crossed the creek before Maddie had even gotten there.

One by one, Maddie watched her friends brave the creek crossing. None of them treated it like a big deal, not even Emma, whose legs were almost as short as Maddie's, and who couldn't climb a tree or swim a lap to save her life.

"All right, let's go, come on, Maddie," Jamie called.

She looked down at the two-foot drop onto the first rock, and at the three feet between that rock and the next one. Suddenly, the crossing seemed impossible, the perspective stretching grotesquely until it was a raging river. Maddie's heart raced and her limbs froze.

In the middle of the wilderness, at a most inconvenient time, Maddie found herself in the middle of a panic attack.

Eddie hadn't always been so distant. Before he'd lost his job, he had actually been kind of fun. And after her sisters had been born, even though she wasn't his natural child, he'd made sure to carve out special time for Maddie so she wouldn't feel jealous. She was seven years old the day he decided to take her to the pool at the community center.

It wasn't very deep in the kids' shallow end, which was separated from the grown-ups' deep end by a thick concrete wall tiled with green. Maddie had never been a fearful child and had been climbing trees, drainpipes, and anything she could get her hands on since she was a toddler. So she jumped into the water and was happily splashing when Eddie had crouched by the lip of the pool.

"Hey Mads, betcha can't walk from this end of the wall to the other," he'd laughed.

"Betcha I can!"

"All right, let's see, small fry."

The top of the wall was almost submerged in the chlorinated water, which lapped from both sides up onto the slick tile. But Maddie thought nothing of it and stepped out like a tightrope walker in her little pink two-piece with the purple butterfly on the chest. She looked back at Eddie, who smiled and clapped.

"Are you sure it's allowed?"

"It's a free country, anything's allowed," Eddie said. "G'on. Trust me. I'll go meet you at the other end."

She held out her arms and walked out into the middle, inching one foot after another along the smooth tile, feeling the rough grout in between with her little toes.

"Watch out, honey," a woman called from the shallow end where she was playing with her young daughter. "I don't think you should be up there. It's not safe."

"My dad says it's okay," Maddie said. "He's right over—"

And then she fell.

Her right foot slid left and she lost her balance, coming down hard on her shoulder before she slipped below the surface of the deep end. She looked up as she sank down, seeing the ceiling ripple through the bright blue water that stung her eyes.

Eddie got to her within ten seconds, but by that time she'd swallowed a mouthful of water and scraped her cheek against the edge of a tile. He'd taken her out for ice cream after, but she didn't stop shaking for an hour. She just kept feeling herself fall and seeing the world retreat slowly from view.

"Maddie!" Jamie yelled. "What are you waiting for, a taxi? Let's go."

"No." She backed away and shook her head. "I can't."

"Yes, you can," Jamie sighed. He jumped to the rock in the middle of the creek and held out his arm. "Trust me," he said.

Maddie burst into tears. "I don't trust you!" she yelled. "I can't do it! You can't make me!" She leaned on a tree and sobbed as the rest of the WOW group stared at her from the far bank. She squeezed her eyes shut and tried to catch her breath, but she was so afraid that she could already hear the splash she would make when she dropped into the water.

"Hey," Jo said, appearing beside her. She had made the splashing noise when she crossed back over; it made Maddie feel better to know she wasn't as crazy as she thought. "What's going on?"

"I don't know," Maddie said, keeping her face against the cool bark. "I'm just afraid."

"Of what?"

Maddie took a deep breath and felt her lungs expand. She wasn't going to stop breathing. It had all been in her head. "Falling."

"I won't let you," Jo said. "Neither will Jamie, even though he's obnoxious."

"I don't think I can do it yet," Maddie said. "I need to sit for a minute."

"Okay," Jo said, squatting next to her as Maddie dropped to her knees.

"Hey, what's going on?" Jamie yelled. "We've got to make ten more miles before dark!"

"You can wait a few minutes," Jo shouted back, annoyed. "She'll be fine." She turned back to Maddie. "You'll be fine," Jo said, stroking Maddie's back. "I promise. I'll be right here. And then we'll go over together."

Maddie kept her eyes closed. She took a few deep breaths. She tried to remember that she wasn't at the Fayetteville community rec center; it was hundreds of miles away. And she wasn't even in the wilderness. Wilderness was thick and messy, with blinding brush that tugged at your skin and hair, pulling you down. She was on a path, and she wasn't alone.

"I'm ready," she said after a few minutes. She took Jo's hand, she said a prayer, and she stepped off the edge.

Jo

Reunion: Day 2

BY THE TIME SHE AND SKYLAR GOT BACK TO THE beach, Jo was exhausted. She might have been the only one who hadn't had an emotional breakthrough so far at reunion, but she still felt spent and decided to clear her head with a swim.

The water was cold and gray, just the way she liked it. Jo knew that a lot of people preferred white sand and crystal blue waves that looked like they'd been Brita filtered, but she'd take Wexley Island over some cookie-cutter paradise any day. She loved the way the muddy lake bottom squished between her toes, and the crisp, fresh, slightly floral smell of the unsalted water. "We're lake people," her dad always used to tell Jo, as her mom watched them swim from the porch of the rental house. "Your mother is landlocked."

She knew that her friends thought it was weird how much she loved camp and how devoted she was to it, but it was hard to explain that sometimes it literally felt like all she had. Her dad had bought the property less than six months after the divorce, and Jo knew it had been no coincidence that he wanted to stay near Onan, the site of the

Putnam family's annual vacations. She knew this because her mother had called it, more than once, his "bizarre, sad attempt to cling to something that no longer exists." Jo had just nodded—she was eight years old at the time—but even then, she knew she was clinging, too. Who wouldn't want to live in their happiest memories all year long?

Jo bobbed in the lake and looked back at Maddie and Skylar on the beach, noting how ironic it was that she was literally treading water and watching her friends live their lives. She dunked her head, and when she resurfaced, she saw Nate walking down the shore toward their towels. He spotted her and waved, and she smiled. She had to hand it to him—the guy had great timing.

"Hey," Jo said as she waded back in, her hands instinctively reaching up to wring out the ponytail she no longer had.

"Hey yourself," Nate said. "I was hoping I'd catch you before you headed back." He handed her her towel. "Maddie also said to give you this." Nate held up a piece of blue fabric.

"What . . . *is* that?" Jo looked over at Maddie, who gave her an enthusiastic nod.

"I don't know. It's Skylar's. I think you're supposed to wear it," Nate said.

"Oh . . . right. Thanks." She finished drying off and wrapped the sarong awkwardly around her waist. Out of the corner of her eye, Jo thought she could see Maddie shaking her head.

"So, listen," Nate said, "I was hoping we could hang out tonight after dinner."

"Sure," Jo said. "What's everybody want to do?"

Nate smiled shyly. “It’s not everybody. Just me.” Jo could see the fear in his eyes as he waited for a response, and the realization hit her: *He’s asking me out.* Jo had never been asked out before. Well, there was that one time at the camp dance when they were twelve that an older guy named Jason had asked her to slow dance, but it later turned out to have been a dare, so it didn’t count. She studied Nate’s face. It was objectively handsome. And he was nice—*so* nice. She knew that the normal thing to do when a nice, cute guy asked you out was to say yes. But then they’d have to have an awkward date, and awkward talks, and she worried it would all just be too awkward.

“I don’t know, Nate . . .” She didn’t want to hurt him, but she also wasn’t in the mood to deal with more emotional melodrama, on top of everything that was going on with her friends.

“Did I mention I make a *really* good bug juice?”

She smiled. “Thanks, but—”

“And you look beautiful in that, um . . .”

“Sarong?”

“Right. That sarong. Well, you do. Look beautiful in it.” He shifted his weight nervously.

She blushed. “Thank you,” she said. “I would love to, seriously, but this weekend is so crazy and . . . I mean, I’m basically running camp. So I don’t really have time.”

“Oh, come on,” he said. “That’s not true.”

She crossed her arms defensively. “Actually, it is,” she said. “I have to get everyone back on the boats, get them back to camp safely, oversee dinner, prep for capture the flag . . .”

"I'm not saying you're not the backbone of this camp, because you are," Nate said quickly. "But you've scheduled this weekend down to the nanosecond. I know because I helped you with most of it. So I also know that everything has already been taken care of. And even if it wasn't, your dad's around. I think he's camp director or something." He smiled and crossed his arms, imitating her with a skeptical eyebrow raise. "So, actually, I can't really see how you don't have time for an hour with me by the lake, especially if I take your dinner shift."

"You don't have to do that," Jo said, softening her stance.

"What if I already did?"

"Then . . ." She looked over at Maddie, who nodded vigorously while pretending to read her book. Jo sighed. She did like Nate, as a friend anyway. It was just an hour. It probably couldn't hurt. And she'd still have time to review her capture the flag strategy with the girls. "Okay," she said.

"Yeah?" His eyes lit up.

"Yes, but I only have *one* hour. I'll meet you by the fire pit at eight." She turned and started to walk away. "And no beer!" she called over her shoulder.

When she reached the towels, she balled up the sarong and tossed it at Maddie and Skylar, who were grinning stupidly. "Why, hello, cupids," she said. "Do you have your bows handy? Because I'd like to smack you with them."

"Come on," Maddie said. "He's adorable. And he's so into you. Look at him!"

Jo glanced back at Nate, who was still standing at the water's edge watching her. She gave him a limp wave and he smiled. Jo had to admit that she did feel *something* when she talked to Nate—an uneasiness roiling in her stomach. But was that butterflies or nausea at the thought of kissing him? Jo hoped she'd be able to tell the difference by nightfall.

Emma

Reunion: Day 2

"I HOPE WE GET BACK IN TIME TO CATCH THE END OF dinner," Adam said as he started to row. The dingy red canoe had scared Emma at first when he'd pulled it out of the brush, but then she realized it was kind of perfect. She and Adam may have capsized in a canoe when they were ten, but now they were riding off into the proverbial sunset in one. She couldn't think of a better metaphor for taking risks and facing her fear.

"I know, I'm hungry," Emma said, reaching her arms around Adam's waist.

"Hey!" he laughed. "Not while I'm driving." Emma picked up her oar.

"Should I help?"

"Nah, the water's calm," Adam said. "I'll let you know if I need you."

Emma rested the oar across her legs and looked up at the stars. She couldn't wait to get back to the others and tell them about her and Adam. She'd been talking about kissing him for so long, they might not believe that it had actually happened. She was so proud of herself. Emma had never been afraid to raise her hand in class or volunteer for a committee, or even apply to Brown, which was a reach school even for someone with her GPA. But letting go and showing Adam how she felt had been the bravest thing she'd ever done, and so far the rewards were more than she had hoped for. She leaned forward again and kissed the back of Adam's neck. He startled, and the canoe wobbled.

"Down girl!" His voice was firm but friendly.

Emma drew back, feeling a little rejected, and he looked over his shoulder.

"I just don't want to capsize," he said. She smiled.

"Sorry, I'll try to control myself."

"Thanks," he said. "I want to make good time. I need to find the guys and find out what I missed."

What he *missed*? Had Adam been spending the afternoon wishing he was back on the beach chasing Frisbees and snapping towels with his friends? Emma suddenly felt a little uneasy.

"I thought you had a pretty good time," she said.

"Believe me, I did," he said. "I just need to find Nate. We were supposed to plot our capture the flag victory." He laughed, and she relaxed a little. "I bet Jo's looking for you for the same reason."

"Yeah, you're probably right," she said. "But . . . I was kind of hoping we could hang out tonight. Maybe go down to the rocks. Except this time you can get some." (Did that sound slutty? She didn't care.)

Adam didn't answer right away, and Emma wished she wasn't

staring at his back. In the same way that it was almost impossible to read someone's tone in an e-mail or a text, it was hard to have a conversation with someone's shoulder blades. It seemed like Adam was acting a little cooler toward her since they left the beach, but maybe everything was fine. She took a deep breath and tried not to worry.

"What do you think?" she asked after a few seconds.

"That sounds awesome," he said, "but let's just see how the night goes."

Emma's heart sank. They'd spent over an hour making out after the sun set, and if anything she'd been the one who'd insisted they head back before it got too late. He'd seemed upset to have to leave, and she'd literally had to pry his hands off her. What could possibly have happened to make him change his mind?

Adam didn't miss a stroke, his oars cutting through the water with a wet thunk and a whoosh every three seconds. Birds shrieked in the branches of trees back on the mainland.

"Sure," she said quietly. "We'll see."

"Hey, don't be mad," he said. "I just have a lot to do."

"Like what? Drink beer by the lake?" Her tone was teasing, but she meant it to cut a little bit.

"Emma," Adam said, dragging his oar against the current. "I'm a counselor now. I actually do have stuff to do."

"I know," she said. "I just thought things would be different now that we . . ."

"They *are* different." He turned and gave her a wink. "But come on, the world doesn't stop just because we kissed."

Emma sat back and stared at the sinewy muscles moving underneath the damp fabric of his T-shirt. She wanted to say that something had changed in him, but had it, really? Adam had always been hot and cold. It was just that they'd raised the stakes back there in the water, and now his hot ran scalding and his cold made her numb. She didn't think that was what love, or whatever this was, was supposed to feel like.

She waited, though. She wanted to give him the benefit of the doubt. Maybe he was thinking of something to say that would make it feel okay again. Maybe he would apologize and tell her he was just scared because he'd never felt this way about anyone before, and that she was different. That was what he owed her, not the stale sandwich cookies that were already giving her stomach cramps.

But instead, he just went on rowing. Adam didn't say another word to her the whole way back to camp.

Jo

Reunion: Day 2

JO ADJUSTED HER SARONG AS SHE APPROACHED THE fire pit. After they'd gotten back to the mainland—once again without Emma, who hadn't answered any of their texts—Maddie and Skylar had helped her get dressed for her . . . meeting.

"It's *not* a date," Jo had said more than once, but that didn't stop them from fussing over her like the moms backstage on *Toddlers & Tiaras*. Maddie had tied the sarong so that it crisscrossed over Jo's chest and fastened behind her neck like a halter top. Jo made her promise to double knot it, since she didn't generally trust things without a built-in sports bra, or at the very least sleeves.

As promised, Nate was waiting for her when she got to the campsite, standing awkwardly and stoking a small fire.

"Wow. You look amazing," he stammered.

She smiled. "Thanks. I like your . . ." Nate was wearing the same basketball shorts and tank top he had been wearing earlier, although he'd changed his shoes and added an open flannel shirt. ". . . sneakers," Jo finished.

"They're limited edition," he said. "I got them on eBay." Jo nodded politely. "Oh, I got you these." He picked up a mason jar full of wildflowers. "Don't get mad. I only picked up the ones that had already fallen on the ground." Most of the flowers looked to have been dead for a number of weeks.

"That's sweet," Jo said, pretending to admire them. "Thank you." She wished she had just worn her camp T-shirt and jeans; she felt so awkward in the dress, like she was some sort of low-budget teen catalog model. Nate gestured for her to sit on a blanket he'd draped over one of the logs, and Jo sat carefully, keeping her thighs glued together. He presented her with what he referred to as a "cheese plate," which consisted of four Kraft Singles surrounded by a sunburst of string cheeses.

"So," Jo said, unwrapping a plastic-covered slice, "how was your day?"

"Pretty good," Nate said. "Did a lot of capture the flag strategy." He winked. "Obviously I can't tell you about that, though."

"Haha," she said. "Right."

"What about you?"

She racked her brain for some interesting tidbit she could share from her day that didn't involve her friends' sexual missteps, and then realized she couldn't do it—any of it. She couldn't exchange pleasantries with Nate, and she certainly couldn't do it wearing a ridiculous sarong. It was *Nate*. He was supposed to feel familiar and comfortable. In fact, this was the only time she could ever remember not feeling comfortable around him.

"You know what?" she said. "Not that the fire and the flowers and the blanket and the cheese aren't all great, but can we not do this formal date thing? It's kind of freaking me out."

"Oh, God, yes," he said, sitting down next to her with a sigh of relief. "Sorry. I got the idea from—"

"Adam?"

"Yeah! How'd you know?"

"Overproduction is kind of his style." She rested her arms on her knees—terrible posture; her mother would wince—and looked at him. "But it's not yours. And I like that."

"Good," he said. "I prefer to set the bar low."

"That's not what I meant!" she laughed. A breeze blew through, sending sparks shooting up into the smoke. Jo shivered; she wasn't used to being outside at night with a bare back.

"Do you want my shirt?" he asked, starting to take it off.

"No, I'm fine." She'd done the polar bear plunge in the Atlantic Ocean in the middle of January. She could handle it.

"No, you're cold."

"Quit being so chivalrous."

"Stop being so stubborn!"

Jo laughed. "I'm sorry," she sighed. "I can't."

"I can live with that," Nate said. "Just don't call me Stay-Puft, okay? It hurts my feelings. I used to be fat."

Jo's mouth fell open, and Nate started to laugh.

"Relax, I'm kidding!"

"Fine. I guess I deserve that." She nudged him with her shoulder.

"I'm sorry I tried to blow you off before," she went on. "This reunion is just really intense, and I wasn't sure I wanted to add any potential . . ." She realized too late she'd talked herself into a corner. "Whatever," she finished awkwardly.

"Wow," he said. "Whatever it is, it sounds like you're having a much more exciting weekend than I am. My highlight so far—other than right now, obviously—was beaning Loring in the face with that Jell-O."

She laughed hollowly. "It's not exciting so much as stressful."

"What?" he asked. "Keeping Emma and Skylar away from Adam?"

"Oh, I've given up on that," she said.

"Then what's up?" He looked at her, and his face was so open and guileless, she wanted to tell him everything. Not just about Skylar and Emma and their tug-of-war that she was now caught in the middle of, but about Maddie and the five-year-old letter she'd found on the last night of camp that had made her realize her own best friend didn't trust her.

But she hadn't even talked to Maddie yet. She didn't know how to bring it up. Could she ever? She looked at Nate, and he smiled reassuringly. It was exactly what she needed.

"Well, maybe you can help me," she said hesitantly. "I need some advice. But I have to be vague, since it's a delicate situation."

"I'm listening," he said.

Jo took a deep breath. "Say you knew someone who was lying about who they were."

"That sounds intense." He started to unwrap a string cheese and then thought the better of it.

"This person, you know, they don't *mean* to lie," Jo continued, feeling the tension that had been building in her shoulders all weekend release with each word. "They're just so ashamed by the truth of their life that they *think* they have to lie."

"What are they lying about?" he asked.

"Just . . . what makes them who they are," she said.

"Why is who they are so bad?"

"Who they are isn't bad," she said. "They're great, but there are things they don't tell anyone that keep them from being . . . I don't know. Free, I guess?" The main thing she wanted to tell Maddie was that she didn't care who her parents were or what kind of house she lived in. Those things didn't make a person good—just look at Sunny Sherman, whose parents really *were* jet-setting rich people. She had Maddie's imaginary life for real, and she would never be half as good a person, or a friend, as Maddie. But to tell Maddie that would be to admit that she'd read her file and invaded her privacy. It would embarrass her.

"Okay," Nate said, smiling. "Now you lost me a little."

"They just wish they would fit in. And be more like everyone else, and not have anything to hide."

Nate considered this for a minute. "Well, I don't think this person should be ashamed of anything," he said. "I'm just sorry they feel like no one would understand." He looked her in the eyes and put a hand on her knee. "Tell them they can talk to me, okay? I know what it's like to feel like no one really sees you. I know—"

Jo leaned over and kissed him. She couldn't stop herself. It felt kind of like playing goalie in soccer—she didn't even think, she just dove. It wasn't the great kiss of her dreams—he was taken by surprise, and so she ended up kind of kissing his top lip and front teeth, and it only lasted a second—but it still felt like she'd always hoped it would feel, like the night sky opened up overhead and the stars started falling out.

Her heart raced as she sat back and smiled. Nate looked shocked, his mouth still frozen mid-word.

"Wow," he whispered. "I was not expecting that."

Jo bit her lip. "Me neither." She started to lean in again, but he pulled away.

"I'm sorry," he said. "But I'm confused."

"About what?"

"I just thought—" He shook his head, his lips moving slightly like he was trying to find the right words. "I mean, aren't you . . . a lesbian?"

"What?!" She shoved him, nearly toppling the cheese plate. "Why would you think that? I just *kissed you*!"

"Because . . . that whole speech you just gave about lying about who you were . . . was that not what you were saying?"

"No!" She jumped up.

"I am *so* sorry," he said, his face a mask of regret. "I never should have said anything. I don't *want* you to be a lesbian. I have a crush on you!"

"Well, you must have thought I was at least kind of gay before, if that made you so sure."

"I swear I didn't!"

"It's my hair, isn't it?" she demanded, narrowing her eyes. "That is such a cliché, you should be ashamed of yourself."

"No! I love your hair short! Can we please just forget I said anything?" He reached for her arm but she dodged him.

"Or maybe," she went on, energized by the sudden surge of rage she was feeling, "it's because I don't suck at sports, or wear skirts and little heart necklaces that say BFF on them."

"Don't put words in my mouth," he yelled. "I said I was sorry. I'm glad you kissed me."

"Good," she said. "Duly noted."

Jo spun on her heel and stomped back into the woods, not caring that the branches scratched and tugged at the loose threads of her dress. She hoped they ripped it off. She felt naked already, anyway. And clearly, no clothing—no skin and bone and muscle, even—could protect her where she really needed it. No wonder her friends were so moody, Jo realized. Once you opened your heart, you couldn't close it again. It just sat there like a moving target on your chest, at the mercy of whoever happened to be aiming at you.

Jo

The Third Summer ♦ *Age 12*
First week of First Session

"Friendship Rule: Best friends stand up for you when you need them."

THE LOW TIDE EXPLORATION—A PERFECT ACTIVITY for the balmy holiday afternoon—had been going well until the counselor in charge, a busty blonde named Whitney, had taken a phone call from her boyfriend—who, she'd informed the campers, was off in college studying theater and was "kind of a big deal" since he'd gotten cast in a toothpaste commercial as the voice of a cartoon molar. But the call was not going well, and Whitney had stormed off down the beach yelling into her cell, and when she hadn't come back ten minutes later, a few of the older boys had started a game of spin the bottle with a Coke left over from lunch.

Jo didn't feel like playing for a number of reasons. One, it was one p.m. and sunny, and weren't kissing games supposed to happen after dark? Two, kissing games were definitely not allowed at Camp Nedoba, no matter the time of day. And three, she had never been kissed. That was the most important reason. When Jo imagined her first kiss, she pictured a quiet moment with a guy she really liked, maybe after she beat him in a really high-stakes game of air hockey.

She pictured nervous butterflies and closed eyes and soft lips. She did not picture the sun beating down on a sweaty glass Coke bottle and a bunch of twelve-year-old boys with weird facial hair and acne. This was nobody's idea of romance, and flies buzzing around their discarded sandwich crusts were definitely *not* the same as butterflies.

But everybody else seemed pretty into the game. Maddie and Skylar actually seemed *excited* to kiss the guys in the circle. Emma was hanging back around the periphery, but she wasn't exactly *not* playing—probably because Adam Loring was there.

"Hey, get in, Joey," yelled a skinny fourteen-year-old named Greg. Greg had a crew cut and an overbite, and had almost been sent home from camp the previous summer for trying to light one of his friend's farts with a burner starter he'd stolen from the mess hall.

Jo made a face. "It's *Jo*," she said. "And no thanks. Somebody has to look out for Whitney. Or *my dad*." She hoped that would be enough to make him leave her alone.

"Lame," Greg said.

"You can still sit with us," Skylar said. "You don't have to play." Jo reluctantly wedged herself between Skylar and Maddie.

"I'm not playing," she said loudly.

"You sit in the circle, you're playing," Greg said, leaning in for his spin.

"Don't worry," Maddie whispered. "I'll dropkick him if he tries anything."

Jo wrapped her arms around Maddie, wishing like always that they could live together all year round, and not just for the four weeks of camp.

"Oh, I get it," Greg said. "You're a lesbo."

"Shut up and spin!" Jo shouted.

Greg twisted the bottle back and forth, taunting her with a leer, before letting it fly. Jo watched the blue-green glass flash in the sun as it spun, slower and slower, getting closer . . . and closer . . . and closer until it finally landed just shy of her, pointing at Skylar's left knee. Greg's friends slapped him on the back and Skylar sighed dejectedly. In the five minutes they'd been playing, she had already kissed most of the guys in the circle, crawling out time and time again on all fours with her golden waves hanging down so low they almost brushed the sand. If any of those boys worked as hard in school as they did at making the Coke bottle land on Skylar, Jo realized, they could probably skip a grade.

Skylar pecked Greg on the lips and quickly sat back down.

"Second time is supposed to be tongue!" Greg cried, scowling.

"You wish," Skylar said. She leaned forward and spun the bottle for her turn, and all the boys sat with rapt attention. After a few seconds, the bottle came to rest, pointing at Adam Loring.

"Yes!" Adam jumped up and pumped his fists like a boxer doing a victory lap around the ring. Jo glanced over at Emma nervously. Emma never said it outright, but Jo was pretty sure she had a crush on Adam. They had been spending a lot of time together lately. Emma caught Jo looking and turned away, pretending to be interested in a sailboat out on the lake.

"Ugh, Adam, you are so weird," Skylar said.

"You know you love it," he said, getting back down on his knees and leaning in for his kiss. Skylar tried to peck him, but he smushed his face into hers and grabbed her chin. Skylar shoved him away, but when she sat back down Jo saw that she was smiling and blushing.

"Best kiss of my life," Adam said.

"*Only* kiss of your life," Skylar teased.

"I get another one, though," Adam said, reaching for the bottle. "Who's it going to be? Which lady is feeling lucky today?" None of them were, as it turned out; the bottle landed on Greg. "Do-over!" Adam cried, but Greg snatched the bottle before he could get it.

"Nope, that means you get skipped," Greg said, smiling. "My turn again." He flicked his wrist and the bottle whipped around. Jo looked back over at Emma to make sure she was okay, and so she didn't even notice that Greg's low whistle of satisfaction was intended for her. "Yes! Gotcha! I knew I would get you!"

Jo looked down at the mouth of the bottle, a perfect little round O that matched her own mouth as it dropped open. She felt her face turn bright red. The older boys started slapping their hands on their knees and chanting "Kiss! Kiss! Kiss!" A few of the older girls joined in, along with Adam—of course. Adam loved any sort of spectacle, even if he wasn't a part of it.

"No way," Jo said, but the crowd drowned her out. She looked at Skylar and Maddie for support but they were busy laughing at Greg, who had gotten to his feet and started doing comical calisthenics, stretching his lips wide and blowing raspberries like an athlete warming up for an event. Jo craned her neck to look for Whitney.

How long could a fight with a talking tooth really last, anyway? Why didn't her dad hire more responsible counselors?

"I'm ready," Greg said, beckoning to her from across the circle.

"Dream on," she said, giving him the finger.

"Playing hard to get. I like it." He leaned forward, and Jo saw beads of sweat clinging to the sparse hairs on his upper lip. *This cannot be my first kiss,* she thought.

"NO!" At first Jo thought she was having an out-of-body experience brought on by stress, but then she realized that it was Maddie who had screamed, not her.

"She *said* she's not playing, jerkface, so leave her alone." Maddie stood, moving in front of Jo, and put her hands on her hips. She was so tiny compared to Greg that it was like watching David face off with Goliath. Greg sat back on his heels and rolled his eyes.

"Fine, Freckles. It's not like I would do anything anyway, since her dad runs camp." He whispered something to the friends sitting next to him and they laughed.

"Didn't you recently almost get expelled?" Emma piped up from behind them. "I bet instigating a kissing game with a bunch of young girls wouldn't help your case."

"We could have you out of here faster than you can say Clearasil," Skylar snapped. Jo reached into the sand and grabbed the Coke bottle, flinging it into the nearby trees.

"Game over," she said. She stalked off through the woods, trying to breathe deeply; the air in Onan always calmed her down, not like the frigid air conditioning at her mom's house, scented liberally with seasonal Glade PlugIns, or the thin, stuffy air at school, which always made her feel like she had to take a nap. She took a few gulps and felt a little better, but when she stopped to wait for the others, in the clearing by the old toolshed, Jo realized she was shaking. She was usually so good at standing up for herself, but she'd frozen for a minute back there.

"I'm sorry," Maddie said, ducking into the clearing with Skylar and Emma trailing behind her. "I shouldn't have tried to fight your battle. I know you are more than capable. Actually, I'm kind of surprised you didn't hit him."

"Don't worry about it," Jo said. "I needed the backup."

"*I* should have stopped it before it got that far," Skylar said. "I forgot that you'd never . . ."

"It's embarrassing," Jo mumbled at the ground.

"I've never, either!" Emma said. "That could have been me. Except no boys even *want* to kiss me, so at least you have that."

"Yeah, if I change my mind I know those flaky, sweaty lips are waiting for me," Jo joked, almost gagging at the thought. She couldn't really imagine kissing *anyone* yet, but Greg was especially disgusting.

"Well, none of you should be embarrassed," Skylar said. "My first kiss was during spin the bottle and it was awful. The guy shoved his tongue down my throat like . . . like an octopus tentacle!" The girls shrieked. "It wasn't the way I wanted it to be at all," Skylar said, wrinkling her nose at the memory.

"Mine, either," Maddie said. "It was on the railroad tracks

behind a trailer park! So romantic!"

"A *trailer park*?" Skylar asked incredulously. "Did you know someone who lived there?" Maddie shrugged.

"Boys are always ruining things," Emma said. "We could have been collecting rocks or climbing trees or something, instead of worrying about them putting their tongues in our mouths."

Jo nodded gravely. "I shouldn't have let it happen," she said. "They took advantage of my authority."

"Jo, no offense, but—you're *twelve*," Maddie said, hugging her.

"Well, we have to be able to do something," Jo said. "Let's make a deal. We still have three weeks left, and the boys aren't going to stop being annoying."

"They can't," Maddie sighed. "It's in their DNA."

"So let's make this summer about us doing what *we* want to do. No boys pushing us around, tricking us, or ruining our fun. And no kissing."

"Hey!" Skylar cried.

"How about . . . unless it's someone special that we really like?" Emma suggested.

"Fine," Jo said. She knew that made her safe. None of the boys at Camp Nedoba seemed special to her. She hoped they never would.

Emma

Reunion: Day 2

RUNNING THROUGH THE WOODS BACK TO THE cabin with tears streaming down her face was becoming a theme in her relationship with Adam, Emma realized. Only last time she was in this state she was dying to turn around and go back to him, and this time she couldn't get far enough away.

He'd barely said good-bye. He'd offered a hand to lift her out of the boat once they'd reached the mainland, but then he'd just hugged her and kissed her forehead. Her *forehead.* He might as well have given her a noogie.

"Come find me later," she'd said, meeting his eyes for the first time since they'd left the island. *I dare you to not to be a coward,* she thought. *I dare you to come find me tonight and prove to me that I didn't just make a huge mistake.*

"Yeah," he'd said, "definitely." And right then she'd realized precisely why people tried not to hook up with their friends. Coming from any other guy, she would have believed it. But she knew Adam. She knew that the scar on his shin was from crashing his bike when he was seven. She knew that he picked all the melon out of his fruit salad. And she knew from his tone that he was feeding her a line. Like she was anyone. Or, more accurately, like she was no one.

Emma had forced herself to turn and walk away at a normal pace. It was only once she was sure he couldn't see her through the trees that she'd started to run.

She burst through the door of Souhegan prepared to sob while her friends held her and then listened to her perform an exhaustive recap of her entire day, followed (hopefully) by the consumption of something full of trans fats. But the scene she found threw her for a loop.

There they were, the three of them, sitting and laughing in sweatpants and tank tops, flipping through magazines just like she hoped they would be. The setting was right, even down to the props: an open bag of Cheetos, teardrop-shaped bottles of candy-colored nail polishes, someone's iPod cranked up to full volume so that it was audible through the headphones, Katy Perry's vibrato reduced to a thin warble that sounded like the Dormouse from *Alice in Wonderland*, babbling inside his teapot to a techno beat. Everything was what she expected—except for the people.

Aileen, Jess, and Kerry looked up as she came in, their mouths dropping open.

"What happened to *you*?" Kerry asked, her eyes drifting down to Emma's muddy shorts and scratched legs.

"Just a bad canoe trip," Emma said. She braced herself on the edge of a bunk bed and tried to catch her breath. "Where is everybody?"

"At dinner, I think?" Aileen said, opening one of the nail polishes and turning her concentration back to her toes.

"Skylar and Maddie were here when we got back," Kerry said. "I think mini-Ma . . . Jo went on a date."

"A date?" Emma said. "Are you sure?"

"Pretty sure," Kerry said. She leaned in conspiratorially. "Reunion makes everyone desperate."

"Seriously," Jess groaned. "Sunny needs to move on."

Aileen looked up from her nail-painting and frowned at Jess. "Stop saying that," she scolded. "We need to let her make her own decisions."

"But Mark is such a d-bag," Jess cried, pulling her tight curls up into a bun. "I literally cannot listen to one more monologue about how he was the one that got away."

"I'm just saying, we're not gonna change her mind," Aileen said.

"Sorry," Kerry said, rolling her eyes and smiling up at Emma. "We're just having a little bit of drama this weekend."

"Believe me," Emma said, kicking her muddy flip-flops out into the grass, "I understand."

She took a long shower in the vast, white-tiled room, grateful for the late-night solitude and for the din of the steamy streams that ricocheted off the seafoam green floor. It was calming white noise, and she needed to be calmed. She didn't know what to think about

Adam. They'd gone from such a high high to such a noncommittal middle that she started to think she might have done something wrong, something to make him change his mind. Maybe if she had agreed to stay overnight with him . . . maybe if she had waited that morning and gone over in a boat with him . . . maybe if she had just been more confident the night before, on the sandbar, or at the bonfire, or at dinner . . . maybe if she had never left camp . . . maybe if she had kissed him the last night of their last year . . . maybe if . . . maybe.

But she knew playing that game never went anywhere. It was simple logic, the kind of stuff she'd learned in elementary school: an exclusive disjunction. *If* she had done things differently, *then* things would be different. But she hadn't. And neither had Adam. They had done things, and those things had consequences, and now she had to face them. And no amount of self-flagellation under a terrible low-flow showerhead was going to change that.

When she got back to the cabin, her skin scrubbed raw and pink, and her hair wrapped turban-style in a thin towel, Emma found Jo, Maddie, and Skylar in their beds, sleeping, reading, and listening to an iPod, respectively. The other girls had moved their slumber party back over to their side, but Sunny was still nowhere to be found, and Emma found herself hoping that she was off somewhere with Mark Slotkin, locked in a passionate embrace—one that would not end with a big blow off in a tiny boat.

"Hey," she whispered, poking Skylar's arm. Skylar rolled over and pulled out her earbuds. Her eyes still looked red and tired.

"Where have you been?" she asked. "You keep leaving."

"I know," Emma said. "It's a long story."

Skylar propped herself up on her elbows. "I'm really sorry about last night."

"It's okay," Emma sighed. "Let's talk tomorrow. I'm exhausted."

"Okay . . ." Skylar was looking at her funny, like she was trying to read her face, but eventually put her earpiece back in and closed her eyes. Emma could hear strains of what sounded like the Pixies.

She sat on her bunk and dried her hair, keeping one eye on the door. Adam might come by—after all, he'd said he would. Maybe she wasn't giving him enough credit. With this in mind, Emma put on a pink tank top with no bra and a pair of black silky pajama shorts.

"You look nice," Maddie yawned, leaning over her bunk. "Got a hot date later?"

"I don't think so," Emma laughed. "Hey," she said, lowering her voice. "They said Jo went on a date? Is that true?"

Maddie shook her head and grimaced. "Don't ask," she whispered. "She's been in a bad mood ever since she got back."

"Don't talk about me like I'm not here," Jo grumbled with her face in her pillow.

See? Maddie mouthed, and turned back to her book.

Emma climbed into bed and stared up at the initials she'd scribbled onto the underside of the bunk. *E + S = BFF*. She wished it still felt true. She had never needed her friends more, but even though they were so close she could touch them, they'd never felt farther away.

Emma

Reunion: Day 3

EMMA WOKE WITH A START. SHE'D BEEN DREAMING about being out on the lake again with Adam, in the canoe. Only this time, they were in the middle of a thunderstorm and the lightning was hitting the water all around them. Emma was terrified and kept crying out for Adam to hold her, but he just kept rowing and rowing without turning around. A huge clap of imaginary thunder had woken her up, and for a few confused seconds she thought the storm must be real, especially when she heard tapping on the outside of the cabin, like heavy raindrops. But through the window right next to her bed she could see early moonlight on the grass outside, and it was dry. Emma sat up. Maybe Adam had finally come to apologize.

"Do you hear that?" Jo whispered. She was peering through the slats of the adjoining bunk. Emma nodded, just as a paper airplane flew into the cabin and landed on Jo's lap. If it really was Adam, he had terrible aim.

"What the—" Jo jumped out of bed in her sports bra and shorts and was headed for the door when half a dozen other paper planes came whizzing in, hitting her in the legs and chest.

"*Now*!" cried a male voice. Fists beat against the cabin walls from the outside. Across the cabin, Sunny screamed. Emma was freaked out, but she was also pretty sure that serial killers didn't usually take the time to fold origami before making their attack.

"Incoming!" Jo yelled, diving down into Emma's bed. Maddie sat up in her top bunk and banged her head on a ceiling beam. Across the cabin, Sunny screamed as a silhouette appeared in the doorway. Emma thought for a second that it *might* be Adam—was this some kind of grand gesture? Because if so it was really weird so far—but as the figure stepped into the cabin she saw it was Matt Slotkin, wearing a tank top and pajama bottoms, and holding Jo's megaphone.

"On your feet, ladies," he shouted through the loudspeaker. Emma heard movement above her; Skylar was finally stirring. Three more boys clambered into the cabin, shining flashlights into the girls' faces. Once her eyes adjusted to the glare, Emma could make out Mark, Bowen, and Zeke.

"Did I stutter?" Matt yelled. "On your feet. *Now*!"

"What the hell do you think you're doing?" Jo demanded, standing up and shielding her eyes. "Is this some weird wake-up call?" She looked at her watch. "It's not even five."

"Silence!" Bowen yelled, and Jo flipped him off.

"We're just paying you a visit to make sure you're in shape for the big game today," Mark said, circling the cabin and banging on the bunks of the girls who hadn't gotten out of bed yet. Emma saw Sunny shoot him a withering look. She stood up and crossed her arms over her chest, wishing she had kept her bra on. Adam was nowhere to be seen, but she was sure he had known about this—and maybe even helped plan it. It felt even more humiliating than being stood up.

"What are you talking about?" Skylar yawned, climbing down the ladder with a sheet wrapped around her.

"They're making sure we're tired, is what they're doing," Jo said angrily.

"That's it, Putnam, drop and give me twenty," Zeke yelled, pointing at the floor. "And you!" he waved his flashlight at Maddie. "Start doing jumping jacks." This was not the sensitive art wunderkind Emma remembered, who used to make glazed vases by the dozen.

"Oh, shut *up*," Skylar groaned. "What are you even doing here? Why are you even friends with them?"

"You guys can't make us do anything," Jo added. "We outnumber you!" She sneered at the boys, who had momentarily stopped their attack to pretend they were fighting each other with light sabers.

"Don't worry, there's no way I'm jumping up and down with no bra on, regardless," Maddie said.

"Well," Zeke said, turning to the twins and shrugging, "if they won't do the boot camp I guess we should just go to plan B and take their clothes." Bowen and Mark started grabbing suitcases and heaving them out onto the grass.

"No!" Sunny cried, guarding her bags. "I'll do squats! I need to work on my glutes anyway."

Jo snatched the flashlight out of Matt's hand and shined it back in his face. "You think taking our clothes is going to keep us from beating you today?" she asked, narrowing her eyes. "It's just going to make us beat you worse."

"You can beat me naked anytime, sweetheart," he taunted. Jo punched his arm, hard, and he cried out in pain.

Emma watched the boys ransack the cabin. She didn't really care if they took their suitcases; probably they'd just stack them in a pile on the basketball court or something obnoxious like that. What she did care about was why Adam wasn't with them. It was pretty clear he was purposefully avoiding her.

"Is Adam with you guys?" she asked Zeke as he grabbed her bag of toiletries from the windowsill. He ignored her.

"Hey," she said, a little louder, "where's Adam?"

"Who cares?" Jo shouted, still focused on her shouting match with Matt. "He's probably sleeping off a hangover—or hooking up with someone random." She shot Skylar a quick look—but not quick enough for Emma not to notice. And she had known Skylar for too long to miss the guilt written all over her face. Emma could still see the boys stomping around, but for all intents and purposes, the cabin went silent. Blood rushed to her head along with a wave of white noise.

"Why did you just look at *her*?" Emma heard herself ask, in a much louder voice than she intended.

"What?" Skylar and Jo asked simultaneously.

"Ohhhhhh, snap," Matt said gleefully, covering his mouth with one hand.

"I thought you said you were going to tell her," Jo sputtered.

Skylar looked at Emma nervously. "I don't know what you're talking about," she said to Jo.

"No one looked at anyone," Maddie said. "Let's just all calm down, get these jerks off our property, and go back to sleep."

"No," Emma said sharply, staring at Skylar, who fidgeted under her sheet. "Why would she look at you, Sky? Tell me *what*? Why would you know anything about Adam hooking up with anyone?" Jo wasn't the kind of person who misspoke. For her to connect Adam and Skylar in that way at four in the morning, there had to be a reason. And if there was one . . . Emma couldn't finish the thought. Nothing had happened. They wouldn't do that to her.

"Can we please not talk about this with them here?" Skylar begged. Bowen shined his flashlight in her face and she winced.

"Wait, you're not denying it?" Emma heard her voice rising even more; she could barely control it. "You hooked up with him?" Skylar looked down at the floor. "LOOK AT ME!" Emma screamed, and reached out to yank Skylar's sheet.

"Em, please," Skylar whispered. "I'm in my underwear."

"You didn't care about being in your underwear last night in the lake!"

"Does anyone have any popcorn? This is better than *Girls Gone Wild*!" Matt laughed, and Jo lunged at him again.

Emma's mind raced through the past three years, through all the e-mails and texts Skylar had sent from camp, complaining of her boredom and recounting funny stories of her escapades with the other counselors, barely mentioning Adam. Whenever Emma would try to subtly work him into correspondence, Skylar would just say that Adam was Adam. The same. Annoying, yet lovable. And Adam, G-chatting her late at night, referring vaguely to his girl problems, had never once indicated that the girl in question might be the friend Emma had trusted most in the world.

"Get out!" Emma screamed. She wasn't sure who exactly she was talking to, but as far as she was concerned, they all could leave.

"Calm down," Zeke said. "Everyone knows Skylar gets around. Is this really news?"

Skylar looked like she'd been slapped. Even though Emma didn't want to speak to her—maybe ever again—she also wanted to dropkick Zeke in the balls and send him flying into another state. Luckily, Jo was on top of that. She shoved him, hard, and the boys finally got the message. They filed out noisily, and Sunny and her friends followed, sneaking peeks at Emma as they left, like they were slowing down on the highway to rubberneck at a car crash.

"Just say it," Emma said, looking Skylar in the eyes. "I want to hear it from you."

"Yes," Skylar said softly. "We hooked up. But it's over. And I never meant—"

"*When* was it over?"

Skylar sat down on Jo's bed. "Thursday night."

Emma let out an involuntary sound that fell somewhere between a laugh and a sob. "Great," she said. "This is very educational. And when did it start?"

"Emma, please," Skylar whispered. "I didn't mean for it to happen."

"When. Did. It. Start?" Emma said, slowly and patiently, like she was speaking to a mentally disabled person. She wanted the words to hurt.

"The last night of camp," Skylar said quietly.

"What, last summer?"

Skylar paused, and just like that, Emma knew.

"No. The year you left."

Emma had only ever fainted once—after staying up all night to finish a final paper on feminist symbolism in *Moby Dick*—and she remembered feeling at first like she was being drawn back in space, seeing her computer screen through a pinhole that swiftly got smaller and smaller against an ocean of black. The same effect was happening now. Skylar, Maddie, and Jo suddenly seemed far away. Emma flashed back to the moment she'd turned away from Adam on the rock. She'd spent that night crying into her pillow while Jo and Maddie tried to cheer her up with junk food and card games, but the person she'd needed had been Skylar. She'd been so worried when she didn't come back to the cabin. Knowing now where she'd been that night changed everything. It rewrote history. Emma could barely wrap her brain around it.

"How could you do that to me?" Emma yelled. "That night, out on the shore, you told me to go for it. You knew how much I liked him. You *knew*." Skylar kept her eyes down. "And then . . . you just took him? That same night? You could have had *anyone*. What is *wrong* with you?"

"I know," Skylar said softly.

"And then you tell *her* first?" Emma asked, pointing at Jo.

"I only found out today," Jo said, walking over to the window on the far side of the cabin. Skylar and Maddie still stood frozen in their places, like onlookers in one of those naked hallway dreams that still tormented Emma the night before each new school year.

"Still, you could have said something. You could have warned me!" Emma knew she was lashing out, but she didn't care. It felt like Jo and Skylar had conspired behind her back to keep the secret, which was almost worse than Skylar and Adam.

"I know you're upset, but this isn't about me," Jo said.

"No, it's about a friend who does the most hurtful thing one girl can do to another girl," Maddie said, turning on Skylar. "I can't believe you just sat there while I talked about Charlie and Christina, and you didn't even flinch!"

"We're talking about Adam," Emma said testily, "not Charlie."

"I'm sticking up for you!" Maddie cried.

"She's right, let's just focus on one love triangle at a time," Jo muttered.

"Sorry I'm so annoying." Maddie stalked off to stand by herself near Aileen and Kerry's bunk.

"Don't be a drama queen," Jo groaned. "We all listened to you yesterday, and it's time to listen to Emma right now."

"Don't talk to me like I'm one of your campers," Maddie said.

"Then don't act like one!"

"Stop it!" Emma shouted. "This isn't about either of you. This is between me and Skylar. You guys should just leave."

"So we have to watch the entire I'm-In-Love-With-Adam series for five years but we get booted from the live finale?" Maddie snapped. "That's fair."

"I want them here," Skylar spoke up. "At least Jo." Emma ignored her and turned to Maddie.

"I didn't say I was in *love* with him," Emma cried. "And why are you being such a bitch all of a sudden?"

"I've been exactly where you are," Maddie said. "Exactly. But you don't care. It's only a big deal when it happens to you."

"Excuse me for being more involved in my own life than yours," Emma sighed. "It's called subjectivity. Plus, we only found out about Charlie yesterday!"

"Jo knew."

"Well, apparently Jo knows everything!" Emma said, putting her hands on her hips.

"Are you kidding?" Jo cried. "No one tells me anything, and when they do it's only because they don't have anyone else to talk to. Skylar only latched on to me because you didn't make it as a CIT."

"Latched on?" Skylar repeated angrily. Then, to Emma: "You applied? You told me you decided it wouldn't look good on your resume."

Jo shot Emma a nasty look. Over the course of the last few

minutes, they'd all shifted position so that each girl occupied one corner of the cabin, like a human map of continental drift.

"Do not talk to me," Emma snapped.

"You can't just shut me out," Skylar said.

Emma wished she could literally turn her back, but the top bunk frame directly lined up with her chin. So instead she sat on her bed and looked out the door, away from Skylar. Sunny and Co. were lined up on the grass a few feet away, listening intently. Everyone on the girls' side could probably hear them.

"Did you sleep with him?" Skylar asked.

"Wow, that's really none of your business," Emma said. She instantly wished she had just said nothing. She wanted Skylar to think she had done it.

"Please tell me you didn't," Jo said.

"We can't *all* be celibate," Maddie sneered. "Who cares if she did? Good for her. Don't be so repressed."

"I am not repressed!" Jo cried.

"Please, you live in a fantasy world. Everything's about your precious camp; you don't give a shit what's going on outside of it. You're like Peter Pan—you even have the haircut! No wonder you're a virgin!"

Jo gasped. "Take that back!"

"No," Maddie said. "It's true."

"Nothing you say is true and you know it," Jo said.

"What?"

"I can't believe anything you say. You're my best friend and I don't even know who you are."

"You're *insane*."

"What is she talking about?" Skylar asked Maddie.

"Don't talk to me, either," Maddie said. "This whole weekend you've been acting like everything was normal! This," she gestured to the entire room, "is *your* fault."

"You can't just blame her," Jo said. "What about Adam?"

"Adam wasn't part of the pact," Maddie snapped.

They all got quiet. Emma looked down at the watermelon backpack, which had been kicked halfway under the bed in the fray.

"Best friends don't keep secrets," she said. "Best friends treat each other with respect." She looked up at Skylar. "Best friends never talk behind each other's backs." She got up and reached for the framed photo, which was sitting on the windowsill between their bunks. "So much for friendship."

"I said I was sorry," Skylar said.

"Actually, you didn't," Emma snapped.

"I'm sorry, Emma," Skylar said, wiping tears away with the corner of her sheet. "You have to believe me. I'm so, so sorry."

"That's not good enough!" Emma yelled. "Tell me why. Did you just want to hurt me?" Her voice was getting hoarse. "Did you just not care? Are you really so insecure that if one guy breaks up with you, you have to steal someone else's?"

"You didn't want him!" Skylar cried. "All you did was talk about him for years and then you didn't even want him."

"You don't know what I wanted!"

"It doesn't matter now," Skylar said. "No matter what I say happened, you're not going to forgive me."

"Why should I?" Emma said, her eyes flashing. "You lied to me! You lied to me for *three* years!"

"Try eight," Jo said, glancing at Maddie.

"Do you have something to say to me, *Johannah*?" Maddie asked.

"Never mind," Jo mumbled.

"No, please, I'm all ears."

"I know, okay?" Jo sighed. "I know you lie about your family."

Maddie's face went white. "Did he tell you?" she asked quietly.

"No," Jo said. "I found the letter. And some other stuff, in your file." She shifted uncomfortably.

"And you decided not to say anything?"

"What was I supposed to say?" Jo said. "Sorry you're poor? Sorry your mom's in jail?"

"It's not jail!" Maddie cried through tears that were pooling on her bottom lashes, threatening to spill down her cheeks. "It's court-ordered rehab! And you have no right to talk about her! You don't know her!"

"Maybe I would if you gave me a chance!"

"Wait, I thought your mom was a consultant," Emma said, confused.

"Her dad's not a doctor, either," Jo said.

"What is going on?" Skylar asked helplessly.

"You are so entitled," Maddie spat at Jo. "You have no idea what it's like not to have everything handed to you."

"You don't even pay to come here!" Jo cried. "My dad basically has you on welfare."

Skylar turned to Jo. "Are you listening to yourself? That's your friend!"

"You have some convenient double standards," Emma spat.

"I would have been there for you," Jo yelled at Maddie, "if you'd let me."

"Oh, really?" Maddie said. "'Cause it sounds like you just pity me. Which is pretty ironic coming from someone who still acts like she's twelve."

"I do not."

"Oh, please," Maddie groaned. "Yes, you do. You know, everyone makes fun of you. *Everyone.*"

"Yeah, I do know," Jo said. "I also know that if I wasn't my dad's daughter, you guys wouldn't be able to do half the things you do. I pull so many strings for you, you have no idea." She turned to Skylar. "Why do you think you never got busted for drinking? Why do you think no one called the police when Emma and Adam didn't come back from the island? I do so much and nobody ever thanks me."

Emma had been so busy trying to follow the verbal volley, she'd almost forgotten what had happened with Adam before she found out about him and Skylar. Fresh pain flooded her chest and forced its way up her throat and out her mouth, like a water main bursting.

"Thank you," she shouted bitterly. "In fact, thank you all for being such good friends." She turned to Skylar. "And thank you especially, Sky, for taking Adam for the team. I'm so glad you had my best interests at heart."

"Look," Skylar said, "I know you like to feel like the victim, but it's not like you were always such a great friend to me. Ever since we were twelve it's been all about Adam. I was just your consolation prize whenever he didn't have time for you."

Emma gasped. "That is not true! Just because I talked about him sometimes . . ." She held up the photo and shook it at Skylar. "You were my best friend."

"It wasn't just sometimes," Jo said quietly. "It was all the time."

"Stay out of it," Maddie snapped. "You don't understand anything about what it means to like someone that much."

"I was a good friend!" Skylar said. "You wouldn't even have tried to go for Adam if I hadn't helped you."

"So you're saying I owed you?" Emma screamed. "I owed you *him*?"

"Oh my God, get over yourself! I didn't do it to punish you!" Skylar yelled. "Some things aren't about you!"

Emma froze. If it wasn't about her—if it wasn't some effort on either of their parts to feel closer to her—then it was just about Adam and Skylar falling for each other. And that was even worse. "Well, it wasn't just a coincidence," she said stonily. "You *chose* him. On purpose."

"Maybe he chose me!" Skylar said indignantly. Emma couldn't control herself any longer. In a burst of anger she hurled the photo at the far wall of the cabin, where it smashed and shattered, raining glass onto the floor.

"Whoa," Jo said, holding up her hands. "Calm down. I think we all need a time-out."

"It's too late for time-out," Maddie said.

"I have to get out of here," Skylar said, grabbing a dress off the floor and pulling it over her head. She ran for the door in her bare feet.

"Are you going to find Adam?" Emma called after her. "Tell him I say 'screw you.' But not you literally. Because he's already done that." Skylar paused in the doorway and looked back, her eyes filled with hurt. Emma felt a mixture of satisfaction and self-loathing. What had happened to her? What had happened to all of them?

She sat back down on her bed and surveyed the damage, noticing for the first time since the raid started that the floor was littered with paper airplanes, like the wreckage from some horrible accident. Jo crouched down and started to clean up wordlessly, but Emma couldn't do anything but lie down and close her eyes. She was too exhausted to pick up the pieces.

When she finally fell asleep again, just as the sun rose over the pines, she dreamed again about the storm on the lake, with the lightning touching down all around her in the black water. But this time, she was in the boat alone.

Jo

Reunion: Day 3

CAPTURE THE FLAG DAY HAD ALWAYS BEEN, historically, Jo's favorite day at camp, and for reunion she had been excited to really do it up. If the reunion was the Super Bowl, capture the flag was its halftime show. She'd bought a tin of eye black, like football players used to cut down on glare, and had been planning to put it on before sunup, "kidnap" the girls, and lead them in an authentic army training boot camp workout that doubled as an inspirational pep talk, like the one near the end of her dad's favorite movie, *Hoosiers*. But when she'd opened her eyes and looked blearily at her watch, it had already been almost nine. And then the early morning's terrible fight had come flooding back. And for the first time in her life, Jo had found herself wishing that capture the flag didn't even exist.

Emma, Skylar, and Maddie were all still sleeping, their peaceful faces belying the heartache of just a few hours ago, when Jo, dressed in a black T-shirt and jean shorts, had crept out of the cabin, slipping into her Converse sneakers on the grass outside to avoid waking anybody up. She wasn't ready to face any of them yet—least of all Maddie.

Jo jogged down the path back to the center of camp, not sure exactly where she was going. Overnight, it felt like Nedoba—her home, her playground, her sanctuary—had transformed into a minefield. She knew that her friends (or maybe former friends, she thought with a stab of remorse) were back in their beds, but Nate could be anywhere, and the thought of running into him after their awkward kiss and his misunderstanding and her hot-headed tirade made her want to hide in the barn loft until reunion was over.

It wasn't the first time she'd been asked point-blank if she was gay. Jo was used to it. The people who asked were usually either antagonistic kids at school, actual lesbians, or her own mother, who put feelers out about once every six months ("Are there any boys . . . or other people . . . you're interested in these days?"). But no guy Jo liked had ever asked. Certainly no guy who liked her back. It was just awkward all around. To be able to face him, she decided, she would need a very large coffee.

She was walking across the Green to the cafeteria when she tripped over someone lying in the grass.

"I'm so sorry," she said, stepping back.

"Huh?" The person rolled over. It was Adam. He was still in his clothes from the day before and bleary-eyed. He squinted at her for a second and then yawned. "Oh, hey," he said casually.

"Oh, *hey*," she said, her voice dripping with sarcasm. But it failed to penetrate the bubble of oblivion Adam tended to float in. He rubbed his eyes and smiled sleepily. "Where were you last night?" Jo asked.

"Just hanging out," he said.

"Didn't feel like joining the party?"

"What party?"

"The one in our bunk. At four in the morning. When your idiot friends raided our cabin." She gestured to the pool, where an overalls-clad Gus was grumpily fishing underpants and lip gloss tubes out of the water with a net.

"They went through with that? Sorry," Adam said, sitting up and stretching. "I thought it was a joke."

"You think everything is a joke, don't you?" Jo said, resisting the urge to stomp on his hand or deliver a swift kick to the kidneys that would sideline him for days.

"What's going on over here?" A blond girl Jo recognized from the year ahead of theirs walked over holding a paper cup of coffee in each hand. She had a sunburn across her nose and thin, straw-colored eyelashes. She sat next to Adam and handed him one of the coffees. "Tired of me already?"

Jo was dumbfounded—after Skylar on Thursday night and Emma on Friday, Adam had then moved on to yet *another* girl. He either had sexual ADD or some kind of moral malfunction.

"We're just old friends," Jo said through her teeth. She stepped over Adam's legs and walked a few feet before turning around. "By the way, *Emma* was looking for you last night," she said. "And she knows everything. You'll never get another chance. Enjoy your day!"

Adam's eyes widened, and Jo flashed him a smug smile. She wouldn't even need sugar in her coffee, that coup de grâce had been so sweet.

Jo found her father in his office opening boxes of bright green bandanas and checking them off on an inventory sheet. At Camp Nedoba, to avoid injury, everyone played capture the flag with a bandana hanging out of his or her back pocket or waistband, so instead of tackling, players just yanked the bandanas out. It was like a pacifist, sportier *Lord of the Flies*.

"Hi, honey!" Mack said, tossing a bandana to Jo. "How's my favorite girl on her favorite day?"

"Okay, I guess," she said, sipping her coffee. The momentary high she'd gotten from seeing Adam process the fact that his long con on Emma had been busted was wearing off quickly. Adam wasn't her real problem.

"Just okay? This is the day you've been waiting for since, what, birth?"

Jo tried to smile, but suddenly it all felt like too much. It was the day she'd been waiting for with bated breath for months, but she'd ruined it before it had even started.

"I really messed up, Dad," she said.

"I doubt that," Mack said. He put down his checklist and sat down in his ergonomic desk chair.

"I let you down," she said. "I let people drink beer the other night, by the lake."

"I see," he said, frowning. "Did you buy it?"

"No," she said.

"Did you drink it?"

"Some." She couldn't even look at him.

"A lot?" he asked. Jo remembered the orientation video she'd watched her first year on staff, which had not so subtly reminded them that drinking on camp grounds could prove fatal in a number of terrible scenarios.

"No!"

"Okay, good. Did anyone get hurt?"

"Not physically," she sighed.

His mustache twitched. "What do you mean?"

"We had a fight," Jo said. "A *bad* fight." She felt her throat closing up and tried to breathe. She sank down to the floor, and Mack crouched next to her.

"You and the girls?"

Jo nodded miserably. He studied her face for a moment and then drew her into a hug. She pressed her face into his shirt so hard that when she pulled away she left tear stains—two perfect almonds, like the eye holes he used to cut out of black pillow cases so that they could play ninja when she was home sick from school.

"Sweetie," he said, "everyone fights. I'm sure it will blow over. These things always do."

Jo shook her head. "Not this time," she said. "Emma and Skylar were screaming at each other. And I really hurt Maddie. I said awful things. I called her a liar."

"What did she lie about?" Mack asked, getting up and turning back to the stack of bandanas. Jo wasn't sure if he was playing dumb or just not listening.

"Dad," she said with a heavy sigh, "I *know*. About your . . . arrangement."

"Oh." Mack looked concerned, but not surprised. He sat back in his desk chair and got the stern look he always got when he was thinking about how to phrase something.

"Why didn't you tell me?" Jo asked.

"It wasn't my secret to tell." Mack sighed. "You shouldn't be so hard on her—or yourself," he said finally. "Sometimes we do things we're not proud of, especially when we're scared. Do you remember when I bought the camp?"

Jo nodded. "When mom left." But then his words sunk in. "Wait, you're not proud of that?!" Jo had already had too many shocks for one weekend. If her dad renounced the camp she loved, she would spontaneously combust.

"No, I *am* proud of what I've done building this camp," he said. "But I'm not proud of how unwilling I was to face the reality of my life at the time. This was such a special place to me—it was where your mom and I came on our honeymoon, and where we brought you every summer after you were born. When I moved here it was because I wanted to live in those memories. I didn't want to move forward, I just wanted to go back."

"I wanted to go back, too." Jo remembered the first days she spent in Onan without her mom, when everyone from the general store clerk to the gas station attendant had asked where she was. "She had to work this summer," Jo would tell them brightly, when her dad was out of sight in the cereal aisle or busy filling up the tank. She'd been, Jo realized with alarm, no better than Maddie.

"I know you did, honey," Mack said. "And that's why I wanted you here every summer. But now I wonder if I did you a disservice."

Jo felt her face crumple. "Do you think there's something wrong with me?" Maybe Maddie was right—maybe she was repressed. Not a late bloomer but an unwilling one.

"No," he said. "You're my daughter, and I'll always think you're perfect."

"Other people think I'm weird."

"Why?!" He was honestly dumbfounded, and Jo was reminded of how many times he'd told her she was beautiful during her adolescence, when all she felt was awkward and plain.

"Because I live here," she sputtered. "Because I dress like you and not like mom. Because I'm not . . . normal."

"Who wants to be normal?" he asked. "I don't care if you're normal. I don't think your mother cares if you're normal. I don't think your friends care if you're normal. I think they love you because you're you."

Jo looked out the window, which perfectly framed the top of the barn rising out of the hill past the cafeteria. Her dad was right. That was exactly how she felt about her friends, too. She could have said that to Maddie, instead of letting her stubborn anger get the best of her. Jo closed her eyes and tried to breathe through the swell of shame she felt.

"I think," Mack said, helping her up from the floor and kissing her on the cheek, "that what you need is to go and make things right with your friends." He looked at the clock above his desk. "Because you've only got two hours before the game starts."

Jo shook her head furiously. "I can't play, Dad," she said. "I can't focus. We'll never win; we're not even *speaking*." Tears filled her eyes again, and she wiped them away with her arm.

"Hey, hey, no tears!" Mack said, grabbing her shoulders and looking at her with a warm, crinkly smile. "Nobody said you had to win. But you can't quit. My daughter, my delightfully abnormal daughter, doesn't quit. I know capture the flag is fun, but it's more than a game. It's about building teamwork and bringing people together. Which sounds like what you girls might need right now."

Jo nodded. He was right. They needed something that would force them to work toward a common goal. They needed to be there for each other, the way they'd promised they always would be. They had to play. She just wasn't sure how she would convince them.

Emma

Reunion: Day 3

EMMA STOOD AT THE BELGIAN WAFFLE STATION sipping her Styrofoam cup of weak coffee and hating pretty much everyone. She had been doing okay, all things considered, when she'd left the cabin, having successfully avoided making eye contact with either Maddie or Skylar, but as consciousness washed over her in the harsh morning sunlight, a new wave of nauseating rage came rolling in. She still felt hurt and horribly betrayed, but it felt better—more productive—to focus on the anger now, and the rising steam from the waffle iron just helped to set the mood.

She was angry at Adam for being such a generally sucky and selfish person and terrible non-boyfriend-slash-ex-friend. She was angry at Skylar for being so thoughtless and dishonest. She was angry at Jo for telling her what she sort of suspected but didn't want to know and she was angry (even though she knew it was irrational) at Maddie for having a personal crisis that stole focus from her own. She was also angry at the waffle maker for taking so long and for dripping the batter out onto the tablecloth even though Emma had poured in exactly the right amount using the provided measuring cup and at the coffee for being so thoroughly crappy and unsatisfying. Mostly, though, she was angry that she didn't have anyone to take her anger out on. So when Adam finally showed up, it was almost a relief.

He was alone and freshly showered, and seeing his wet hair combed back reminded Emma of the previous day's water sports. Now, his little speech about how Skylar had grown so attached to him and was projecting her longing for closeness with Emma onto him struck her as possibly the most supremely douchey thing anyone had ever said. How had he been able to feed her those lines with a straight face?

If Adam saw Emma seething quietly by the waffle station, he didn't react. Instead, he just waved to someone across the cafeteria, plucked a cup from the stack near the coffee urn, and started fiddling with the knobs.

Finally, the waffle iron beeped and Emma turned the handle to release the asymmetrical but delicious-smelling contents. She doused it liberally in maple syrup and even added a fat curlicue of whipped cream. Having a healthy sense of irony, she was overjoyed that the kitchen workers had set out a bowl of maraschino cherries. She set one on top of the waffle with a satisfying feeling of schadenfreude. And then, as she balanced her plate in one hand and crossed the room to where Adam was standing, Emma saw Skylar and Maddie waiting in line at the buffet table separately, but both staring at Adam, too.

Things were about to get interesting.

"Hi," she said, startling Adam as he continued to fail at pouring himself a cup of coffee. Adam startled and flipped on the switch, sending hot decaf splattering onto his flip-flop clad feet. He cursed and jumped back. People looked over. Emma saw Maddie smirk.

"Hey," he said, avoiding her eyes and wiping at his legs with a napkin. "Um, good morning."

"Actually, it's not such a good morning for me," she said, stretching her lips into a thin smile. Adam finally managed to get his cup under the spigot and fill it. "Aren't you going to ask me why?" she said.

"I, uh, I ran into Jo." he muttered.

"Oh, good," Emma said loudly. "So you're caught up. So you already know that last night a bunch of your friends came into our bunk, yelled at us, took our clothes, and stacked them on the diving board. Right?" He looked down at his coffee. "And that after that was over, I found out that you've been hooking up with my best friend for the past three years, ever since the night I refused to kiss you."

"Emma," he said, keeping his voice so low it was barely audible. "I know you're upset. And believe me, I want to explain. I know I owe that to you, but can we not do this right here?"

"Where would you like to do it?" she asked.

"Um . . . outside?"

"Great idea," she said. "Follow me." She walked past Adam, shoving her waffle into his chest with as much force as she could muster from such close range. The only flaw in the execution was that she didn't get to see his face right after it happened. But the people in the buffet line did.

As she pushed through the double doors, she heard Maddie start to slow clap.

"I guess today is a two-shower day," Adam said as he emerged behind her, his shirt wet and still streaked with syrup. Emma was waiting on the lawn out front, sitting cross-legged and picking idly at grass.

"I wasn't sure you'd actually come out," she said.

"I didn't really have anywhere to go."

"There's the back exit."

"Come on, I'm not a total coward."

Emma crossed her arms. "Then where were you last night?"

"I'm sorry about that," he said. He kept a distance of about two yards and stayed on his feet—the better, Emma thought wryly, to dodge additional carbohydrate attacks.

"That's not an answer," she said. Adam just squinted into the sun, looking like he'd rather be somewhere—maybe anywhere—else.

"You know, I was fine before I came back here," Emma went on. "I wasn't looking for anything to happen this weekend. But then we hit it off again, and . . . I'm just trying to understand why you would go after me if you didn't actually want me."

"I did want you," he said, without moving.

"But not anymore?"

He looked flustered. "No, I didn't say that."

"You don't say *anything*," she said, standing up, her voice getting strong and angry. "Nothing real, anyway. You want to know why no one 'gets' you, Adam? Because there's nothing to get. You're just as superficial as you pretend you are!"

He looked down at his feet, and Emma felt her anger surge again. Not only had he hurt her and hurt Skylar, but he'd tried to come between them—knowingly. He didn't care about either of them. He only cared about himself.

"Do you even know what you want?" she asked. What she meant, really, was *who* he wanted. But she realized that if she let him choose, like they were two toys on a shelf, she would just be playing into his already massive ego. And she didn't want to give him the satisfaction.

Adam looked at her as if he was formulating actual words that might one day work their way through his lips and out of his mouth when Skylar pushed through the doors of the cafeteria clutching a cup of coffee. She stopped when she saw them, and something that looked like fear flickered across her face.

"You know what?" Emma said. "You don't have to know. You can have each other. I'm done."

She turned and walked back toward the main path, focusing her eyes on the ground in front of her. This time, she was determined not to run.

Emma

The Second Summer • *Age 11*
Last Week of Camp

"Friendship Rule: Best friends don't fight dirty."

"HOLD STILL."

Emma stood behind Skylar, delicately holding a sticky, tangled strand of her long blond hair. She didn't want to hurt her, but she had to pull on it a little to see what she was dealing with. Under the bright lights of the empty shower room, she examined the thick wad of purple gum that had been embedded in the hair three inches from Skylar's scalp.

"Okay," Emma said, holding out a hand like she was a doctor asking for a scalpel. "Give me the peanut butter."

It had happened after lunch, when they were dropping off their trays. Skylar and Emma had been standing in front of Mark and Matt, who were taking turns burping letters of the alphabet. It made the lasagna in Emma's stomach lurch.

"That is so gross," Skylar had said.

"You're gross," Mark had shot back, taking a deep breath and then repeating it in a long belch. "*Groooooooooossssssss.*"

"Yeah, but there's two of you so you're twice as gross," Skylar had laughed. And that's when Matt had planted his gum.

They'd already tried ice (Jo's idea), Vaseline (Maddie's), and olive oil (Skylar's). It looked like someone had cooked an omelet on Skylar's head and then covered it in kindergarten paste. Luckily there were no mirrors around.

"How bad is it?" Skylar asked.

"Pretty bad," Jo said, peering over Emma's shoulder.

"It's not *that* bad," Maddie said. Skylar reached her hand up to feel.

"Don't touch it! You'll just make it worse." Emma looked at the butterscotch-colored snarl and tried to figure out how to start. She only knew about the peanut butter trick because she'd seen her mom take gum out of her brother Kyle's hair once. She decided not to tell Skylar that Kyle had ended up with a crew cut.

"I wasn't sure if I should get chunky or smooth," Jo said. "So I got both. And some Reese's peanut butter cups, just for snacking."

"I think we should go with smooth," Maddie said.

"Definitely," Emma said. Jo unscrewed the lid from the jar and Emma dipped her pointer finger in, coming up with a scoop the size of a quarter.

"Are you sure this will work?" Skylar asked.

"No," Emma said. "But it's our last chance."

"I smell like a compost pile!" she cried. Emma smeared the peanut butter onto the gum and started to knead it with her fingers.

"My mom says boys only tease you if they like you," Maddie said encouragingly.

"That doesn't make me feel better," Skylar moaned.

As she worked, Emma tried not to smile. But Skylar always seemed so cool and confident, seeing her pitch a fit was kind of funny. Emma wondered if that made her a bad friend.

"Okay," she said. "Comb, please."

The gum had gotten stiffer and less sticky, but it didn't budge when Emma dragged the plastic comb through the knot.

"Ow!" Skylar yelled.

"*Sorry*!"

"Maybe you should pull harder," Jo suggested, biting into a Reese's cup.

"No," Skylar said. "Don't do that."

Emma worked for a few more minutes, even letting Maddie have a try, before declaring the experiment a failure.

"I'm sorry," she told Skylar. "I did everything I could."

"So what now?" Skylar sniffled and wiped her nose on her sleeve. "We can't just leave it in there."

"I think," Maddie said gravely, "we're going to have to operate."

Maddie had experience cutting her little sisters' hair back home, so she did the honors while Emma and Jo held Skylar's hands, offered her candy, and assured her that she was going to look fine. Emma wasn't really all that sure—not all girls could pull off short hair, even the pretty ones—but she tried not to show it.

"You're so beautiful," Jo said. "This won't change it."

Skylar squeezed her eyes shut as the scissors snapped shut and the gum fell to the floor in a tangle of golden hair.

"I could give you a mullet if you want to go emo," Maddie said. "Then the back would still be long."

Skylar grimaced. "Now you're just trying to make me look bad." She looked at Emma and squeezed her hand. "Everyone's going to look at me, Em," she said quietly. "They're going to laugh."

"No, they won't."

"The boys will. Especially the twins."

Emma knew that she was right. The boys would never let her live it down and would make fun of her every chance they got. She couldn't let that happen.

"Can I have the scissors?" she asked Maddie.

"You want to try? Be my guest." Maddie handed her the nail scissors—which they'd borrowed under false pretenses from their counselor, Beth—and stepped back.

Emma smiled at Skylar as she brought the scissors up and snipped off a huge chunk of her own hair.

"Emma!" Skylar cried, her hands flying up to her mouth.

"What?" Emma asked innocently. "Is there something on my face?" She handed the scissors back to Maddie. "I guess I'll need a haircut, too," she said.

Maddie grinned. "Mine's a pain in the ass in summer anyway," she said, clipping off a handful of her auburn curls.

"You guys are nuts," Jo laughed, clutching her long black ponytail protectively.

"Come on," Emma said. "All the pro athletes shave their heads. It cuts down on wind resistance." She wasn't sure that was actually true, but it seemed to make Jo happy.

"Okay," she decided. "But just because I don't want to be left out."

By the time they were done, the shower looked like a petting zoo, and the girls moved over to the sinks to admire their handiwork. Emma almost didn't recognize the girl staring back at her in the mirror. The choppy bob Skylar had given her didn't look half bad—it actually made her look a little older, she thought, and more stylish.

"Wow," Skylar said, meeting Emma's eyes in the mirror and giving her a grateful smile. "I thought we were twins, but it turns out we're quadruplets!"

Emma nodded, and looked down the line at the faces of her friends, which all looked new without so much hair. They looked different than they had before, but anyone could see that they belonged together.

Jo

Reunion: Day 3

JO STUDIED HER REFLECTION IN THE BATHROOM mirror. After her talk with her dad, she had changed into a black tank top, brown jodhpurs (she'd wanted real army fatigues, but camouflage wasn't allowed during capture the flag thanks to a male counselor who had painted himself brown and green one year, hidden in a tree, and scared a female camper so badly she'd had to be taken to the ER), and black boots, and then she'd slicked her hair back with pomade, strapped her cell phone and a granola bar to her calf, and applied two thick stripes of eye black across her cheeks.

She knew she was overcompensating with the outfit, but Jo needed all the celebratory spirit she could muster. Because somewhere along the path on the walk back to Souhegan, she'd realized something she'd been trying to deny for a long, long time: it was time for her to go. Her dad was right. She needed to move forward, to grow up, to stop holding on to the past. And that meant leaving camp. For a while, anyway. She had to convince the others to band back together for one last hurrah. Jo took a deep breath and tried to smile. She was preparing for the rally of a lifetime.

Skylar was back in bed, with her blanket covering her head. She, Emma, and Maddie had all come back from breakfast separately, still, it seemed, in terrible moods. Emma was paging through a thick novel and Maddie was doing her makeup, and neither was talking to anyone. Jo tried to ignore their chilly stares and cued up her iPod to play Wagner's "Ride of the Valkyries." She'd seen it used to powerful effect in *Apocalypse Now* and hoped it would make a compelling motivational soundtrack for the day.

As the surging strings and triumphant horn calls filled the cabin, Maddie looked up with a death glare.

"Please turn that off," she said.

Emma nodded in agreement. "Seriously, Jo—*no*. Not today."

Skylar, true to form, didn't stir until the crescendo.

"Ladies," Jo announced, "last night is in the past. Today is a day that will live in infamy."

"That was Pearl Harbor," Emma snapped.

"Fine," Jo said. "But today will, too. Because today is the day that we finally claim victory against the boys in capture the flag."

"I'm not playing," Emma said. "Give it up."

"You're crazy," Maddie sighed.

"We first played capture the flag together eight years ago," Jo continued, ignoring them. "It was a cloudy Sunday in August, and even though we were small in stature we had big dreams. Unfortunately, we didn't make it off the Green before all our bandanas were snatched, and we had our first taste of defeat.

"The following year we amped up our game but fell victim to a classic fake out by a group of senior boys who led us into the north field and ambushed us," Jo went on. "Our third summer we had to forfeit when Maddie lost her glasses and ran into a tree. The next year was a dark time, when two weeks of rain made the ground so muddy that capture the flag had to be canceled. And during the last game we played together, we literally touched greatness when I was at last able to get my hand around the boys' flagpole—"

"Poor word choice!" Maddie yelled, but Jo could see that she was trying not laugh, even while scowling.

"—only to be tackled by an eleven-year-old in an ILLEGAL move that was upheld for reasons unknown by a member of *my own family*." Jo clapped her hands together and held them underneath her chin, saying a little prayer. Everything about the previous two train wreck nights could be made right if she could only pull this off.

"Now," Jo said as she reached into her duffel and pulled out four green bandanas still in their crisp cellophane wrappers. "Before you guys even got here, I took the liberty of ordering custom bandanas for us this year for solidarity and good luck." She slipped a bandana from its sleeve and unfolded it to reveal the Camp Nedoba logo, surrounded in a circle by all four of their names.

"That's sweet, Jo," Emma said, the bite gone from her voice. "But nobody's in the mood."

"And what does . . . *katiff fatwah* mean?" Skylar asked groggily, hanging her head over the side of the bunk and squinting at additional letters printed on the four corners of the fabric.

"That's CTF FTW," Jo corrected. "Capture the Flag For the Win." She sighed. "I know I can go overboard and be a little stubborn sometimes"—she looked at Maddie—"and I know that no one but me wants to spend all day running around in the woods after a plastic flag. But guys," she said, swallowing hard, "I need this. *We* need this. And I can't do it by myself. So, please, let's suck it up and show Adam and Nate and Charlie—in absentia—that we're not afraid of them anymore. And that we won't let anything keep us apart."

No one said anything for a few minutes, and Jo started to worry that she'd misjudged the situation. She should have started with the sincere part and left the jokey theatrics to the end after she'd won them over with her heart and loyalty.

"I think I need more coffee before I can deal with this," Skylar said finally, clambering down from her bunk.

"I need a shower," Emma said.

Maddie capped her lip gloss and let out a deep breath. "I don't know," she murmured.

"Lucky for you, I do," Jo said, blocking the door. "I've been waiting for this game my whole life."

"That's really sad," Maddie said.

Jo paused, wondering if she should tell them about her decision to quit. It would be *so* much easier to get them on her side with the added push of a little sympathy. But no, she decided. She didn't deserve a victory that was won by manipulation.

"Maybe," Jo said. "But who in this cabin *doesn't* need a win today? Who doesn't need to feel better about themselves? We all came here—or stayed here, as the case may be—expecting different things out of this reunion, and so far I think it's safe to say we've all been disappointed." Skylar stood still at the edge of the bed, staring down at the floor. Emma hugged her knees and let out a deep breath. Maddie stared off at the corner of the cabin where the glass from the photo frame still lay in glittering shards, her nostrils flaring.

"We need this, you guys," Jo said. "I don't know about you, but I'm not going down without a fight. So come on—who's with me?"

Emma

Reunion: Day 3

WHEN EMMA SAW THE CROWDS OF CAMPERS LINED up on the Green, on opposite sides of a bright yellow line of caution tape that had been stretched across the grass, she knew she had made a terrible mistake. She thought Jo was just being her normal over-the-top camp self, wearing the eye black and playing the weird opera, but almost everyone else had shown up for the game with the same level of commitment. People wore face paint and had prearranged team outfits. Even Meredith, Allie, and Ruth wore matching pink ringer tees and white denim shorts. They looked like the Easter Bunny's harem.

Mack came out ten minutes before the start time to thunderous applause, wearing his referee T-shirt and whistle along with a pair of incongruous butter-colored Crocs. He dragged his Adirondack chair to the edge of the caution tape and sat down with his Thermos full of coffee, winking at Jo, who was already toeing the line, peering through a set of binoculars to try to see signs of the guys' base camp.

Capture the flag had always been Emma's least favorite camp

activity, a full day of running around in the woods trying not to get tagged out by fellow campers on the opposing team. It took speed, strategic thinking, and a lot of paranoia, so it had always been intimidating—but the reunion game set even higher stakes. It was girls versus boys, for starters. And of course it was still the JEMS versus . . . each other.

Jo's speech had been hard to say no to, but Emma, Maddie, and Skylar still weren't really speaking. They all had the same expression of anger and skepticism mixed with abject fear. And they were the least visually coordinated group: Maddie was in her blue tank top, grungy Keds, and white capri pants—which had taken a beating over the past two days and were covered in dusky dirt splotches that looked like bruises and welts; Skylar was wearing a forest green romper that seemed to have been made from old sweatpants (somehow she was still pulling it off, though, which just added insult to injury as far as Emma was concerned) with Converse high-tops; and Emma had on the workout clothes she'd packed but never used: a pair of black running shorts and an old T-shirt of her dad's that read NEW YORK CIVIL LIBERTIES UNION. Jo had asked Emma to bring her watermelon backpack, but Emma would sooner have run the course completely nude, so Jo carried it. The combination of the infantile backpack and the Lara Croft–style wardrobe made Jo look like she belonged in a mental institution. *Which she kind of does,* Emma thought with a smirk.

"Okay!" Mack yelled. "The game starts in a few minutes and everyone needs to go back to their base, but I just want to go over the rules, for those of you who may have forgotten or who may be trying to circumvent them . . . ." He looked right at Jo when he said it.

"This yellow line marks the border between the two sides of camp. Each team will start back at their bunks, and on my signal you'll be free to travel anywhere on camp grounds in pursuit of the other team's flag. Rule number one is that you must cross this line going back and forth—and while the Green will be a battlefield of sorts I want to take a moment to stress that these are *not* the Hunger Games, so please, don't get carried away. Which leads me to rule number two: no tackling." A group of boys booed.

"That's right," Mack repeated. "No tackling. If someone relieves you of your bandana, you're out, and when you get tagged out, you stay where you are until you hear my whistle that signals the end of the game—no sneaking off. And no inappropriate touching. You're grabbing the bandana, not the person. The body may be a wonderland, as John Mayer says, but for our purposes today it is *off limits*."

Emma bit her lip to keep from laughing, and out of habit looked over at Skylar. But Skylar had her headphones in and hadn't even heard. Overhead, the clouds were looking ominously gray.

"Ready?" Jo asked. They were clustered back on the girls' side, standing around a dead pine stump. Emma sighed and put her hands on her knees. She had never felt less ready for anything. She had a headache from drinking too much coffee, and the thought of sprinting made her stomach flip.

"I think I'm going to throw up," Emma said.

Jo looked down at her watch. "Do it now," she said. "We only have twenty seconds."

"You're not getting out that easy," Skylar said, stretching her calves.

I'm not the one who's easy, Emma thought, but she kept her mouth shut. She knew she had lost it during the fight and had said some things she didn't mean. She wanted to talk to Skylar more about it, but first she needed to hear a real apology, not just a series of excuses. She couldn't believe that Skylar had made it seem like the betrayal was somehow her fault.

"No more sniping," Jo said. "Today is a new day. We're in this together."

"Whatever," Maddie sighed. "Let's just get this over with."

"Okay, on my count," Jo said, lowering herself into a runner's stance. *Three . . .* Jo mouthed. *Two . . . ONE!* At the sound of Mack's whistle, girls broke off from the cabins in all directions. The older girls in pink jogged off toward the woods that led back behind the barn, while Sunny, Aileen, Jess, and Kerry hung back to "defend" the flaccid red flag Jo had planted in the dirt behind a picnic table, staring uninterestedly at their cell phones. But per Jo's instructions, Emma started down the main path toward the Green, bringing up the rear of their disjointed team. She watched Maddie's red ponytail swing back and forth as she focused on her breathing and tried to ignore the burning sensation in her lungs, which were exhausted from all the crying and screaming and did not seem at all amused that Emma had chosen this particular moment to rediscover physical fitness.

Jo's preferred route, which she had outlined to Emma, Maddie, and Skylar in a series of e-mails dating back to April—and reviewed again that morning—was fairly simple: they would head straight for the border line, wasting as little time as possible, and then divide and conquer to make it across the Green, around the well, and over to the woods on the northern border of the boys' side without being tagged out. Then they would regroup and lay low, edging together around the boys' bunks through the thick, almost impassable woods on the eastern side and ambush them from behind. It was an ambitious strategy even under the best of circumstances, but with their communication hovering somewhere between stony silence and open hostility, Emma knew they didn't have a chance. She half hoped that one of the boys would tag her right away and put her out of her misery.

When they got within sight of the border, she panicked even more. The boys playing "guard" were exactly the ones she'd hoped to avoid until later in the game, when, hopefully, she would already be unconscious from dehydration. There were the usual suspects: the twins, in matching sports jerseys; Bowen, looking unconvincingly thuggish in heavy beige hiking boots; Zeke, whose hair was still hanging in his eyes like a mop; Nate, who waved limply to Jo as she reached the Green, as if unaware that he was supposed to look intimidating; and Adam, who had opted to change out of his syrup-covered breakfast wardrobe and had a look on his face, as he saw first Skylar and then Emma, like he was about to be run over by a bus.

"Play fair, everybody!" Mack yelled from the sideline as he saw the teams begin to face off. The boys, on defense, adopted crab-like wrestling stances. Emma looked frantically for a hole in their lineup, but the slowest person—or, at least, most exhausted—was probably Adam, and she really didn't want to get anywhere near him if she could avoid it.

A few yards ahead, Jo sprung forward and sprinted across the caution tape, easily passing between Bowen and Matt Slotkin, who stumbled forward with the grace of two garbage trucks. Emma saw Jo double back to pluck Zeke's bandana out of his back pocket as she bounded away.

"That's for Skylar," she yelled, holding it over her head.

It *would* feel pretty good to beat them, Emma realized, feeling a sudden rush of adrenaline. But she had to get past them first. She took advantage of the fact that the others had reached the border line before she did—Nate had run after Jo, the Slotkin twins were fumbling for Maddie, who darted back and forth in a double helix pattern around the gazebo, and Bowen was following Skylar toward the well, slowed considerably by his choice of footwear. Adam, however, had hung back. He stretched his arms out as Emma approached.

"You have to listen to me," he said.

"No," she panted, breaking left and narrowly dodging his reach. "I don't." She sprinted as fast as her legs would carry her, hearing his footfalls right behind.

"You can't outrun me," he yelled.

"You're probably right," she called back over her shoulder, tasting bile. "No one runs away faster than you do." She felt his fingers brush the back of her shirt and she stopped abruptly and turned around. Adam barreled into her at full speed and they both fell clumsily to the ground.

"Hey!" she heard Mack yell. "No tackling!"

"Don't you dare tag me out," she panted, rolling back onto her knees and standing over Adam, who was examining a scrape on his palm. "Please, just leave me alone."

He looked up at her. "I can't."

"Clearly, you can." She glared at him. "I waited for you all night last night."

Adam looked pained. "I just didn't know what to say," he said. "I didn't want things to change between us."

Emma looked out at the woods, knowing that every second she stayed behind was widening the gap between her and her friends. Plus, the other boys could be waiting for her under the trees, where she was even less sure-footed. She looked down at Adam and shook her head.

"It's too late," she said, and sprinted all the way to the trees without glancing back.

Once she'd survived ten minutes without running into anyone or breaking her ankle, Emma started to think that there must be a patron saint of girls with no sense of direction watching over her. She wandered skittishly, jumping at every rattling branch and chirping bird, wishing she had brought her cell phone just in case she needed to call the sheriff's department to airlift her out. Luckily, she occasionally caught glimpses of the lake to her left through the trees, so she knew she was heading in more or less the direction that Jo had mapped out. Emma just hoped she found the others before she got too far and crossed over the invisible Camp Nedoba property line into the neighboring farmland.

She finally came upon them after about a quarter mile. They were sitting on a fallen tree, Jo in the center and Skylar and Maddie on either side, facing in opposite directions. The open watermelon backpack was wedged between Jo's boots.

"There you are," Jo said, zipping it up. "I thought they might have tagged you."

"Not yet." She snatched the backpack away from Jo.

"Relax, I didn't take anything." Jo got up and fished a compass out of her pocket. "By the way," she said, tossing it to Emma. "Use this next time."

"Did you get Adam's bandana at least?" Maddie asked. Emma shook her head, and Skylar laughed.

"What's so funny?" Emma tossed the compass on the ground, and its dial spun wildly in the dirt.

"You two need to *stop,*" Maddie yelled. "If I hear his name again, I'm going to explode!" As if on cue, thunder cracked above them.

"Great," Jo said. "Thanks a lot."

"Sorry, I also forgot to tell you, I control the weather," Maddie said, rolling her eyes. A light rain started to fall, and Emma turned her face up to the sky. On the bright side, maybe this meant the game would be canceled.

"Okay, new plan," Jo said, retrieving the compass.

"We go back and stop playing?" Emma asked hopefully.

"I second that," Maddie said.

"No," Jo said. "We look for shelter and wait out the storm." The rain was already getting heavy, slapping the ground with rapid-fire smacks that quickly turned the rust-colored dirt into slick mud.

"Where are we supposed to wait?" Emma asked.

"There's the treehouse," Skylar said, flicking wet hair off her shoulders.

"No way." Emma remembered the rickety box, built on the sagging limbs of a thick oak tree, that had been a favorite hideout of theirs until a camper fell and broke his arm the year they were twelve, and Mack declared it unsafe.

"That's ten minutes out of our way," Jo said, shielding her face from the rain with one hand. "And there's no ladder."

"Never stopped us before," Skylar said with a shrug.

Maddie looked unsure. "I don't know if I can make the climb in this weather."

"I can't make it at all," Emma said. She tried to remember the exact wording Mack had used in his rejection letter. "My wilderness skills are somewhat lacking."

"Well it's a good thing you've got us, then, city slicker," Jo said, blowing droplets out of her eyes.

Even though it loomed like the top of the Empire State Building in her memory, Emma was relieved to find that in reality the old tree house was really only about ten feet off the ground, and the branches of the oak started at four feet, so it wasn't as treacherous a climb as she had feared, even for a relatively uncoordinated person. Unlike the barn loft, however, the tree house was in perpetual motion, swaying gently back and forth as the driving wind and rain whipped through the woods.

"That's not comforting," she said as they stared up at the wet, gray wood, which had torn away in spots, exposing thick, rusty nails. The doorway was boarded shut, but the windows, which were about two feet square, were open to the elements—and to potential squatters.

"It'll have to do," Jo said. She put her hands on the lowest branch, pressing down on it a few times to make sure it would hold her weight. Then she vaulted herself up and swung a leg over, until she was straddling it like a horse. "The bark's definitely slippery," she called down as she climbed, the soaked bandana hanging from her belt loop like a piece of overcooked spinach. Emma watched as Jo tried to pull herself up on one of the thick, knotty branches that supported the tree house floor. She almost had a grip on one of the windowsills when her foot shot out from under her and she dropped almost two feet, hanging on precariously with her left elbow.

"Be careful!" Maddie yelled. "Use your feet like I showed you!" Jo smiled down at her with a look of grim determination and managed to get her legs back into position. A few minutes later, she was waving at them from the window.

"See? Piece of cake!" she called.

One by one, they climbed. Maddie had no trouble navigating the wet branches, and despite her lack of form, Skylar's lanky legs and arms helped her reach the window in just a few long steps. But when it was Emma's turn, the tree house once again seemed perilously high.

"I'm soaked already," she called up. "I'll stay down here . . . be a lookout."

"Woman up," Jo yelled. "We did it, and so can you."

Maddie stuck her head out the window, her wet curls sticking to her forehead. "Just hug the branch!" she cried. "It'll feel stupid, but just hug it and then wrap your leg up around it." Emma put one hand on the rough, clammy bark. It didn't seem worth it, but she couldn't let the others think she had no follow-through. Especially since she knew now that was how they all thought of her—all talk, no action. So she reached up, hugged the branch for dear life, and kicked her right leg until her ankle found purchase on a knot. She shimmied her way onto the branch and looked up. Skylar was actually smiling, and at first Emma thought she was laughing at her again. But then she reached an arm out the window, spreading her fingers wide.

"You can do it, Em," she said. "Just climb one more branch and you can grab my hand."

She was right. No sooner had Emma managed to drag herself up the next two feet or so, than she felt Skylar's long fingers close around hers, and then Jo leaned down to grab the other arm, and before she knew it she was crouched in the corner of the six-by-eight-foot wooden box, listening to the water drum down onto the sloped roof. Miraculously, there were only a few places where it was dripping through.

Emma's already threadbare shirt clung to her skin, and she shivered as she took off her backpack and settled in against the wall, hesitant to put her full weight on it, afraid that it would fall away like wet pulp.

"Hey," she said, smiling at Skylar as she blew fat raindrops off the tip of her nose, "thanks."

Skylar put her hands over her face and mumbled something through her fingers. As she pushed her wet hair back over her scalp, Emma noticed that she was shaking.

"What?"

"I said, I'm sorry." Skylar's face was pale and gray, her normally sea-green eyes glassy. "I am so, so sorry."

Emma took a deep breath of the chilly, damp air. Her muscles ached. She was so tired, she didn't feel like fighting anymore. "I know," she said. "Me too."

"What I did was wrong," Skylar said quietly. "But you have to believe me that I didn't do it maliciously. That night on the beach, after Zeke left me—"

"I don't need to know," Emma interrupted her. She already

knew enough to believe that Skylar was telling the truth. After all, she *had* rejected Adam, even though, in her mind at the time, she had just been avoiding getting hurt in the future. Skylar had been rejected, too, and somehow, somewhere between the fire pit and the rocks, she and Adam had crossed paths. The rest of the details were too painful to think about, and besides, Emma knew the basics from the first-edition copy of *Our Bodies, Ourselves* that her mom had given her when she turned thirteen. No matter who said or did what, they had found each other that night, and there was no way anyone could undo it. None of the barbs she had thrown at Skylar in the past twenty-four hours had helped. And neither had her fight with Adam, although the waffle punch had felt pretty good.

"I just wish you had told me sooner," Emma said.

"I should have," Skylar said. "I just didn't know how. I thought you'd hate me."

Emma shook her head. "I could never hate you." It was true. She had tried, for the past ten hours or so, to hate Skylar, but the fact was she'd only felt so hurt and angry because she loved Skylar so much. And that hadn't changed, underneath everything.

"I'd do anything to take it back," Skylar said.

"Did it make you happy?" Emma asked. "Even a little?"

Skylar nodded and wiped her eyes.

"Then I wouldn't want you to. You were right. I had my chance, and I threw it away. He wasn't mine. And if I could go back, I would probably run away again. I wasn't ready."

"We can't go back," Jo said suddenly. She looked up at them and frowned. "I thought we could, too, but we can't. We can't ever go back to the way things used to be. We can only move forward."

"Thanks for the tip, Gandhi," Maddie said. "But they were kind of having a moment there." Jo looked at her angrily for a second and then burst out laughing. Maddie smiled and shook her head. "Sorry," she said. "That was bitchy."

"No, I deserved it," Jo said. "And I'm the one who needs to apologize. I don't care where you come from. That doesn't change who you are. And when I found out, I should have reached out to you, instead of assuming it meant you didn't trust me."

Maddie was quiet for a minute. "I don't know why I didn't tell you," she said. "I just wanted to be a different person here. Like the Witness Protection Program or something." She laughed. "It seemed like a good idea when I was ten, anyway. And then I felt like I'd already started it, so I had to keep going. Plus it was nice to have a pretend family who didn't let me down."

Emma smiled at her; she had no idea how Maddie could have been so brave for so long, making the trip from North Carolina all by herself even as a little girl, just to be with them.

"Is it really bad?" Emma asked.

"No," Maddie said. "I mean, my parents have issues, and sometimes they screw up, but they feed and clothe me and my sisters and try to do their best. They love us as much as they're capable of loving people who aren't themselves. I could have it a lot worse."

"That definitely puts my family problems in perspective," Skylar said.

"What's going on?" Jo asked.

"Just that my dad thinks I'm talentless and should give up on art school."

"He's crazy," Emma said. "If it makes you feel better, my parents think I don't work hard enough."

"You?" Skylar asked incredulously. "All you do is work."

"Right? Thank you!" Emma said, feeling vindicated. If anything, she felt like she needed to take on less responsibility. She definitely wasn't going to retake the SATs again, she was sure of that much. She wasn't even sure she liked Brown. NYU had a great writing program, it wasn't a reach school, and it would mean she could go back to New York, where she already had at least one built-in friend who also happened to be extremely cute. Not to mention an eccentric aunt whose apartment she could sublet.

"My mom thinks I'm a standoffish lesbian," Jo blurted out. "So does Nate, by the way."

"Nate does not!" Maddie said.

"Maybe not after I kissed him."

"What?!" Maddie cried excitedly. "Why didn't you tell us?"

"World War III was unfolding," Jo said.

"I finally made out with Adam," Emma said. She looked at Skylar apologetically. "I'm sorry if that's weird. But it was something I needed to do."

"No," Skylar said. "I'm happy for you. Is that weird?"

"Yes," Jo said. "Friends don't let friends share boyfriends."

"He's not my boyfriend," Emma clarified.

"Mine either," Skylar said.

"I guess this is a weird time to bring it up, but Adam and I are engaged," Maddie said. They all cracked up.

"You guys," Jo asked once the laughter died down. "When did we stop being best friends?"

"We never stopped," Emma said. "We just *lapsed*. I tried to keep in touch, but . . ."

"Life gets in the way," Skylar finished.

"Exactly," Maddie said.

"Hey!" Emma suddenly had what felt like a brilliant idea. "Why are we wasting our last day soaking wet in a tree? Let's forget about the game and go back to the cabin for the slumber party we never got to have last time."

Skylar clapped excitedly. "I would love that," she said.

"Me too," Jo said, clearing her throat. "But first we have to win this game."

"Says who?" Maddie asked. "Don't you think our time together is more important than a cheap little flag?"

Jo looked down at her feet. "It's not the flag," she said softly. "It's what the flag stands for."

"What?" Emma demanded. "Cutthroat competition? The humiliating vanquish of an enemy?"

"Shut up," Jo laughed, and then looked up at her somberly. "It's my last chance to win."

"What are you on?" Skylar groaned. "There's next year, and the year after that, and the year after that . . ." She smiled.

"Nope," Jo said, "that's where you're wrong. You guys . . . I've decided that this is my last summer at Camp Nedoba."

"But I thought you loved this place!" Maddie cried.

"I *do* love it," Jo said. "This is my home. Literally. It's my family. It's basically my whole life. I love it. But Maddie, you were right. I shut out everything else."

"I was upset," Maddie said. "I said a lot of things I shouldn't have. Like about your hair. I *love* your hair."

"Thanks," Jo said. "It was a big change, but I got used to it. And that's why I know I'll be okay if I don't come back next year."

"But . . . where will you go?" Skylar asked.

"I have no idea," Jo said. "Maybe do a coaching internship or something. I haven't really thought about it. I just decided today."

"Did you tell your dad?" Emma asked. She couldn't imagine camp without Jo. It almost felt like it couldn't exist, like when Emma drove up next summer, all that would be left was a big crater.

"Actually, he kind of gave me the idea."

"Wow," Skylar said, leaning back against the treehouse wall and drawing her knees up to her chest. "It's the end of an era."

"Or maybe," Emma said, gesturing to Jo to toss her the backpack, "it's just the beginning of a new one." She unzipped it and carefully removed the bulging portfolio that held the pact. Apart from a few small water stains on the outside, it was fine. "I took it home," she said sheepishly. "I know it's supposed to stay on camp grounds." She decided not to add that the pact had been collecting dust under a box of super absorbent maxi pads (with wings!) in her bedroom closet.

"Well," Jo said, visibly relieved at the change of subject, "I think we can safely vote Emma as our next virgin sacrifice."

"Spoken like the only other eligible member," Emma laughed.

"Can I see that?" Skylar said. She carefully unwound the leather tie that bound the portfolio together. Index cards threatened to spill out onto the wet floor, and Emma scooted over to hold them in place while Skylar ran her fingers over the map. "Look!" she said, pointing to a drawing of the tree house. "We've come full circle."

Emma nodded and squeezed Skylar's arm. Their friendship hadn't ended, not by a long shot—it just needed to be renewed. Keeping her right hand on top of the precarious pile of pact rules, Emma fished at the bottom of the portfolio with her left and slipped out the thin, folded sheet of notebook paper covered in foil stars that marked their very first contract. They had all written their pledges on the same sheet of paper, folding it over four times and signing it at the bottom.

"I know you said we couldn't go back," Emma said, looking at Jo, "but I think in order to move forward we need to start back at the beginning. I move that we renew the vows we made at the end of our very first summer." She looked at the bottom of the sheet, under their loopy, childlike signatures. It was dated July 27. "Oh my God, you guys. We started the pact *exactly* eight years ago today."

"It's a sign," Skylar said.

"I'll start," Jo said. "Rule #3: Best friends always share their candy." She hung her head. "That is so poignant, you guys. I think I might cry."

"It still applies," Maddie said. "Especially if you consider Adam candy." She winked, and Jo made a face.

"Well, maybe a Milk Dud," Emma said.

"Or a Dum Dum!" Skylar added.

Jo handed the paper to Maddie.

"Rule #4," she read. "Best friends don't forget you when you leave camp."

"Awwww," the others said in unison.

"I know it's hard to believe, but I was never a sap before I met you guys," Maddie said, her chin wobbling. "You ruined me."

"Rule #2," Skylar read, putting an arm around Emma, "Best friends never take off their friendship anklets." She held up her own bare ankle. "Well, that's what did it, guys. Mystery solved."

"Good," Emma said, "we can share the blame." She took the sheet of notebook paper and read her charmingly rounded ten-year-old print. "Rule #1," she read. "Best friends never forget what brought them together." She smiled. "I'd like to add, 'or what pulled them apart.' So it never happens again."

"Seconded," Skylar said.

"Deal," Jo said.

"Aye, aye captain," Maddie said.

Emma heard a thrush start singing and looked out the window. She'd been so distracted, she hadn't even noticed that the rain had stopped. Jo noticed, too.

"Great," she said. "Let's re-up on this thing so we can get back to kicking ass today."

"Can't wait," Maddie said drily. "Does anyone have a pen?"

Emma grinned and reached into her backpack. "I still have *the* pen," she said, pulling out a Gelly Roll with a hot pink cap. She signed her name at the bottom and passed it back around the circle.

As the sun finally peeked through the clouds, they re-sealed the pact and climbed back down to finish what they'd started.

Jo

Reunion: Day 3

JO COULD TELL THEY WERE CLOSING IN ON THE BOYS' camp. After so many years spent exploring the property end to end, she could identify her location by smell, and the boys' side had a distinctive, pungent odor of dirty sweat socks and Doritos.

After they had climbed down from the treehouse and finally shared a much-needed group hug, Jo had applied eye black to all of them, and with their stringy hair, muddy clothes, and dazed expressions, they now looked like some sort of zombie football team.

"What do you do when we get close to the tree line at the southern end?" she quizzed Maddie now, as they batted through the brush, their faces slick with sweat and their arms covered in scratches.

"I climb the tree," Maddie said, looking comically determined under her eye black, "and I look out and I tell you where everyone is positioned."

"Good. And then Emma, what do you do?" she called back.

"Run through their base to distract them!"

"Right. And then?"

"Throw up from running too hard."

Jo smiled. "Just aim for Mark Slotkin," she said.

When they got within a hundred feet or so of the clearing behind the boys' cabins, Jo tied Maddie's hair up in an elastic and then covered it with her black bandana, like a skull cap. Then Maddie shimmied up the side of a tree like a squirrel until she was straddling a branch twelve feet off the ground.

"I think I've earned my merit badge in thigh chafing this weekend," she yelled down.

"Shhhhh!" Jo whispered. "Do you see it?"

"Yeah." Maddie leaned forward and peeked through the branches. "It's gonna be a bitch getting to it, though."

"Why, where is it?" Even though she was exhausted, Jo wished she had thought to climb the tree herself. She couldn't stand not knowing exactly what they were up against.

Maddie slid back down the trunk and wiped her hands on her shorts. "It's on the roof of the bathroom," she panted. "They're all just sitting up there trying to throw cards into a puddle."

"Distracted and dumb, just the way I like them," Jo said, smiling.

"But how do we get up there?" Emma asked. "I can't exactly run across a roof."

"Don't worry," Jo said. "There's a ladder built into the side of the building. If we surprise them they won't have time to run."

"That's the thing, though," Skylar jumped in. "You know those guys, and they probably *will* run, and someone will fall off and break something. We can't go up there." Jo grimaced. Skylar was right.

"Then we'll just have to make them come down," she said.

Saying a silent prayer to her Abenaki ancestors to aid her in kicking some serious ass, Jo made her move.

When Jo came walking up through the center of the cabins, goose-stepping like a soldier in her riding boots, the boys on the roof sprung into action—which, for them, meant just standing up and looking confused.

"How'd she get past the well?" Bowen asked, elbowing Mark.

"Doesn't matter," Mark said. "She's ours now. "Hey, Jo!" he yelled as he lowered himself onto the ladder, "You wanna bend over and give me that bandana or am I gonna have to chase it out of you?"

"Remember, no tackling," Nate said nervously. Matt and Bowen cracked up.

"You are so whipped," Matt said, slapping Nate in the back of the head with his bandana. Jo looked away. She felt bad for dodging him when he so clearly wanted to make amends. She knew they needed to talk eventually, and she wanted to tell Matt and Bowen that Nate was ten times *both* the men they could ever hope to be, but that would just embarrass him and make things worse. So instead, she stuck to the plan. She held up an apple, polished it on her shirt, and took a big, showy bite.

"Wait a second," Adam said. Mark stopped his descent. "Where did you get that?"

"Dude," Matt said. "Who cares? We have Doritos."

"I'm not *hungry*," Adam said. "That apple came from my trunk."

"And that's not the only thing," Emma said, stepping down out of the Wawinak cabin, where the boys were staying for the weekend. "Turns out Adam is kind of a hoarder." She held up a plastic bag full of condiment packets and fixed him with a steely gaze. "Either you really love mayo, or you've got a serious problem."

"Get out of my stuff!" Adam cried. "I thought you told me to leave you alone."

"I did," Emma said. "I'm just acting as a concerned friend."

A lightbulb finally went off in Bowen's head. "They're in our bunk!" he shouted. Jo grinned and kept chewing the apple. Who knew how long it had been in there, commingling with Adam's ironic statement tees, but it was mighty good.

"Here's something interesting," Maddie said, peeking out of Wawinak's door frame. "Tinactin: Fast-acting relief for jock itch!" She batted her eyes. "I won't say where I found this, but I will say that this particular gentleman also enjoys a nice lavender sachet in his undies."

"Maybe that's what caused the jock itch," Emma said.

"That's it," Mark yelled, jumping down to the ground. "Game over. You might as well just hand us your flag now."

"Well, that wouldn't be any fun," Jo said. Mark was fifty feet away, but he was a quarterback, and even though he had a hundred pounds on her she knew he could move. She tossed the apple in the dirt and bolted for the woods just as Mark leaped for her.

Jo ran track in the spring, and her event was the four-hundred-meter dash, but she was used to sprinting in super lightweight sneakers and flimsy shorts, not jodhpurs and knee-high leather boots. She felt herself slowing down no matter how fast she pumped her arms, and she could hear Mark's thunderous steps getting closer and closer. A few yards from the edge of the woods, she realized that she'd miscalculated the distance; she would never outpace him. If she wanted to stay in the game she would have to use her size to her advantage and get somewhere he couldn't reach. She lunged for the nearest tree and started to climb. Luckily, the old oak had a split down the center, and Jo was able to wedge her hand in it, using her grip to hold her weight while she wrapped her legs around the trunk, pushing in toward the tree and out to the sides through either foot like Maddie had taught her. She frantically pulled up with her hands, feeling her fingernails tear against the rough bark, and finally swung a leg up and over the split just as Mark reached her. She angled her butt away from him so that he couldn't grab her bandana, and kicked at his hands with her free leg, splattering mud all over his face. When she accidentally landed a blow on his jaw (against official capture the flag rules, but Jo reasoned he had it coming), he stumbled back long enough for her to climb out of reach.

Jo caught her breath and looked down at the scene below. All the boys except for Adam had left the roof. Matt Slotkin was taunting Maddie, shuffling back and forth in front of the cabin door with his arms outstretched as she pelted him with whatever she could find: balled-up socks, belts, Speed Stick deodorants. Bowen was chasing Emma around the bathrooms, slowed considerably by his choice of footwear, and Nate was hanging back, peering out into the tree line. Jo smiled. It impressed her that he was smart enough to realize there was one of them missing, but she still had to get him out of the way.

"Hey!" she yelled. Nate looked up and shook his head.

"Oh, so you're talking to me now?" he asked. "Don't tell me you want my help getting down."

"I'm afraid to jump with Frankenstein here barking up my tree," she said, glaring down at Mark. "But if you come over and help me, I'll surrender."

"Oh, please!" Nate cried. "That is such an obvious lie." Even from a distance, she could tell by his body language that he was mad. "You're on your own," he said coldly.

Jo watched Skylar sneak out of the woods behind him and wished that she could enjoy it more, without the guilt that was creeping under her skin, almost making her want to call a time-out and talk things out with him. *Almost.*

"That's okay," she yelled. "A few seconds of your attention was all we needed." Nate turned around, but it was too late. Skylar snatched his bandana and held it over her head triumphantly. Maddie let out a whoop and Matt looked up to see what was going on just as she beaned him in the head with a hacky sack. She scurried out of the cabin and tore his bandana out with a flourish, performing a series of grand jetés down the path. Mark glowered at Jo and raced off to defend the flag.

"Adam!" Mark yelled. "They're coming up! Watch your ass!" Skylar reached the ladder just as Bowen and Emma rounded the corner but before Mark could make up the distance.

"What the—" Bowen cried, and Emma stopped short, tripping him. She grabbed his bandana and fell to her knees, grinning, just as Mark came thundering out of the woods, heading straight for her. Jo held her breath. He was going in for a tackle.

"Mark!" Adam shouted sharply from the roof, abandoning his post at the flag. "Don't hurt her! It's just a game, man!" He ran for the ladder but stopped short when he saw Skylar. Jo could see Adam looking back and forth between Emma on the ground and Skylar on the ladder, trying to decide what to do. Mark showed no signs of stopping, and Emma didn't have anywhere to go other than into the side of the building. Adam finally turned and went for the lip of the roof. *He's going to jump,* Jo thought, feeling sick. But Adam didn't have time. Skylar got to the top of the ladder and lunged for him, holding him back by the shirt as she handily plucked the bandana out of the waist of his boxers. On the ground, Emma dropped and rolled, narrowly dodging Mark's leap. He hit the grass with a thud and slid into the wall, where Maddie relieved him of his bandana.

"THAT'S RIGHT!!!" Maddie cried, holding her spoils in the air like a gladiator.

"Whoooooooo!" Jo yelled, climbing back down the tree and jogging out to join her friends in a sweaty embrace. *This is what it must feel like to win the Olympics,* she thought as the adrenaline flooded her system. She couldn't wait to tell her dad that she had done it—not only had she brought her friends back together, but she'd led them to victory. "Get it!" she yelled to Skylar, who stood on the roof a few feet away from the bright blue flag, which was waving picturesquely in the wind. Jo wished she had brought her camera; she would have loved to put a picture in the Nedoba newsletter. The only thing that took some wind out of her sails was seeing Nate moping dejectedly by the bathroom door. But she would deal with him after the game, Jo decided. Plus, she was still kind of upset. She might have overreacted, but it was only because he'd jumped to conclusions about her, just like everybody else.

Jo looked up at the roof. Skylar should have been back on the ground by now; they would need to get going—they still had to make it back to base without getting tagged. But Skylar was circling the flag hesitantly, pulling her hair up into a ponytail and gazing off into the distance. "What are you waiting for?" Jo yelled, getting impatient. "Let's go!"

"I call time-out," Skylar said finally.

"Time-out?" Jo panted. "There are no time-outs in capture the flag!"

"Sorry, Jo," Skylar said. "Time-out." She looked down at the girls with a faint smile. "I think I have a better idea."

Skylar

The Second Summer ◆ *Age 11*
Middle of First Session

"Friendship Rule: Best friends never leave each other behind."

"I HATE THIS GAME." SKYLAR SAT DOWN IN THE GRASS on the edge of the north field and started picking wildflowers, nervously slitting the bases of the stems with her thumbnail and threading them into a wreath. She knew she didn't have time to waste, but she was getting frustrated. It felt like they'd been playing manhunt forever. They'd started after breakfast, and now they were out in the woods at least half a mile from the cafeteria, the sun already so unforgivably hot that her hair was sticking to her neck in clumps. Plus, her legs were itching from wading through the bushes—walking in circles, as it turned out. But she couldn't quit and go back for lunch, or jump in the lake to cool off, because Jo was gone, and they had to find her. The boys, who were the "hunters," had tagged her and hauled her off to their "jail" when she had gone back to try to cover their tracks. Now it was up to the other girls to hunt the boys and free Jo.

Growing up, Skylar had never even been allowed to play tag because her parents said it was inhumane to call a person "it." Instead, she had a Loop 'n Loom that she used to make dozens of potholders while her friends played outside. She felt comfortable in the wilderness—she'd gone camping plenty of times before starting at Nedoba, even once at Joshua Tree in California on a family trip—but the whole concept of hunting creeped her out, even if it was just a stupid game.

Maddie paced back and forth in front of Skylar, kicking at the dry dirt with her Keds, which were still white in spots since they'd only been at camp for two weeks.

"We've got to *do* something," she huffed. "We can't just sit here smelling the flowers."

"I'm *thinking*," Skylar said. But she knew Maddie was right. One of them had to step in and lead—but no one seemed to want to take Jo's place . . . even though she wasn't there. Skylar looked over at Emma, who was crouched on the ground planting a stick in the dirt.

"What are you doing?"

"Trying to find true north," Emma said. She took a step back and studied her work, wiping her hands on her jeans.

"It looks like you're burying a hamster," Maddie said.

"No, see?" Emma motioned to the grass. "I just mark off where the shadow falls with a rock, and then we just wait a while and see which way the shadow moves to figure out what's west." She smiled proudly. "I saw it on TV."

"You're like Map from *Dora the Explorer*," Maddie said. Skylar smiled down at her lap.

"That's great, Em," Skylar said. "But I can tell you what's west. The lake is west. If you listen hard you can hear people splashing."

Emma looked crushed, and Skylar leaped up, placing the daisy chain on her head with a flourish. "You get a Girl Scout badge, though." Skylar hadn't been allowed to join Girl Scouts, either. According to her father, the cookie business was "like a Ponzi scheme."

"What are we waiting for?" Maddie said, balling her fists. With her unruly red curls and tiny limbs, Maddie looked about as intimidating as a cupcake, but Skylar knew it wouldn't help to mention that.

"Lead the way," she said, stepping aside.

Maddie hesitated. "You're taller," she said. "You can see farther."

"But you have better shoes," Emma pointed out. Skylar and Emma were both wearing flip-flops.

"How about we all go together?" Skylar suggested. She linked arms with both of her much shorter friends, feeling like a gangly Dorothy navigating the yellow brick road.

"Lions and tigers and bears—oh my!" Emma whispered. Skylar squeezed her hand. Emma always seemed to know exactly what she was thinking.

"Except instead of lions and tigers it's just boys making armpit farts," Maddie said.

"Well," Skylar reasoned, "at least we'll be able to hear them coming."

Ten minutes later, they'd found nothing but a broken ping-pong paddle and a pile of what Emma identified as "probably deer poop."

"This is the least exciting chase ever," Maddie sighed.

"We're not chasing them; they're chasing *us*," Skylar reminded her. It was hard not to jump every time a squirrel scampered up a tree. The boys could play rough sometimes, and Skylar didn't want to put anything past them. Just the other day, Matt Slotkin had given Skylar an Indian burn on the lunch line for no reason. Her mother would have said that boys bothered her because they liked her, but Skylar knew that kind of teasing, and this wasn't it. This was meaner. Wherever they were, she knew Jo was giving them more trouble than they'd bargained for.

"Look!" Maddie said after they'd walked a few more yards, pointing at the path in front of them. Skylar could see a little red dot mixed in with the dirt clods.

"What is that?" she asked, crouching down.

"A berry, probably," Emma said.

"Nope!" Maddie reached out and plucked the red thing off the ground, brandishing it proudly. She pointed to a faint but unmistakable white *S* in the center. "It's a Skittle! It's a sign!"

"A sign?" Emma asked skeptically. "Of what, littering?"

"No," Maddie said. "Jo left this for us to find. She's leading us to her prison . . . like Hansel and Gretel!"

Skylar started to laugh, but then remembered that Jo had been known to stash candy in the pockets of her cargo shorts on more than one occasion.

"Okay," she said. "If we find another Skittle, we'll follow them."

They found a purple one next to a log at the crest of the next hill, and soon they were closing in on the old toolshed near the lake, which had been abandoned for decades.

The shed looked like something out of a horror movie. Set in the center of a "clearing" that had since become overgrown with weeds and stinging nettles, it seemed to sag inward, dark and gray, with boarded-up windows and a fine, sickly green moss crawling all over its roof. The boys had barricaded the door shut with a rusty shovel. When she saw it, Skylar instantly thought of all those horror movies her older brother made her watch whenever their parents went out to dinner. A couple of young girls wandering into a creepy cabin in the woods . . . nothing good ever came of situations like that. Skylar felt chills. And the most disturbing thing about the whole scene was that the boys were nowhere in sight. The girls hid behind a thick oak and deliberated.

"It's too quiet," Emma whispered. "It's a setup."

"I know," Skylar said quietly. "They've got to be watching us."

Maddie started humming the music from *Jaws*.

"Do you think she's actually in there?" Emma wondered. "I figured she'd be ninja-kicking the door or something."

"The Skittles don't lie," Maddie said.

Skylar grabbed a pine cone off the ground, took aim, and lobbed it into the clearing. It ricocheted off the front of the shed and rolled off into the brush.

"Hey, jerks! Are you still out there? Open the door!" Jo's voice was muffled but still sounded impressively angry.

"She's in there," Emma laughed.

"And the boys aren't," Skylar added. "If they were, they would have reacted. They must have doubled back to find us." She was proud of herself. She had led them to Jo —with the help of some bite-sized candy, but still— and now they could break her out and spend the rest of the day on the dock eating ice-cream sandwiches.

"Two birds, one cone," Emma said admiringly.

"Jo!" Maddie cried, running for the shed.

"Shhhhhh!" Skylar looked around for signs of life as she waded through the weeds, with Emma right behind her.

"*Maddie?*" Jo sounded confused.

Skylar and Emma moved to help Maddie lift the shovel out of the door handle, and within seconds they were reunited with Jo, who stood with her hands on her hips in the musty air, the light streaming in through cracks between the window boards, illuminating the dust particles that floated around like allergenic snowflakes. Skylar could see an old lawnmower in one corner and a wall full of shovels. *It* was *like they were in a horror movie,* she thought. Or a really boring episode of *Antiques Roadshow*. But Jo's scowl disappeared as soon as she saw her friends.

"Wait, where'd the boys go? How did you find me?" she asked.

"We found your trail," Skylar said.

Jo looked confused. "What trail?"

"Haha, we totally got you guys!" Adam Loring yelled, coming out from behind the shed. The Slotkin twins and Nate joined him, forming a circle around the girls.

Skylar arched an eyebrow at them and crossed her arms. "So, what, you guys were just hanging out until we came by?" she asked. "That's a wimpy move."

"So's following a trail of candy," Matt said, looking proud of himself.

"Stop talking to them," Mark said. He drummed his fingers together like a cartoon villain. "They're *all* our prisoners now." The girls were trapped against the front of the shed.

"Stop being such losers," Skylar groaned.

"You'll have to tag us first, anyway," Emma said. That gave Skylar an idea.

"Get inside," she whispered to the others.

"What? No way, it stinks in here," Jo said.

"Get in," Skylar hissed. "We tagged you back in, and if we get in the shed and hold the door shut they can't tag any of us out again." She looked over at Emma, who gave her a supportive nod. "Go!" Skylar cried.

They all piled into the dank room and closed the door, throwing their collective weight against the inside of the door to keep the boys out.

"Hey!" Adam yelled.

"I told you we should have tagged them," Nate said.

"I'm not sure this is going to work," Jo panted.

"Trust me," Skylar said. "The lunch bell is going to ring any second."

It was quiet outside for a minute.

"Maybe they got bored," Maddie said hopefully.

Just then they heard the sound of the shovel barricade being moved back into place. Skylar's heart sank. She'd been a leader all right—and she'd led her friends right into a trap. The Girl Scouts probably wouldn't take her even if she paid them.

"Hey!" Emma yelled, banging on the inside of the door with both fists. "This is not funny!"

"Yes it is!" Mark's voice was thin, like he was farther away all of a sudden. "'Cause we're going to go jump off the dock now. You guys are stuck. We win!" Skylar heard faint laughter from outside the cabin.

"That's not how it works!" Jo yelled, grabbing a hoe and whacking the door like an action hero, nearly decapitating Maddie in the process. She dropped it on the floor with a clatter. "Great," she sighed. "Thanks for the company, anyway."

Skylar wiped an inch of dust off an ancient workbench and sat down, taking shallow breaths of the stale, metallic air as the lunch bell finally started ringing in the distance, just missing its cue. Emma sat next to her and tried to start a game of MASH, but Skylar wasn't in the mood. Her afternoon was officially ruined. She hated feeling embarrassed. She hated being inside on days that were perfect for swimming. She kind of hated Jo for making them play manhunt in the first place, and she definitely hated the boys for making up their own stupid rules. *Why,* she thought, tracing a curlicue into the dust by her thigh, *couldn't the girls be the ones to make up the rules once in a while?*

Skylar

Reunion: Day 3

"WHAT ARE YOU WAITING FOR?" JO REPEATED, LOUDER this time. Skylar looked back at the blue flag rippling in the breeze. She looked down at her grimy knees and her muddy romper and her arms, which were latticed with faint scratches. She looked at the black dirt buried under her chipped nails. She looked down at Adam, who was sitting quietly by the edge of the roof where she'd tagged him, and at Emma, still on the ground after nearly being flattened by Mark Slotkin. She looked at Maddie, who was catching her breath, and at Jo, who was staring up at her like she was insane, the black smears under her eyes shimmering with sweat. Then she walked over to the ladder and climbed down empty-handed. She knew Jo wouldn't—and maybe couldn't—understand, but she also knew it was what she had to do for the JEMS to be able to start over. At a certain point, she reasoned, when things got bad you had to just let go. The way she'd finally cut herself loose from Adam. The way she knew she had to deal with her dad and his selfish, misguided attempts to steer her life in the course of his choosing. Some people didn't change, Skylar thought, but she did. She *had*. And she wasn't willing to waste another minute playing by someone else's rules.

"Look," she said, gathering the girls into a huddle. "We tagged them all out. They're trapped here. And yeah, we could take the flag and crawl back through the woods and dodge more boys and make it back to base for a big win—"

"Which was the original plan *we all agreed on*," Jo interjected.

"—but what would that prove?" Skylar asked. "That we beat them? Look around—we already have." Mark and Bowen were splayed out on the ground, while Nate and Matt were busy picking up the toiletries the girls had tossed out onto the grass. And since Adam had been tagged all alone on the rooftop, that was where he had to stay.

"Let's go to the lake and lie out in the sun and enjoy our last full day together," she said. "We all deserve a rest."

Jo looked crushed. "We've come this far," she said. "That's ruined if we forfeit!"

"No, it isn't," Emma said, stepping up next to Skylar. "Like you said this morning, the important thing is that we came together. I didn't think we could, but we did, Jo—don't you see how amazing that is? So who needs a bandana? Who needs a flag?"

"I'm glad we made up," Jo said. "It's not that I'm not happy about that, I just . . . I need this, too." She looked around pleadingly. "Come on, guys. It's my last summer. One more push, for old times' sake?"

Skylar felt suddenly torn. She wanted nothing more than to abandon the game, but she also wanted to give Jo the victory she so desperately needed. Didn't she owe her that, for being her (somewhat unwilling, but steadfastly loyal) rock over the past three years? Maddie was already tightening her ponytail elastic in preparation for the next battle. Skylar looked over at Emma, who frowned and shrugged, wiping sweat off her temples.

"I don't know," Skylar sighed. "We're wet and sore and exhausted. I almost lost my best friends and now I feel like I can breathe again for the first time in three years. And frankly, no trophy is going to trump that."

Skylar glanced up at Adam, sitting on the roof by himself. Adam was so rarely alone that he looked out of place, like a scarecrow that had been put up there as a prank. But maybe some time to examine his feelings would be good for him. With no one to flirt with or make witty asides to, Adam would have to figure out what he really wanted. Skylar knew it wasn't her, that it would never be her, but she hoped it was something, or someone, who could make him better.

"We captured them, Jo," she said. "But we don't need them anymore."

"I agree," Jo whispered through clenched teeth—the boys, done licking their respective wounds, were all craning to hear what was being said—"but we are not just walking away." Maddie looked up at the flag and narrowed her eyes. The sun was so bright now that even with the eye black they had to squint.

Skylar leaned forward and rested her palms on her thighs, which were practically vibrating from all the running. She didn't want to admit that she wasn't sure she could make it back across camp without collapsing.

"So, what, you're not even taking the flag?" Mark said petulantly, pulling himself to his feet. "That's such a girly cop-out."

Maddie's eyes flashed. "Oh, we're taking the flag, Jock Itch," she said, bounding over to the ladder. She climbed up to the roof, breezed past Adam, and pulled the flag loose with one hand. Then, just as quickly, she was back on the ground, jogging off down the path toward the lake. "Come on!" she called over her shoulder.

Skylar wasn't sure what Maddie had in mind, but the direction she was headed suggested that whatever it was didn't involve sprinting, and that was good enough for her. She linked arms with Emma and a slightly bewildered Jo as they followed behind at a somewhat slower clip.

"Hey!" Nate yelled after them. "When's the game going to end, then? We can't stay here all night!"

"Sure you can," Skylar called back as they started down the path toward the shore, already feeling the breeze blowing in off the water, blessedly cool on her sweaty skin. "At least you've got a bathroom."

But as the wide mouth of the lake came into view at the end of the familiar wooded path, Skylar felt her confidence start to falter. They'd reconciled after the big blowout that morning, but so far the whole weekend had been about old times. About trying, and failing, to be their old selves. Whatever new phase of friendship they were heading into was completely uncharted territory.

Jo

Reunion: Day 3

BY THE TIME THE OTHERS CAUGHT UP TO MADDIE, she was already on the dock, her now completely ruined trademark Keds squeaking with each step on the damp planks. Jo appreciated that Maddie had refused to leave the flag behind—it felt much more like a victory to take it with them—but she selfishly didn't want her to toss it into the lake. Jo knew that she should feel accomplished. She'd made things right, just like she'd promised her father she would. But she still had a nagging feeling that something wasn't quite finished yet.

"Wait!" she shouted as Maddie wound up to pitch the flag into the water like a javelin.

"Come on, Jo," Maddie said, hesitantly lowering her arm and resting the bottom of the stick that served as a makeshift flagpole on the dock. "It's over. It's pointless."

"She's right," Emma said, gently squeezing Jo's hand.

"You can be the one to throw it if you want," Skylar offered.

"Can't I just . . . keep it?" Jo asked. "Like a memento?" As soon as the words were out she knew how petty she sounded.

"No," Maddie said, her normally bright eyes darkening. "I know it might sound stupid, but *I* need to do this."

"Me, too," Skylar said.

"Me, three," Emma said.

Jo thought about what she had said back in the treehouse, that it wasn't the flag itself that was important, but what it stood for. At the time she'd thought that the flag simply stood for winning the game and lording it over the twins and the rest of the people who'd mocked her for years. But seeing how sad and limp it looked in Maddie's hands, she realized that it wasn't a symbol of victory, after all. It was a symbol of everything they needed to leave behind. She looked out the water and immediately spotted the weather vane of the Putnams' rental cottage, the sun glinting off the brass like a diamond. Maybe Skylar's Buddhist leanings had finally rubbed off on her, but Jo found herself thinking that it couldn't be a coincidence.

"Okay," she said. "Let's all do it, then. Together." They stacked their fists one on top of the other and sent the flag sailing into the lake.

"No more secrets," Maddie said, grinning.

"No more fighting," Emma said, throwing an arm around Skylar's waist.

"No more camp," Jo said, her voice breaking.

"You wish!" Skylar said. "There are four more weeks."

"Oh," Jo laughed. "Right." She had forgotten that within twenty-four hours, the campers would be back for second session.

"And one more night of reunion," Maddie added, wiggling her

eyebrows lasciviously. "Which means you can have another 'meeting' with Nate."

"Thanks, but I'm afraid that boat has capsized," Jo said glumly.

"You'll never know until you talk to him," Emma said.

"And if this is your last summer, you might not have another opportunity," Skylar said.

"No excuses," Maddie cried, grabbing Jo by the elbows and beginning to steer her back toward the boys' camp.

"Hey, why does this conversation feel so familiar?" Jo laughed.

"Because we're right," Skylar said.

"Take it from me," Emma said. "If you get a last chance, you don't want to waste it."

Jo didn't need any more convincing.

She found Nate in the boys' bathroom washing mud off his face. While her sturdy boots had served Jo well during the game, now they clacked loudly on the tile floor, robbing her of the element of surprise. When he looked up and saw her behind him in the mirror, he shook his head.

"You're following me into the bathroom?" he asked without turning around. "You ignore me for a whole day, except to publicly humiliate me, and now you show up next to the urinals."

"I like to set the bar low?" she joked.

He shook his head. "Sometimes I don't get you, Jo. I mean, I thought I hit the jackpot when you said you'd go out with me. But after you freaked out, I realized you're mean to me about seventy-five percent of the time."

"I'm not mean," she said. "I'm . . . challenging."

"I'm getting that sense," he sighed.

"And in my opinion, nothing that's not a challenge is ever worth it."

"Is that why you never liked me?" He met her eyes in the mirror and leaned on the sink, and she noticed his triceps flexing underneath the skintight arms of his T-shirt. Jo had been noticing a lot of details like that lately. It seemed like all the girls' sex talk had finally gotten to her. She took a deep breath of peroxide-scented air to clear her head.

"I do like you," she said.

"You don't act like it."

"I know," she said. "But I'm trying. This is me trying."

Nate smiled a little, but he still didn't turn around. "You know," he said. "Just a general tip: If you don't want people to think you're gay, you probably shouldn't use the men's room."

She crossed her arms. "That's not funny."

"Oh, come on," he said.

"Here's the thing about me," she said. "I'm not a lesbian. Not that I haven't ever thought about it, because you're not the first person to tell me that. But I'm not. And pigeonholing anyone like that is not okay."

"Jo—" Nate started, but she cut him off.

"Also, not all lesbians have short hair or play basketball, FYI. Just like not all straight girls like makeup or stupid TV shows about morons who compete with each other to marry some guy who spends all his time running shirtless in slow-motion staring into the middle distance. Some of us are just a little different, but that doesn't mean we don't have the same feelings." She swallowed back tears. "It doesn't mean we don't stay up at night thinking about kissing the guy we like for the first time, or that when that moment finally happens, we don't get scared. Because especially for different girls, it's not always easy for someone to like you for who you are, and not for who they wish you would be."

Jo spun around and clenched her jaw. She didn't want him to see how upset she was.

"Are you done?" he asked. She felt like throwing something at him. She'd finally opened up to him and he cared more about scrubbing dirt from his cuticles.

"Yeah," she said bitterly. "I'm done." She bolted for the door and had already grabbed the knob when she heard his sneakers squeak on the wet floor, felt his hand on her waist. She turned to tell him where he could put his overly friendly paws and was surprised to find that his face was an inch from hers.

"Good," he said. "Because I have something to say, too." He kissed her, pushing her back against the heavy door and reaching his hands up to touch her hair, his thumbs tracing trails down her neck. When he pulled back, he smiled. His face was smeared with sweat and eye black. He looked ridiculous. "Wait—are you crying?" he asked.

She shook her head defiantly, feeling the tears spilling onto her cheeks. "No," she laughed, wiping a wrist across her nose. "Shut up."

"See, that's the thing," he said. "I like that you tell me off when you're crying. And that you call me out for making stupid jokes. I like that you work out but eat crap all the time. I like that you're so strong and don't apologize for it, and that you're so beautiful but you don't define yourself by it." He reached down and took her hands. "I *do* like you for who you are, Jo," he said. "I always have. You just haven't noticed."

This time, she kissed him.

Maddie

Reunion: Day 3

MADDIE STARED AT HER PHONE AND STEELED herself. She'd been sitting on her bunk for almost ten minutes, scrolling through her contacts and letting the highlighted bar hover over "DO NOT ANSWER!!!!," never allowing herself to actually hit the call button. She hadn't spoken to Charlie in months, but after throwing the flag into the lake, she was fired up. She didn't feel like hiding from him—from anyone—anymore. Escaping wasn't fixing anything in her life, and being with her friends reminded her how brave she used to be. She'd ended her junior year wandering the halls of Cross Creek High like an outcast, but she refused to play the part of the humiliated ex-girlfriend when she went back in the fall. Her heart may have been broken, but she was still standing. And she would be damned if she let a guy try to knock her down again, much less with a cowardly text. *If I can climb a twelve-foot tree and outrun a quarterback, I can make this call,* Maddie thought. She pressed her thumb down and held her breath.

She almost couldn't hear the sound of the ringer over her own heartbeat, but after three and a half rings, Charlie picked up.

"Hello?" He was trying to act like he didn't know who it was. Maddie rolled her eyes dramatically at the empty cabin. Who didn't have caller ID on a cell phone?

"It's Maddie," she said.

"Oh . . ." She heard some shuffling in the background. "Hey." She would have bet a hundred dollars he was lying in bed playing video games in his boxers, if there had been anyone around to take the bet. But Jo had gone off to throw herself at Nate, and after the rest of them had showered and changed, Skylar and Emma had headed over to the big end-of-game pizza dinner in the mess hall. To be honest, Maddie had never felt so grateful to be alone. She wasn't sure she could do this otherwise.

"Listen," she said. "I want you to not talk and not hang up for sixty seconds while I say something. Can you do that?"

More shuffling. "Okay."

"Great." She cleared her mind and willed the right words to come. "First, that was a shitty text you sent. What happens between me and Christina is between me and Christina, and even though I know you'd like to think of yourself as in the middle of us, you're not. If we want to mend our relationship and be friends again, you have no part in that. No part. So yeah, I knew it was her birthday, and no, I didn't call, and that is exactly zero of your business." She paused and listened for some sign that he was still there. He coughed. She dove back in.

"I'm not going to yell at you for sleeping with her, or for lying to me about it, because I know that wouldn't do anything. What's done is done, and I hope you feel terrible, honestly, but I'm not looking for an apology anymore. What I *do* take issue with is your letting me become a joke at school, like I was just some girl you screwed, and like you never cared about me. So when I get back in September, I expect that to stop, and I expect you to make sure it stops. And if it doesn't stop, know that I'm not gonna take it anymore." Maddie's heart was racing. She was on a roll.

"What you did to me was horrible and unforgivable," she said, standing up, trying to picture him right in front of her, with his hair in his face and his hands in his pockets: the Charlie slouch, she used to call it. "And I'll never regret anything more than I regret sleeping with you. But I'm not your victim any more than you were the love of my life. And if you only remember one thing about me, I want it to be that. Have a nice day now." She hung up and dropped the phone, her hand was shaking so hard.

Maddie sat back down and stared at her suitcase, which sat in the center of the cabin with its Southwest Airlines tags still attached. In a massive stroke of irony, her baggage had found its way back to her just as she was ready to let it go; the suitcase had been sitting on the steps of Souhegan when she got back from capture the flag. Now that she had taken care of the Charlie business, Maddie felt entitled to a change of clothes that actually fit her, as well as some underwear that didn't seem to be constructed of dental floss—she had spent the weekend in Skylar's "emergency thongs" (Maddie didn't even dare ask).

Showered and dressed and emotionally purged, Maddie decided to take a walk down to the Green. As soon as she stepped outside, the air seemed crisper, the colors looked brighter. It was like Souhegan had been swept up in a tornado and landed in Oz. Maddie smiled. She almost wanted to skip. She'd stood up for herself, she'd been articulate without getting nasty, and she'd said her piece. And even though she hadn't let Charlie get a word in—because, she reasoned, nothing he could say would make it better, and there were a lot of things he could say that would only make it worse—she finally felt like she had closure. For one of her problems, anyway. She had a list of other people who deserved phone calls—and none of them would be as easy as Charlie's. It was a literal list, scribbled on the palm of her hand with a Sharpie:

Mom

Christina

Eddie

Bio Dad (?)

The last one was a question mark, for obvious reasons. Maddie didn't have his phone number. She didn't know if he had another family. She didn't even know if he knew she existed. But the main reason he got a question mark was that Maddie didn't know if she needed to look for him anymore.

Of course, she was still curious. She wanted to know what he was like and whether she was like him, and who on his side had the curly red hair that was both her trademark and, in more humid climates, the bane of her existence. But the more she thought about it, the more she realized that her biological father and Camp Nedoba—which were only linked by their location in the state of New Hampshire, as far as she and the Google search bar knew—served a similar purpose.

The year Maddie turned nine was the same year her mother started coming home from work smelling funny. It was also the year Eddie lost his job at the auto shop and settled into his permanent spot on the basement futon, in front of Orioles games. She'd always wondered about her "real" dad, but the forces that drew her to the computer that day in the library had nothing to do with him. She just needed to get away. At that age she was naive enough to think she could just pick up and go live with him, and that he'd welcome her with open arms and endless patience, and maybe a even canopy bed.

She hadn't found him. But she'd found camp. She'd found Mack. And through a series of events that still seemed unbelievable, she'd gotten the escape she'd so desperately needed.

Maddie didn't have Mack's name written on her hand, but she still ended up at the door of his office. It was almost six, so she wasn't sure if he'd be there, but when she rapped on the screen door, his big, deep voice told her to come in.

"Hello again," she said as she poked her head into his office. Mack was sitting at his desk, typing on his laptop underneath a framed Abenaki tribal flag, which coincidentally had the same colors as a Girl Scout badge.

"Maddie!" he said. "I heard you were the MVP of capture the flag this afternoon."

She smiled. "Did Jo tell you?"

"No, I saw Emma and Skylar at the pizza party. It just finished up. Why weren't you there?"

"I . . . had some cleaning up to do," she said.

"Well, is there anything you need?" He pushed his laptop away and sat back in his chair.

"No," she said. "I guess I just wanted to say thank you."

"For what?"

"For *everything*. For letting me come here, for keeping my secret—which I know put you in a weird position—and for just . . . being there for me."

"Maddie, it's been entirely my pleasure." He smiled, and she ran over to give him a hug.

"I had an okay time, too," she said with a smile. "Oh! Also, I was wondering, is registration open for next summer?"

"September first," Mack said. "Why?"

"I want to get my sisters up here," Maddie said. "Harley just turned eleven, and Mae'll be ten by next summer. I know they'd love it here. And before you say anything, I want you to know that I'm going to pay for them to go here. Full tuition. I've been saving up my paychecks, and by winter I'll have enough."

Mack looked at her with a glint in his eye. "That's fine," he said.

"But you know, relatives of staff members go to camp for free. If you feel like applying." He tapped his pen on his desk. "Just something to think about."

"Thanks, I will," she said, her face breaking into a slow smile.

By the time the screen door banged shut behind her, Maddie had a singular purpose. She ran across the Green and up the hill to the barn, vaulting herself up the beams more sure-handedly than she ever had, not caring that her clean white jeans were getting covered in dust. She crawled through the boxes of junk, back to their corner, and reached into her back pocket for her Sharpie.

After she was done, she stepped back and admired the letters she'd printed in thick black marker, stark and strong against the rough, gray wood:

MADDIE RYLAND WAS HERE.

And even better, she knew she would be back.

Emma

The First Summer ◆ *Age 10*
Last Morning of Camp

"Friendship Rule: Best friends never forget what brought them together."

"ONE . . . TWO . . . THREE . . . SMILE!"

Emma squished in closer to Skylar and squinted into the late morning sun. She and her seven bunk mates were packed onto Nashua's narrow front steps, and Adri and Tara, their co-counselors, were taking photo after photo with everyone's cameras. Emma's cheeks hurt from smiling for so many photos, but if it meant she got to stay with her friends for even just a few extra minutes, it was worth it. She couldn't believe that it was already time to go home. The first summer had flown by. It almost felt like a dream, and sometimes she had to look down at the friendship anklet Skylar had made for her—a thin leather strap threaded with deep blue wooden beads—to remind herself it had really happened.

"Can't I *please* get my phone back from Mack?" Sunny Sherman—whose real name, at least according to the permanent marker on her trunk, was Allison—whined to Tara. She was pouting because her camera battery had died.

"No phones until checkout," Tara said, firmly but kindly. "Now, one more time—SMILE!"

"No faces this time, Maddie!" Adri called.

Emma glanced over at Maddie, who had folded her tongue into a loop and crossed her eyes.

"I think the mosquito bites have gone to her brain," Jo said, elbowing Maddie gently in the side. Maddie stretched her lips into a wide, fake grin, batting her eyelashes.

"That's better," Tara murmured, snapping away.

"Can you get one with my camera of just the four of us?" Jo asked. "No offense," she said to Sunny.

"It's okay, I know you need your precious JAM time," Sunny said with a sniff.

"It's *JEMS,*" Emma said defensively. The other three girls—Aileen, Jess, and Kerry—seemed pretty nice, but Sunny had rubbed her the wrong way from the very first day, when she'd picked up Harold and said with a laugh that she didn't even know they *made* Pound Puppies anymore.

"Whatever," Sunny said, hopping up with a smirk. She crossed her arms and looked at Adri. "Can we go to the Green now? I know my dad's waiting. He told me I could watch a movie on the ride home. *And* stop at Dairy Queen." Skylar snickered.

"For her they should call it Dairy *Princess,*" she whispered, but Emma raised a finger to her lips. As annoying as Sunny could be, she didn't want to start a fight on the very last day.

"I can take these four down the hill," Adri told Tara, struggling to pick up Sunny's oversized suitcase.

As they started off down the path, Emma heard Kerry whisper, "You have a TV in your *car*?"

"Okay, ladies, show me those gorgeous faces!" Tara fumbled to find the button on Jo's point-and-shoot. Skylar slung her arm around Emma's shoulders and squeezed, and Emma beamed at the camera. Out of the corner of her eye, she could see Maddie sticking out her tongue. "Now say 'camp'!" Tara cried.

"CAMP!" they yelled. The flash went off.

"That one's a keeper," Tara said proudly.

While they waited for Gus to load their trunks into the back of his blue pick-up truck, the girls clustered on Jo's bed, since it was the only one that still had sheets. Jo was staying for second session, but they all promised to come for the whole summer next year. Emma never would have thought she could be happy away from her parents for a month, but now she felt bad that they were on their way. She worried that she might not even be able to pretend that she'd missed them.

"What if I just don't go home?" she wondered aloud, as Maddie sat behind her, braiding her hair. "What if I just hide in my trunk until everyone leaves, and then live in the barn until next summer?"

"Shhhh!" Jo whispered, nodding her head at Tara, who was leaning against the doorframe reading a paperback. No one could know they'd made a secret rope ladder to get up into the barn loft.

"If you stay, I'm staying," Skylar said, retying the knot on her own matching anklet. She'd made them for the whole group, one in what seemed like a never-ending series of craft projects. Leaf rubbings, nature paintings, picture frames made out of sticks and beads—Skylar's bunk had been so cluttered with knickknacks that she'd had to give some of them away to the counselors to make room for more.

Emma wished that she had more tangible objects to take home from camp. Aside from the anklet and a very lumpy mug she'd made for her mother in the pottery studio, all her memories were in her head. Her "roses," as Adri and Tara would say. It was a Camp Nedoba tradition that every night before they went to bed, the girls went around the cabin telling the best part of their day (the "rose") and the worst (the "thorn"), and then the counselors would sing them to sleep. Jo's dad thought the ritual was a good way to keep things in perspective, celebrating the good moments and letting go of the bad ones.

"Awesome," Emma said, trying to focus on the fantasy of staying at camp, and not on the fact that at any minute, Tara would be rounding them up to leave each other for a whole year. "We can go swim in the lake every day."

"And drink bug juice at every meal!" Skylar laughed.

"I can learn to play the trumpet!" Maddie offered. She adopted a thick Southern drawl. "I'll only charge y'all a dollar a show. More if I tap dance."

"You'd never survive the winter," Jo yawned. "The barn has no heat. The lake will give you hypothermia. And if the kitchen's closed, who would make the bug juice? Or the waffles? You'd starve." She rolled over lazily and put her head in Emma's lap, and Emma marveled that just four weeks earlier, they'd all been strangers. She hadn't known that Skylar only used conditioner, never shampoo, because of a regimen her mother had picked up in France, or that Maddie could deal a deck of cards with one hand just by flicking them off with her index finger, or that Jo liked to sneak spoonfuls of coffee and sugar into her milk carton in the cafeteria when the counselors weren't watching.

"It was a joke," Emma groaned, tugging playfully on Jo's ponytail. "Obviously we can't stay. I just . . . really want to."

"Me too," Maddie said quietly, in her normal voice. "I had the best summer of my whole life."

"You'll be back next year," Jo said. "It's not the end of our lives."

Maddie tied off Emma's braid with an elastic. "Still," she said. "It's a long time. Send me that picture. I don't want to forget what you look like."

"Send it to *all* of us," Skylar said. "We should make an e-mail list."

"Phone, too!" Emma added. She rooted around in her backpack and pulled out a notebook.

"E-mail me before you call," Maddie said after she hesitantly recited her number for Emma. "My house can be . . . chaotic."

Emma looked down at the short list of letters and numbers, which only took up four lines, not counting the heading she had added in bold capitals:

JO

EMMA

MADDIE

SKYLAR

Still, it didn't feel like enough.

Emma would have given anything to do a *Freaky Friday* body swap with Jo and spend the next four weeks being awesome at diving and eating Belgian waffles topped with M&Ms instead of sweating in front of a fan in the Medford library reading the autobiography of Frederick Douglass for extra credit, or helping her dad build a bocce court for the senior citizens' center. Even just sitting around watching TV for the rest of the summer like a normal kid suddenly seemed hopelessly boring, and going outside would be pointless, since there was no lake or barn or arts and crafts cabin filled with spools of every color of lanyard.

It wasn't that Emma didn't have friends—she even had a best friend, Anna, who had nothing to do but hang out since she'd broken her leg in the spring. But suddenly, compared to Skylar, Anna seemed kind of (Emma hated to think it, but it was true) boring. She didn't know how she would make it through the school year.

"I have an idea!" Emma said. "Before we leave, let's make a pact that we'll always be friends."

"Pinky swear?" Jo asked, extending a finger.

"No, something more . . . official," Emma said.

"Blood sisters?" Maddie asked excitedly.

"*No,*" Tara intoned from the door. "And whatever you're writing, make it quick."

"There's this thing called an exquisite corpse," Skylar said.

"Like a dead person?!" Jo asked.

"No, well, not really. It's a drawing thing. One person draws something and then folds over the paper, hiding everything but the very edge, so the next person continues the drawing without seeing what the first person drew—and then you keep going until you have a full page." She tucked a stringy piece of hair behind her ear and smiled self-consciously. "It's pretty cool."

Jo looked confused. "What does that have to do with anything?"

"I get it," Emma said. "We all write part of the pact but we don't read what anyone else writes. Right?"

"Exactly!" Skylar grinned.

"Top secret," Maddie said. "I like it."

Emma tore a new page out of her notebook and selected a pink rollerball pen.

FRIENDSHIP PACT, she wrote in flowery script. Below that, she recorded the date and time. She folded over the top and thought for a minute before writing her rule. Then she folded the paper again and passed it to Skylar, who chewed on the pen cap and then started to write, her sharp, skinny elbow bouncing wildly. Jo chuckled to herself while writing hers—she probably didn't take it that seriously, Emma thought. But Maddie clearly had her rule already in mind, because she put pen to paper with no hesitation. When she handed the pact back to Emma, it was a thick rectangle. Skylar made the executive decision to decorate it with red foil stars, so that it would stand out from the dozens of other crumpled notes that filled Emma's backpack.

"Now what?" Emma asked. "Do we read them?"

"No," Skylar said. "Let's wait until next summer. It can be like a time capsule!"

In the doorway, Gus cleared his throat. "You ladies are gonna be a living time capsule if you don't get your butts moving," he said, hoisting Emma's trunk onto his shoulders. "Don't think I won't leave you here."

Jo rolled her eyes, but they all got up and started moving toward the door.

Emma looked down at the folded piece of notebook paper. It would get crushed in her backpack, but she had no other place to put it.

"Hey, want me to keep it here?" Jo asked, holding out her hand. "That way it never leaves camp." Emma smiled gratefully and passed it to Jo as she followed Skylar down the steps and out the door. Jo shrugged like it was no big deal, but to Emma, it was.

This way, in a small way, a part of her would always be at camp.

This way, a piece of all of them would never leave.

Emma

Reunion: Day 3

"CAREFUL, DON'T SET IT ON FIRE!" JO SAID. EMMA looked up at the others, standing over her in the darkness. The flame of the match in her hand was licking at the edge of the paper lunch bag between her feet, but she knew what she was doing. Emma carefully lowered her hand down and angled the match toward the tiny wick of the votive candle. "Come on . . ." she whispered. Finally, it lit, and she pulled her fingers out, shaking the match before it burned her. The bag glowed amber in the darkness, illuminating Skylar's, Jo's, and Maddie's faces against the purple sunset. Behind them, through the trees, Emma could hear laughter and shouting wafting up from the fire pit. But after the day they'd had, none of them had felt like going to a big party. They just wanted to be together on their last night, and unlike their *last* last night, this time they wouldn't leave each other's sides.

It had been Skylar's idea to make the floating luminaries, and in just an hour in the arts and crafts barn, she'd whipped up four little rafts made of twigs bound by hemp cord. She'd even made four little masts with four construction paper sails, on which she'd painted each of their names. They were so beautiful, Emma almost didn't want to send them out on the water. Luckily, she had motivation.

"We don't have all night," Jo said, looking back at the trees. "It's only a matter of time before people start wandering out here to pee."

"And here I didn't think anything could make this moment more special," Maddie said.

Emma lit another match and reached for the second bag. "I'm going as fast as I can," she promised.

Jo sat down next to Skylar and dug her toes into the sand. She was back in her Camp Nedoba T-shirt and cargo shorts, but she'd looked different ever since she'd come back from talking to Nate. It looked like someone had lit a votive inside her, too.

"I can't believe the kids are coming back tomorrow," Jo murmured.

"I know," Skylar said miserably. "I need like twenty-four hours of sleep."

"We'll make it an early night," Emma said as she lit the final candle. "Unless you guys want to rage."

"No thank you," Skylar groaned. Jo clapped her on the back. "Turning over a new leaf, are we?"

"Yeah," Skylar said, smiling. "I think I'm gonna take it easy for a while. Read some books. Write some terrible poetry. Maybe do some SAT prep."

Emma shuddered. "You can have all of my books," she said. She stepped back and admired the rafts, the candles flickering like trapped lightning bugs. "Okay, we're ready to launch."

They waded into the lake in their bare feet, holding the bags gingerly so that the flames stayed lit. When they got past the softly breaking waves, they set the rafts down on the surface and gently pushed them forward into the black water. Even though the lake had cooled to a shivering temperature, none of them made a move to go back to the shore. Instead, they clasped hands and watched in silence as the lanterns floated away.

"There we go," Maddie whispered. The rafts bobbed in the moonlight, each to their own rhythm.

"Here we are," Emma said, squeezing their hands. She looked up at the sky, and a tiny light flickered above them. Emma gasped. "Was that a shooting star?"

The others looked up, and for a silent minute they all waited. But then the light flashed again.

"Nah, just a plane," Jo said.

But none of them moved. Instead, they just stood in the water gazing at the stars until it finally got too cold to stand.

By the time they got back to the farewell bonfire, the crowd had thinned considerably, owing to a game of beer pong that was taking place on the boys' side, according to Aileen Abrams, who had filled them in when they'd crossed paths near the tree house. Sunny and her friends had been avoiding them since that morning; apparently one of Sunny's Louis Vuitton purses had sustained water damage when the boys raided the cabin. "I could take your dad to small claims court," she'd huffed to Jo. Once she was out of sight, they had all agreed that the only appropriate retort would be to short-sheet her bed later.

They sat down knee to knee on the seniors' log and held their hands over the fire, which was dwindling but still warm enough to make Emma's legs stop shaking. Jo found a few forgotten marshmallows at the bottom of a nearby milk crate, skewered them onto sticks, and passed them around. Emma held hers low over the flames, letting them lick at the bottom until it got sooty and black.

"Mind if we join you?" Emma looked up to see Nate coming through the trees. But he wasn't alone. Adam followed behind, staring intently at the ground. It was becoming his signature stance.

Jo jumped up and gave Nate a hug.

"I missed you," she said. Emma glanced at Maddie and raised her eyebrows. It was a new side of Jo she'd never seen. "But *he*'s not welcome." She crossed her arms and glared at Adam, and Emma smiled. It looked like the old Jo was still alive and kicking.

"It's okay with me," Skylar said. "As long as it's okay with Emma."

"It's okay with me," Emma said, keeping her gaze on the fire. She wasn't sure if it was, really, but she was too tired to fight anymore.

"Do I get a vote?" Maddie asked in a tone that suggested if it were up to her, Adam would get hog-tied and put on a spit.

Nate sat next to Jo, draping an arm casually around her shoulders, and Adam looked around as if trying to compute where he could sit that would keep him the farthest away from a potential slap. After hesitating for a second he settled next to Emma, leaving a few feet between them. But the wind conspired against her; she could smell his Old Spice mixing in with the smoke, and in spite of everything, it still made her heart beat faster. She inched closer to Skylar, who stared straight ahead like she had blinders on.

"Belated congratulations on your win today," Nate said. Jo beamed and leaned into him. Nate had always known just what to say to her, Emma thought, and Jo had finally started to listen. Emma was glad someone was getting a neat, happy ending, because as she inched away from Adam on the log, she realized once and for all that it could never be them.

"I'm guessing I'm not getting that kind of reception," Adam said, attempting a joke. Emma gave him a withering look.

"If you're going to pretend that you don't know why you're not exactly the guest of honor, the exit's that way," she said, pointing to the path.

"Sorry." He paused. "I know I really screwed up," he said softly. Emma didn't respond. She'd been giving Adam a lot of thought that afternoon, and she still wasn't sure how to word what she wanted to say.

Her instinct was to hurt him the way he had hurt her, to reject him the way she felt rejected. But she'd already engaged in petty warfare at breakfast and during capture the flag, and now, maybe thanks to the chilly evening breezes, she had cooled off considerably. Adam wasn't evil, he was just confused. And so was she.

Because the more thought about it, the less she felt like she really wanted Adam. What she had wanted was the second chance, the possibility of changing course. She'd been holding on to the idea of Adam for so long that he'd become the focus of a need that had nothing to do with him. After all, she'd gotten her second chance. She'd gotten her best friends back. And the course correction she'd needed wasn't to fix the past, it was to face the future, and to have the courage to make choices that would make her happy. Emma didn't need a MASH game or a paper fortune teller to let her know Adam wasn't one of those choices.

"It's for the best," she said finally. "I think what I was trying to do this weekend was kiss you on the rock three years ago."

"What?" He looked confused.

"I like you," she said. "And I want to be your friend, if we can do that. But I think the idea of us together is better than the reality, you know?"

Adam got quiet. "Do you regret yesterday?" he asked.

"No," she said. "I needed that." Plus, he had been a great kisser. But the less she dwelled on it, the better.

"I'm sorry I freaked out afterwards," he said. "I just felt like I didn't deserve you, and I didn't know what to do with that. I've never felt that way before." Emma felt Skylar's leg tense against hers, and she pushed Adam down the log a few feet and scooted over.

"Anyway, I think you're right," he went on. "The idea of you was kind of overwhelming. Like, I had you on a pedestal for so long, actually being with you was way too much pressure."

"You had *me* on a pedestal?" she asked. Her marshmallow, now blackened, fell into the coals.

"Don't look so shocked. You're pretty awesome."

"You too. When you're not being a jerk." She smiled at him and he shook his head.

"See, I told you, Emma. You get me."

"Sometimes I think so," she said. She fought one last, powerful urge to kiss him—just on the cheek, but still, she reasoned, unwise—and then shifted back over to Skylar. They watched Adam get up to leave, his face falling into shadow as he turned away from the fire.

"Are you okay?" Emma asked.

"No," Skylar said, leaning her head on Emma's shoulder. "Not yet. But I'll live."

Nate got up to follow Adam, after giving Jo a kiss and one last proposition.

"Hacky sack tomorrow?" he asked. "Before the munchkins attack?"

Jo smiled. "You got it," she said. Once he was gone, she patted the log next to her and Maddie leapt over, wrapping her in a hug.

Skylar stared out into the fire. "He's not the one, huh?" she said, exhaling heavily.

Emma shook her head. "Nope."

"He is for someone," Maddie said. "In thirty years when Adam reaches maturity, I'm sure he'll make some poor woman very happy."

Emma knew Maddie was right. Adam Loring had been her first crush, but he wouldn't be her last. And while she would always remember with a bittersweet ache of nostalgia how it felt to love him from afar, she'd grown out of him since camp, just like the old watermelon backpack, or her stuffed animals (well, except for Harold; she still slept with him sometimes). Luckily, not everything felt too small, like the low-ceilinged cabins or the tiny paper cups that only held three sips of water. The people who really mattered had grown up with her.

She listened to Skylar's even breath, and the crackling logs, and the reedy song of the crickets beyond in the grass. *This is my rose,* she thought. *This moment.* Her heart hurt, but in a good way, the way a muscle hurt when it had been pushed to its limits and had to tear to strengthen. The night air was cool on her face and the fire was warm on her legs. She was with the people who knew her best in the world, and she knew herself better, too—better than she had when she'd turned off the highway just two days earlier, at the old oak with the blue flag tangled in its branches. Emma felt a sudden urge to say something meaningful to her friends, something that would tell them how special and irreplaceable they were, and how lucky she was to have them in her life, even if only for a few days a year. She wanted to tell them how she would always be there for them, and how she would never, ever again throw them over for a guy, no matter how hard she fell.

But as they sat together, holding each other under the darkening sky, she realized she didn't need to tell them. They already knew. They had always known.

Skylar

Reunion: Last Day

SKYLAR TOOK A DEEP BREATH AS SHE STOOD BEHIND the double doors that would lead her out of the calm sanctuary of the cafeteria and back into the fray. It was almost ten, which meant that the new session's campers were already arriving, making painful, loud, and public detachments from the family members who had driven them there. The Green was a maze of luggage, frenetic campers, and frazzled parents, and Skylar had taken twenty minutes to toast her bagel to a Cajun crisp just to avoid going back out. She took a swig of her coffee and steeled herself. She wasn't ready to start another four-week marathon, much less one that involved seeing Adam every day, but she had no choice.

She slipped on her Ray-Bans and walked over to the gazebo where Jo and Mack were seated behind a folding table, registering the new campers.

"Need anything?" she asked Jo. Nearby, a group of girls shrieked at an ear-splitting decibel.

"A lobotomy," Jo deadpanned. "Or money to pay for my future

hearing aids."

"What?" Mack said, putting a hand to his ear.

"See?" Jo said. Skylar laughed.

"What's my bunk this session?"

Jo sighed. "You were supposed to check last week and have your stuff moved in already."

"Oops," Skylar said. "But in my defense I was having a very intense weekend with my best friends."

Jo gave her the side-eye. "You're with the twelves."

"Yes!" Skylar was thrilled. Twelve-year-olds were old enough to be seasoned campers, but not old enough to think they knew everything. They were her favorites.

Just then, a tiny girl with black curls walked up to the desk and tapped Skylar's arm.

"I'm supposed to find my counselor, Jo," she said shyly. "Are you her?"

"No," Skylar laughed. "I wish. That's Jo." She pointed, and the girl smiled. "You are so lucky," Skylar whispered as Jo turned to grab a welcome packet. "Jo is the best counselor you could possibly have. Do you know that she actually grew up on this camp? She knows everything about it, and she'll make you feel at home in no time."

"Do you really know *everything*?" the girl asked.

"Pretty much," Jo said.

"Can you show me where my bunk is?"

"Sure," she said, grinning as she handed Skylar her clipboard.

Skylar watched with a smile as Jo led the girl up the path to her new home, at least for the summer.

"Excuse me," someone said a few minutes later, as Skylar was frantically trying to keep track of Jo's registration system. "I'm trying to find my best friend."

"Um, sure, what's her name?" she asked hurriedly, checking the clip board.

"Skylar MacAlister." Skylar could feel Emma's smirk before she even lifted her head. "Hi," she said, turning away from Mack and whispering, "*Help me.*"

"Overwhelmed?" Emma asked.

"Just a tad." Skylar held up a stack of disorganized registration forms. "Apparently I am incapable of alphabetizing."

"The key is to burp it," Emma said, laughing.

"What's so funny?" Jo asked, walking back, with Maddie following close behind and dragging her recovered suitcase.

"Some things never change," Skylar said, looking out at the chaos on the Green, where boys were running wild and pairs of girls were taking kissy-face self-portraits before their counselors confiscated their cell phones.

Emma sighed. "I guess I should probably get out of here before someone blocks my ride."

"I just called a cab," Maddie said. "I'll walk over there with you."

"We *all* will," Skylar said. She felt a lump forming in her throat.

She wasn't ready to say good-bye, especially not to Emma. She'd spent the last three years without her, and now even just a month seemed insurmountable. But she knew it would be good to have fewer distractions, especially of the late-night variety. She would need to do a lot of work to make up what she'd missed the past semester at school. Maybe if she took some college credits in the fall, she could even catch up and graduate with the rest of her class.

"You're sure you don't want to stay?" Skylar asked, throwing her arms around Emma and Maddie as they walked. "I'm pretty sure we could hook you guys up with a job at the hash brown station."

"As tempting as that is," Emma said, "I have to go back to New York and finish up my internship. But . . ." She smiled. "There's always next summer."

"Wait, are you going to apply again?" Skylar asked. She tried to control her glee.

"Maybe," Emma said. "You never know."

"Well, I'm definitely going to," Maddie said. "My sisters can come for free if I'm a counselor."

"What?" Jo cried. "I finally leave and now you're coming back?"

"You can always come visit during reunion," Maddie said, sticking out her tongue. "Plus, someone has to keep an eye on Nate for you, make sure he's eating his Wheaties and doing his push-ups."

"That is *not* funny," Jo said, pushing her. Skylar hoped one day when they talked about all the drama that had happened surrounding Adam Loring, they would just laugh.

"Fine," Skylar said as they crossed the middle of the Green. "I guess I'll just have to stalk your Facebook photos late at night while I cry into my Diet Coke."

"Please *don't* do that," Emma laughed. "I'll be in touch more now, I promise. I know I haven't been a great friend—"

"It's *me* who's been the bad friend," Maddie interrupted.

"So have I," Jo said.

Skylar looked ahead at the parking lot and suddenly stopped short, nearly tripping Maddie. "You know what I just realized?" she said, examining the balding patch of grass beneath their feet. "We're basically standing on the exact spot where we met."

"You guys!" Maddie cried, tearing up and dropping her bags.

"Don't you start," Jo said, rolling her eyes.

"Maybe there'll be a plaque some day," Emma said.

"Oh, definitely," Skylar said. "I'm hoping for life-sized statues."

Maddie clapped. "You can sculpt them!"

Skylar didn't want to move. She wanted to sit down and turn her face up to the sun and remember what it had felt like the first time she saw Emma sitting on her trunk, clutching her backpack and looking around cautiously. Skylar liked to think there had been something guiding her that day, steering her toward the girl who would be her rock as she navigated the treacherous emotional terrain of adolescence. But she knew if she said it out loud, they would just pile on her for being a hippie. So Skylar kept quiet—until they got to Emma's car, anyway. Then she fell apart.

"Oh, Em," she said, her face crumpling. "I'm gonna miss you so much."

Jo slammed the trunk shut, interrupting their reverie.

"I'm sorry to make this quick," she said, "but I have to get back to the insanity."

"I guess this is good-bye, then," Emma said, pulling her into a hug.

"Just for a year," Jo said.

"But the past three days felt like a year," Emma said. "An actual year is going to feel like . . ."

"Forever!" Maddie said, practically leaping onto Jo.

"Hey, give me a break. I'm trying to be stoic here," Jo said, her voice wavering.

"That reminds me," Skylar said, winking at Emma and Maddie. "We have something for you."

She reached into the back pocket of her cutoffs and slipped out the miniature replica of the boys' blue flag that she'd made while waiting for the luminary rafts to dry.

"You deserve a memento," Skylar said.

"You *earned* it," Maddie added with a wink. It was just a twig and a flap of construction paper, and Skylar thought it looked pretty dinky, but Jo looked at it and promptly burst into tears.

Gravel crunched as a yellow cab turned into the parking lot and pulled to a stop next to them. A portly, pony-tailed driver got out and Jo hurriedly composed herself.

"Hello again, prom queen," he said to Maddie with a smile. Emma raised her eyebrows quizzically and Maddie laughed.

"It's a long story," she said. "And a whole 'nother life."

Once Maddie's cab had gone, and Jo had been called back to the gazebo, Skylar turned to Emma and smiled sadly.

"Where were we?" she asked.

"You were about to ugly cry, I think."

"Right." It didn't take much work for Skylar to choke up again. "I love you," she said, hugging Emma tightly.

"I love you, too," Emma said. "Thank you for being my best friend."

"Don't worry about it. You're stuck with me for life." Skylar grinned through her tears. "I never want anything to come between us ever again."

They hugged once more before Emma got into the driver's seat and adjusted the rearview mirror, wiping her eyes.

"I'll text you when I get home," she said.

"You better."

"Love you."

"Love you more."

Skylar watched the green station wagon roll up the gravel toward the access road and saw that Jo had affixed a bright yellow I'VE GOT A FRIEND IN CAMP NEDOBA! sticker to the rear bumper, on top of the liberal Jesus one. Emma's aunt was going to be so confused.

When she turned back to the Green and scanned the crowd, she saw Zoe Dawson, one of her favorite elevens from the previous summer, leaning against the chain link fence around the swimming pool with a group of girls. Skylar walked over, hoping she didn't look as sad as she felt.

"Are you my Pennacook girls?" she asked.

"Yes!" they cried. She started to gather them to head back to the bunk when a car pulled into the parking lot and a tall brunette hopped out. The girls started to scream with glee.

"That's Quinn," Zoe said, jumping up and down excitedly. "We weren't sure she was going to make it this summer." Quinn ran across the green and the girls enveloped her in a group hug. When they broke apart, Zoe flashed an embarrassed smile. "I know it seems like we're overreacting," she said. "But we really, really missed her."

"I get it," Skylar said. "No one loves you like your camp friends do." She felt herself tearing up again and turned away so that her new campers wouldn't see. "Now, come on," she said brightly. "Let's go get unpacked."

Emma

The First Summer ◆ *Age 10*
First Day of Camp

"You've got a friend in Camp Nedoba!"
—*Official Camp Nedoba slogan*

EMMA SAT ON HER TRUNK IN THE MIDDLE OF THE lawn, looking up at the wooden sign creaking in the breeze. Camp Nedoba. She couldn't believe she was finally there.

That morning, Emma had woken up in her own bed, looking out at the same maple tree branch she'd seen every morning since she was five and her dad had cleared out his study so that Kyle would finally stop bugging him about getting his own room. The foliage changed—from flowery bright green buds in May to fat summer leaves the color of steamed broccoli to golden-orange in October, before it went bald for the winter—but the branch was always there, rising behind the lavender shutters like an arm reaching up to wave hello. Until, now, it wasn't.

Emma's stomach flipped and she drew her knees up to her chest, staring hard at her sparkly pink toenails and willing herself not to search the parking lot again for her parents' car. She knew they were gone. If her best friend, Anna, had been there, like she was supposed to be, everything would be perfect. They'd been excited about their first summer at sleep-away camp all year, until Anna had broken her leg horseback riding in May and couldn't go anymore. Emma had begged her parents to let her stay home, too, but they'd already paid the deposit. "Besides," her mom had said, "you'll make new friends there." Emma sucked on her bottom lip to keep from crying. After her parents had taken her through registration, the tall man with the megaphone had told her to wait with her things for one of her counselors to come show her to the cabin. But she'd been waiting for ten minutes already and nobody had come. All the other, bigger kids seemed to travel in packs, shrieking and laughing and stomping off toward their cabins, which all had weird, unpronounceable American Indian names. What did *Nedoba* mean anyway? It could be some kind of code for a child labor farm, for all Emma knew.

She had been away from home once before, but only for a weekend, and that had been with her grandparents at Disney World. Here, she knew no one, and there weren't even any people walking around dressed like cartoon characters to make her feel better. Emma hung her head and felt the tears drop onto her kneecaps. She was embarrassed, but the fear overwhelmed her, and she couldn't even run somewhere to cry in private because she didn't know where anything was. Opening one of the wide-planked wooden doors could lead to a bathroom or to what the brochure had called its "state-of-the-art pottery kiln"—Emma had no way of knowing. She felt suddenly, irretrievably lost.

"Hey!"

Emma turned toward the voice and saw a tall girl with messy

blonde hair and a baggy sweatshirt, dragging a purple trunk and a matching duffel bag over to where Emma sat. She waved, and Emma looked behind her, sure she must be talking to someone else. But then the girl plopped down on the grass a few feet away and raised a hand to her eyes to shield her face against the sun. She was beautiful. If she brushed her hair, Emma thought, she could probably be in a commercial. But then the girl's big green eyes narrowed with worry. "Are you okay?" she asked.

Emma sniffed and clutched her new backpack to her chest. It was painted to look like a watermelon, with stripy green straps. She felt even more ashamed now. The blonde girl looked at least thirteen. She probably thought Emma was being such a baby.

"I'll be fine," Emma said. "It's just my first year."

"Me too," the girl sighed, dropping her things and plopping down on the grass. She fished in her pocket and brought out a smooth turquoise stone with rings on it like the inside of a tree. She held it in her palm and showed it to Emma. "My mom gave me a rock to rub whenever I miss her, but so far it's not doing anything."

"It's pretty, though," Emma said. The girl examined it for a moment before tossing it on the grass.

"Yeah, pretty stupid," she said, and then laughed. Emma laughed, too. They grinned at each other. Emma's stomach seemed to right itself almost instantly.

"I'm Skylar, by the way," the girl said. She reached out her hand and Emma noticed that Skylar had purple painted nails and was wearing multiple silver bangles. Emma made a mental note to hide her Pound Puppy when they got back to the bunk. Skylar did not look like the kind of girl who brought a stuffed animal to camp.

"I'm Emma," she said. They shook.

"Have you ever been to camp before?" Skylar asked.

"Nope."

"Me neither. Do you have any brothers or sisters?"

"An older brother," Emma said.

"Me too!" Skylar cried. "Are you from around here?"

Emma shook her head. "Boston."

"I'm from Philly," Skylar said, playing with her bracelets. "We drove eight hours to get here."

"Wow," Emma marveled.

"I know. My dad went here when he was our age. It's really important to him for some reason. Probably because I'm an artist like him." Skylar's eyes brightened. "Hey, do you like drawing?"

"Yes . . ." Emma wasn't actually very good at art, but even though she'd only known her for sixty seconds, she already wanted to be just like Skylar.

"We're twins!" Skylar declared with a grin.

"Maybe *fraternal* twins," Emma joked.

Skylar looked at her, squinting in the sun. "We could totally do a *Parent Trap,*" she said. "You in?" She studied Emma's face seriously for a second and then broke into a radiant smile. "I'm kidding, relax."

"Oh, good," Emma said. "I don't think I can walk on stilts."

Skylar laughed. "Hey, want me to draw you?"

"Really?"

"Yeah, I love doing portraits." Skylar unzipped her duffel and took out a thick sketchbook covered in multi-colored marker spirals. She brandished a pencil and held it up to her left eye, squeezing the other one shut. "For perspective," she explained.

Emma sat still as Skylar started sketching. "Should I put down my backpack?" she asked, trying not to move her mouth.

"Nah, I'm just doing your head," Skylar said. Out of the corner of her eye, Emma could see Skylar's left elbow bouncing as her hand moved across the page.

"Well, you guys seem to be getting along!" Skylar stopped drawing, and they both looked up to see a teenage girl with a curly ponytail and freckles sprinkled across her nose jogging over from the gazebo. She was out of breath and clutched a clipboard. "Sorry I'm late. I'm Adri, one of your counselors. Welcome to Camp Nedoba!"

Skylar and Emma smiled nervously at each other.

"None of the other girls from our cabin are here yet," Adri said, looking at her list after they recited their names. "Well, except for Jo. She's around here somewhere. Her dad owns the camp, so she already knows everything." Adri winked and dropped her voice to a whisper. "Or thinks she does, anyway."

In the distance, Emma saw the tall, mustachioed man from the Camp Nedoba website walking with two girls, both about Emma's age. One was dark-haired and the other had red curls like Annie, from the movie. As they got closer, Emma could see that the red-haired girl had recently been crying. She wished she could reach out to her, like Skylar had done for Emma, but she would have to wait until the adults left.

"Adri," the tall man said, "this is Maddie Ryland. She was a late addition so she might not be on your list."

"Hi, Maddie," Adri said brightly, crouching down to her eye level. "Don't worry, we're going to have so much fun this summer, you won't even miss home."

The tall man smiled at Adri and bent down to whisper to the black-haired girl. "Now, Jo," Emma overheard him say. "Remember, I told you Maddie really needs a friend here. Please be nice to her and show her around."

"Why do *I* have to?"

"Because you're my right-hand girl!" he said, ruffling her hair. Emma saw her smile proudly, and then looked away before she got caught eavesdropping.

"All right, ladies, why don't I take you back to the cabin so you can get settled?" Adri said. "You can have your pick of the beds." She put her arms around Emma and Skylar. "I think you two should share a bunk," she said. "What do you say?"

Emma smiled. "That sounds good."

"Definitely," Skylar said.

"You can be my bunkmate, I guess," Emma heard Jo say reluctantly to Maddie.

They left their trunks behind—Adri promised that the

counselors would drive them over to the girls' side later—and started walking up the hill that led to a dirt path shaded by tall pine trees. As they passed the basketball court, Emma noticed a short boy with big ears in a giant Boston Red Sox jersey talking excitedly to one of his counselors.

"I know karate," the boy said. "Wanna see?"

"Later," the counselor said wearily.

"Wanna hear a joke?" the boy went on. "What do you call cheese that's not yours?"

"I have no idea."

"Nacho cheese!" The boy cracked up, and the counselor smiled tolerantly.

"Gonna be a long summer," he called to Adri as she passed.

"Nah," she laughed. "I've got some quality girls here."

Skylar shifted her duffel bag to her other shoulder and reached out her hand, grinning at Emma. Emma took it gratefully. Maybe it wasn't such a big deal that Anna wasn't there with her. Maybe her mom was right; she would make new friends. She already had one, one that was cooler than anyone Emma had ever met back in Boston. The breeze lifted Emma's ponytail off the nape of her neck, and she felt a chill of excitement shoot down her spine. Summer camp might not so bad after all, Emma thought to herself with a smile. It was only four weeks.

And how much could her life change in four weeks, really?

Acknowledgments

MY DEEPEST AND MOST HEARTFELT THANKS ARE DUE TO:

Jocelyn Davies, for holding my hand through first-time authorship with limitless patience and cheerleading; Ben Schrank, for his trust and guidance; Rebecca Kilman and everyone else at Razorbill, for their tireless enthusiasm and support; Laura Bernier, for playing matchmaker; Beth Ziemacki and Michael Stearns, for being my pro bono consiglieri; Zoe LaMarche, for being my sounding board and forever favorite person; Ellen Chuse and Gara LaMarche, for their unconditional love (and free babysitting); Lisa Mueller and Ben Iturralde, for adopting me as family long before it was official; all of my friends—especially Emily Barth Isler—for their excitement and encouragement throughout the writing process; Adrianna Muir and Tara Tracy, without whom I would never have made it through adolescence, let alone three summers' worth of camp; and of course to Jeff and Sam Zorabedian, without whom I would simply never make it, period.